THE GINGER GRIFFIN

THE
GINGER GRIFFIN

A Novel
by

Ann Bridge

LONDON

CHATTO & WINDUS

1934

To

Eric and Nellie

" Recollections, above all, of horses—of their courage and foolishness, of their light feet upon the cold December fields and of their sweet breath and eyes in dark and scented stables."

A Journey from Peking

NOTE

Of the characters in this book, the Bong alone is drawn from life. All the rest are purely imaginary.

A. B.

Chapter One

MONSIEUR JOURDAIN was astounded to learn in middle life that he had been speaking prose for half a century. And many people are surprised, and even a little indignant, on being told that in their relations with other human beings they generally act on a theory. They use, they say, their instincts, their emotions—a flair they have for such things. All this may well be true, but their flairs and instincts nourish and support their theories about other people. And the lamentable truth remains that we have, ultimately, only our theories to guide us. We can never know all; but upon the accuracy of our theorising will depend the measure of intimacy and fulfilment that we achieve. Though we are reluctant to realise it, the successful and perspicacious theorists are the brilliant, the satisfying friends. But the most brilliant may be baffled, be left in doubt—Time alone shows, very often, how far our theory was correct. Or Time may play us a bad trick—allow us to learn, too late, that our theory was all wrong, or—more bitter still, that though we did not venture to act on what we thought, we were really right all the time.

Perhaps, after all, the wisest are those who employ the minimum of speculation on the facts before them. At least they avoid disappointment. Mrs. Grant-Howard, whom we meet powdering her nose on one of those large shabby leather sofas which rather infrequently adorn the corridors of the Foreign Office, certainly belonged to this latter group. She dealt mostly in facts, interpreting these rapidly in accordance with a few well-cut ready-to-wear theories which her husband sometimes accused her of having bought at Selfridge's. She was inquisitive and amused, but the obvious was her sphere—making very few outside shots, she made correspondingly few mistakes. "Certainty First" would undoubtedly have been her slogan, if she had felt the need of slogans.

The corridors of the Foreign Office might seem to some an odd place in which to powder the nose and otherwise restore the appearance. But Mrs. Grant-Howard was no respecter of places or persons. Neat, small, assured, her primary assumption about the world, made quite unobtrusively and nicely, was that it existed principally for the convenience of people like herself. Finding her nose in need of powder, and being in the Foreign Office, she powdered her nose. She was waiting for her husband, who was seeing the Private Secretaries about his next post. She waited without agitation. Nugent Grant-Howard was on excellent terms with the powers; he called the Private Secretaries Walter and Noel; he was able, personable, efficient and, above all, *coulant*; he was a rising and successful man. Not such as he are sent to Bogota against their will.

A door further along the corridor opened, and a man emerged—a tall good-looking man, neither young nor old, whose whole appearance and manner was of an extreme and accomplished smoothness. His left arm embraced a sheaf of papers, his right hand held a cigarette. Seeing Mrs. Grant-Howard, he went up to her with— "Hullo, Joanna! What are *you* doing here?"

"Waiting for Nugent—he's seeing *them*," said Mrs. Grant-Howard, nodding her head vaguely down the corridor.

"Oh, are you off again already? Do you know what you'll get?"

"No."

"Well, you and Nugent must come and lunch with me before you go," said the smooth man. "Goodbye!"— and he titupped rapidly off down the corridor, still embracing his papers.

Mrs. Grant-Howard continued to wait. Other men, equally ageless and of a similar uniform smoothness, came and went, opening doors and carrying papers; messengers bearing red boxes passed to and fro on flat and silent feet. Joanna had had time to think—twice—that the Foreign Office was the stuffiest and ugliest place in London, when at last her husband joined her.

Nugent Grant-Howard was tall and thin, with brown hair brushed up rather stiffly above the ears, where it was turning grey, in the approved diplomatic fashion; his very small moustache was also brushed upwards. In his manner and general appearance he was every bit as smooth and ageless as the men with papers who opened doors, and like them he wore spats; but instead of papers he carried a soft black felt hat and a gold-topped cane.

"Well?" asked his wife.

"Peking," he replied briefly.

"Pe*king!*" said Mrs. Grant-Howard, with the accent on the last syllable. "I never thought of that. What a curious idea! Will it do for Dickie? And is there riding?"

"They say it's a very healthy post, and perfectly suitable for children," replied Grant-Howard in the completely colourless tone which in diplomacy implies doubt. "The riding," he went on more briskly, "is first-class, and the cheapest in the world. Quite average ponies for a tenner, and plenty of polo." As they talked Mrs. Grant-Howard had risen from the sofa, and they now moved away along the corridor, descended some stairs, and still discussing this new venture, emerged on to the

Horse Guards' Parade, and strolled across it in the
direction of Jermyn Street and lunch. "Well, we'll take
Dickie, then—that's settled; and Jane must look after
the others, as usual," said Mrs. Grant-Howard at length,
in a tone of finality. Dickie was her son, aged seven—
"the others" were her two daughters, both of school
age, and continually succoured during their parents'
prolonged absences by Nugent's sensible and devoted
sister, Lady Rosemere, otherwise Jane. The children
thus disposed of, she reverted to the new post—"Who's
there?"

"Boggit—do you remember him?"

"Vaguely—a nice fat man. But I can't remember his
wife."

"He hasn't got a wife—he's a bachelor."

"Oh, *what* a let-off!" Joanna breathed quite deeply in
her fervour. "No chef-ess means such a saving of wear
and tear. Who else?"

"Rupert's there—the greatest possible luck! And
George Hawtrey is Second Secretary."

"A tall rather un-clever one, who's mad on sport, and
talks about Uganda?" Mrs. Grant-Howard's slighter
diplomatic acquaintances were usually ranged in her
mind with these small, concise and frequently rather
pungent verbal labels attached to them. Rupert Benenden's was on the tip of her tongue—"that clever quarrel-
some young man, who writes"; but he had also a warning
tag in her mind, with "Nugent's friend" on it—and the
labels of people who bore this tag were seldom uttered
aloud.

Grant-Howard at once rose in defence even of Mr.
Hawtrey. "George isn't half bad—in fact, he's really
very nice, as you'll find out when you've had the chance
of getting to know him. But it will be marvellous to
have Rupert there."

"Yes, rather," said Joanna, amiably. But her mind darted back to the practical—"And we start when, do you say?"

"They want us to sail on January the fifth. Oh, and by the way, I believe you'll have to chaperone a girl on the way out."

"A girl! What girl?"

"Her name is"—Grant-Howard as he walked removed one pair of horn-rimmed spectacles and substituted another; then he extracted a slip of paper from his pocket-book and read out—"Miss Amber Harrison."

"Who is she, and why have we got to take her?" asked his wife, as he replaced his pocket-book and reversed the order of his spectacles again. The frequency, skill and speed with which he performed this operation was still, after fourteen years of marriage, an unfailing source of incredulous amusement to Joanna.

"She's going out to stay with an uncle in Peking— old Bill Harrison. He's a brother of that consul who died after being shot up, a few years back—do you remember?"

"Is *he* a consul?"

"No—in business. But Anstruther says he's a tremendous horse-coper, so he's quite a useful person to put under an obligation."

"Why is she going out to him? Hasn't she any parents?"

"They didn't tell me why," said Grant-Howard, who always took questions in their order, as if they occurred in a memorandum. "Yes, she's got a mother all right —her father died round about a year ago. Do you remember Lady Julia Harrison, who has that lovely house in the Cotswolds? You've been there with the Freemans. This is her girl."

"The woman who gives the parties!" said Joanna, suddenly illuminated. "Yes, I remember, perfectly well. But I thought she married the girl to some peer."

"That was the elder one—this is another. And they want an escort for her."

"Well, I don't wonder she wants to go away!" said Joanna unkindly, reminiscences of Lady Julia and her parties beginning to crowd into her mind. "That woman is every sort of snob in one—social, intellectual, political! But I expect she'll be a great bore. How old is she?"

"That you will be able to ascertain from her passport," said Grant-Howard smoothly—"they didn't tell me."

"Amber — *what* a silly name!" said Mrs. Grant-Howard. As they passed into the discreet restaurant, "Gemma!" she exclaimed suddenly.

"What?" asked her husband, startled.

"The other sister—the one who married. Amber and Gemma! Isn't that the nadir of affectation?"

"It is pretty steep, certainly," said Grant-Howard. "But the girl didn't christen herself, my dear."

"No," admitted Joanna, with grudging justice, as she stood looking about her, in search of the friends they had come to meet. "I wonder why she wants to canter off to China, though—whether she's running away from all the Amber-and-Gemmering, or from a young man."

"She may be trying to run away from herself," said Grant-Howard. A woman standing next to him turned her pretty painted face towards him with a startled glance at this remark, but his wife paid no particular attention to it. She was accustomed to Nugent's habit of suddenly spilling a wineglassful of his peculiar philosophy into the pool of ordinary conversation. "Here they are!" she said, as a couple entered the door.

"Tom! Judy!" And between the handshakings she announced "We're going to Peking!"

While the Grant-Howards were canvassing Miss Amber Harrison's reasons for going to China, the subject of their speculations was riding slowly along a hill-track in Gloucestershire, munching a ham-sandwich, and deep in thought. She had ridden over to a house near Stow to show, and if possible sell Major, the efficient and companionable hunter which she rode, to a newcomer to the neighbourhood, and she had succeeded in her mission. Mrs. Crutchworthy had bought the horse, had promised her a good fat price for him, and had even agreed to take delivery of him a month later, just before Amber sailed. Nevertheless, Amber's forehead was puckered with rather discontented speculation. She loved Major, and she wasn't sure if she approved of Mrs. Crutchworthy. She liked the groom—a decent man; but she wasn't sure about the mistress. Amber was very seldom sure about people. It didn't take her long to make up her mind about a horse; if she kept her eye on one through a day's hunting, she generally knew all she needed to know by the end of it. But people! You could keep your eye on them for weeks and months, talk to them and be talked to, and still not be sure about them. Amber was not very sure even about herself, ever. She knew she was not as beautiful as Gemma— lovely Gemma, with her Titian hair, her perfect, delicate profile, and her incredible skin. Amber's hair was darker than Gemma's, off the true and perfect red; her skin was a warm honey-colour—again, off the true and perfect white; there was a slight bump on the bridge of her honest nose, on which, to her mother's disgust, a faint golden powder of freckles was liable to assemble in spring. Amber would not have minded all this much if it had not, so manifestly, disappointed her mother.

She was always disappointing her mother. She couldn't talk properly to the brilliant people who came to the house. She did try—hard; she wanted to please her mother, she wanted to please the people themselves. Amber was as innocently anxious to please mankind in general as a bob-tailed sheepdog puppy which blusters about, sniffing and wagging its foolish tail. She did please some people. But not the right ones, and not in the right way, she felt. She couldn't make those little light witty remarks about books and pictures—if a book had interested her, she wanted, if she talked about it at all, to sit down and chew it over for twenty minutes, and get at the bottom of it. But the talk always sailed on ahead of her—one little light clever remark, or two at most, and off it skimmed, leaving her baffled, her contribution suspended. And she would glance furtively at her mother to see if she had noticed; nearly always, she had—nearly always, there was that half-closing of Lady Julia's eyes, or that slight compression of her fine lips, which told Amber that she had failed again. And failure took the stuffing out of one so frightfully.

It had all been much easier while her father was alive. Either because he expected very little, or because they understood one another, he had never seemed to be disappointed in Amber. But then Daddy had not been much good at the brilliant people and the little light remarks either; Daddy, she said to herself, with a small giggle of amusement, had been a bit of a disappointment too! But he had been an impenitent disappointment, as she was not; and as they slipped away together, happy confederate truants, into the safe world of horses and the people who dealt with horses—"A lot of damned highbrows!" he would ejaculate. (It always amused Amber so much that when he made this and similar disparaging remarks about highbrows, he used to shove his own bushy and projecting brows up so far that they over-topped the Triplex spectacles which his short sight com-pelled him to wear, even out riding, by nearly an inch.) "Come on, my pretty!" he would call to her, as they swung towards some savage-looking obstacle—"let's see what you can make of it!" And as often as not, what she made of it called forth the cheerful "That's *right!*" which so thoroughly put stuffing into her.

Amber had been jogging absent-mindedly along the old green road in the pale winter sunshine, eating her sandwiches and occasionally slapping the reins con-fidentially on Major's shining coppery neck. Having finished her lunch, she crumpled up her sandwich-paper into a ball and shot it over the dry-stone wall into the beech wood which bordered the track, brushed the crumbs from her shabby breeches and jacket, and put her horse into a canter. A quarter of a mile further on the turf track crossed the high road, and beyond it dropped suddenly into one of those deep-sunk valleys which intersect the Cotswold uplands. This was her direct road home—down into the vale, up the further rise, and a couple of miles along the ridge beyond, to drop again from it into her own valley. But she did not take it. She pulled up on reaching the road, and sat frowning in her saddle at the wavering columns of smoke which rose from an unseen house below her, hidden among a group of trees—then with an energy which surprised Major she turned his head to the left, and gal-loped like mad along the roadside turf for nearly a mile. "Fool!" she muttered as she galloped—"Fool! fool!" Then drawing rein she crossed the road, and took a slanting lane which led down into the dip. "Cut it out!" she said aloud to herself, in a sort of anger, brush-ing the smarting tears from her eyes—"You must cut it out!"

Mrs. Grant-Howard's chance shot about running away from a young man had not been wholly wide of the mark. Amber was going two or three miles out of her way simply to avoid passing a small Cotswold manor-house whose wrought-iron gates had been to her, for nearly a year, the secret portals of Paradise. It was a very simple story. When Captain Arthur Griffiths had come into Gloucestershire from, it was believed, New Zealand, three years before, he had met with a civil if slightly restrained welcome from the inhabitants. This, since he kept a pleasant bachelor establishment, a good table, and two or three decent hunters, had grown gradually into a rather complacent acceptance. He dined with his neighbours, he shot with them, and with them, regularly, he hunted. He rode straight enough to satisfy old Tom Harrison; he talked well enough to please Lady Julia. He was often at Riddingcote. And Amber had enjoyed him. She had felt curiously safe in enjoying him. People who satisfied both her parents were rare—so rare that it must be safe to enjoy them. The world of people and ideas and books was not closed to Amber, nor in the least without interest—it was only that, compared to her mother, to Gemma, she acquitted herself in it so deplorably; whereas in her father's world of horses and woods and walls and stiff jumps she got on all right. She had been turned defeatist in her mother's world by defeat— like a horse, she used to think, that has once been overridden and afterwards won't race. But Captain Griffiths moved easily in both, and in either made her feel secure and adequate—more, successful, admirable.

Of course she had fallen in love with him. He was more intelligent and amusing than her hunting young men, more mature and somehow more solid than the youthful intellectuals from Oxford who flooded Riddingcote at week-ends. He had displayed first interest in her, then admiration; he had somehow brought a quietly increasing intimacy into being between them. On this for some months she had rested, happy and sustained, gaining confidence from a relationship obviously approved, veiling even from herself its secret possibilities of rapture.

As she rode down the lane now she remembered with tormenting clearness the day when those veils had been removed—when intimacy had first spilled over into tenderness, and happiness had wakened into bliss. Riding home together after a day's hunting, something he had said, something he had done, had wakened in her a new piercing certainty. Oddly enough, she remembered far less vividly what had evoked it than the feeling itself. They had parted at his gate—he had pressed her to go in for a hot drink, and she had resisted; she felt such an urgent need to be alone with her joy, to let it show itself, fill her. Down the valley the road passed through a marshy place, where the stream expanded on either side into reedy stretches of water, masked and fringed with thickets of alder and sallow. In the soft February starlight she had stopped here, deliberately; she wanted to hear the silence, to smell the damp leafy smell of the sedgy pools, to see the stars shine back from the dark water, and watch the young moon low between the dim tracery of slender twiggy branches. These things, she felt, could somehow express for her this new flooding sensation—could make the inexpressible wonder visible, audible. She suffered her bliss to possess her, as it were, in their shape; in this vision of familiar things felt and seen as she had never seen or felt them before. In those moments when she sat motionless on the valley road they stamped her emotion indelibly with their image, made it ring with their hidden universal harmony. Tremulous, over-brimmed with realised rapture, she had at last

ridden slowly home.   And the next day her father died of
a stroke.

It seemed to Amber that everything had gone forward
swiftly after that night.   That pause by the marsh had
been a pause in her life, really—a moment of suspension
between two epochs.   In her loss and sorrow she had
turned to Arthur Griffiths for support and consolation—
more blindly, more directly than perhaps she would
otherwise have done.   But she felt quite sure of him—
her father had liked him, her mother approved; his
feelings for her he had shown.   It was all right, it was
safe, even for her, uncertain as she usually was.   Her
idea of him seemed perfectly watertight this time.   And
so, innocently and simply, she had precipitated her
disaster—her theory of safety and comfort to be found
from him, had forced Captain Griffiths, presently, to the
admission of the secret of his outwardly cheerful life.
He was married, and his wife, a hopeless drug-fiend, was
in a police asylum in the Antipodes, on a charge of opium
smuggling.   He had meant to be guarded—he *had* been
guarded, up to a point: but he had fallen honestly in
love with Amber, and had given himself ever so slightly
away on that ride home.   Her sorrow and her simplicity had done the rest.

Pityingly, honestly, as the admission was made, the
shock for Amber was fearful.   All that he left unsaid of
her share in the business, her own consciousness lashed
her with, searingly, when she went over it in her mind.
In honesty she could not blame him more than a little—
his one slip he would quickly have rectified, she could
guess, by a sheering off, if her grief had not made this
seem impossible.   To guard his secret, she could not
wholly and suddenly sever relations with him, and the
poor child passed some weeks in a misery hard to ex-
aggerate—meeting him in public with an air of cheerful-

ness that consorted ill enough with a face white with
strain, meeting him in private not at all.

She was driven at last to the first really independent
action of her life. Her father had left her £300 a year
for herself—perhaps the most perspicacious thing Tom
Harrison ever did. And she presently announced to the
horrified Lady Julia that she was going out to Peking
to spend a year with Uncle Bill and Aunt Bessie.

Old Bill Harrison had been in England and paid a
visit to Riddingcote during the last year of his brother's
life. He had taken greatly to Amber, and Amber to him.
He looked like her father, except for his queer, liverish,
far-eastern complexion; he had the same shrewdness and
impatience with mere cleverness, and an even greater ob-
session with horses. They had gone to the Grand National
together, and old Bill had been hugely tickled by his
niece's determined backing of a rank outsider simply
on his looks and on his remembered form three years
previously in some obscure West Country point-to-point.
The outsider had come in first at fifty to one, and Amber
had made a hundred pounds. Uncle Bill's heart was
hers, after that. "Whenever you feel like it, you come
and stay in Peking with me and Bessie," he said more
than once. "I'll show you some riding there. China
ponies look like pigs—no necks, you know, and no withers
—but they're as honest as gold. You come out to us."
Amber had remembered this, and without a word to anyone, in her extremity, she wrote and proposed a visit to
Uncle Bill. His answer was even warmer and kinder
than his original invitation; she was to come, and come
at once—they would love to have her, they would give
her the best time they could. And Aunt Bessie put in a
few lines of pleasure at the prospect of "a young thing
in the house to cheer up us old fogies." Thus armed,
Amber had tackled her mother. She met all Lady Julia's

objections and questions with a new and immovable stubbornness. She wanted to go, and she was going— going to see the world and to be with Uncle Bill, whom she liked. She was twenty-two, and she had the money— and no one could really stop her. Lady Julia tried appeals to her affection. Amber was affectionate in return, as she had always been; but not, as always hitherto, compliant. Astonished, hurt, Lady Julia at last accepted defeat, and turned her energies to putting a good face on it at home, and making the visit as much of a social success as possible abroad. She bothered the Foreign Office, where she had friends, about an escort; she wrote to Sir James Boggit, whom she knew, engaging his good offices in Peking. "Such a chance for the dear child to see that marvellous civilisation!" she told Gloucestershire. "The most intellectual people on earth," she told the Vice-Chancellor, smelling a rose as they strolled in the garden. Meanwhile Amber, indifferent and unhappy, but resolute, set about collecting her kit and selling her hunters with a certain gloomy practicality. And to-day she had sold the horse Major. In five weeks, she reflected, as she completed her detour and started up the further ridge towards home, it would be over and she would be gone. Suddenly the idea seized upon her with intolerable force —gone! and that house no longer within her reach, either for sight or avoidance. Urged by an uncontrollable impulse of misery, she swung the astonished Major round in his tracks, clattered down the hill again, and galloped furiously back across the heavy sodden pastures to a small thorn-crowned knoll which commanded a view of the low grey garden-front, the lawn and the pretty gates of Captain Griffiths' home. There she drew up, and sat, staring through tear-blurred eyes at the house the sight of which she had just ridden three miles round to avoid.

Chapter Two

AS Amber drove through the unfamiliar dark and rainy streets to Fenchurch Street Station, and assembled her authoritatively labelled luggage in its lowering yellow gloom, on the day of her departure, she felt the very minimum of enthusiasm for her coming adventure. To take ship and go East may well be—almost certainly is—one of the best remedies for a broken heart, but from the point of view of the heartsick it is nevertheless a pity that the start should be so depressing. Anything more gloomy and unappetising than Fenchurch Street and Tilbury, particularly in January, it would be hard to imagine. Pale and chilly, she stood beside her mother on the platform, and went through the introductions to the Grant-Howards with a sort of neutral resignation. Lady Julia had tried hard to bring about a meeting—indeed a whole series of meetings—before the actual start, but she had been defeated by Joanna's most reasonable plea of not having a moment, really; and a bare ten minutes, without Amber, in Brown's Hotel was all she had achieved.

To the girl's confused eyes they presented an immense crowd, these people who were to be her companions for the next six weeks. Mr. and Mrs., by an effort of attention, she got firmly placed, but there was a whole troop of boys and girls; there were female attendants, apparently, of all sorts; there were numbers of people coming up with books, with flowers, with boxes of chocolates and magazines; men who drew Mr. Grant-Howard aside and talked to him in low tones and with absent expressions

which suggested State secrets, women in pearls and furs
who kissed Mrs. Grant-Howard and told her she really
must write *this* time.   Lady Julia, with Gemma and her
husband, seemed a very modest lot by comparison—so
few as to be almost negligible, Amber thought.   Except
Gemma.   Gemma was never negligible.   Even the men
who stood talking to Mr. Grant-Howard with their eyes
on their boots, in the approved diplomatic manner, if
they happened to look at Gemma looked a second time
and a third.   Amber drew a curious momentary consolation from this fact—she was feeling diminished and
isolated, about to be plunged into this group of important
strangers, and Gemma's inevitable effect somehow re-
inforced her.   Then looking at her brother-in-law's face
of chronic devotion, she experienced such a sharp pang of
desolation that she could hardly bear it.   If only Arthur
had been there, *could* have been there!   If only she had
had his face to hold to.   She turned into the carriage for
a moment, and rearranged her coat, her book—simply to
get a few seconds to hide her face, to pull it together; she
was disconcerted, when she emerged, to find Mr. Grant-
Howard's eyes suddenly fixed on her intently.

The train chugged out.   Hats were raised, hands and
handkerchiefs waved, the Grant-Howard children shouted
and capered on the platform.   There ensued a cold and
smoky interlude of journey, like the pause between
pulling out one tooth and the next.

At Tilbury there were fewer people, but still some.
By dint of following other passengers through a trackless
waste of railway lines and station buildings, they found
themselves at last on the dock-side, with the peculiar
buff and black bulk of the P. & O. boat towering above
them.   Amber had never seen a liner before from close
to, and was startled by its size, though in reality this
was one of the smaller and older boats, and quite unim-

pressive to more experienced travellers. They went on board; with the help of an equable but abstracted chief steward and an openly harassed Goanese they found Amber's cabin—a single-berth one, to herself, on the port side; and Amber got her first conscious prick of entertainment from the small ingenuities of the folding basin, the furniture, the nets above the berth, the port-hole. It seemed almost impossible that in such a minute apartment one should make a home for six weeks. She moved about, examining everything; reading the rubrics of regulations fastened to the bulkhead, trying to work the electric fan, while Lady Julia fussed because the luggage had not reached the cabin. "Presently! Presently! It will come soon. Don't worry!" said the stewardess, professionally consoling and cheerful, and rustled starchily out, Lady Julia looking after her with marked distaste for her powdered nose and waved yellow hair under the stiff cap.

There was a tap at the door, and Mrs. Grant-Howard appeared. "Oh, here you are—how nice. Port-side too—you are lucky!" Amber had no idea why she was lucky to be on the port-side, and was too shy to ask. "We're starboard, alas," Mrs. Grant-Howard went on, "come and see where we are!" They repaired to the other side of the ship, through passages with that strange smell of paint, steam heat and hot salt water peculiar to P. & O. boats, and found the headquarters of the other party. In Joanna's cabin her maid was already fussing about; in the adjoining one Miss Carruthers, the governess, was cheerfully supervising Dickie Grant-Howard's attempt to discover whether his body would really go through the port-hole. "He mustn't do that—port-holes are forbidden," said Joanna with calm decision. "Dickie, come and say how-do-you-do to Miss Harrison."

"If I cam gep my heab through, I oughp po be able po

gep my boby through," said Dickie, reluctantly scrambling back. "How bo you bo?" he said, holding out a small and already filthy hand to Amber and Lady Julia. While Lady Julia murmured something amiable to Joanna about the comfort of having at least *one* child with her, Dickie studied Amber with a long steady stare. "I palk like this," he finally said to her confidentially, "because of my plape." He opened his mouth and projected horribly into view an object like a black plum, with screws in it. "*Dickie!*" Miss Carruthers deprecated. "Ip's po emlarge my jaw," Dickie pursued, unabashed. Amber laughed. "I cam palk quipe orbimarily withoup ip. I'll show you." He was about to implement this promise, but was prevented by Miss Carruthers. "Take him on deck," said his mother easily—"the luggage won't be here for ages." She offered the services of her maid, Burbidge, to Amber. "Miss Harrison is in Number 114, on the port-side, Burbidge." She was being kind, with a competent kindness which struck Amber as nearly as professional as the cheerfulness of the stewardess. Amber, however, didn't mind this in the least—she was quite without the moral fads of more sophisticated people. The fact that Mrs. Grant-Howard talked to her rather as a vet. who knows his job talks to a strange horse she found engaging rather than otherwise. She studied her chaperone covertly as they proceeded on deck, rather approving of her smallness, her neat build and perfect finish, which reminded one of a very smartly turned-out Welsh pony. "My husband has a cabin up here, with his papers," Joanna said to Amber, in a tone of amusement, and indeed in a moment they came upon Mr. Grant-Howard standing at the door of a deck-cabin into which a steward was carrying large black tin boxes which bore a variety of legends in white lettering: "Mr. N. L. Grant-Howard, Union of Socialist Soviet Republics," "Mr. N. L. Grant-Howard, H.B.M. Embassy, Madrid"—and so on. The tin boxes impressed Amber deeply; they gave her quite a William le Queux thrill, a sense of moving in a larger world of mysterious and important affairs. Lady Julia entered into conversation with Mr. Grant-Howard, and Amber strolled off along the deck by herself. It was raw, rainy and foggy—the picture presented was of a rather blurred etching of shapes of ships, masts and funnels, across a foreground of brown dirty water, with straws and orange-peel and bits of paper floating on it. Amber's momentary thrill died down—she felt chilly and homesick and depressed. She turned back towards the group, towards her mother. "'The Chinese dynasties—so restful, so impartial!'" she heard Lady Julia say to Mr. Grant-Howard as she approached.

Something should really be done about the departure of ships from Tilbury. It is not suggested that there should be a band playing and coloured ribbons of paper to throw and to hold, as they have at Vancouver and Yokohama; that would merely be to add an element of the false and the grotesque to a situation which is already at once boring and poignant. But the situation itself should be cut short. An immense curtain, or a smoke-screen, should be interposed between the quay and the ship from the moment that the last see-er-off has left the vessel, which would then steam rapidly away. It is intolerable, having embraced fervently, having murmured last words and taken farewells possibly heart-breaking, then to be called upon to stand, either on the quay-side or on deck, for half an hour, for an hour—looking up, looking down, shouting the hearty nothings suited to such a wide publicity; being cheerful, being amiable; calling one another's attention to irrelevant details—the activities of the crane, the winch. And when at last the

ship does move, the slowness, the unbearable delibera-
tion with which she manœuvres herself out into the
channel, while one still gazes, still shouts; and then at last
waves, waves, waves the hand, the handkerchief, at the
receding quay, at the diminishing figures, till gradually
they diminish to vanishing-point, become indistinguishable, and one is free to go below and have lunch.

Just such a protracted leavetaking occurred to fray
Amber's nerves. She was not passionately devoted to her
mother as she had been to her father, but she was aware
of a general painful emotion, of a sharp breach with the
familiar and the homely, which focussed itself on the erect
and fashionable figure of Lady Julia below on the quay,
among the straw and paper and packing-cases. The one
thing which lightened it all was Dickie's interest in everything. "They've gop pwo mopors om boarb!" he
shrieked to his own Grannie, who stood below. "They're
going po Porp Saib!" Nevertheless by the time they
went below to lunch she was thoroughly overwrought.

The saloon steward met them at their entrance and
asked Mrs. Grant-Howard with a certain formality if she
would like to sit at the Captain's table? and disposed them
there—Joanna on his right, Amber on his left, Nugent
and Miss Carruthers opposite. Dickie was to eat at the
children's meal-times under Burbidge's supervision. The
Captain was not there—his vacant swing-chair presided
like an empty throne over the table. While the Goanese
stewards brought course after course of an ample meal,
the party, now fairly confronted, began the inevitable
process of a mutual stock-taking.

"Are you a good sailor?" Nugent asked of Amber
across the table.

"I don't know," Amber replied rather vaguely. "I've
only been across the Channel and back."

"One can be quite as ill in the Channel as anywhere,"

said Nugent, helping himself to curry. "Were you ill? Have some curry—it's the best thing you get on these boats."

"No, thank you—I hate it. No, I wasn't, but it wasn't rough," replied Amber.

"I'm definitely bad," said Mrs. Grant-Howard resignedly. "Miss Carruthers swears she's not—don't you, Miss Carruthers?"

The governess blinked politely. "Oh, I call myself an *av*erage sailor, Mrs. Grant-Howard."

"Burbidge declares she's a good sailor, but I'm sure she'll be sick," Joanna chattered on. "Servants think it so frightfully unrefined *not* to be sea-sick." She continued to talk with competent amiability, with the kindly intention of putting Amber at her ease; while she talked she studied her with an expert eye. Pretty—yes, definitely pretty, with that skin and that mass of hair; not outrageously lovely like the sister, Lady Thingummy, of course, but that was really uncalled-for! Cleverly dressed, too—that would be the mother—and a good figure. She seemed very mousy and quiet; good style, thought Joanna, but the style of fifteen years ago—her manner didn't match her modern finished appearance in the least. Well, all the better if she *was* mousy; there would be less likelihood of a need for exertions on the chaperone's part. Joanna was painfully familiar with the idle flirtations incidental to travel by sea—her practised eye roamed over the saloon, trying to pick out the men who would be likely to flirt with Amber. It was only two-thirds full—the rest would come aboard at Southampton, of course, including the Navy; there were sure to be reliefs for the China squadron. Her eye lit on no one noticeable—the men were all either very old or incredibly young, she thought, as she concluded her brief survey.

Amber, anxious as always to do the right thing, responded politely to all Mrs. Grant-Howard's remarks. She was quite aware of her scrutiny; she recognised at once that particular expression as of one who runs his eye over a horse. But as the meal proceeded her attention became increasingly focussed on one thing—the effort to control her voice. Unreasonably, maddeningly, she found herself wanting to cry—wanting more and more violently to cry. She could not have said why—her loss of Arthur, her parting with her mother, with her horses, with Riddingcote; the plunge into the unknown, these polite strangers—all combined to weigh her down with a desperate sense of severance, of isolation. She held out somehow till the end of the meal released her; then she went off to her cabin, losing herself several times on the way in the white-walled electric-lighted passages which moved with a faint perceptible motion of their own—the strong throbbing forward thrust of the ship.

The Grant-Howards sat in the green sofa-ed saloon and took their coffee. "Well, what do you make of her?" Joanna asked of her husband. She was always more interested in Nugent's point of view than in her own.

Nugent lit a cigar rather carefully before replying. Then he blew out a cloud of smoke and said "Nothing, so far," and began to read *The Times*. After a moment or two, he lowered it again, exchanged one pair of spectacles for another, and observing "She has beautiful legs," resumed his paper.

Joanna, however, was quite accustomed to talking to her husband through a newspaper and pursued her meditations more or less aloud. "Lady Julia's even worse than you said, Nugent. Heavens, what a woman!" Nugent grunted. "The girl doesn't seem a bit like her," Joanna went on—"she's out of date, somehow. I think she's got an unfashionable mind." Nugent continued to grunt, in a manner apparently satisfactory to his wife,

who resumed, "I don't imagine that she'll be much bother
—she doesn't look at all the sort whom every man on
board will run after. She isn't"—she paused for a word
—"she isn't very *notice*able."

"Her legs are," said Grant-Howard, making his final
contribution to this rather one-sided conversation.

It is impossible to feel that a voyage has really begun
while there is a call at another home port in prospect.
There is a certain suspense; the possibility of last visitors;
meanwhile the passage down the Channel seems merely
like a trip on a penny steamer. The *Kalwoona* berthed at
Southampton at 7.30 next morning, and sailed again at
5.30. In the interval the Grant-Howards did in fact receive a number of callers who dashed down to the dock
in cars; parcels and letters for them came aboard; they
walked ashore, and Nugent Grant-Howard dealt with
some eleventh-hour details by telephoning to the Foreign
Office. Amber went ashore with them, feeling rather
lost and lonely—no one had come to see her, nor sent her
a last letter. And Nugent's telephoning suddenly put an
idea into her head which, for weeks afterwards, she
blushed to remember.

It came over her, like a sudden sickness, that she
could not, simply *could not* leave England without once
more hearing Arthur's voice—and there was nothing to
prevent her from ringing him up! Insidiously, this idea
presented itself to her at the moment as a good one;
what more simple and natural than to say goodbye, in a
friendly way? It was 4.30, and he would almost certainly be in for tea, because the meet that day was close
by. Making some excuse about buying a book, she left
the others and slipped off. She found a telephone, ad-
vertised by a blue-and-white notice outside a small and
rather grubby teashop, and hurriedly put her call
through. There was not much time; she was at least

ten minutes walk from the dock. She ordered a cup of
tea, while she waited—ten minutes it would be, the exchange said—and sat sipping it nervously, gazing round
with discomfort at the dirty tables, the fly-spotted walls,
the blowzy and suspicious-looking woman who presided
over the shop. In those minutes her courage began to
ebb; her idea seemed less good, less natural; what would
Arthur think? Would he realise how cool and casual
and friendly her intention was? She began to stare with
horror at the telephone-box into which she must soon
go and cope with this situation of her own creating.
Then the bell rang and she darted in. "Your Broadway
call." "Is that Broadway 379?" she asked, troubled at
the wavering tone of her voice. But it was not—they had
given her 375. The check filled her with desperation,
banished her fears—she *must* get him! She banged on
the receiver, and gave the number again; holding the
line, she looked at her watch. Ten to five already! She
would just do it, if they were quick. If only the Grant-
Howards didn't begin to worry about her. Should she
give it up? Would Arthur understand? Oh, what *had*
she better do? But if only she could hear his so familiar
voice just once more it would be something to go on,
would make it all more endurable, this journey. Distracted with irresolution and unhappiness, she stood in
the stuffy box; perspiration sprang out on her skin, tears
began to sting maddeningly behind her eyes. She looked
at her watch again—two minutes to five. She would
have to go! And then: "There you are! Hold on,
Broadway!" rang in her ear.

It was a man's voice at the other end, and for a moment
she thought it was Arthur. But it was only Benson, his
man. No, Captain Griffiths had not come in yet. He'd
expected him half an hour ago; the agent was waiting
to see him—something must have kept him. Would she

leave a message? What name, please? Stammering
that it didn't matter, Amber replaced the receiver. No
good—no good; and probably it would have been no
good if she had got him! Feeling completely desolate,
she paid the huge fee and left the shop. She missed her
way twice, and it was twenty-past five when she ran up
the gangway, pale, breathless and embarrassed, to find
Nugent Grant-Howard waiting for her, watch in hand,
at the top. She apologised. "It would really have been
more inconvenient for you than for us if you had missed
it," he said—and the easy casualness of his words was
soothing to Amber's taut nerves. He looked her over
and saw that she had no book. "Would you like tea
in your cabin?" he said. "Oh, *can* one?" "Of course—
I'll have it sent down." And as he watched her pretty
well-dressed figure disappear along the deck—"Poor little
wretch!" said Nugent to himself.

Chapter Three

THE Peninsular and Oriental Line is a unique institution. It is a sort of Blackwood's Magazine in being; like it, a microcosm of that other unique institution, the British Empire. To travel by it is an education in itself. For it is quite possible for conscientious and high-minded people to spend half a lifetime in England, reading their newspapers and devoutly paying their income-tax, without, so to speak, meeting the British Empire at all. To such it is a geographical expression or a political abstraction, regarded as a rule with vague complacency, but it is not a thing to be reckoned with; it is on the periphery of their lives, an affair of background, making no claims on them that cannot be liquidated by regular payments to the Inland Revenue Department. But on a P. & O. boat the conscientious English citizen suddenly meets the British Empire face to face. There is a Kipling smack about the whole thing, from the crossed flags on the tins of duty-free and blessedly cheap cigarettes to the Sunday services in the saloon, with the Union Jack draped over the piano. The formerly remote institution now confronts this quiet person—as a living organism or as a vast machine, according to his cast of mind; in either case he is soon made aware of claims and duties with respect to it, which he must fulfil or forfeit his self-respect. A frightful sense of collective responsibility pervades the ship— frightful, that is, to the timid individualist. He is called upon to promote sports, or to take part in sports promoted by others, and he does so, unresisting; he "lends a hand," he responds to heartiness, he sets an example—he who perhaps never darkened the doors of a place of worship at home parades for church in the saloon on Sundays; he learns at last that he is not his own man, as he had obscurely supposed, but an active servant of something rather bigger than himself.

The British Empire, however, like one's fellow-passengers, is seldom much in evidence until after Gibraltar, if, as usually happens, it is rough in the Bay. It was rough in the Bay on this occasion, and first Mrs. Grant-Howard, then Dickie, then Grant-Howard himself vanished from the public ken, in common with most people. Amber, to her own great surprise, did not feel in the least ill; the steep rush of water, the sight of a heaving skyline only fifty yards away, the soaring plunges of the ship—up, over, down—filled her, in spite of her sick heart, with a curious exhilaration. She would stand for hours, wrapped in a coat and mackintosh, on the drier parts of the deck, watching the impassioned relations of ship and water, and come down with spray-damp hair and colour in her cheeks to eat a hearty meal in the thinly populated saloon, where she and an elderly Naval officer were now the sole guests at the Captain's table. The Captain praised her; and indeed there is no sense of superiority so subtle and irresistible as that of the good sailor over the sea-sick. She even enjoyed her own staggering progress along the passages and up and down-stairs, and helped Miss Carruthers, who kept on her feet but could not eat, in her ministrations to the stricken family and to Burbidge, who fulfilled Joanna's worst anticipations.

But the Bay does not last very long, and about the entrance to the Straits passengers, bearing a strong resemblance to sick flies, began to crawl once more about the deck; by the time they were twenty-four hours into the

Mediterranean the British Empire had already made itself felt. Even Amber was seized upon by the inexorable machine and learned that she had obligations towards such unwonted types of British subject as very immature youths going out to businesses in Malaya, and flirtatious girls with little vulgar shoes, speaking with a strange sub-American accent, which puzzled her greatly till she found out from the elderly Naval officer that they all came from Shanghai. She had never met anyone like them before, and in England would have gone to her grave without meeting them at all; but the moment you approach the East this terrific national solidarity makes itself felt, and grasped by the British Empire, held indeed firmly by the elbow by it, she was introduced to these people. With and for them she sat on various sub-committees which drew up rules for a variety of amusements: a deck tennis committee, a dance committee, a concert committee, a fancy dress committee. These bodies were the creation of Nugent Grant-Howard, who, on the first evening in the Mediterranean, as the principal British official on board, was forced by some obscure pressure into the position of Chairman of the Entertainments' Committee. He stood up in the saloon, flanked by the Captain and the Purser, and made a short witty speech which dealt almost entirely with the formation of sub-committees for everything. He called so many of these into being that there was no business left for the main committee to transact, and he never in point of fact took any further part in the activities of entertainment till he made a final speech off Singapore. When his wife remonstrated with him about this—she also sat on several of the sub-committees—Nugent said that decentralisation was half the art of government, and went on reading China Print out of his tin boxes.

Amber had been surprised to hear him make such a

funny speech. It had never occurred to her that it was
in the official character to be amusing, and it cut across
her incipient theory of Grant-Howard, as a learned, serious, important and rather intimidating person, of whom
it was almost a moral obligation to be a little afraid.
Like everyone else, she saw very little of him—he sat in
a deckchair outside his cabin, wearing a pair of tinted
glasses and surrounded by his tin boxes, reading, reading, all day long. People walked past him, doing their
daily five miles round the deck; hurled quoits along the
planking, threw rope-rings into buckets and practised the
ukulele—Nugent remained unmoved, absorbed in the
past and present history of China, as revealed in masses
of pale-green Foreign Office papers. When Dickie accosted him, as he did at least twice a day, with "Whap
are you boing, babby?" Nugent invariably replied,
"Learning about China, Dickie. Don't touch those
papers. Where is Miss Carruthers?" At meals he exchanged a few rather caustic jocosities with the Captain,
a stout dapper quizzical little man, who gave the impression of having at least two sweethearts in every port, and
who amused Amber by his methods of conversation.
Obviously, the necessity of talking to two total strangers
at all meals for four weeks on end, year in and year out,
calls for a special technique, and Captain Heron had
developed it to perfection. He never involved himself
in any topic which demanded the smallest mental effort;
indeed he reserved his fire more completely than anyone
Amber had ever seen, although he conscientiously talked
all the time. He began each meal by an enquiry as to
appetites; went on to discuss the food and recommend
particular dishes with great knowledge and cogency, and
ended by telling two or three funny stories. He never
mentioned books, politics, religion, personal or international relations, or the passengers; his stories were

generally about the Scotch or the Goanese. Very occasionally he was lured by the elderly Naval man who sat on Amber's other side into telling some nautical tale, and then he was enthralling, for he told them very well; but he was at no time a bore, which considering the conversational material he employed was little short of a marvel.

Amber indeed, in spite of herself, began gradually to enjoy her voyage. She had not in the least foreseen the curious solace which the eye can purvey to the distracted human mind, and was startled by the first little thrill of excitement which took her at the sight of Cape St. Vincent —the yellow monastery with its tall pharos, perched so precariously on the bare headland, the cliffs silvered to the top with a plastering of salt from the high-flung Atlantic spray. She could not help being excited during the hot hours they spent ashore at Port Said, by lamplight and moonlight, to find herself actually in Africa, walking on sand, the shadows of palms reaching to her very feet, and polyglot greedy Levantines addressing her as Mrs. Asquith or Mrs. Cornwallis West. "For your vyfe!" said a Levantine to the elderly Naval officer, draping a string of sham turquoises round Amber's neck as she sat drinking lemon-squash, and ogling them both horribly. "She's not my wife," said the N.O. curtly. "For *not* vyfe!" said the Levantine, unabashed, adding another string, and Amber laughed out, ringingly. Mrs. Grant-Howard, across the table, looked up in surprise—she had not heard Amber laugh like that during the whole voyage so far.

Then there was the delightful strangeness of putting on cotton frocks and white shoes in January, as they passed through the Canal and the heavenly heat began, and Amber realised why she was lucky to have a cabin on the port side, in the shade. And there were moments of overwhelming excitement. One morning in the Red Sea she

came up on deck at sunrise and saw on the port beam a
coast of high blue mountains, with what she took for white
mist about their feet, and deeper blue of distant forests
in the valleys. It was some moments before she realised
that this was the coast of Arabia, a rainless and barren
land, whose only mists are drifted sand and its only foliage
the blue shadows of bare rocks. They passed close to
Perim, the low and sun-baked island with its oil depôt
and coaling station, swept all day by the shadows of great
yellow kites and dusky skuas. Sights like these left Amber
with the feeling of having definitely acquired something
of value—of having put a gold piece, as it were, in her
pocket. And just because these gold pieces were so totally
unrelated to Arthur, they took her mind off him, left the
raw place of her pain untouched for hours at a time.
There was nothing to remind her of her home circumstances; every hour and detail of this life on board ship was
new and different. Grant-Howard dragooned his whole
party into the correct tropical régime. They paraded at
6.45 every morning on deck and did physical jerks in
bathing-gowns, before a swim in the sail-bath and an
early breakfast. At this hour Nugent unbent. He forced
Miss Carruthers to learn to dive, with a precarious take-
off from the bulging and unsteady sides of the bath; Amber,
who could dive, was taught to open her eyes under water.
"Yes, you can, perfectly well, if you choose, Miss Harrison.
Go in and try again!" In the afternoons Amber lay in a
chair, watching the shadow of the rails slide to and fro
across the deck as the ship moved, and the majestic and
orderly progress of immense white clouds across the sky
from horizon to horizon. Then indeed she did sometimes
think about Arthur, with a sullen gnawing pain; but if
she caught sight of a group of flying-fish, the skimming
blue and silver creatures distracted her attention. Or
she fell to wondering why none of the writers about tropic

seas had ever mentioned that there were clouds in the
Indian Ocean—that, indeed, the great feature of the
Indian Ocean was this unending procession of clouds, like
sheep moving all day long to a Cotswold fair. The
thought of the Cotswolds hurt again, sharply, as she remembered their great green slopes crowned with woods,
and runs there with Arthur or her father; but then she
was never left for long, she was sure to be summoned to a
committee, or to practise for a competition. The young
men besieged her a good deal too—she was one of the
prettiest and quite the best-dressed girl on board. Arm-
our-plated in her feeling for Arthur, they meant nothing
at all to her, which perhaps accounted for the ease with
which she handled them. Her behaviour called forth
Mrs. Grant-Howard's commendation. "She's no trouble
at all," Joanna said to her husband—"she's frightfully
good with all those creatures. Do you know, Nugent,
I'm really beginning to think she's rather nice, though
she never *says* anything."

"She's too young to say anything. Most of the young
can't say," said Nugent.

"Do you like her?" asked his wife.

"I like the way she swims," said Nugent. "And of
course her legs," he added, as an afterthought.

But Nugent had been keeping an eye on Amber, in
spite of his preoccupation with China. The young
always moved him a little: to a wistful half-envy of their
youth itself, with its ardours and possibilities; to an amused
pity for their inexperience and the hoops through which
they would certainly be put. It had become clear to him
that Amber was traversing a hoop of some sort—her face,
on her hurried return to the boat at Southampton, had
told him that much. He was touched too by her lack
of assurance, the timidity of her desire to do the right
thing with people, which he discerned behind her pretty

manners; and he wondered whether it was due wholly
to her present trouble, or to some deeper cause. Anyhow, he decided, it was time he found out a bit more
about her.

"Isn't that like the West Coast of Scotland?" he said
to her one morning, coming up to where she stood leaning
on the rail as they steamed down the Straits of Malacca,
and indicating the coast of Sumatra. It was a damp
overcast day, and the soft rounded contours rose blue and
misty from a still, colourless sea. "Those hills might
perfectly well be somewhere in Arran or Kintyre," he
went on. "Isn't it funny to think that instead of blue
hares and sheep and grouse, they are full of snakes and
leopards? They look so quiet and harmless." Amber, a
little embarrassed at finding herself the sole object of his
attention, murmured a vague assent. They continued to
gaze on Sumatra till—"Is the world bigger than you
thought?" Grant-Howard asked her suddenly, turning
to her with a quizzical expression. Somehow this reminded her of her father in the most comforting way, and
forgetting her embarrassment—"Much!" she answered
readily.

"Are places important to you?" Nugent pursued.

"Yes—in a way," she answered, doubtfully again, uncertain if he was "being clever to her" as she privately
called it.

"In what way?"

"Well, in two ways, really," said Amber, hesitatingly,
and encouraged by his "Which two?" she produced her
small thought: "There are the places you know well—
they are frightfully important in one way; they're like
a house you live in."

"Yes, good—well?"

"Then there are the places you just see, like that,"—
she waved vaguely at Sumatra. "They're very exciting,

I think. Of course I've not seen many before this time,
but each one I see makes me feel—somehow much richer
than before."

" 'The traveller who bears home bags of gold,' "
muttered Nugent.

"Oh, but *just* that! Is it a poem?"

"Yes it is—and by someone you'll soon meet," said
Nugent, smiling at her sudden animation.

"Oh, who?"

"A man called Benenden—he's First Secretary in
Peking. But go on about your bags of gold. What is
your biggest nugget so far?"

"Something I saw in the Red Sea"—and she went on
to tell him how she had mistaken sand and shadows, for
a moment, for mist and thick trees. "You see, that has
in a way given me Arabia for myself. Not the desert
and camels and horses part—that belongs to the people
who've told one about them. But the barrenness. Can
you see that it makes it seem drier than ever to have
fancied for a moment that I saw it with moisture and
trees, the things it can never have?"

"Yes, of course it does," said Nugent. He was impressed himself by the vividness of the girl's impression.
She had eyes, anyhow. "I wish I'd seen that. Tell
me," he went on, "which do you think most important—
these places one just sees, or the ones one knows fearfully
well?" He had already got a good deal and wished to
draw her out further.

Amber considered. "I've seen so few strange places,
it's hard to say. But I think probably the familiar ones
are. These new ones are exciting, but the others you
know well are really in a way a part of you, and"—
she hesitated—"and of other people." He noticed
the quick nervous look she shot at him, to see if she was
going to be thought silly, and said at once—"Yes, I

know what you mean. Places and people *do* get mixed up."

"Oh, *don't* they?" She was getting quite excited at being so thoroughly understood. "Do you know how a place can be *affected* by a person?" she said, staring away at Sumatra. Getting near the bone, thought Nugent— he said aloud, "Do you mean a place getting so connected with someone in particular that it seems coloured with them, like a dye? So that really you can't see it or think of it apart from them?"

"Yes," said Amber, and nothing else. It was exactly what she did mean; before the blue outline of Sumatra rose a picture of the pool among the sallows on the road between Thornhays and Riddingcote, which during those miserable months at home had not ceased to echo with a ghostly tune of Arthur, and her mistaken happiness. This thought frightened her with its intensity; she moved her hands restlessly on the rail—she mustn't go back to all that! She began to wish to escape, only she hadn't quite the courage. But Nugent noticed the movement of her hands, and led the conversation back to the strangeness of places—Penang and Colombo, which they had just seen. When Mrs. Grant-Howard came up a little later with some question and carried her husband off, Amber was left with a definite sense of comfort. However clever and important Mr. Grant-Howard might be, one could talk to him; and he kept on at a subject, didn't skim off with the little light remarks. She felt almost at home with him. And to feel at home with anyone was a release from the slight strain of living for a month among people one didn't really know.

For the rest of the voyage, too, whenever she acquired what Nugent had called a nugget, she thought of the line he had quoted—"The traveller who bears home bags of gold"—and speculated about the author, the man with

the funny name which she hadn't quite caught, Ben something. The words had captured her imagination, because they corresponded so closely to her own feeling.
Amber had met plenty of poets—Lady Julia ran rather
to literature—but it was a surprise to her that people in
the diplomatic service should write anything but despatches, or whatever they did write. She collected one
more supreme nugget too. After leaving Singapore they
steamed for a couple of days up the China Sea—the
weather turned rainy, rough and chilly, and they shivered
after the heat of the last fortnight. And then one morning Amber woke to calm and clear skies, and her first
glimpse of China. Not a landfall—no landfall could have
been so lovely and astonishing. No—through her port-
hole, in the early light, she saw a distant fleet of
junks, their square sails looking like a cloud of great
brown and golden butterflies on the silky blue and prim-
rose of the water. Oh, wonderful! She hurled on some
clothes and ran up on deck, where she stood gazing at
them, enchanted and stirred by her first movement of
genuine curiosity about China for its own sake, and not
simply as the place where Uncle Bill lived. There must
be something remarkable about a race which could make
of a fishing-boat a thing as lovely as a butterfly. She said
something of this to Grant-Howard at breakfast, and he
gave her one of his quick appreciative looks from behind
his glasses. "Yes, and had you thought of them as sea-
men at all? Most English people don't—their idea of the
Chinese is a whole race paddling about ricefields in grass
hats."

"Mr. Grant-Howard, why do people say '*John* Chinaman'?" Miss Carruthers asked at this point.

"I haven't the least idea," said Nugent.

"They don't say it in China—we call 'em Daniels,"
said Captain Heron. "You'll see, in Hong-Kong."

"Why Daniels?" Miss Carruthers wanted to know. But Captain Heron could not satisfy her.

"I wonder what they call us?" Amber hazarded.

"Big-noses, or foreign devils," the Captain told her. "They think us simply hideous."

In Hong-Kong Amber did see, or rather hear, the Royal Navy calling the Chinese "Daniels," and it made her laugh whenever she heard it. But from Hong-Kong onwards the voyage became, she felt, more and more a succession of Consuls. Wherever Mr. Grant-Howard went, Consuls seemed to spring up before him like mushrooms, and afterwards she remembered each different port chiefly by the peculiarities of its Consul, as American tourists remember places chiefly by the peculiarities of the food. A huge whiskered Consul-General from Canton came down to meet Mr. Grant-Howard at Hong-Kong, where they lunched with His Excellency at Government House at the bottom of the hill, and dined with him at Mountain Lodge on the top. A thin learned Consul-General, and a whole troop of lesser ones appeared at Shanghai, where the party changed into a smaller boat to proceed to Tientsin; one of the lesser Consuls took Amber shopping in the French concession, and she learned that good blue-and-white china costs more in Shanghai than in London. The smaller boat was very small indeed, and it grew colder and colder; they made a sort of nest of rugs on deck, abaft the saloon, and camped there in the sun, watching the icicles which hung from the rails dip up and down against the bitter bright blue of the sea. At Chefoo the Consul was a long melancholy person with an umbrella; he and Grant-Howard stood on the deck talking, and staring at one another's boots in the way that Amber began now to connect with official business. The Wei-Hai-Wei Consul, who appeared the moment they anchored, like all the rest, to talk to Nugent, was a

little youthful man with bright eyes and long eyelashes—
he looked, not at his boots, but at Amber, and she decided
on these grounds that he wasn't a proper Consul at all.
When he had gone ashore, and they were steaming away
from the wintry brown and white hills that mount guard
over the harbour, she spoke of it to Nugent. "Is that
little man—Mr. Green, was he?—really a proper consul?"

"Well, he's a vice-consul, really, but he's acting Consul
there for the time being. Why?" asked Nugent. Amber
explained, and Nugent roared. Joanna, hearing him
roar, glanced across to where they stood together at the
rail, and registered a further note of approval of Amber.
Someone to keep Nugent content was always an acquisi-
tion—"if she amuses him, we must see plenty of her in
Peking," she thought to herself. She had gathered even
in London that Peking was intellectually a desert. Not
that Amber seemed strikingly intellectual, but Nugent
never took any interest in complete mutts, however
pretty. They had to *be* pretty, but they had not to be
fools, or too affected, in order to amuse him.

As it turned out, they were compromised into seeing
plenty of Amber from the outset. When they berthed
at the bund in Tientsin there came on board to greet
them, not only the inevitable Consul-General, a cadaver-
ous man with a face like a lawyer and a bitter smile,
but a neat stoutish little woman, in whose round face a
look of worry was superimposed on an evident natural
jollity, who was greeted by Amber as Aunt Bessie. Aunt
Bessie was in trouble. Old Bill Harrison had been seized
with some internal complaint while duck shooting near
Pei-tai-ho, and had been hurried into hospital at Tientsin,
where he now lay, watched over by Aunt Bessie from an
hotel close by. Amber could not go to the house in
Peking alone—"So you must just stay here with me, dear.
I'm afraid it will be rather dull for you, as I am with

your Uncle most of the time." The Grant-Howards, on
learning how the land lay—the Consul-General confided
to Nugent that "Old Bill" was pretty bad—immediately
offered to take Amber on to Peking with them and look
after her till the Harrisons were able to come back to their
own house. Aunt Bessie, though she made some formal
protests, was obviously relieved at the suggestion and finally accepted it gratefully.

"She may be a help to you," said Nugent to Joanna.
"She's rather good with Dickie."

"Oh yes," said Joanna easily. "I shall like to have
her." She was thinking that Amber was even better
with Dickie's father, who was really more of a proposition
than Dickie. Very small boys don't suffer from bore-
dom, at any rate. "It's an excellent plan," said Nugent's
wife. So it was still under the auspices of the Grant-
Howards that Amber entered Peking.

Chapter Four

THE Grant-Howard party left Tientsin on the morning after their landing in a slight and rather exciting atmosphere of uncertainty. There was a small war on, and their train was the first to go through to Peking for some days—indeed there was a certain doubt as to whether it would run right through. They sat crammed in a small coupé adjoining a long coach full of Chinese; a soldier with a rifle stood in one door-way, while a military executioner, a curved sword with a blade seven inches across slung at his back, patrolled coach and coupé alike. The fact that he wore elastic-sided boots and grey cotton gloves added, as Nugent observed, to his charm. Nugent sat reading some tele-grams which he had got at the Consulate; Joanna was writing letters on her knee; Dickie kept asking Miss Carruthers if the executioner couldn't be persuaded "po pake off his sworb, so as I cam see if ip will cup!" Miss Carruthers was very repressive; she thought the exe-cutioner a most dangerous and objectionable travelling companion; she was feeling train-sick, and resented the fact that she had to shove past the sentry every time she wanted to get into the lavatory. It was embarrassing enough, travelling with gentlemen, anyhow, Miss Car-ruthers thought, with a hostile glance at the unconscious Nugent: but really, to have to push a yellow Chinaman with a fixed bayonet away from the very door! It was not at all well arranged. Burbidge stared out of the window, and at intervals sniffed. There certainly *was* an odd smell all through the carriage—when the executioner came past, Burbidge sniffed harder than ever. She leaned across to Amber once—"Don't you think he smells of acetylene, Miss, that man?" she enquired confidentially, in a whisper. Amber's one visit to Italy enabled her to correct Burbidge; the smell was not acetylene, but garlic. "Comes to much the same thing, Miss," said Burbidge, putting Eau de Cologne on her handkerchief—"I never could abide acetylene—not even on a bike, I couldn't. It turns me."

Amber, like Burbidge, sat staring out of the window. This was China! She saw a flat landscape, mud-coloured and absolutely bare except for innumerable small round mounds, anything from three to ten feet high, scattered through the fields, as though a whole army of giant moles had been at work. These, she learned from Nugent, when Dickie routed his father out of the telegrams with an enquiry, were graves. The soil was dry, with a dusty bonelike dryness such as she had never seen. At intervals they passed villages, groups of one-storey houses built of and plastered with mud, with thatched roofs—they were as brown as the soil they stood on. Groups of little spindly orchard trees made a pattern on the skyline from time to time, like blue and biscuit-coloured lace; and the shadows between the houses were blue. It had a certain beauty in spite of its dreariness, this immense expanse of landscape in two colours only, pale brown and pale blue, with its extreme simplicity of design; Amber remembered that Pater had said something very knowing about economy of detail in a landscape being so valuable and tried to remember what it was, but her attention was deflected by a trainful of wounded soldiers which they passed just then. Dickie screeched with excitement—"There's a man with bloob om his bambage!" Slowly the train trailed on across the brown country, past ramshackle brown stations plas-

tered with flaring yellow advertisements of American
cigarettes, till at last it crept through an archway,
rumbled along between a frozen canal and a high grey
wall, and drew up beside a platform in a bare draughty
station. They had arrived.

The considerable group which awaited them on this
platform Amber sorted out gradually during the introductions. Henry Leroy, the Commercial and Oriental
attaché, was the big heavy black-haired Irishman with a
booming voice. The small *pincé* man with a thin, nervous,
kind-faced wife was Mr. Hugo, the Consul. Consuls
again! Then there was a very tall handsome red-haired
young man with an eyeglass, a clipped moustache and a
horsey walk, whom everyone called Joe, but who was
introduced to Amber as Mr. George Hawtrey; and a
rather smaller man, mouse-brown and rather untidy as
to hair, with his coat-collar half turned up and a brilliant
smile, whom everyone called Rupert and who was not
introduced at all. In the background stood a gaunt
lame individual in gaiters, presiding over a group of
Chinese in neat quilted black cotton jackets and trousers
bound in round the ankles with white garters—waving
his hand at this group—"Jamieson will see about your
stuff," said Leroy to Grant-Howard—"We'll go on. The
cars are outside the Water-gate." And ignoring their
luggage as if it did not exist, he led the party off down
the platform, which was a yelling mass of Chinese—soldiers
and coolies mixed up with bundles of merchandise
and crates of fish, professorial figures in long grey gowns
with horn spectacles and umbrellas; mail-bags, railway employees—all struggling and shouting as if in the
throes of a first-class riot. It seemed to Amber very
unwise to abandon their possessions in such a mob; she
wished she had managed to snatch her dressing-case, as

Miss Carruthers had done. But no one else seemed to mind. Grant-Howard was walking between Leroy and Mr. Hugo, already talking business, she gathered from the scraps that floated back—"Wang's attitude is the crucial factor," "Likin is always the trouble." Hawtrey was escorting Joanna, and talking hard already. "Of course you're going to ride, Mrs. Grant-Howard? Splendid! We must get you fitted out with some ponies at once. They're not really fully broken, you know, but you'll manage them all right once you get the trick of it. Leroy and I will put you on to some." Joanna made some appropriate response. "Oh, no trouble at all, Mrs. Nugent. You must come out to our temple and try some there. My friend Harry Leicester has one or two that would just do you, I think. He's a very good fellow, Leicester. We share a temple, you know. And Nugent must come up to Huai Lai and shoot a goose soon. The shooting's pretty good. Of course it's nothing to what we used to get in Uganda—but it's not too bad, not too bad." His voice, rather high and curiously soft, ran on and on, as they trailed down a cinder-path under an immense forbidding smoke-stained wall—Amber began to feel hungry. The rather untidy young man was now walking beside her—as they approached an archway which pierced the wall he pointed to it and said, "That's the Water-gate!"

"Oh, really," Amber replied, looking at it.

The young man looked at her sideways. "You don't know what the Water-gate is in the least, do you?" he said, twinkling at her with a pair of light blue eyes; eyes so very light as to be startling in his tanned face. He had a mouth rather like a fish, and he pursed it up at her now, quizzically.

"No," said Amber.

"The troops got in that way when they raised the siege

of the Legations in the Boxer rising in 1900," he said. "It's an historic site."

"Oh," said Amber, and looked at the arch again. "Wasn't it guarded?" she said. The arch was high, and so broad that a dozen men could march through it abreast—to enter it, as they were now doing, seemed too easy a matter to fit such an event.

The young man burst out laughing. "You have the true historian's outlook, evidently," he said—"and observe historic sites with an accurate and sceptical eye. But—no; it wasn't like this then. It was only a conduit with a grating and water in the bottom. They really had quite a job to get in—it was all quite proper."

Amber laughed. The tone of the young man's voice as he apologised for the Water-gate, and his pursed fish's mouth amused her. She was wondering if he could be Benenden.

"There are quite a lot of historic sites here," he went on. "If you have feelings about the Flag, and all that, you can go and have them at the Jade Canal gate, where there are bullet-holes in the wall. I'll take you. *Do* you have feelings about the Flag?" he asked, peering at her.

"I did on the boat," said Amber. This seemed to amuse the young man; he laughed again, not loudly, but with a sort of intensity of amusement that was very engaging. "Service in the saloon on Sundays? The Navy singing?" he said. "Oh, I know——"

"Benenden, put Miss Harrison in my car," said Leroy loudly. "You two can walk." Amber found herself in a car with Miss Carruthers and Dickie, driven by a smart Chinese chauffeur. She caught a glimpse of a high European building as she was driven off down a broad walled street, planted with an avenue of immature and leafless trees, towards the Legation. Tired, hungry, excited by the strangeness of everything, she was yet conscious of a small stir of interest—the mousy man *was* Benenden.

The two young men, meanwhile, strolled back together towards the Legation, following the cars. "Mrs. Nugent looks all right," Hawtrey observed, pausing to light a cigarette.

"It's most extraordinary the way all the tallest men in the Service marry these *minute* wives!" burst out Benenden, talking with extraordinary energy and very fast. "Roger and Dacres and Leftwich and Killin and Tommy Armstrong. Every blessed one of them over six foot, and deliberately arranges to go through life beside a little dot of a woman. And generally plain with it!"

"Mrs. Nugent's not too bad," said Hawtrey. "She's not exactly a *femme fatale*, but she's quite chic. Not like poor Frosty-face, the *gouvernante*. What's *her* name, by the way?"

"Don't know. Never heard it. Forgotten it. What's it matter, anyhow?"

Hawtrey didn't seem to think it mattered much either. "I like the looks of the girl," was his next remark.

"It's one more girl, anyhow," said Benenden. "Not that girls of that age are particularly interesting as a rule, but it is something to dance with."

"My dear fellow, that's your own fault. The place is full of nice girls, charming girls; only you are so frightfully fastidious, you won't see anything of them."

"No, I damn well won't!" Benenden burst out. "I won't go and dance with typists and secretaries, just because I'm short of a petticoat. I'd sooner go without." He pulled a pair of fur-lined gloves out of his pocket, drew them on, humped his shoulders and said "Filthily cold it is."

"They're British, after all," said Hawtrey, ignoring the

last remark. He threw out his chest a little and said—
"Out here it's positively a duty to keep in touch with one's
nationals. Places like this are the front line trench, you
know. When you've been out here as long as I have——"

"Oh, stow it, Joe! Damn national solidarity!"
Benenden, like most people who knew Hawtrey at all
well, knew at the beginning of one of his high hurried
orations precisely what *clichés* he was going to use before
the end.

"Oh, well, you know——" Hawtrey was quite un-
ruffled. He returned to the subject of Miss Harrison.
"She's a pretty girl. She looks thoroughly well bred,
and *rangée*, you know. Naturally, my dear fellow, I prefer that, just as you do, just as you do."

"It's possible for girls to be too *rangées*," said Benenden
gloomily—"though not usual, I admit." They had entered the Legation compound by this time, and at the
grass square Benenden swung off to the left.

"Coming to ride this afternoon?" Hawtrey called after
him.

"No, thanks."

"Do you good, you know—make the blood run."

But Benenden, without replying, entered a low grey
house backed against the wall of the compound, and disappeared. Hawtrey walked off to his own house and
lunch.

On the following morning Nugent Grant-Howard was
sitting in the room already allocated to him as a study,
surrounded by his tin boxes, methodically arranging his
papers in the drawers of a large heavy writing-table.
The room was a tall grey box, with two French windows
draped with blue curtains giving on to an arcaded verandah, which ran round two sides of the house. It bore
signs of the process of "setting-in"—besides the boxes,
piles of books lay on the floor, while others were already

in position in the shelves on both sides of the fireplace.
A small tree of white lilac stood in a corner by the window,
delicately distinct against the grey wall, curiously frail
and fresh among the solid blue furniture; on a long narrow
table three shallow earthenware bowls held violet plants
in full bloom. Nugent's eye rested on them as he paused
for a moment to light a pipe, and he leaned over and
sniffed the nearest bowl with a sort of gratitude. Well!—
if the house *was* ugly and the furniture worse, it was something to have flowers like this in February. And that
chef man with the profile like a Roman Emperor and the
long pigtail could cook! Inured by long habit to the
rigours of moving-in in many capitals, Grant-Howard
had been astonished by the ease with which it happened
in Peking, and amused by some of its features. That
parade of the servants, for example—conducted by the
fellow with the game leg, Jamieson, the Legation Constable. The domestics, in their white or blue clothes, had
all filed past, each making a curious sort of reverence,
while Jamieson spoke their names. There seemed to be
no end of them—a dozen or fifteen, at least—and most of
them had been in the house for years. Only Liu, the
Number One, a little wizened fellow with a face like a
monkey, spoke any English to mention—how Joanna
would manage he didn't know, except that Joanna always
did manage. And by Heaven, how those servants had
worked the day before! They had lunched off borrowed
stuff—Mrs. Hugo had arranged all that; but by dinner-
time wine, silver, linen—every blessed thing had been
stowed somehow, and they had eaten a first-rate dinner
off their own plate and china, as if they had been there
for weeks. That child, too, Amber, had worked like a
horse, and shown she had quite a head on her shoulders.
Nugent laughed suddenly, remembering the episode of
Amber and the Minister, the previous afternoon. Amber,

under Joanna's instructions, had been sorting sheets in
the hall, which was a sea of linen and blankets surrounded
by a shore of packing-cases, when Sir James walked in to
pay a call of welcome. Amber, hearing a voice asking
for Mr. Grant-Howard, looked up from where she knelt,
flushed and dishevelled, and said in some confusion—
"I'll find him. Are—are you a consul?"

"Certainly not," Sir James replied, with some asperity
—and then, taken with Amber's prettiness and obvious
embarrassment, "a Pro-consul," he chuckled. Nugent,
through his study door, had been a spectator of the little
scene, which passed before he had time to rescue Sir
James. But it had done no harm, he thought. Boggit
was on the whole a good fellow, and a fairly easy chief
to *ménager*. And now Nugent found his mind running
off on the too familiar track, of how this new post was
going to work out for him. He knew so well what it involved, and here it was all to be done over again—getting
on with his Minister, getting on with the Chancery; taking stock of the *chers collègues*, finding out which of them
mattered and which of them didn't, and then getting on
with *them*. He leaned back in his chair, a little wearily,
and puffed at his pipe, thinking how boring the business
of getting on with the *chers collègues* was going to be. But
it was absolutely essential to doing the job properly. He
had of course also to find out what, precisely, the job was
—what problems awaited solution, what was the most
fruitful line of advance—all that. This prospect did not
bore Nugent—he liked nothing so well as getting his teeth
into a situation, and working it through. And here in
China, it was bound to be peculiarly interesting and absorbing, getting to grips with this strange race. That
part of it was all right. But there were always two
aspects to every post—the job itself, and the effect on one's
career. Nugent was pretty well acclimatised by now to

that curious sense of isolation, remoteness, and of almost complete non-comprehension by the authorities at home, which assails all diplomatists on foreign service. In that remoteness and isolation, so much, so painfully much, depends on one's minister. He can blast a whole career in one private letter. Nugent had seen this happen, and a prickling of discomfort ran over his mind, like a shiver over the skin, at the thought. China was apt to be a grave of reputations. So far his own career had gone very well, without his needing to worry much; when he had been in any way conspicuously placed abroad, hitherto—in charge, for instance—the right thing to do on the spot had not been unduly unpopular at home. But this was sheer luck; very often it *was* unpopular—and what then? Oh, well, one must trust to luck—and he'd treated Walter and Noel pretty well. After all, the Private Secretaries were the people who mattered most in the long run.

Shouts outside roused him, and he looked up. Slightly distorted by the glass of the double windows, he saw the blue-clothed figures of two of the house-coolies trundling an immense wooden barrel across the garden, while Dickie, minute but solid in his reefer and beret, commanded them with gestures and shrill cries. As Nugent watched, his face changed suddenly, almost out of recognition. The weariness, the careful diplomatic calm left it, and like a light switched on suddenly in a dark room, pride and tenderness illuminated his eyes, his lips—the whole man glowed with them as he looked at his son. The little monkey, ordering them about like that! When the procession with the barrel had disappeared behind a fringe of evergreens, Grant-Howard turned back to his papers. But the current of his thoughts had changed. He was aware of a certain vexation with himself for having allowed his mind to dwell on his career at all. That his

E

children, that Dickie, should come to a healthy maturity was really what mattered—and that they should grow up intelligently honest, aware of interior values. Changing his spectacles to examine a paper more closely, Grant-Howard thought how tremendously important was this question of integrity in the inner life; how trivial, relatively, a mere career. And what, exactly, did one do to make one's children realise it? Oh Hades, this telegram didn't belong in this series at all! Where the devil was the file it did belong in? He became absorbed in the routine of his job once more.

He was still shuffling his papers about and swearing gently and pleasantly to himself when the door opened and his wife came in. Joanna sat down in a blue armchair and began to laugh.

"What is it?" Nugent asked.

"This place is so comic!" she said. "We've got a new name!"

"Sounds very Biblical," said Nugent—"how have we acquired it?"

"Oh, Mr. Hugo has been in about it, with another little man, very learned. Apparently we must have a Chinese name, for the servants and so on; and if you leave it to them, they make up one which means sewers or bitches. So an official one has to be given out."

"And what is ours?"

Joanna consulted a slip of paper—"Kang Ho-Wu," she read out. "That's the nearest the Chinese can get to Grant-Howard. They haven't settled what it means yet, exactly."

"But they must *know* what those words mean," protested Grant-Howard, taking the paper and scanning it. His swift and orderly mind revolted from vagueness in any form.

"No—not necessarily," said Joanna, with the equable

firmness which Nugent found so restful in his wife. "The learned little man explained it all. The *sounds* may mean heaps of things—it's the characters which matter. He's going to find some characters with frightfully exalted meanings to fit those three sounds."

"How crazy!" was Nugent's only comment, as he handed back the slip.

"I'm going to learn Chinese," Joanna next announced. "Leroy will get me a teacher, he says."

"You won't have time," said Nugent dampingly.

"Oh yes, I shall," said his wife easily. "Though not much, I admit. Sir James sent Mr. Benenden across with this just now." She held out a small paper-covered book. Nugent examined it—"Oh yes, the diplomatic list."

"He's ticked the ones *I* call on," Joanna proceeded. "The new arrival calls first here, you know—but only on potatoes as large or larger than oneself. The others call on me."

"Well, that lets you off with chef-esses and counsellors' wives—not too bad."

"*And* Military Attachés," she reminded him. "And then there's an appalling lot of outside people—heads of Banks and Hospitals and God knows what. And the Posts and the Salt."

"Well, you must be careful to do it properly and only go to the ones you've got to," said Nugent. He made this kind of remark quite mechanically, being perfectly well aware that Joanna was the most thorough and socially efficient of wives.

But the list had brought him back into the cautious watch-your-step frame of mind, the curiously artificial atmosphere of diplomacy; that atmosphere in which no one ever says anything or goes anywhere or does anything without keeping a watchful eye on all the possible effects and repercussions of their words or actions. Naturally this is most acute in a new post, when all one's social surroundings are *terra incognita;* but to some extent it persists always, at once exciting and enervating.

His wife, however, rated his remark exactly at its due worth. "Oh, that will be all right," she said.

"It's a pity Leroy's wife is at home—she would have put you right. Who shall you ask?" Nugent enquired.

"The Private Secretary—that's what he's for," said Joanna, getting up. She also went and smelt the lilac-tree. "Heavenly these flowers are," she murmured. "Mr. Hawtrey has asked us to lunch tomorrow—shall we go?" she said.

Nugent pulled out his little engagement-book and looked at it. "Yes—by all means. What do you think of George?" he asked, facing round to her. He felt a sudden urgent need for a touch of reality, for some breath of the homely simplicity of conjugal criticism, as a relief from the atmosphere of calls and telegrams.

Joanna gave him a shrewd affectionate glance: "If I were clever, I should call him stupid," she said. "At present I call him remarkably good-looking!" She laughed. "I'll tell you more tomorrow." She picked up a single fallen blossom of the lilac, stuck it in the thick hair above Nugent's right ear, and left the room. Nugent turned back to his papers. He did not smile, but he felt he had got what he wanted.

A little later the door opened again, and Miss Harrison entered, her arms full of books. "Mrs. Grant-Howard thought you would want these in here," she said—"shall I put them on the shelves or on the floor?"

Nugent rose and peered at the titles; he bent to peer, and his head, with the lilac-blossom stuck in the grizzled hair, came close under Amber's face. Amber smiled, amused. "Oh, the floor, I think. Here, I'll take them,"

said Nugent, straightening himself up.   He surprised her
smile.   "How do you like Peking?" he asked her, smiling
too.

"I think it's enormous fun," said Amber.   "The servants are so fascinating.   It's like living in a cinema to
watch them.   *Two* men brought my morning tea!   Oh,
and Mr. Grant-Howard, have you noticed the face of
that tall one called Chang?"

Nugent had not.   "What about it?"

"It's like a Saint's face in a German drawing."

"I should doubt his having a Saint's character, though
he can undoubtedly fold clothes," said Nugent, in his
most man-of-the-world manner.   Amber felt rebuffed.

"I must go," she said.   "I promised to help Dickie.
He's started to build a 'forpress' in the upper garden."
At the absurd word a gleam of that illumination of pride
and tenderness came again into Nugent's face.   "Oh,
that's what the barrel was for," was all he said.   But
Amber went off with a new facet to her growing theory
about her host—that his man-of-the-world-iness was only
skin deep.   Then what was underneath?

Chapter Five

MR. GEORGE HAWTREY prided himself a good deal on the excellence of his housekeeping. His bungalow was comfortably, almost richly furnished, with Chinese curios superimposed on a basis of solid furniture taken over from his predecessor, and diversified with a sprinkling of trophies from Uganda. The whole effect was agreeable and slightly incoherent, like Hawtrey himself. On the morning of his lunch-party he had left the Chancery a little early, and was now congenially engaged in giving the final touches to his arrangements —tasting the cocktails, chivying the boys and arranging the name-cards. Cigarettes—where were the Virginian cigarettes? Here there were only Russian and Turkish! Chin, his Number One, said Mastah not order *wu wu wu* (555's). He was told, explosively, to get them, and a coolie went flying from the back regions to the canteen.

Hawtrey continued to plan his table. Mrs. Grant-Howard must of course go on his right—she was a counsellor's wife; but who sat on his left was more difficult. Madame de Bulle, the wife of the French Fourth Secretary, had a technical claim as being a diplomat's wife— but then Countess Stefany was of much higher rank socially, though her husband was merely a buyer of Chinese antiques for a big Vienna-Paris firm. In the end he plumped for the Countess; Mimi de Bulle was a sportswoman, whatever you might think of her morals, and above such petty considerations. Harry and Lydia Leicester of course were merely chemical fertilisers, and apart from her beauty and his good nature had no social

claims at all—she could sit on Grant-Howard's left and
Mimi on his right, and they could all talk horses. He
half regretted having asked Mimi and Count Stefany
together, now that that girl was coming—one always
did ask them together, but English girls—! They really
were very awkward, they knew nothing about anything,
and they had a way of opening their eyes as wide as a
baby's, when they were shocked, and saying nothing at
all. Well, if she was going to live for a year in Peking,
she must begin to learn, thought Hawtrey to himself,
humming "*La donna è mobile*" a little out of tune, as he
placed a card with "Miss Harrison" on it between Harry
Leicester's and Benenden's; he dropped his eyeglass, and
before he found it, trod on it; calling to Chin to clear up
the glass chips, he went into his study and got another
from a box on the mantelpiece. But she looked a nice
girl, a pretty girl, Miss Harrison—after all, what was
there to touch a nice well-bred English girl? He hoped
Herman and Mimi would behave. If only they would
stick to horses! That really was the main concern of all
of them. If the G.-H.'s wanted to ride, you couldn't do
more for them than to introduce them at one go to the
Leicesters, who simply lived for horses: to Mimi, who had
the best racing-stable in Peking, except perhaps Old
Bill's, and to Herman Stefany, who was quite the most
brilliant horseman in the place.

"*Er-ch'in-ch'ai t'ai-t'ai lai-loh!*" announced Chin, and
Hawtrey went into the drawing-room to greet his guests.
By Jove, she was a pretty girl, now she was all dolled up!
And Mrs. G.-H. was very fresh and chic, too, in those furs.
A certain amount of screaming outside heralded the
entry of Madame de Bulle, a large round-about French
Canadian, whose dress and make-up were carefully
designed to give the maximum impression of impropriety,
and succeeded. She flung herself on Hawtrey, thrusting

her arm through his—"Ah, Joe, *mon ami, figure-toi que* Huron, *mon beau* Huron, *a quelque-chose de grave!*" Hawtrey glanced at Amber over Mimi's head—sure enough her eyes were wide as an infant's. He hurriedly detached Madame de Bulle sufficiently to present her to Mrs. Grant-Howard, and then the Leicesters came in— Harry small, neat, dark, with a mouth so like a jockey's that one expected to see a straw in it; Lydia tall, slender, ashen-blonde, her face as still as a flower—except for her very vivid blue eyes there was no life or colour in her face at all. There were more introductions; the Stefanys arrived, and hard on their heels Grant-Howard and Benenden, completing the party. When everyone had nibbled an olive or two, drunk a cocktail, and flung a minute cigarette with a straw mouthpiece into the fire unfinished, they went in to lunch.

Sitting at the round black lacquer table, incredibly smothered with yellow roses in the month of February, Amber observed her fellow-guests. Mr. Leicester on her left was talking about ponies to Madame de Bulle; on her right Rupert Benenden was eating his soup with humped shoulders and a general appearance of gloom. This was really a relief to her—too humble to feel that she had much claim on the attention of others, she liked to be able to study them undisturbed before she was called upon to make the effort of conversation herself. The Stefanys attracted her attention first. The Countess was very tall and dark, and quite perfectly dressed, but Amber was absorbed by her face; she had never seen so much animation in a human visage before. It was impossible to tell if she was beautiful or plain, because her face was never still enough to be seen. This Amber found curiously fascinating. She turned her attention to the husband. Count Herman was slight and fair, with an over-sweet smile which he used all the time, but Amber thought his eyes looked a little malicious. He, too, was talking about horses to Mrs. Grant-Howard; everyone was talking about horses; she could hear her host's high voice and frequent laugh referring to horses across the table. This ought to have made her feel at home, but for some reason the familiar jargon, in a setting so unfamiliar as this room with the scroll-paintings on the walls, the masses of yellow roses on the table, the discreet boys in white moving silently over the rush matting, merely had the effect of emphasising her sense of strangeness. Most of all perhaps, it was odd to hear a kind of talk she knew so well, in the mouths of people so unwonted to her home-bred eyes—Count Stefany with his sleek un-English fairness, his wife with her dark grace and unbelievably perfect clothes, or that Madame de Bulle! Impossible to imagine them in Gloucestershire. She found herself looking at the Grant-Howards, who so recently had also been strangers, with a sense of reassurance—now they represented the familiar; they were her safety here.

Mr. Leicester presently turned his dark jockey's face to her and asked her if she rode? Amber said that she did.

"Good! You must come out and see our temple at P'ao-ma-ch'ang," he said. "It's a charming place. We do all our riding from there. We share it with Joe, you know." Amber did not know. "Joe," he called across to Hawtrey, "I'm telling Miss Grant-Howard that she must come out to the Temple of the Excited Insects and try some ponies there." Hawtrey made some indistinguishable reply. Amber opened her mouth to say that she was *not* Miss Grant-Howard, but Mr. Leicester was too quick for her. "We might be able to put you on to something that would suit you," he went on, turning again to Amber—the faintest flavour of the salesman crept into his manner, to her amusement. This at least was familiar.

"You'll keep your ponies in the Legation Stable, I suppose?" Mr. Leicester pursued. "Do you know how many you'll want, at all?"

"I expect I shall keep them at my uncle's—I believe he has a stable," Amber replied.

"Aren't you staying in the Legation, then?"

"Only till they come back; then I go to the Harrisons."

"Oh! Oh, you're Old Bill's niece, that he was talking about. I apologise—I got you wrong. Oh well, he'll put you right, of course." Mr. Leicester's tone altered considerably at the mention of Old Bill. His air of salesmanship vanished. "He'll get you the best of everything," he said, almost ruefully. "Do you read, Miss Harrison?" he went on. "That is much rarer here. Everyone rides in Peking, but practically no one reads, except me and Benenden." Amber noticed that he did not wait for her reply. "We read, don't we, Benenden?" Mr. Leicester continued, talking across her. Benenden made no answer. Still untroubled, Mr. Leicester went on—"By the way, what did you think of that last book of Rotherham's I lent you? Have you finished it?"

At this point Hawtrey's voice rose across the table. "Miss Harrison, you must have some of this. This is bustard—our Peking speciality. Most unusual, you know, and delicious—really delicious. My boy gets them specially." Amber helped herself rather gingerly from the breast of an enormous bird to a slice of dark brown meat which looked like mutton, and tasted like venison, with a reminiscence of grouse. It was delicious, as Hawtrey said. But Benenden was now replying to Leicester, across her. "Yes, I finished it—I don't like it," he said.

"Oh, don't you?   It's written with tremendous punch, don't you think?"

"It's got a sort of vulgar violence, if you call that punch," said Benenden.   "Look here, Harry, you were in the War and so was I, but *we* don't spend our time either bleating that the War has wrecked our lives, or bellowing like angry bulls at our fathers for having caused it.   Aren't you getting rather fed up with all these books that do?   It simply isn't true that the War was made by the old men in Clubs—and it's even less true to pretend that it wrecked our lives.   It *ended* lives enough, God knows, but it didn't wreck all the others."

"I think Rotherham is tremendously sincere, though," said Leicester.

"Oh, sincere!   My dear Harry, a little boy of six kicking and yelling on the floor is tremendously sincere, he's showing terrific 'punch,' as you call it, but we don't extol him for that."   Leicester laughed, and Amber laughed too — Benenden's own violence was curiously engaging.   "It's childish temper, that's what it is — it isn't a mature book.   One expects the young in their twenties to rage against the established order, and scream hysterically about the older generation; but if a man hasn't outgrown all that by the time he's thirty, he's no damn good.   This man Rotherham was all through the War; he must be nearly forty, and yet he's still in a screaming temper over it.   That's silly, you know."

"I agree with you up to a point," said Leicester—"I still think the actual writing is extraordinarily competent. And he does know what he's talking about."

"My dear chap, we *all* know what he's talking about! So why talk about it?   He's got no monopoly of the War. Why can't he let it alone?   It was nasty enough while it lasted.   What is even *more* silly and sickening, if possible," Benenden went on, talking faster and faster and with more and more emphasis, "is these *young* novelists, who were being trundled about in perambulators while the War was on, and now take it upon themselves to stand up and curse the older generation too, and say that *their* silly neurotic little lives have been blasted. If your life is blasted, let it *be* blasted, blast it! But don't write it up, for God's sake! Who cares?" He drank some wine, while Leicester laughed out. Benenden suddenly turned to Amber and said, "What do *you* think, Miss Harrison?"

"I—I don't write," she faltered, taken aback.

"No, but you read, don't you? Do you agree with me about these sort of books?"

A sudden memory of certain young novelists who had tormented her with their cleverness at Riddingcote came into Amber's mind, and with a little revengeful impulse she said—"I think I agree with you that it doesn't much matter if some writers' lives *are* blasted." Benenden looked at her with surprise—his eyes said "Oho!" though he merely pursed his mouth—this was quite unexpected. Leicester roared; "One for you, Rupert!" he said. Amber blushed furiously—she had forgotten for the moment that Benenden wrote. "Oh, I didn't mean that," she said.

"But that's a very sensible thing to mean," said Benenden. "It doesn't in the least matter if most people's lives are blasted, if only they'll keep their mouths shut about it. Besides, it's generally their own fault if they *are*. Isn't it?"

"I expect so," said Amber limply. This last shot of Benenden's brought her down from her little flight of animation like a bird with a broken wing. Of course it was one's own fault—her misery over Arthur was her own silly, silly fault! It all rushed over her again, making her feel lost and small—involuntarily her eyes sought

the Grant-Howards. To her relief, Joanna at that
moment rose, with polite smiles at the Countess and
Madame de Bulle, and the ladies left the room.

In the drawing-room Mrs. Grant-Howard and Countess Stefany, seated on an immense sofa, their feet on
the jazz-looking skin of an okapi, at once began a brisk
conversation about mutual friends in Buda-Pesth, while
Madame de Bulle started a toilette of such a drastic
nature that Amber was quite embarrassed. She pulled
off her hat, combed her thickly-waved and very improbable orange hair, and besides the usual application
of powder and lipstick, she did things to her eyebrows
and lashes with a small black brush, which like the rest of
her face equipment lived in a large silver case of many
compartments. While she made herself up, she chattered in French to Mrs. Leicester about reducing exercises with the most extreme frankness; Amber could
not understand all she said, but frequent references to
"les hanches" caught her ear. She thought Madame de
Bulle a dreadful person. She went over, coffee-cup in
hand, to look at a leather shield, strangely decorated,
which hung on the wall. She tilted it sideways, to see
how it could be attached, and came on a gummed slip of
paper on the back, on which was written in a very neat
small hand—"Given me by my friend Ban-to-bu, Chief
of the Ngamba, on my birthday, Oct. 10 ——, for killing
a lion which bothered him.—G. H." This inscription
pleased Amber—it showed her host in a nice light, she
thought; she liked the simplicity of "bothered," she
liked the description of the chief as "my friend." She
thought of Hawtrey's face as she had just seen it—handsome, with that clean race-horse look about the regular
features and the narrow red head, though the eyeglass
and the little moustache gave a touch of fashion which
rather repelled her. She tried to imagine him in con-

versation with his friend Ban-to-bu, and found it possible, but difficult. What she had so far heard of his conversation seemed to her formal and rather foolish. And yet there was something likeable about him—his smile was reliable and kind.

Her meditations were interrupted by Madame de Bulle coming up to her, putting her arm affectionately into hers, and leading her, to her great embarrassment, to a small divan. "You are the niece of my old friend Beel 'Arrison—we shall be friends together, isn't it?" she observed, pulling Amber down beside her and patting her hand. "You ride also? You love ponies, like eem? That is good. Then we are friends." She threw off these professions of friendship with a sort of voluble ease which disconcerted Amber very much — she was not accustomed to being patted by strangers, and her theory about this stout improper-looking person was already cut and dried. "Beel and I, we are—'ow do you say?— *concourants*," Madame de Bulle went on, with a loud jolly laugh; "'e always seeks to beat my ponies in the races, and I seek to beat 'is. 'E 'as some very good ones, but so 'ave I." She laughed again. "You will come and see my ponies—come to lunch with me at P'ao-ma-ch'ang, yes?" Amber made some polite response. "You will see Huron—'e beat your uncle's pony, Norsecliffe, last year." She was making some enquiries as to Bill Harrison's state of health, when the men rejoined them; in the general reshuffle which ensued, Amber found herself talking to her host.

"Well, Miss Harrison, I hope you'll like us," he began, turning his eyeglass on her. "A Legation is a funny place, you know—a little world! And all sorts in it. Benenden, you know—you've been talking to him; he's one of our learned ones. He and Leroy. Have you met Leroy? He's a great man, is Henry. Odd combination, you know—knows more about China than almost anyone living, and yet he's a terrific sportsman, the best polo-player here. I'm not learned," Hawtrey went on, with a cheerful laugh—"but after all, that's not the only thing in diplomacy, as you'll see, my dear Miss Harrison. The Minister isn't learned either—he and I are a sort of *bloc du bas-front* in the compound." He laughed again. "Have you met the Minister?" he asked her.

"Just," said Amber. "I made rather a bad break with him, I'm afraid." The evident amiable intention of Hawtrey's *compte-rendu* of the Legation had begun to put her at her ease, and she told him how she had asked Sir James if he was a consul. Hawtrey laughed. "Poor old man! How did he take it?"

"He said, 'No, a proconsul,' " said Amber.

"Now that's exactly like him! He does think pro-consularly," said Hawtrey. "That's very character-istic." Hawtrey nearly always said the same thing twice over, in different words, as Amber was beginning to notice. "Do you know the story of old ——" he continued, "who was sent as Minister to Brussels, when the *maître d'hôtel* in the restaurant thought he recognised him and called him Monsieur le Consul?—'*Le service consulaire, c'est une belle carrière, je ne dis pas le contraire—mais moi, je suis Ministre!*' " Hawtrey told this story with a rapidity and perfection of indignant French intonation which made Amber laugh. "That's the attitude of all Ministers to the life, my dear Miss Harrison. Ni shên-ma? " he said to a servant who now approached him; "Excuse me, please, Miss Harrison — the proconsul is on the telephone!" He gave his high laugh and hurried from the room.

"Where has Joe gone?" Mrs. Leicester asked in a languid voice, drifting over to Amber.

"To speak to the Minister on the telephone," Amber replied.

"It would have to be the Minister, if Joe was rung up in the middle of a party," said Mrs. Leicester, looking very faintly amused.

"Why?" asked Amber innocently.

"Oh, because Joe is like that. Diplomacy is the breath of his nostrils. But he's a dear." She pulled her furs up round her thin shoulders, so that the fine soft darkness touched her pale face, and said, "Joe's very innocent, really—that's why we all like him." She looked sideways at Amber and said, "I expect you are rather innocent too, aren't you?"—and again she looked faintly amused. "You won't like everything in Peking, or everyone, but you can be very happy here, if you choose your people and your occupations. You ride, don't you?"

"Yes," said Amber.

"Well, if you stick to that, and to people like Joe, you'll be all right," said Mrs. Leicester. She looked thoughtfully at Amber, with her blue eyes in her still face, and then gave a tiny laugh. "You want to ask me why I'm saying this to you the moment we meet, don't you? Never mind about that—remember it when you leave. Most girls who come to Peking leave it engaged, generally to the wrong man; and nearly all women leave Peking with a broken heart. But your Aunt Bessie won't tell you so! She's never noticed! Have I been impertinent?" she asked, with a faint, charming smile.

"Oh no!" said Amber. She did not in the least know what to make of Mrs. Leicester's sudden *démarche*, but she liked her face, and her own natural impulse towards amiability in all circumstances was uppermost. Murmuring that they would meet again, Mrs. Leicester drifted away.

Walking back alone—Mrs. Grant-Howard had gone straight on in her ricksha to pay calls—Amber first drew a deep breath of relief. The stinging glittering air, the flooding cold sunshine, were delicious after the hot rooms in the bungalow. And suddenly she decided to walk about and explore the compound a little. She strolled down a straight drive, bordered with small leafless trees, looking with interest to right and left—at a large handsome Lutyens-y house in a pretty garden, at various low ugly buildings whose use she could not guess, but which were in fact the dispensary, the electric-light plant, the artesian well and the sanitation system. Well, if that was a diplomatic luncheon, it was rather dull, Amber thought regretfully, as she walked along; except Benenden and that strange Mrs. Leicester, no one had been very interesting. Worse, she felt that these people were going to be rather hard to like and get on with; there was something—what was it?—almost *unreal* about them which made them as intimidating in their way as the clever people at home. And thinking of luncheons at home caused Amber, from sheer force of bad habit, to wonder how she had acquitted herself. Oh dear, her mother would not have been best pleased — she had really said nothing at all, done nothing but listen. There hadn't been much chance, actually—at lunch itself Mr. Leicester and Benenden had done all the talking, and Mr. Hawtrey talked like—like a waterfall! She had liked listening to Benenden—she wondered why he was so violent; more than violent—so bitter. How awful of her to have said that about writers' lives being blasted, thought Amber, blushing again at the memory.

Her thoughts were diverted at this point. She had reached an open space of dusty dead-looking grass, round which several groups of ponies were walking, led by Chinese grooms in nondescript trousers and black

F

sateen jackets. So these were China ponies! They were absurd—so tiny! Like children's ponies for sale at Stow market. And so stocky and short-necked. But here and there was a shapely one, with a faint look of breed about it. One or two groups now left the circular track round the manège, and were led off towards a gateway in a red brick wall; Amber, always drawn by horseflesh as by a magnet, followed, and found herself in a large yard, surrounded on all four sides by solid brick-built stalls and loose-boxes. Several ponies stood against the north wall, tied to rings; down the centre of the yard ran a sort of open-sided barn, with a small building at one end of it. Outside this building, on a wooden chair, sat an old, slender and completely bald Chinese, wearing jódhpores, a black jacket and velvet slippers, smoking a little black and silver pipe. At the entrance of the ponies he took his pipe from his mouth, and without otherwise moving, emitted a loud stream of what appeared to be curses of the most violent sort. The *mafoos* in charge of the ponies replied in accents equally loud and violent, but set quietly about the business of unblanketing and grooming their charges. Now the old man noticed Amber; he at once rose to his feet, bowed deeply and addressed her as Missy. He spoke English of a sort, and talked a great deal about how well he knew Mastah Ha-lee-san—it was some time before Amber realised that this individual, whose ponies so welly good, was her Uncle Bill. The old man was anxious to do the honours of the stable, and showed her several ponies by the wall which he said belonged Ssu-ch'in-ch'ai—seeing that this conveyed nothing to Amber, "Mastah Haw-to-lee" he brought out triumphantly. He yelled at an underling, who ran to raise a stone slab in the floor of the central barn and hauled up something on the end of a string from within; the underling then approached Amber with a grimy little bundle of butter-muslin, which contained neatly peeled carrots. The old man indicated that she was to give these to Haw-to-lee's ponies; she was doing so, asking their names, happy and contented again in the safe world of horses and those who dealt with horses, when Haw-to-lee himself appeared.

"Ah, Miss Harrison! Is Wang introducing you to my string? Good. I've just come up to see about this fellow's shoes. They shoe atrociously here, you know—atrociously, on the whole." Hawtrey now entered into an examination of the shoes of a large and rather ugly pony, hideously mottled about the face in purple and white; he and Wang kept up a flood of highly technical conversation, half in Chinese and half in English, while Hawtrey made asides to Amber at intervals. "This fellow Pertinax came from your uncle's stable—he didn't much want to let me have him, but I ride over a stone heavier than he does, so I need a weight-carrier. . . . No, Wang—*pu-shih! Nakö fah-tzu pu hao!* Now show that hind foot." While two *mafoos* scuffled with Pertinax, who had no wish to exhibit his feet, Hawtrey continued to discuss the pony. "Old Bill calls all his stable after newspaper men, because he says all China ponies are half rogues!" He gave a cheerful high giggle. "Mind!" He caught Amber by the shoulder and pulled her unceremoniously to one side, as Pertinax lashed out. "He does that—he's a stubborn brute—Pertinax is just the name for him. But those chaps call him Hua-ma, the Flower Pony."

"Why on earth?" Amber asked, looking at Pertinax's hideous face.

"Oh, those spots all over his head. Anything spotty is *Hua*—the same as small-pox," said Hawtrey airily. "Now, Wang!"—a further examination. "He's not fast enough to race," to Amber—"but he's turning into a decent paper-hunt pony. Do you ride at all, Miss Harrison?"

"Yes, I do," said Amber.

"Capital—that's really excellent. I hope you'll let me mount you sometimes, till your uncle comes back. It would be the greatest pleasure. This fellow now, the Gazelle"—he led Amber up to a graceful creamy pony with dark points—"he'll do you splendidly, you know." Amber liked the look of the Gazelle, though wondering secretly, as all Europeans wonder when first confronted with the China pony, whether her feet would not touch the ground when she was mounted on him. Hawtrey continued to show her all his ponies, with much conversation and a certain rather naïve complacency; he was somehow much nicer among horses than he had been at lunch among people, though she was still amazed at the number of times he said everything—by the time they left the stables she found it quite easy to imagine him with his friend Ban-to-bu. As they walked down a curving drive towards the Counsellor's house—"How did that old man—Wang is he?—know that I was Uncle Bill's niece?" Amber asked. "I've only been here a day."

"Oh Lord, he'd know all right! The Chinese know everything," said Hawtrey. "Don't know *how*, but they do. So do all the other people, as a matter of fact. Living in a Legation is like living in a film studio, you know, with the sound recorder going all the time. 'The night has a thousand eyes, and the day a million!'" He laughed, clearly expecting Amber to laugh too; for a wonder, she recognised the quotation, and did. "That's Rupert's, as a matter of fact," he said, as he left her at her door.

Amber went into the house thinking again about Benenden—Hawtrey's last remark had brought him back to her mind. On the whole she thought him rather disappointing—he was so bitter and violent, not in the least like a poet, a happy collector of visual nuggets. As she went upstairs and took off her things she found herself still wondering *why* he was so bitter. But as Hawtrey recrossed the compound his thoughts were more varied. He hoped to God that that old scoundrel Wang really would do what he was told and not what he thought best about Pertinax's forefeet. He hoped to God the Minister hadn't heard that ass of a new archivist say "Righty-oh" to him over the telephone; and settled exactly what he would say after tea to the said archivist. He decided not to go to Mimi's cocktail party after all, but to stay and finish that draft and get Yee Hsing round to alter those new jódhpores at the same time. Blasted fool for making them so loose! Finally he thought of the girl he had just left. She seemed rather nice—anyhow she wasn't an absolute man-eater, so far as you could see, which was one mercy; and not a crashing highbrow either. He'd certainly give her a ride. In fact he found himself hoping quite actively that old Bill wouldn't get well and come back too damned soon.

Chapter Six

"NOW, for Sunday, dear lady, there's a little plan. Rothstein wants me to take you all to lunch at his villa at P'ao-ma-ch'ang, before the paper-hunt. Quite a good thing to do, you know—one meets every-one, and his cook is first-class. And one must support *le sport*: it holds people together, it really does hold them together a bit. I always say the Diplomatic Body would go to pieces in a week without golf and the paper-hunts!"

So Sir James to Joanna over a cocktail. Joanna asked who the amiable Mr. Rothstein might be?

"Oh, a Hamburger, and a great racing man. He's in alarm-clocks," put in Sir James in parenthesis and ex-planation. "But he's been here twenty years and he knows a great deal—a useful felloh, quite, you know, on occasion. His wife is English. No, nobody you would know. But she's a harmless little person. And they have this cook. These Sunday lunches are his little weakness — an amiable weakness, you must confess! You'll come, then? You and Nugent, and the—ah—the consular young lady!" He bowed to Amber. "Excel-lent. I'll collect you after Church."

"And you're lunching with us tomorrow?" said Joanna, as the Minister rose to take his leave. "I don't know what you'll get—the boy said he was giving us roast tailor!"

Sir James laughed. "Tailor—very good! Now let me see—what would that be? Oh yes, teal, of course! They're in now. Excellent."

From December to early March the lives of those who

70

ride ponies in Peking are dominated by the Sunday paper-hunts. These take place at or near P'ao-ma-ch'ang, the suburb close to the race-course, where all race-owners, and plenty of others beside, have a villa or a temple, and keep their stables; it is, in fact, the centre of that sporting life of Peking to which Sir James Boggit attached so much importance. The main feature of these paper-hunts is that there is no paper. The winner of the previous week's hunt merely lays a flagged course over eight or nine miles of open country, along which are constructed jumps consisting of mud walls or fences of *kaoliang* straw; round this course he conducts the field, giving a couple of checks; after the last check the field races home down the "run-in," for the two cups, a light-weight and a heavy-weight cup. There are roughly three types of riders: the competent owners, who ride their own ponies and are always well up—of such were Leroy, Hawtrey, Harry Leicester and Count Herman; the young and penurious men who are too poor to keep ponies of their own and ride those belonging to stout race-owners with cigars, like M. Rothstein (this class was always referred to by Hawtrey as "the hired assassins"); finally a motley crowd of rather indifferent riders on still more indifferent mounts who for one reason or another feel that they gain face by riding.

On Sundays, therefore, a general exodus takes place to P'ao-ma-ch'ang by car; lunches are consumed in the villas and temples, and then the paper-hunt is witnessed by a large crowd. The onlookers stand and shiver in a cruel wind, up to their ankles in sand, watching a cloud of dust disappear; after a prolonged interval the cloud of dust reappears, and they have the fun of seeing whether their husbands, sweethearts or jockeys will fall or be rolled on at the last two jumps or not. After which everyone drinks cherry brandy, the two cups are handed out by some woman, the lottery tickets are drawn and the proceedings close till next Sunday, when they begin all over again.

Most of this information was imparted by George Hawtrey to Miss Harrison on the following Sunday, when she and the Grant-Howards, escorted by the Minister, appeared at M. Rothstein's luncheon. The house was a new, garishly painted villa, set down baldly on the naked earth without any apparent attempt at a garden, and flanked by a large range of clay-walled stables; the icy wind caught their faces, hands and ankles as they left the car, and made them shiver. They were ushered into a room nearly as bare and ugly as the surroundings of the house, where some forty people were already drinking cocktails, and met their host, a large man with a peculiarly kindly and pleasant, if somewhat heavy face. It was suffocatingly hot, and the noise of forty people, screaming as they only scream in a low-ceilinged room, was deafening: the Grant-Howards suffered various introductions, and Amber, left standing rather lost, was distinctly relieved when Hawtrey came and took her under his wing to go in to lunch. He was dressed for riding; an orange leather waistcoat exactly the colour of his hair was a conspicuous feature of his costume, and the riding clothes emphasised with a touch of gallantry the real splendour of his height and build, as set sails emphasise the splendour of a ship. Lunch was served in another room, as bare and ugly as the first, and as cold as that had been hot; the food was marvellous, as Sir James had foretold—the champagne incredibly profuse. Hawtrey made it his business to instruct Amber in the various personalities seated at the vast table—giving instruction apparently afforded him a peculiar satisfaction. "That little abject on your right," he hissed in her ear as they sat down, "is Mimi's husband, de Bulle. He's going to ride today for the first time; watch him—he won't eat a bite!" Amber cautiously regarded her neighbour. He was a small fair French-man with a timid expression, whose hands trembled slightly as he helped himself to *hors d'œuvres*. Hawtrey pointed out their hostess, a big cheerful blonde—"that's Dolly Rothstein, sitting opposite to Dickie Roberts—he rides for them, you know. They say she was a barmaid, but she's a jolly good sort." Amber despaired of re-membering even a third of all the information she was given; she listened with half an ear, and looked about her. Madame de Bulle was carrying on a quite blatant and very noisy flirtation with Count Herman; further up the table she noticed Mrs. Leicester looking unwontedly animated, talking to a dark and extraordinarily handsome man. "Who is that next to Mrs. Leicester?" she asked.

Hawtrey hawed—he seemed slightly embarrassed. "That's Bruno," he said at length.

"What is he? a diplomatist?"

"Oh Lord, no—he's a Bessarabian—in business." He lowered his voice. "It's supposed to be tobacco, but actually he's made his thousands out of selling rifles to the various war-lords. Of course Bessarabia signed the Arms Embargo like all the other Powers," Hawtrey hurried on, giggling slightly, "but in point of fact no one observes it but us. It puts us in a damned awkward position, too. The Transalpians sold Wang a dozen commercial aeroplanes last year; Harry Leicester hap-pened to see them unloaded, and they all had bombing attachments! So very commercial! Last month Li—that's the Marshal, you know—asked us if we wouldn't sell him some. He specified the bombing attachments." Hawtrey giggled again. "Of course we told him we couldn't authorise that, and he was frightfully miffed. Poor old Leroy had a fearful job trying to explain to him

about the Arms Embargo. 'But the Transalpians sign
it too,' he said, 'and they sell to Wang, my rival. If you
are my friends, you sign it and sell to me!' He believes
now, of course, that we are really backing Wang."

After lunch, the whole assembly hustled into their
various cars, and bumped off along sandy roads to witness
the paper-hunt. Villas as bare and ugly as Monsieur
Rothstein's stood about in the fields—here and there the
grey wall of a temple overhung the road. At the foot
of a hillock tufted with small bare trees and crowned
with a green-shuttered house, which Sir James pointed
out as his country residence, they came to an open sandy
space, where the cars stopped and everyone got out.
Mafoos were leading blanketed ponies up and down,
whistling to them; men in greatcoats and riding-boots
stood about smoking; the sand, ankle-deep, got into
Amber's and Joanna's shoes; it was intensely cold. At
this point Benenden joined them, muffled up to the ears
and looking very chilly.

"Hullo, Rupert, aren't you riding?" Nugent asked him.

"Not me—I leave that to Joe and Leroy," replied
Benenden. "They're our die-hards. Look, there they
are."

The riders were now mounting, and Hawtrey and
Henry Leroy were both visible among the crowd—
Leroy's big black head covered with a fur cap with ear-
flaps, Hawtrey conspicuous by his orange waistcoat.
He was riding Pertinax. Dickie Roberts was among the
"hired assassins" on a graceful piebald. Harry Leicester
came by on a strangely coloured pony, café-au-lait with
dark brown points, like a Siamese cat; he waved to the
group. Bruno was talking to Lydia Leicester, who stood
patting his pony's neck; Amber noticed the unfortunate
de Bulle wrestling with his mount, a fidgety chestnut,
whose bit was obviously hurting its mouth; she guessed

that he had made the usual mistake of the nervous amateur and had got his curb too tight, a precaution which generally leads to discomfort if not disaster. The chestnut's uneasy shufflings presently brought him quite close to where she stood with the Grant-Howards, and now she could see the pony mouthing and wriggling his constricted jaw, and the agonised dismay on the rider's face. This was more than she could stand. She went over to de Bulle. "Your curb is too tight—let me alter it," she said.

"'E bulls," gasped de Bulle—he was a Lorrainer, and spoke with a curious Teutonic burr; "*c'est mieux ainsi*, Mademoiselle."

"No—he'll pull much less if I loosen it," said Amber firmly, and taking the bridle in her hands she worked at the bit. The chestnut lashed out at her, and a *mafoo* came running up—he held the pony's head and Amber loosened the chain. "There!" she said—"now you'll both be more comfortable." And indeed when the chestnut's head was released, he stood more reasonably.

"*Merci infiniment*," said de Bulle. "Ze worst of zese China bonies is, zey bull zo!" he added as he moved off.

Benenden glanced curiously at Amber when she rejoined the group. "What were you doing?" he asked her.

"He'd got his curb ludicrously tight," said Amber. "I just loosened it."

"Do you know a lot about horses?" Benenden enquired.

"No, not a lot, but I know that much," said Amber.

"But how did you know it was too tight?"

"I could *see*—it was hurting the pony's mouth."

"I believe you *do* know a lot about it," said Benenden, looking rather quizzical.

"Rupert, what is all this about? What exactly *is* a paper-hunt?" asked Joanna, in a confidential tone.

Benenden proceeded to explain, at some length. "I

expect it will be a loathsome course today," he continued,
"because Stefany won last Sunday. He's a crack rider;
he used to jump for the Hungarian international team,
and he sets a course according! Hullo, they'll be off in
a moment."

The riders were indeed getting their ponies into line,
and the spectators moved away to one side. A man in
a tweed suit exhorted the competitors to keep level;
eventually the Master blew his horn rather faintly, and
off they went—down a slope to a large ditch, over it, and
sharp left-handed between two flags; almost at the turn
was a low mud wall, a thoroughly awkward jump: Amber
saw Pertinax refuse twice, before Hawtrey cudgelled him
over, and the whole troop disappeared in a cloud of
yellow dust.

Mrs. Leicester came up with Madame de Bulle.
"They're going round by the Sand Temple," she said;
"we're going to cut across to the bank to see them pass"
—and walked on.

"Anyone like to go? It's no distance," said Benenden
to the party generally.

"I should stay here, if I were you, Mrs. Nugent," said
Sir James. "It's frightful walking in these fields."

"I think I will," said Joanna. "My shoes are full of
sand as it is."

"You?" said Benenden to Amber.

"Yes, please," said Amber. The sight of horses jumping had stung her blood, as it always did—her eyes were
bright with excitement; she longed to see more. She and
Benenden accordingly set off after Mrs. Leicester and
Madame de Bulle. They ploughed through deep loose
soil for some distance till they reached a small track,
which they followed to the foot of a great bank of earth
some thirty feet high—Benenden took Amber's hand
unceremoniously and tugged her up it at a run. Madame

de Bulle and Mrs. Leicester were on the top, a few paces away, with Rothstein and one or two others.

From the bank they could see out over a wide stretch of country, all brown and bare—here and there some spindly willows or a dark group of pines broke the monotony, and a line of very unreal-looking pink and blue mountains presided over the horizon. The wind was piercing; it raised little eddies of dust along the bank and across the sandy stretches below them. Amber shivered —it all looked exceedingly dreary and strange to her. Strangest of all was the idea of riding a point-to-point fetlock-deep in loose dusty soil, instead of across the green slithery meadows of an English meeting. And suddenly, seeing all that in her mind, she felt a rush of home-sickness—the home-sickness of the eye, which is so much more potent than any other. Benenden stood watching her; he wondered what she was thinking of, but he said nothing. He had been rather intrigued by her prompt and decisive action over de Bulle's horse. Amber as a matter of fact was just recalling her last point-to-point at home— Arthur had been there—when her eye was caught by something. To the left of where they stood, the bank, which was actually the remains of an ancient fortification, bent round at right angles and ran far out into the fields; at its foot, beyond the bend, she noticed two red flags, with a yellow *kaoliang* fence between them. "Good heavens, is that supposed to be a jump?" she asked Benenden, pointing to it.

He looked. "Yes. That's a typical *schweinerei* of Herman's."

"But it's a ridiculous place!" Amber was beginning, indignantly, when cries of "*Les voici!*" and "Here they are!" from further along the bank interrupted her. Some distance away to the left a cloud of dust appeared—as it approached they could pick out various figures in it, before they were cut off from view by the intervening fortification.

"Now we shall see some smashes," said Benenden. Amber hardly heard him—she was again feeling that dancing thrill of the flying blood at the sight of a race, with a little extra quickening of excitement because she had a focus for her emotion.   She knew Hawtrey—therefore she wanted Hawtrey to win; she had someone to *feel* about.

A rider on a white pony appeared now on the top of the bank just opposite them; for one moment he was silhouetted against the blue sky, then slithered and skidded down the slope.   It was Count Herman.   At the bottom he pulled up dead; then, neat and light as a cat, he lifted his pony over the *kaoliang* fence in a standing jump. Amber could not restrain her admiration for so pretty a piece of horsemanship.   Others now appeared on the skyline — Hawtrey and Bruno, Leicester and Leroy. Pertinax sidled down the bank sideways like a crab, refused and ran out, was brought back, and crashed half over, half through the fence.   Meanwhile Leroy, to her amused delight, rode down the slope at an easy angle, wrenched his pony round, and cantering back, took the fence in a sideways jump.   "*What* an old soldier!" she murmured.   He was first away after Count Herman. Bruno's horse fell coming down the bank; he picked himself up, with a loud "*Maldito cascado!*"—remounted and popped through the gap left by Pertinax, as did a crowd of others.   Last of all came de Bulle and a small towheaded man on a black pony.   The chestnut was obviously out of control; seeing the slope below him, he shied away from it; de Bulle turned him round, and incautiously used his whip; the pony plunged furiously forward down the slope and fell, knocking over the black, whose tow-headed rider had dismounted and was leading him down. Without warning, a struggling heap of men and horses lay beside the *kaoliang* fence.

"Good! Budgen's taken a toss!" said Benenden in a satisfied tone. "Don't go!" he added, catching Amber's arm as she started forward—"they're probably quite all right." Indeed it appeared in a moment that they were —Rothstein and Madame de Bulle hurried down the bank, but by the time they reached the group both de Bulle and the man referred to as Budgen were on their feet, and the chestnut, riderless, was streaking off after the rest of the paper-hunt as fast as he could go. The black pony was lame, and the tow-headed individual, looking very crestfallen, started to lead him home. Amber and Benenden could hear Madame de Bulle scolding her husband vigorously.

"Wretched François! Listen to Mimi taking it out of him!" said Benenden, grinning. "Come on, let's go back and see the finish." Amber wanted to do this too, and they set off at a round pace. She felt rather out of conceit with Benenden, all the same — she didn't like the malicious pleasure he appeared to take in other people's discomfiture. This, like his bitterness over Rotherham, didn't fit in at all with her theory of the poet. "Why were you so pleased at that man's getting a fall?" she asked him at length, a little out of breath with walking in a fur coat through the heavy going.

"Budgen? Oh, because he's a swine," said Benenden easily. "I'll tell you about him another time. But he is a swine, and if he'd broken his neck just now I'd have thrown up my hat." "Come over here," he went on, as they approached the crowd at the post—"if we go a little way down this side we shall see the end of the run-in."

Accordingly they clambered up on to a little mound. "That's where they'll come, down that gully and through those trees in the dip,"—he pointed with his stick. "The run-in's always the same. Here they are!"

Down the gully indeed a speck appeared, and then another, and another, dust flying behind them. Triumphant yells from a crowd of Chinese in blue near a jump in the dip arose as two riders crossed it, only a length apart. Amber strained her eyes to identify them and saw that it was Harry Leicester and Hawtrey, Leicester leading: they swept through the trees, Hawtrey gaining a little, and approached the last jump at the foot of the long gentle rise which led up to the post. As they approached this jump, a mud wall, Amber saw Hawtrey suddenly swing to the right, and thought that Pertinax was going to run out. No, he was over, right at the wing —but Leicester's pony appeared to skid sideways, just when he should have risen to the jump, and cannoned into the wall, shooting his rider over it. Hawtrey had not seen this, and rode on; but the third figure now crossed the mud wall, well to the right, like Hawtrey, and revealed itself as Bruno, coming up fast. A length behind, half-a-length, almost alongside—up the rise they came, riding a terrific finish; shouts rose from the crowd of Europeans: "Bruno! Bruno!" and "Come *on*, Joe!" But though Bruno's black hung on Pertinax's quarters, he could not overhaul the spotted pony, and in a little roar of cheering Hawtrey passed the post first.

"Good old Joe!" said Benenden. Then he looked at Amber. Her lips were parted with excitement; she was glowing, she was eager—she was very pretty! "You were excited," he said. "Why? Did you want Joe to win?"

"I always am excited at a race," said Amber—she thought Benenden's question rather forward. "I can't help it. But let's find the others, shall we?"

They found Nugent. "Joanna's gone home," he said.

"The Minister had to get back, and she was cold, so she went with him. He's sending the car back for us." Benenden and Hawtrey both accepted the offer of a lift, and after a hurried prize-giving by Mrs. Rothstein, the whole assembly packed into the waiting cars and started back to Peking.

"By George, old Stephanotis just about excelled himself today," Hawtrey said, as they bumped along in the Minister's roomy saloon. "He must have had that last jump watered; the take-off was a sheet of ice. Leicester says he's going to report it to the Stewards."

"Oh, *that* was why you swung out," exclaimed Amber.

He turned to her, pleased—"Ah, you noticed that, Miss Harrison. Yes—saw it just in time." He continued to regale them during the whole drive home with an account of the humours and perils of the paper-hunt. At one jump he was next to de Bulle, and heard him muttering *"Courage! Voici l'obstacle!"* to himself. "Old Henry went up to Herman at the first check and asked him where the paper hoops were for us to jump through, and whether he hadn't better start the next lap standing on the saddle, so as to be ready for the other circus events. Herman wasn't at all pleased." Everyone, it seemed, was indignant with Count Herman's line and his arrangement of the jumps; de Bulle as well as Leicester was meditating a protest, and so was Schroff of the American Guard. Amber could not help remembering the Minister's remarks to Joanna about *le sport* holding people together; she felt that the day's events furnished a rather curious instance of the promoting of international solidarity, but was too shy to say so. Benenden, however, with his usual keenness of eye, noticed her expression and said: "What is amusing you?" She told him, and the three men were de-

G

lighted. "How the Diplomatic Body sur*vives le sport* is always the miracle to me," said Benenden.

"I shall give them—ha-ha!—a diplomatic hunt next Sunday," said Hawtrey complacently, as the car passed in at the West Gate of the compound. "And tomorrow you're coming to try the Gazelle at the Temple of Heaven, aren't you, Miss Harrison?"

"Rather!" said Amber.

Chapter Seven

THE Grant-Howards now settled down into the usual Peking social routine of lunches, dinners and cocktail-parties—diversified for Nugent by his work in the Chancery, and for Joanna by the task of house-keeping, and bearing the brunt of the family correspond-ence. House-keeping in Peking has certain peculiarities, foremost among which is the question of "squeeze." Joanna was nothing if not practical; she knew how largely successful diplomacy depends on a good table and a well-run house; to ensure success she wisely began by consulting the authorities, like Mrs. Hugo and Henry Leroy. From them she learned a great deal about "squeeze." It was, apparently, ruled by the strictest conventions. The cost of any given article bore an exact relation to the official rank of the household con-suming it. Whereas a chicken in the market cost some thirty cents, the moment it entered the Legation Gate it cost thirty-five—the five cents being the legitimate "squeeze" or rake-off of the *Kai-mên-ti*, or gate-porter. But the further possibilities of the chicken in the matter of price were endless. If it went to the students' mess, it would figure on the bill at a paltry thirty-eight cents; if to Mrs. Hugo, who was only a consul's wife, at about forty-one; and so up through every grade of diplomatic rank, till it reached the Leroy's kitchen at fifty-four, while the Ministerial chickens cost Sir James Boggit sixty-three or thereabouts. "And you *can't* alter that, Mrs. Grant-Howard—you must just make up your mind to it," Leroy told her, nodding his head. "You pay fifty-eight cents for your chickens and no more, but you won't get 'em for less. And the same with everything else. But look here, you do this. Make your boy write out the cook's bill every day, and check it up in the kitchen, under the *ch'u-tzŭ's* eyes, with your meal-book. Then he'll know you're watching him. And put down your weekly totals. He won't squeeze you too much for the first fortnight, and when your totals begin to grow— and they *will* grow—then you can go for him."

Joanna, characteristically, did not ask how one went for one's *ch'u-tzŭ*—there would be time enough for that when her totals showed vernal symptoms of growth; she just noted down in her mind these extraordinarily illogical facts which Leroy had given her. Following his and Mrs. Hugo's precepts, every morning, escorted like royalty by the No. 1, she proceeded to her kitchen, received the bows of the white-robed cook and his assistants, and stood by while every saucepan and utensil was lifted down for her inspection; examined the icechest, and saw that the vegetables were correctly soaking in a pink solution of permanganate. Once a week she said that something was not clean. "Never mind whether it is or not," Leroy had said. "Just tell your Number One to tell the cook it's dirty; never tell him yourself. That keeps them up to it." So each Wednesday Joanna complained of the dirt on some different and highly burnished article of her *batterie de cuisine*. And every Monday she said that the permanganate was not strong enough.

The Number One then produced the meal-book, and Joanna studied his projected menus for that day and the next, and compared the cook's book with yesterday's meals. Once a week, still acting on instructions, she queried some item; even if they *had* had an omelette and a *soufflé*, the cook had certainly not used 130 eggs! The

reactions of the Number One and the cook to these re-
proaches amused her enormously. The cook would
stand by, his eyes searching now her face, now Liu's, with
eager and puzzled intensity, trying to guess what was
wrong. Liu then turned and spoke to him in Chinese,
whereupon the cook would jabber some passionate
explanation, waving his slender hands in gesticulations
as fervid as those of an Italian prima-donna in *Tosca*.
The Number One would then present the case for the
cook in English, with a fine show of detachment and an
almost legal impartiality. "Cook she say, t'ai-t'ai want
welly good cake—use plenty eggs; *she* say, use not plenty
eggs, cake not good!" Or "Mastah she like welly big om-
lett; small Mastah *she* like welly big om*lett*—use lot eggs."

Sometimes he threw in items of general information—
"China eggs welly small"—to reinforce the cook's case.
All this time the cook stood, watching with searching intentness Joanna's expression, again struggling to discover her reactions to Liu's special pleading. It was
essential to success, Joanna found, to preserve complete
facial control; she must never allow it to appear that she
was amused, as she always was, or half-convinced, as she
sometimes was, by Liu's arguments. She cultivated an
expression of rather stern blankness, and usually ended
by saying, quite unmoved, that seventy eggs was enough,
and walking away. The cook would then break out
into lamentations; but if she had played her part sufficiently well, Liu's defence would crumple up—he would
silence the cook with a firm word, and protest to his
mistress that all should now be well—he would fix. And
a few days later sixty eggs would suffice for precisely the
same items; but, mysteriously, eight pounds of butter
would have been used.

It was all immense fun, Joanna thought, much more
fun than keeping house in any European country. The

resourcefulness, the doublings, the pertinacity of the servants were endless, and formed a daily game, your wits
against theirs. Often, she was sure, they won. But they
were on your side in this, that squeezing you apart, it
was their pride and their glory, as much as—no, much
more than yours, to make your household a thing of perfection. "And anyhow it's all so wildly cheap," she told
Nugent. "*Imagine* getting a cook like this for twenty-
four pounds a year!" Joanna had been alarmed at first
to find five men working in her kitchen, but was relieved
to learn that she only paid wages to two, the *ch'u-tzŭ* and
the next man, whom Liu referred to as "Leeti-Cook";
the others paid the cook for the privilege of working
under him in her exalted establishment. "Leeti-Cook,"
it appeared, cooked when his superior was out, but she
never knew when this was, as no difference was ever
detectable in the uniform and quite delicious perfection
of the food.

For the rest, she took up the routine of life in a new
capital with her usual assured ease. There was nothing
very much out of the way about this part of it, except that
till her car arrived she paid the innumerable calls on
quite unknown people in a ricksha. Going about in her
ricksha amused her greatly. There was of course the
difficulty of directing the coolie, but he had been Guy
Ruthven's before, and apart from a slight tendency to
take her to the Club when in doubt, he did very well.
She got Rupert, or Joe, or Jamieson the Constable, to
tell her the Chinese versions of the names of the people
she had to see, and wrote them down on her calling list.
"Ta-Ch'in-ch'ai T'ai-t'ai, Fa-kuo-fu" she read out
blandly, when calling on Mme. La Salle, the French
Minister's wife; and "San ch'in-Ch'ai T'ai-t'ai, Mei-
kuo-fu" when calling on Mrs. Mencken, the American
First Secretary's wife. Bowling along the draughty

dusty streets of the Legation Quarter, she summed up
in her mind, rapidly, the woman she had just left, or
adjusted herself to what she had heard of the woman
she was going to see. She arranged an At Home day.
"You'll have a *jour*, dear lady, I do hope," Sir James said
to her with some urgency the day after the Rothstein's
luncheon. "It's most important out here, you know,
especially for one's own nationals. They like it, they
like to feel that they can come on a Monday and be sure
of a welcome."

"Why on Monday?" Joanna asked.

"Oh, because that has always been the Legation day—
ever since Lady Jordan's time," he told her. "You'll
find it helps to hold them together," he added.

Amber, who was present, had choked slightly. She
recalled the paper-hunt and was a little sceptical of Sir
James's ideas about holding people together.

Mrs. Grant-Howard raised her dark eyebrows at
Amber over the choke, half in sympathy and half in re-
proof; they were beginning to get on very well together,
they shared small jokes like this. Joanna had rather
wondered at first how she was going to manage about
the girl, in the inevitable process of being entertained
to death on their arrival; she would have no time to look
after her, she feared, and it would be very dull for her
alone with Miss Carruthers. Her fears however were
quite unfounded. The woman shortage in Peking is
chronic and acute, amounting practically to a famine;
the advent of an extra girl was an unmixed boon to a
small society which contained mostly married women,
and a vast surplus of single men. Amber had been seen
at the Rothsteins and the Paper-Hunt and was immediately in tremendous demand; she was expected to lunch,
to dine, to dance, to drink cocktails, from morning till
night.

Amber rather enjoyed all this, in what she herself described to Benenden as "a cinema sort of way." She took everything and everyone as she found them, though she theorised about some of them, in her own fashion. And she had next to no time to think about Arthur. She hadn't really as much time as she wanted for horses, which were still her principal preoccupation in this strange new world. Uncle Bill, though better, was by no means well enough to return as yet to Peking, and Amber soon decided that she must somehow get hold of a pony of her own, without waiting for him.

She had her ride with Hawtrey at the Temple of Heaven, where, after a good deal of fussing about the stirrup-leathers and scolding of the *mafoos* on Hawtrey's part, they rode round a narrow track, between planta-tions of young trees or open wild spinney, for about four miles. Amber was rather disappointed—she had read about the Temple of Heaven and hoped to see it; but all she got was a few scattered glimpses of the great triple dome of deep blue, and a gleam of white marble among dark trees. Hawtrey had given her as much coaching and advice, at first, as if she were a child of six: but he finally returned to the Legation full of enthusiasm, taking all the credit for having discovered that Miss Harrison rode "really *well*—very well indeed, you know. A pretty seat and good hands; a very pretty seat."

The Grant-Howards themselves wanted ponies, and a few days later a ride was arranged at P'ao-ma-ch'ang to try some both of Leroy's and of Harry Leicester's. They all met at Leroy's temple, where the animals waited under a yellow-washed wall, outside a stable-yard with willow-trees in it. Leroy took charge of the proceedings. He would only allow Joanna to ride a pony of his own selec-tion, to begin with—"You'll ride the Mishu Ma, Mrs. G.-H." The Mishu, who owned his peculiar title of the

"Secret Clerk" pony to the fact that he had formerly belonged to a private secretary of the Minister's, now departed, was regarded as a safe animal. Nugent was mounted, after some scuffling, on a black called William Randolf—a discard from Bill Harrison's stable. "He's a fair jumper; Bill only turned him out because he wouldn't train fine enough for racing"—so ran Leroy's commentary. The character, achievements and history of each pony in Peking are as well known as those of the people, if not better. Hawtrey had brought The Gazelle again for Amber; to his evident disgust she insisted on trying the Siamese cat-coloured pony which Leicester had ridden in the paper-hunt. This animal, who rejoiced in the name of Bananas, had a wise head, and more shoulders and more carriage than most China ponies— he had taken her fancy, and try him she would. "He pulls like the devil," Hawtrey muttered in a discontented aside in her ear. "Lloyd-Jones offered him to me when he left, and *I* wouldn't take him. And he's much too hot for you just now."

But Amber was obdurate and off they went, accompanied by half-a-dozen *mafoos* with spare horses—a long straggling cavalcade, winding single-file along the narrow paths of beaten earth through the villages. Here on the outskirts of the city the market-gardeners are always busy; the low wind-breaks of *kaoliang* straw which sheltered the seed-beds shone like pale yellow reeds in the sunshine; peasants in blue were hoeing and raking among them; barrows of produce were being wheeled along the narrow sunk roads, and when the party encountered one of these, they had to scramble up the steep earth banks to avoid them. Presently Leroy decreed a canter—the long file swept swiftly through a wood of small pines, past a horseshoe-shaped graveyard, past a mud-walled farm and into another sunk track. Amber was enjoying the whole thing; Bananas *was* hot, and *did* pull—goodness, you wouldn't have believed one of these little beasts had the strength!—but by gentling him, and letting him have the bit to shake about as much as he liked, she managed all right. Even Hawtrey's displeasure amused her. As they left the track and skirted another small spinney he came and rode beside her, and urged her on no account to buy any ponies from anyone till Old Bill returned. "People here will stick you with anything, my dear Miss Harrison," he said in warning tones, "positively anything. Even Harry stung me frightfully when I first came." But Amber only laughed, and said she thought she should buy Bananas.

Leroy at this moment pulled up, and indicating two gaunt and stag-headed trees standing leafless and solitary about three-quarters of a mile away, said that the company might now "let them out" as far as the Ginkgos, as there were no sunk roads. Let them out they accordingly did—Amber was determined to see what Bananas was good for, and his flying start and turn of speed satisfied her completely. She reached the Ginkgos well ahead of the rest, and finding a handy mud wall, occupied herself in popping him over it, backwards and forwards, with an economy of effort and an easy skill which filled the four men with admiration as they rode up. "By Jove, she rides like a proper horse-coper!" Harry Leicester muttered. He had not intended to sell Bananas at all— the pony was oldish, but he was a good paper-hunter; if he did sell him, he had intended to "stick" the purchaser properly. But Amber's prettiness and Amber's horsemanship got past his guard; she rode back beside him talking horses with a knowledgeableness that matched her skill, and making herself uncommonly agreeable— Amber had bought horses before. On their return to P'ao-ma-ch'ang Bananas changed hands for 130 dollars, or roughly £13. Leroy chuckled as he heard the bargain concluded. "That's the first horse Harry ever sold cheap!" he observed in a booming whisper to Joanna. "The little puss!" was her only reply. Even Hawtrey had grudgingly to agree that the pony was not dear. "I'm not surprised Harry sold him cheap to *you*," he said to Amber, with a certain emphasis, as they drove home, rather squashed together on the front seat of Leroy's old tourer. "We don't often see riding here like yours— most of the women ride like sacks of potatoes, *le genou roulant*, you know, and all that. It will be a tremendous pleasure to have someone here who really *can* ride." Amber found nothing to say in reply to this. "But I hope you will sometimes let me help you, you know, if I can—advice, or any little thing." His voice was different, suddenly; there was a note of sincerity in it Amber had never heard before, and she responded at once.

"Yes, indeed—thank you tremendously," she said.

"You didn't mind my suggesting that you shouldn't buy in too much of a hurry today?" he went on, bending towards her—his handsome head, eye-glass and all, had a curious expression of submissiveness, suddenly. "I— you never quite know, here—" he had lost his glibness, for the moment.

"But of course not. You were very kind. Only I happened to know what I wanted!" said Amber gaily. "And I've got it," she concluded.

She thought, while she bathed and changed on her return, how odd it would be if Mr. Hawtrey were to stop being a joke—because that was really what he amounted to, so far. A nice joke, but a joke, and she liked him best as a joke, she decided. But Mr. Leicester, for his part, confided to his wife that evening at dressing-time that he shouldn't wonder if Joe's goose wasn't cooked at last. "How excellent!" said Mrs. Leicester slowly, "it will do Joe all the good in the world to fall in love. He's sauntered about with that conquering air long enough." She leaned forward to her mirror, examined the line of her jaw critically, and signed to the amah for the face-cream. Smoothing and powdering— "I hope she won't marry him—" she said, and looked again into her mirror.

"Why not?" asked Harry.

"—Too soon," Lydia continued. "It will need a good long spell of adversity to make Joe really marriageable."

Harry pursed his mouth. "There's something to be said for getting the adversity over first," he said drily, as he left the room.

Two days after this conversation Amber lunched with the Leicesters. They lived in a Chinese house in the Tartar City, out near the Pei-t'ang. The Boy had told the ricksha coolie where to go, and Amber, who had no idea where the Pei-t'ang was, sat a little anxiously, cowering in her fur coat, while the blue-coated ragged figure between the shafts ran, ran, ran, just in front of her, his slippered feet patting gently on the cold dust. They passed the great golden-roofed gate-towers of the For- bidden City, and skirted its scarlet wall for some time; then dived into a maze of small streets, all unpaved, with trees standing casually about the roadway, and blank walls on either side. The half-deserted, wholly casual air of this part of the city struck forcibly on Amber's imagination; she would like, she thought, in warmer weather, to sit and meditate like that old man on the canal bank; to do her sewing on those steps where the knife-grinder was at work; or to mug up her Chinese grammar in that sunny corner where the itinerant barber, the stand with the tools of his trade set up before him, was shaving a man's head, and cleaning out his ears with a small ivory spoon. She liked—almost with passion—the serene, leisurely way in which, in these quiet by-ways, any occupation was carried on by the roadside, without comment or haste; there was a freedom and a simplicity about it which drew at something in her with unexpected force. Peking was, in fact, beginning to take hold of her. When the coolie dumped her down at a scarlet door in a high grey wall, sheltered by a group of trees, she had a sense of interruption. And the luncheon which followed, cheerful as it was, gay to the point of noisiness, somehow made little impression on her; the jokes, the compliments, slipped off the surface of her mind like water off a pane of glass. She was glad when it was over—when Mme. de Bulle and Count Herman had taken their leave (neither François de Bulle nor the Countess were present, she noticed with surprise) and the rest were free to depart. She got into a ricksha, proudly said "Ying-kuo-fu" to the coolie, and prepared to enjoy the ride home.

As she re-passed the southern gateway of the Forbidden City, a sudden impulse took her to stop and look at it. "*Man-man!*" she said to the coolie, and experienced a little thrill of triumph when he really stopped. She strolled across to one of the five little marble bridges spanning the moat which crossed the paved area in front of the gate from side to side, their balustrades carved so richly and closely as to look more like ivory than stone. Before her rose the gateway, its double roof of amber-coloured tiles supported on rows of scarlet pillars, with heavy eaves painted in fresh clear colours; it was pierced by three deep tunnels, each with a scarlet door ornamented with rows of golden bosses as large as footballs, and nine in a row—nine being the Imperial number, only Amber didn't know it. The central door was ajar, guarded by a knot of police with rifles, in black and white uniforms; every now and then a Chinese approached them, presented a pass of some sort, and was admitted. Amber was seized with a violent curiosity to see what was inside. She wondered if she could get in. It was worth trying; and taking out a visiting-card she walked firmly up to the police, held it out to them, and tapping her chest importantly, waved her hand towards the door, indicating that she wished to enter. The police took her card, held it endways, passed it from hand to hand, and finally, jabbering in a satisfied manner, allowed her to pass. Amused, excited, triumphant, Amber walked through the red door.

She found herself on a great paved roadway, at least a hundred yards wide, walled in on each side with narrow cloisters, and closed at the further end by another gateway precisely similar to that through which she had come. On her right the greyish green of thujas showed over the yellow tiles of the cloister, and among them the long golden roof of some hidden building, shining in the brilliant light. There was no one about; pale dead grasses stood up in the cracks between the paving-stones; a mouse ran nimbly through the sunshine to some hidden destination. Vast, deserted, desolate—and incredibly beautiful. In pictures seen at home in England, Amber had always rather disliked those curved Chinese roofs, thought them merely comic and in rather poor taste. But here, seen across immense stretches of stone paving, they were splendid with a sort of inevitable splendour. On their great crimson ramps they rose against the sky, the yellow roofs softened by age and dust, and by the dead grass which covered them, to a gold only a little deeper than the thatch on new hayricks.

The supreme wonder of Chinese architecure lies in its use of space. It is not only in the curved pillared roofs, built to imitate the pole-propped tents of their ancestors, that the architects of the Forbidden City betray their nomadic origin. By a strange skill in proportions, by isolating great pavilions in immense stretches of flagged paving, they have succeeded in bringing into their palace courts the endless spaces of the Gobi desert. The eye travels over the lower walls surrounding each mighty enclosure to distant roof-trees, and beyond these to others more distant still, with a sense of beholding mountain ranges hull-down on vast horizons; the gold of the roofs suggests the wonder of dawn and sunset on far-off snows. The world holds nothing to match this, knows nothing on such a scale. Not even Ang-Kor can approach those areas of granite pavement, those miles of scarlet wall.

Amber of course knew nothing about Chinese architecture. She did not even know that by her judicious use of a visiting-card she had entered the Forbidden City through the dynastic gateway which the Emperor himself, in earlier days, only used on such ceremonial occasions as his visits to the Altar of Heaven—which is so seldom opened to foreigners that Sir James Boggit himself had never been through it. She was merely full of delighted wonder at what she saw, and anxious to explore further. She went on to the second gate. Here were more police, but she was ready for them, pulled out a card and passed through as before. She entered another stretch of paved avenue, as large as the first, but the gateway beyond it was even more splendid than the others. From the central portion two mighty wings projected, crowned with blunt tent-topped towers, each capped with a great gilded knob; in the enclosure so formed the groups of police, the one or two Chinese, looked like ants moving about. When she walked over into it the red ramps rose above her head like cliffs. But here the police were for some reason obdurate; she could not get through, and had to turn back. She had caught a glimpse of green through a half-open door in the cloister on her right as she approached the third gateway, and now, unhindered, she went over to it. The cloister was full of timber, broken lumps of marble and decaying rubbish; tiles were falling off it in places, the small door hung crooked on its hinges. Giving it a push, she passed through.

To most people, once or twice in a lifetime, there comes a moment of supreme recognition, when something often heard and never fully believed flashes on eye and mind alike with absolute conviction. Such a moment came to Amber then. She was in Xanadu! Straight in front of her, beyond a small stone Pai-lou, ran a quadruple avenue of thujas, with grey trunks as stout as English oaks. To the left of the avenue lay a broad moat, sunk between huge walls of dressed stone; beyond it rose a grey battlemented wall. And over the wall appeared the pleasure dome! A summer-house, a little pavilion, with roofs in tiers and at angles, fluted up and down; delicate, fantastic, gay—enchanting by contrast with the austere immensity of the grey wall and the greater gate-towers. And oh!—"the shadow of the dome of pleasure floated mid-way on the wave"—it really did. There in the blue moat lay the golden fantasy, the delicate thing. Murmuring the familiar lines to herself in a sort of ecstasy, she walked along the thuja avenue, and now came upon the final wonder. The caves of ice were there too! Sitting down on the low parapet beside the moat, she looked over; below her, in the deep cold shadow of the dressed stone, the thick ice of winter still clung to the wall in broad projecting sheets, and the water was lapping gently in and out under it.

By this time she was quite intoxicated with wonder. Nuggets indeed! Here was Eldorado! Her main thought was to find some way of returning to this magical place, for she guessed that the card trick might not always work.

It was pure marvellous luck so far. Sitting on the parapet, in the sun, she spied about her. Just below the
pleasure-dome, both moat and wall made a right-angled
turn; some distance further on, the moat was crossed by
a bridge, on which traffic was moving to and fro. Presently she saw a Chinese come out through the door
in the cloister and walk along the narrow dusty strip of
ground below the wall towards the corner. At the bend
some little paper hovels encumbered the strip of ground,
and he disappeared behind them; watching carefully—
he had an odd hat on—she saw him reappear and pass
on to the bridge, where he mingled with the traffic and
vanished. So there *was* another way in.

Satisfied that her new paradise was not closed to her,
Amber turned now to further exploration. She was to
be back at five to go with Mrs. Grant-Howard to a choral
practice of part-songs for the St. Dunstan's entertainment, but she had forgotten all about that. Behind the
avenue was a crimson wall, all tenderly stained with
lichen, and over it showed a long golden roof. After
some search she found a little door in this wall, and
passed through. She wandered on and on, through one
red-walled enclosure after another, all full of saecular
junipers or thujas—the "ancient greenery" of Xanadu.
There was not a soul about—the whole place was empty,
ancient and silent, except for the harsh cries of the little
grey egrets which had their home in one grove, and the
Peking crows croaking and quarrelling in another. She
came at last to a paved clearing among the trees; on one
side of it was a three-arched gateway, with something
rather Moorish-looking about its marble carving. As
usual, Amber went in, and found herself in the outer
court of some building whose roof was visible over an
inner wall—by its shape she judged it to be the same that
she had seen from the avenue. Across the outer court

H

where she stood a little moat wound mazily, in the best
Kublai Khan fashion, appearing suddenly from underground on one side and vanishing, presumably into
caverns measureless to man, on the other. It was
spanned by seven little marble bridges; she crossed over,
and went up some marble steps to the inner gate. But
the scarlet doors were shut fast; she could not get in.
Sounds came from within; peering through the crack,
she saw two coolies hammering on a packing-case.
This aroused Amber's curiosity without surprising her—
she had already learned that there are two men and a
packing-case every few yards in China, and frequently
they are hammering at it in the middle of the street.
Since she could not enter, she sat down on a broken piece
of marble in the sun. The court was all overgrown with
dead weeds, their silvery empty seed-heads springing to
a man's height against the stained red walls; over the
tiled ridges appeared the green thujas, with egrets sitting
in them like weather-stained statues; further off still she
could see the shining roofs of the great gates, like huge
golden tents. It was all so still, deserted and forgotten,
in the afternoon sunshine, that but for the occasional
hammering she would hardly have believed that she was
in the actual world at all.

She did at last remember tea and the singing-practice
with Joanna. She lost her way several times among the
thuja-filled enclosures, the innumerable doors in endless
red walls; she was breathless when at last she found herself again by the moat, and ran like a deer down the
avenue. Thank goodness, the little door into the court
before the great gateway was still open! Back down the
paved roadway she sped, the police making no trouble
about her exit, and jumped into the first ricksha she met.
Borne along in the glowing afternoon light, in turns she
was horrified to think of her lateness, and exulted in the

wonders of her afternoon. Lovely, incredible places. She *must* find out exactly what they all were. Good heavens, it was half-past five! And she had no change at all. At the Legation gate she jumped out. She must get some from Jamieson or someone. Darting through the low ugly archway, followed by the protesting coolie trailing his ricksha, she ran slap into Rupert Benenden. "Hullo! What on earth's the matter?" he asked, as the girl recoiled and apologised.

"Give me fifty cents, quick, will you?" said Amber.

Chapter Eight

"WHAT *have* you been doing?" Benenden asked, when he had paid off the ricksha. He had taken in at one glance the girl's starriness of eye, quick breathing, and general air of being fresh from some emotional encounter; for a moment he wondered if she could have come from a rendezvous—he knew that vibrant look in women.

"Oh, in heaven! But I must fly—I'm going out with Mrs. G.-H., and I'm fearfully late," Amber breathed.

"Joanna went out three-quarters of an hour ago," said Rupert repressively, "so it's no good your hurrying. You'd much better come in and have a cup of tea with me. Come on. They had it early at the Erh-ch'in-ch'ai's."

"Oh. Thank you. Yes. Was she worried?" Amber asked as they walked along towards Rupert's house: he observed that she was still thinking mainly about Joanna, and not in the least about coming to tea with him, which increased his curiosity.

"She rang up the Leicesters, but she wasn't really worrying. She doesn't unless it's Nugent or the children," he said. "In here—now sit down and tell me where you've been."

"Oh, what a lovely room!" said Amber.

"Yes. You haven't been here before, have you?" said Rupert as he rang the bell; he was pleased with her exclamation.

It was a lovely room. The walls were covered with rice-paper of the colour of pale parchment, the furniture with tribute silk of a slightly deeper shade: on the floor was an old Chinese carpet in tones of blue and yellow and pale fawn. There were cool blue and yellow cushions on the chairs and sofas, and four bronze pictures on the pale walls, but nothing else. In this clear monotony of colour the abundant flowers and books glowed with sudden significance. It was all very thought-out, very perfect; quite different to Hawtrey's rather miscellaneous surroundings—a poet's room, Amber thought, looking back after her survey of it to its owner. The room fitted her theory of the poet better than Benenden himself. He was sunk into a deep chair, his hair rumpled and his coat collar half turned up as usual—he was watching her with those light intense eyes of his, curiously, quizzically. "Where have you been?" he asked her again.

"That's just what I want someone to tell me!" she burst out. "Have you got a map or a guide-book or anything?"

"There *are* no guide-books to Peking: there are maps in Juliet Bredon. But tell me where you went—this is Indian tea, by the way: do you mind?"

"No." Amber's tone dismissed the tea. She began to recount her adventures of the afternoon to Rupert: she *had* to tell them to someone, and he was there, so he got the full recoil of the explosion, so to speak, made by the Forbidden City in her unexpecting mind. Out it poured, in a flood—the pleasure-dome above, the moat, the ancient greenery, the caves of ice, the water vanishing underground. "It's all *there!*" she said at length, gazing at Benenden with large astonished grey eyes. "How the man could have written it all up like that, without even seeing it, I can't imagine. Someone must have been here and told him. Or *was* Coleridge ever here?"

"It was a dream," he reminded her. "Don't you remember, he started to write it when he woke up, and they interrupted him because a person from Porlock had called to see him—and when he got back to his study he'd forgotten the rest."

"Damn the person from Porlock!" said Amber with energy. She mused, her chin cupped in her hand, staring in front of her. Benenden watched her. He was struck, as Nugent had been, with the vividness of her seeing, and the sureness of her insight into the significance of what she saw: still more was he impressed by the very unusual phenomenon of a fashionable young woman being so violently *émotionnée* by places and buildings. Of course the Forbidden City was enough to *émotionner* anyone, but most of the young women who came to Peking seemed to take it very coolly. Certainly none of them ever had the enterprise to barge their way in through the dynastic gateway, leaving cards all the way! And recalling her account of this, he gave a little snort of laughter.

"What is it?" Amber asked, looking up.

"I'm wondering who will get all those cards you left on the police," he said, still laughing. "The Chief Executive, I expect. I'm really rather jealous," he went on. "I've been here two years, and *I*'ve never found Xanadu. I've never even been into that side. Let's get the map and see what it all is."

Seated side by side on the sofa, they pored over the map, tracing Amber's route: Benenden finally decided that the courtyard where she had "fetched up" must be the outer court of the Temple of the Ancestors, where the Memorial Tablets of the Imperial Family were housed. "But that's the most sacred place of the lot," he said. "No European has ever been in there except once, in the Boxer time. It's always most jealously guarded." He banged his knee. "I *must* get there!" he said, rumpling his hair. "Do you think you could take me—if we could

get in again with your famous cards? Would you remember the way?"

Oh, but they wouldn't need the cards, Amber told
him—she'd found out another way in: and she described
how by watching the man with the odd hat she had
marked down the route from the bridge.

"My heaven, you are a sportswoman!" Rupert cried.
"You ought to be in the gum-shoe brigade! When shall
we go? Tomorrow?"

The idea of escorting the poet to a sight he had never
seen was a delightful temptation, and Amber longed
to say yes. But she held stoutly to her conscientious
scrupulousness, and said that no, tomorrow she was
riding with Hawtrey.

"Damn Joe! You can ride with him any day!
Thursday, then?"

No, not Thursday either. Amber was riding with
Mme. de Bulle on Thursday, to try a pony.

"Oh—well; can you spare an hour from the *sacrés*
horses *any* day this week?" Rupert asked irritably.
"And don't get too much mixed up with Mimi de Bulle
—she's a foul woman. You can't *like* her?" he asked,
turning brusquely on Amber.

"No, I think she's frightful," replied Amber candidly.

"Then why in heaven's name do you go out with
her?"

"Oh well—for one thing, I want to try the pony, and
besides, she keeps on asking me," said Amber.

Benenden looked at her consideringly, his head on one
side. "Why are you so amiable?" he asked at length.
"There's no sense in it. The important thing at the
beginning of any encounter is to show that you are capable of being disagreeable. You never do that, do you?
I've watched you. You're as friendly as a spaniel!"
He offered her a cigarette, and lit one himself. "Aren't

you?" he said, in the half-caressing, half-reasonable tone which people use to a nice child.

Amber was rather at a loss. No one had ever talked to her quite like that before; the caressing tone, the fact that he had watched her, the apparent contempt, or nearly that, with which he had done so, brought so many confused and confusing ideas into her mind that for a moment she simply sat, blushing and disconcerted, in the firelight. At last—"I don't see any harm in being amiable," she brought out.

"I don't see any good in it," Rupert countered. "Who wants it? Certainly not Mimi—she isn't fond of you; she only wants to get in with the G.-H.'s, and uses you as a catspaw, because Joanna is too jolly astute to be got at. People don't respect you if you're so friendly."

His words poured over Amber like an astringent disinfectant—they stung, they almost hurt: he was letting in a cold light on a lot of comfortable preconceptions. She had begun to think Peking a friendly place, this last week or so: her miserable secret consciousness of being diminished and humbled by her mistake about Arthur had found, half consciously, a balm and a tonic in the fact that people seemed to like her, that she was so much in demand. It was beginning to restore her self-respect. And now perhaps it was all a delusion. Her mind flew round her new circle of acquaintances, trying to see if what she had observed matched this new idea. Harry Leicester, determined that she must ride in the Ladies' Handicap which closed the paper-hunting season, and anxious therefore that she should take Bananas out in the two next drag-hunts, to qualify: Hawtrey with his insistence that she should help him lay his paper-hunt course. Was it all a complete sham? How horrid! Anyhow, she wouldn't back down, she thought, with a healthy movement of resentment, and quite unaware how plainly her trouble showed in her face, she said stoutly:

"Well, I was brought up to be polite, and I *shall* ride with Madame de Bulle on Thursday."

"Well, will you take me into Xanadu on Friday?" Benenden asked.

"Wouldn't that be rather unnecessarily amiable?" Amber asked, in a chilly tone.

Benenden shouted with amusement. "Oh you darling! *Touché!* No, you must take me."

"But why? Why you and not Mimi — Madame de Bulle, I mean, and all the rest?"

"Oh, because I'm quite different. In *every* way!" he said, leaning a little on the word; he smiled at her, and there was something forcible and engaging about his smile. "Friday, at three?" he asked.

"Very well," said Amber. She got up to go.

"No—wait a moment: don't go yet. Look here—you want, don't you see, to discriminate about people, especially in a place like this, which is full of all sorts and nearly all with axes to grind. There's not time for everybody, and you want to go for the ones who have got something real inside, who aren't just façades. You see for yourself that Mimi is frightful—then don't waste time on her. *She's* pretty obvious: but don't you see the difference between old James, say, and Nugent? The Minister's a good old thing, but he's much too fat and comfortable, and too much of a diplomat, to be a real person."

"But isn't Mr. Grant-Howard a good deal of a diplomat?" Amber asked, thinking of Nugent in action at some recent dinner-parties.

"Oh Lord, yes, brilliant—but it isn't his *life*. His life is"— Benenden paused and blew—"well, ultimate things. Secretly he adores the spiritual graces. Haven't you got into that side of him at all?"

Amber considered. She remembered little things—
their talk about people and places as they looked at
Sumatra: the swift illumination on his face on the first
morning in Peking, when she mentioned the "forpress."
And slowly—"I've seen the shadow of it," she said.
She paused, considering again: she had thought of
Hawtrey, and was trying to fit him into this new valua-
tion. "How well do you know Mr. Hawtrey?" she
asked at length.

Benenden answered the question in her mind and not
the one she uttered aloud.

"Oh, Joe's a border-line case. When he's being social
he's barely human!" Amber nodded—it was exactly
what she felt.

"The trouble with Joe," Benenden went on, "is that he
values his façade so much—all that eye-glass and 'dear
lady' business. But he's pretty shrewd really." He lit
another cigarette. "And as a matter of fact I don't
much believe in all this lady-killing business either. I
don't say he hasn't had his loves, like everyone else, but
fundamentally I think he's much more simple than he
likes to give out."

"Mrs. Leicester said that," said Amber.

"Oh, she did, did she? Poor Lydia!" He sighed.
Amber wondered why, but catching sight of the clock,
which said twenty to seven, she gathered up her gloves
and prepared for flight—she had a Chinese lesson at
seven.

"I'll see you back," Benenden said when she announced this fact. As they walked across the compound
and up the drive to the Counsellor's house, "Don't you
think it's about time I began to call you Amber?" he
said.

"A month? M-m-m. All right," said Amber.

"Do you reckon it by time?" he asked, peering at

her in the dusk—he sounded half irritated and half amused.

"*You* said it was time!" she protested.

"Yes, but I was reckoning by this afternoon," said Rupert, departing.

Indoors, she first looked into the drawing-room to see if Joanna had returned. She hadn't. Then she had better get as much dressing done as possible before Mr. Lin came, and take the first half of him. Mr. Lin was the Chinese teacher provided by Leroy: Amber and Mrs. Grant-Howard shared him, and by great efforts one or other contrived to be with him for quite a fair proportion of the hour which he spent daily at the Counsellor's house. Amber darted upstairs, bespoke a bath from Burbidge, undressed, whisked into it, whisked out again: she had time to do her hair, but not her face, and slip into a frock, before the Number Two tapped at her door and called "*Lin Hsien-hsieng lai-loh!*"

Mr. Lin was round, fat and comfortable: he wore a black sateen robe and velvet slippers, and a little round satin cap. His broad greenish-white face, the planes so delicately flattened that it looked almost like a plate with two eyes in it, was nevertheless sensitive and humorous. He came of an old Manchu family, now fallen on evil days, and was thankful to teach Mandarin to the foreign devils for fifty cents an hour. He spoke no English at all, and Amber and Joanna learned like parrots, repeating phrases after him and copying them down in little note-books. This method was strongly recommended by Leroy as good for the accent, but involved a great deal of pantomime.

Amber came in now, hurriedly, received Mr. Lin's ceremonious bows and *Nin hao's?*—(Are you well?)—said "*Nin hao*" herself: and taking her copy-book and pencil, settled down to her lesson. Gravely, Mr. Lin began his revision of yesterday's work. "*Wo-ti pi*," he said, touching his pencil. "Waw-dy bee," repeated Amber, touching hers. "*Nin-ti pi*," said Mr. Lin, touching Amber's pencil. "Nin-dy bee," repeated Amber, touching his. "*Nin-ti pen-tzŭ?*" said Mr. Lin, an ivory-coloured finger on her note-book, with a questioning glance. "Waw-dy bendze" said Amber proudly: Mr. Lin beamed. When, encouraged, she indicated Joanna's note-book and said "Erh-ch'in-ch'ai T'ai-t'ai-dy bendze," he clapped his beautiful hands and laughed.

But while Amber was repeating the sounds of "*bee*" and "*bendze*," talking about chairs, tables, sofas, clocks and carpets, and scribbling in her book that She-in-garden-flowers-see-not-could, half her mind was back in Benenden's pale room, listening to him, trying to clear up her thoughts about him. It was, definitely, *fun* to be taking him to the Temple of the Ancestors: it marked Friday with a little luminous dot in her mind. Friday—what was Friday in Chinese? Oh yes, *li-pai liu*. Then there was what he said about Hawtrey. Hardly human!—he was very amusing. That was absolutely true, too. Was it really equally true, all that about not being friendly? Amber wasn't sure—she had a feeling that there was a catch in this somewhere. She could feel the difference, anyhow, between Sir James and Mr. Grant-Howard. ("I today sitting ocean-cart to Pei-t'ang go" repeated Amber, and wrote down this very peculiar description of her ride to the Leicesters' in the ricksha.) That about his adoring the spiritual graces was frightfully interesting. She tried to think exactly what the spiritual graces were. It stuck in her mind that in the little books she used to read when she was confirmed *humility* was always referred to as one of the main spiritual graces. Humility? —Mr. Grant-Howard? She thought of him—busy, learned, ironic; suave in need, caustic by choice—and yet—yes, she thought she saw what Rupert meant, and might meet it in time.

Joanna came in at this point, very glittering in a silver frock, very perfect and complete as to face and hair. Amber rose and said she would go and finish dressing. "Right—can I have your book? Oh, and Amber"— Joanna called her Amber now—"tell Nugent, will you, that that wretched Leopardi has failed tonight, but I've got Rupert instead? The silly idiot cut his head open out riding." (Amber realised that the unhappy Leopardi was the silly idiot.) "And change that one name-card, will you, on the table and on the plan? The rest can stay—you'll be on one side of him and Señor Parados the other: perfectly all right." Amber was aware of a little tiny puff of pleasure, like the half-caught scent of a flower, at the thought of seeing Benenden again so soon; as she left the room she heard Joanna's voice saying "Wo-ti pi."

She changed the cards, then went to Nugent's study to give the message. As she opened the door she heard voices in discussion, and there were Nugent and Rupert.

"Oh, I beg your pardon," Amber began.

"Come in—it's all right, we've finished," said Nugent amiably. "You'll take that back then, Rupert, and give it to Joe to be typed, and we'll let Himself have it to-morrow morning. Well, Mademoiselle, what can we do for you?"

"It was only a message from Mrs. Grant-Howard," said Amber: "about M. Leopardi having failed—but perhaps Mr. Benenden has told you himself."

"Now, now!" said Benenden. "Nugent, don't you think it's time she stopped all this Mr. Benenden business? I'm going to call her Amber—I said so."

"And what did Amber say?" Nugent enquired, changing his spectacles and looking very benevolently at the girl through his other pair.

"She said yes," said Rupert. "Didn't you?"

"Yes," said Amber, smiling—the two men were some-how very pleasant, standing there together by the fire and teasing her. "Well then, Mrs. Grant-Howard said that *Rupert*"—she stressed the word firmly—"would take Monsieur Leopardi's place. And I've seen to the cards. Now I must go and dress."

"You look very dressed now," said Nugent.

"Oh *no*—this was just for Mr. Lin," said the girl, escaping.

"That's a very nice child," said Nugent when she had gone.

"By Jove, she has got a nerve!" said Rupert. "Do you know where she went today?" He retailed the story of Amber's afternoon—Nugent was delighted with the epi-sode of the cards. "She's a very odd mixture," Benenden said at the end: "she has the gift of seeing *things*, you see, with this extraordinary intensity."

"Yes, I know—she was like that on the boat," said Nugent. "You ask her about the coast of Arabia."

"I will. What about it? Oh well, anyhow!—never mind. I will." He laughed at himself. "But she's ab-surdly silly about people—and uncertain about herself. She's childish, rather."

"She's inexperienced," said Nugent. "I'm not sure that she's really as undiscerning as you think. I think she's lost her nerve."

"Why?" Rupert pounced.

"Why do young people lose their nerve?" Nugent enquired of the room at large, blowing out smoke. "Muddled it with some young man, I expect. And her mother is a most crushing woman. She'll get all right."

"She wastes her enthusiasm on such futile things," said Rupert, going back to his own point. "All this fuss about riding, and ponies—*here!* here in Peking! With all this miraculous stuff to see! And she with a quite outstanding capacity for seeing it! Really, Nugent, you must admit that it's very absurd—and *quite* maddening."

"Let her alone, then," said Nugent, with deliberately irritating reasonableness. "Leave her to ride her ponies with Joe. They get on very well." He threw his cigarette into the fire. "Come on, take that stuff across, there's a good fellow, or you'll be late. Dinner's at eight-thirty, and there are no Tuchuns coming, so we shall be punctual."

"Hang you, Nugent!" said Rupert, and went. But while dressing it occurred to him that he and no one else must show Amber the Temple of Heaven, and get her first reactions. At dinner he sat, maddened by the faintly smutty vacuities of the Chilean Third Secretary on one side—Rupert was at the edge of that arid desert of less important men which occurs at every Peking dinner-table—and equally maddened by Miss Harrison's quite needless amiability to Mr. Schroff on the other. She was promising to lunch with them, to escort Mrs. Schroff to the next drag-hunt, and heaven knew what else. When at last he could gain her attention, he told her that he wanted to take her to the Temple of Heaven.

"To ride, do you mean?" Amber asked innocently.

"*Ride?* God help the girl! No, to *see* it," Rupert fumed. "My soul in heaven, don't you *want* to see it? Can't you ride somewhere else?"

"Of course I want to see it," said Amber. "Why are you so cross?" she said, a little irritated in her turn: "people do ride there."

Rupert apologised. He made himself very amiable, and described the altar and dome in a way that made Amber thirst to see them. Before dinner was over, she had promised to go with Rupert before she went with anyone else, though his urgency in demanding this puzzled and startled her. From the head of the table Nugent, watchful, weary and courteous, between the wives of two Ministers, saw how Rupert was letting Amber alone. He smiled.

Chapter Nine

RATHER surprisingly, in spite of the fact that she had looked forward to it so much, Amber's visit to the Forbidden City with Rupert was a distinct success. What she remembered most, looking back on it, was something he said as they sat in the sun on the low parapet above the moat, looking across at the little building she called the pleasure-dome. "That's very nearly comic," he had burst out abruptly—"and yet it's perfectly lovely. It's not a grin, it's a smile—a smile in architecture. Who else has done that?" And he had gone on to talk—more to himself than to her—about Chinese art: "You'll begin to see presently how terribly sophisticated it is—so sophisticated that it's a little amused at itself. There's that hint of laughter about it nearly all the time—a thing Europe doesn't really know in art." She remembered that, it opened such new doors in her mind—that, and his serenity. Not once that afternoon was he prickly or irritable; it was as if those empty ancient places had laid some spell on him of sweetness and peace. She felt that she had caught a glimpse of the poet at last, and she was content.

Their other expedition, to the Temple of Heaven, was delayed by one thing and another. Amber's activities were absorbed by preparations for the Ladies' Hunt, in which Hawtrey and Harry Leicester were determined that she should compete. To qualify she rode out twice with the drag-hunt, which was presided over by Major la Touche, the commandant of the Legation Guard, and a rather withered man called Heseltine. Accompanied by

Hawtrey, she followed an extraordinarily miscellaneous and incompetent pack of dogs of a variety of breeds, known and unknown, across the dusty brown country; halting in the bitter wind while the scent was lost, cast for, and found again, generally by the agency of one minute animal who appeared to be three-quarters Schipperke. But even when she had actually qualified, there was much to be done. Bananas had to be trained, in a sequence of gallops, trots, walks and rests; there were anxious consultations in the yard of the Legation stable after breakfast as to his diet, when Hawtrey, Wang and Jamieson stood round with solemn faces, or shouted in Chinese at one another. It seemed to Amber that the simplest consultation in Chinese had always to be carried on at the pitch of the voice, in a series of loud and ferocious yells. From her bathroom window, which overlooked the servants' compound, she was frequently an observer of the cook's interviews with the purveyors of various articles. An outburst of shouts and roars of the most threatening description would draw her, wrapped in a towel, to the window, where she would watch, fascinated, the scene in the yard below—the pig-tailed *Ch'u-tzŭ*, his Roman profile contorted with emotion, screaming with a wealth of threatening gesture at some men in blue, who replied with equal ferocity, while the rest of the household, like Amber, looked on. But she soon learned that it was only an amicable discussion over the price of eggs or "French onions" (leeks); suddenly the storm would subside, the food be carried into the house; some copper money changed hands, and bowing and smiling at one another with the most friendly courtesy, the parties separated.

Rupert looked on all these activities with a slightly sour eye. The poet once more receded out of view, and he was as prickly as ever, making caustic remarks to both

Joe and Amber about their "infatuation with horseflesh."
Then, suddenly, he was sent off to Shanghai on business.
And so he came to miss Amber's next adventure.

Dickie had set his heart on going to the Forbidden City.
Ever since Amber had told him of what she had seen
there, he was determined to go. His daily trots with Miss
Carruthers on the Wall or in Central Park no longer
satisfied him, and it was "Amber, when will you take me
to the Forbidden Cipy?" all day long. Amber had made
great friends with the little boy. She helped him with
his "forpress" behind the thujas in the upper garden,
under the glass-topped wall of the Soviet Embassy; it now
comprised a dug-out roofed with *kaoliang* straw as well
as the block-house formed by the barrel. Dickie was
meditating an attack on the Embassy—by climbing up a
small tree he had already succeeded in knocking the glass
off quite a stretch of wall, and there was a grandiose project of a tunnel under it, leading from the dug-out. She
assisted him in the arrangement of his Chinese City in
the corner of the loggia—a town in miniature, made with
those enchanting little clay toys which are one of the
most engaging by-products of the Chinese mentality.
Little bridges, little pagodas, little devil-doors, walls,
houses, pai-lous—all most delicately modelled in hard grey
clay; and to people them, minute straw dolls, barely an
inch high, representing with perfect accuracy the familiar
figures of the country-man, the barber, the sweetmeat
vendor, the knife-grinder, and so on. The servants brought
these from the market at frequent intervals to give
pleasure to Small Grandfather. The Chinese as a race
simply cannot resist children, and even Joanna, with all
her detachment, was rather touched by the evident devotion of Liu and Chang to her small son. Ignorant as the
whole party were of China, the idea of danger lurking
in these charming little playthings never occurred to any

of them, and Liu and the rest made their offerings unhindered.

Soon after Rupert's departure Amber found herself
with a free afternoon, and at once suggested to Miss
Carruthers that she should take Dickie off her hands.
Miss Carruthers was delighted, and Amber annexed the
child. A whisper in his ear set him bouncing and capering at the end of her arm like a ball on a string. Nugent
met them as they crossed the compound on their way to
the gate, and Amber saw again that sudden illumination
in his face as he looked at his son. "For a grape ex-
pebishum!" Dickie said triumphantly, in answer to his
Father's "Where are you off to?"

Amber thought there was an unusual crowd about the
public entrance to the Forbidden City, but when they
had paid their fee and passed in she could hardly believe
her eyes. The great open court before the Pavilion of
Audience, which had lain so white and empty when she
went there with Rupert, was thronged now from side to
side with Chinese. Two or three high rostrums or pulpits
had been set up in the middle, from which orators were
haranguing the multitude. Now and then the crowd
made way for some procession to pass up towards the
Pavilion—a troop of Boy Scouts, a file of soldiers, nurses
in uniform, or Girl Guides with long skirts and swinging
black plaits. Bewildered, Amber and Dickie made their
way slowly towards the Dragon Throne Room, wondering
greatly what it was all about. Passing under one of the
walls, they saw that it was plastered with posters of the
most blood-curdling description. Chinese, both in uniform and in civilian dress, were crudely but vigorously
depicted in various eminently anti-foreign activities:
pounding the foreigner with mallets, shooting the foreigner, bayoneting the foreigner, pushing the foreigner
into the sea; leading him in chains, jumping on him with

both feet. Dickie was enchanted; he wanted to linger and examine these admirable pictures, which were thoroughly to his taste. But Amber hurried him on. She was beginning to be a little doubtful. If there were any connection between the obvious intention of these posters and this enormous gathering, she and Dickie might find themselves in difficulties. They had better just see the Dragon Throne, so as not to disappoint the child, and then leave.

Their progress, however, was slow. The crowd was very dense, and surged vaguely in all directions—now pressing out towards the walls to jabber delightedly at the inflammatory posters, now crowding in towards the rostrums to listen to the speakers. Caught in such a movement, Amber and Dickie were carried close under one of these erections; judging by the gestures and expression of the orator, he was using very forcible language about something. They tried to move on, but now Dickie's loud observations drew the attention of the crowd. They thronged round Amber and the child, gazing at them with interest and discussing them eagerly and with apparent pleasure; the more enterprising presently patted Dickie on the head, felt his clothing, and even chucked him under the chin. When Dickie grinned at them their faces wreathed into broad and benevolent smiles—more and more Chinese left off listening to the speaker's imprecations to come and bestow small gentle caresses on the little foreigner. Amber's doubts vanished; these attentions were embarrassing, but obviously not dangerous; the posters must be intended for some other occasion.

Accompanied wherever they went by admiring groups, they found their way at last into the Pavilion of Audience. The Dragon Throne itself was completely masked by an enormous picture of a famous Chinese democratic leader,

wreathed in paper flowers, and the reason for the whole
strange assemblage dawned on Amber. It must be
some anniversary of this national hero, and these crowds
had gathered to do him honour. The press in the
throne-room was terrific, and she was glad when they
were borne forth again into the sunshine. Slowly, as
before, still the centre of much friendly interest, they
made their way back across the crowded court. People
were passing through the great tent-topped gateway
where she had been held up on her first visit, and she
decided to go through. In the court beyond a perceptible human stream set in the direction of the thuja
avenue; she and Dickie went with it, and passed through
doors and enclosures shut before; she quite lost her sense
of direction, and was borne along, unheeding, till with a
shock of surprise she found herself in the outer Court of
the Temple of the Ancestors. But oh, wonder of wonders!
The inner door was open now, and the crowd was pouring into those most venerable, most jealously guarded
precincts.

Amber's colour rose with excitement. If only Rupert
were here! was her first thought. But the next was a
thrill of exultation. Once before, once only, had this
place ever been opened to Europeans—and now she and
Dickie were there! In they went with the crowd, and
she looked eagerly about her, taking stock of everything. The centre of the inner court was occupied by a
large building, capped by that long golden roof which
was so conspicuous from outside. To the left was another building, smaller, and into the open doors of this
the crowd passed, to re-emerge by some further doors
higher up. Like everyone else, Dickie and Amber went
in. A passage had been roughly railed off along one
side; on the other, through the gloom, she could see a
whole series of slim golden tablets, raised on what ap-

peared to be altars; each standing on a carved base, and each bearing an inscription. Since her first visit to the Forbidden City Amber had read up everything that she could lay hands on on the subject, borrowing freely from the Chancery Library, and she knew enough to realise that she was looking at the memorial tablets of the Chinese Emperors themselves, at once the symbols of their immortality and the means of its promotion. Before these, in the past, the filial incense was burnt, the devout prayers said, which ensured the happy continuance of a life beyond the grave. She could not escape a touch of awe, feeling herself in the actual presence both of royalty and of death, which has a royalty of its own. If only Henry Leroy had been there, or anyone who could read the inscriptions, to tell her to which each belonged! But there was no one she could ask, and she was borne slowly by that silent and anonymous pageant of the Imperial past, and out into the open air again.

Dickie was by this time frankly bored. He left Amber and ranged about the Court, where the crowd was not quite so dense. Presently he dragged Amber over to see a discovery. On the ground, among dead weeds and marble fragments, lay a little hen in glazed yellow earthenware, with a small headless figure on its back; it had evidently fallen from one of the roofs, where on each angle sat perched a whole row of tileware dogs and dragons, with one of these small figures at the bottom. It was quite unbroken, except for its head—and in a moment Dickie found this too—it had a loose unglazed stem which fitted into a hole in the neck. The child begged to be allowed to take it with him. Amber looked about her. The inevitable crowd of Chinese was gathering round them, smiling and making comments. "I don't think we can," she said. "I don't suppose it's allowed, and there are all these people about."

"Boo lep me!" Dickie begged.

"No, Dickie. It's no good coaxing," said Amber firmly. "Let's sit and rest here," she added, an idea striking her. "I'll tell you a story."

They sat down where they were on some pieces of broken marble. The hen lay between them. The circle of Chinese pressed closer, delighted with this opportunity of studying Dickie at close range. As Amber told her story, their eyes followed her every movement.

"The stork lived high up in a tree," said Amber, pointing upwards, and the circle of faces was lifted to gaze where she pointed. At the same moment, with her other hand she moved the figure a little nearer to her. "And the eagle came flying over like that"—she pointed again, and again the Chinese stared skywards, while Amber twitched the hen nearer still. Now it was under the skirts of her fur coat; still pointing, still improvising, she worked it up inside her coat till it was firmly lodged under her arm. With a little smile of triumph she rose, ending her story only when they reached the outer court. As they got into their ricksha at the main gate Dickie broke into renewed lamentations that he had not been allowed to bring home "the hen"; when Amber let him see it tucked into her coat he nearly wriggled off her knee with rapture. It was a triumphant couple who scrambled out of the ricksha at the steps of the Counsellor's house, very late for tea.

They had a rather chilling reception, however. Nugent Grant-Howard came out of his study on hearing them in the hall. "Ah—there you are!" The relief in his voice was unmistakeable. "Aren't you rather late?" he said then, more coldly than Amber had ever heard him speak. Before she could explain Joanna appeared from the drawing-room. "Where in the world have you been?" Her voice was almost sharp—Amber looked from one to the other in astonishment.   Nugent was the first to recover himself.

"I'm glad you're back," he said.   "There's rather a fuss going on—some form of anti-foreign demonstration in the Forbidden City.   I heard of it just after you'd gone out, or I'd have told you you'd better keep in the compound this afternoon. Joanna was rather afraid you might have gone there, when you were so late coming back."

For a moment Amber was silent from sheer horror. Then she screwed herself up to it.   "I'm afraid we *were* there," she said.

"Were *where*?" Nugent asked.

"In the Forbidden City.   We didn't know either," she said, feeling like a criminal.   "But it was very nice, really," she added lamely.

"Good heavens!" Joanna burst out, startled out of her usual composure.   "Do you mean to say you took the child there today?   You and he alone?   Really, Amber, I thought you had more sense."

Here Dickie interposed in defence of his beloved Amber.   "Bom'p be silly, Mummie. Ip was quipe all ripe," he said firmly.   "And we've gop a hem."   He produced the little effigy triumphantly.

"But you must have known when you got there that there was a demonstration," said Joanna to Amber. "Yes, Dickie, it's lovely; now run to Miss Carruthers and get your tea."   She turned to Amber again.   "Why didn't you come home, as soon as you saw what was going on?   How long were you there?"

"About two hours, I suppose," said Amber wretchedly. "But I didn't know what it was all about.   There were only the crowds, and processions.   I am most terribly sorry, Mrs. Grant-Howard.   Of course, the posters looked anti-foreign, but the people were so—so fearfully friendly, I didn't think it could be anything to do with us, after the first."

"What exactly do you mean by friendly?" Nugent asked. "Do you mean they spoke to you?"

"We could hardly *move* for them!" the girl burst out, her lip quivering. "They kept coming up to look at Dickie, and smiling, and patting him—they left the speakers to come and see him! How *could* I know? If that's their way of showing their anti-foreign feeling, it's —it's very misleading!" she said, on the verge of tears.

At that, suddenly, the momentary tension broke. Nugent opened his mouth and roared. He laughed till the tears came into his eyes. It was of course partly the reaction from his anxiety. And while he was still crowing with mirth over this unexpected revelation of the realities of an anti-foreign demonstration, Hawtrey walked in.

"The truants safely returned, ha-ha!" he said. "You gave us all quite a fright, Miss Harrison. We thought you'd got mixed up with the demonstration."

"They had! They were in the middle of the whole blessed thing, and apparently had a *succès fou,*" said Nugent, wiping his eyes and changing his spectacles. "Come on, Joanna, give Amber some tea," he said, shepherding them into the drawing-room—and Amber knew that by her host at least she was forgiven. "But of course that's completely Chinese—that's just like these celestial comics," Hawtrey observed, when he had heard how the crowd had turned from listening to the speakers' denunciations of foreign devils in general to pet and admire the particular small foreign devil in their midst. "Hullo, what's this?" he asked of Dickie, who had again unobtrusively presented himself, and was holding up the tiled figure for his inspection. "By Jove, it's a Bong! Where did you get that?" Dickie explained.

"Well, don't let any of your boys see it, or they'll probably clear out in a body," said Joe. "It's the one thing they're absolutely terrified of. It's hideously unlucky."

"Why?" asked Amber and Joanna together.

"Oh, because the Bong is *the* most pernicious of all the Demons. He was caught once, and they secured him in this thoroughly Chinese way—tied him to a hen, and set the hen on the corner of the roof, above the eaves. They say a hen, being the most timid of all living creatures, is safe never to jump down—and she can't get back up the roof-tree, because of the dogs and things behind. You must have seen them on the roofs."

"Yes, I have—and I wondered what they were," said Nugent.

"Well, that's it."

"But why are they afraid of the thing indoors, if they put it on the roof?" Joanna asked.

"Oh, on the roof it's merely a sort of inoculation," said Joe—"but if you bring him into the house he has power, I suppose."

"He *does* look rather like a griffin, with the two heads," observed Amber, holding the creature up.

"Well, don't let the boys see it," said Joe again.

So the Bong was locked away in a drawer among Amber's underclothes, and only shown secretly to selected admirers. Mrs. Hugo shook her head over it, and told Joanna that nothing would induce her to have such a thing in the house, but Joanna only laughed. She took occasion to impress on Amber, later, the unwisdom of letting Dickie be in the crowd, for fear of infection, and Amber, duly penitent, made her peace. Dickie meanwhile was playing with his Chinese toys at the other end of the loggia. His mother watched him complacently.

Chapter Ten

THE Ladies Hunt is usually the last event of the Paper-hunting Season in Peking, and socially the most brilliant. Even the least horsy people come out to see how the T'ai-t'ai's will acquit themselves, and the lottery tickets enjoy a brisk, if rather derisory, sale at the Club. It is a course without jumps. "They tried letting the ladies jump one year, but it was simply a massacre," Hawtrey explained to Amber. "They fell off in heaps—armfuls of them. So Leroy—he was master then—said Never Again." He had been showing her round the course in the spring sunshine, pointing out its main features, so that she might recognise them next day; in the distance they had seen M. Rothstein leading a band of competitors on the same errand. Now, as they jogged home, Joe was giving her a résumé of the rivals she had most to fear. "Mimi will be riding Ontario; of course he can really beat Bananas into fits, but Mimi is pretty sure to lose her way—simply can't carry five miles of country in her head. And Dolly Rothstein will probably fall off, ha-ha! Countess Stefany is a superb horsewoman, but Herman will probably put her on some dud pony, so that she shan't beat Mimi," he went on, with thoughtless truthfulness.

"His own wife? Does he *want* her to be beaten?" Amber asked, her eyes very wide. Hawtrey mentally damned his own folly.

"Oh—er—well! People have these little eccentricities out here, you know, my dear Miss Harrison. Mimi's a good sort, but—well, she's French. *Un peu de rouge, un*

124

peu de poudre, un peu d'amour! That's our Mimi. Live
and let live, you know! And Lydia," he hurried on,
flattering himself that he had got over that rather neatly,
"dear Lydia will probably forget that she's racing at all,
and go for a nice ride alone! But you ought to be all
right. You must keep the Legation flag flying, you
know!"

But Hawtrey had not got out of it so neatly as he
thought. His careless words had been like a slap in the
face to the girl, suddenly revealing in all its potential
ugliness the relation between Count Herman and Mimi,
which hitherto had seemed to her merely puzzling and
in rather poor taste. It was horrible! To want his wife
not to win, and to let it be known that he wished her
rival to triumph. Thinking of it alone, afterwards, her
cheeks flamed with indignation. "The—*indecency* of it!"
she murmured. And to her natural and healthy desire
to do well was added a fierce and resentful determination
to "pip that woman" if she possibly could.

This feeling was intensified next day during lunch
before the race at Harry and Lydia's Temple of the Excited Insects. The Insects themselves were extremely
effervescent. Countess Stefany was there—Count Herman was not—and the indignant colour stole into Amber's
cheeks again when she observed his absence as final, on
the company's sitting down without him. Under the
shock of this discovery, the girl watched with an in-
voluntary, rather painful interest her hostess's absorption
in M. Bruno. Oh no, she told herself presently—*that*
wasn't possible! Mrs. Leicester was English—there
couldn't be anything in that! The countess was being
gracious, gay, delightful; she and Benenden, who had
returned from Shanghai, discussed the English language,
and Rupert used the word "filthy" as an adjective of
literary criticism. She turned to him. "Zere are two

Ing-lish expressions which I sink quite ex-cillent," she said, "ze best and most expressive in ze hol world— 'Filcee' and 'Gosh'!" This unusual view of Shakespeare's tongue enchanted the table. Benenden asked all the women in turns if they were nervous, with pertinacious mischief. "He is really id-yot, zis Benenden," Anna murmured to Amber as they powdered their noses in a small latticed side-room of the court; "in such a moment one is *criblée de nerfs*, but one shall not say so." Amber agreed—and a little prick of desire to shine under Benenden's rather scornful eyes added itself to her other motives for doing her utmost in the race.

The start had its delays. "Keep back, keep back, ladies, please! *Behind* the furrow, Mrs. Shroff." "*Which* furrow?" from Mrs. Shroff. "Major La Touche, do we *go* to the right of the flags, or leave the flags *on* our right?" After more bleats of anxiety or protest from the T'ai-t'ais, and further objurgations from the stewards, the dozen or so of women were got into some sort of alignment, La Touche dropped his hat, and they were off.

The next few minutes were for Amber a whirl of struggle, excitement and confusion. Then she got Bananas, who was pulling, sufficiently in hand to take stock of her position. Hawtrey had advised her to get ahead out of the ruck, in order to avoid jams at narrow places, but to keep behind Mme. de Bulle, "so that she can lose her way for herself." At the end of the first mile she had more or less realised this aim: Mme. de Bulle and Mme. Rothstein alone were ahead of her, the former leading; the others some lengths to the rear. With flying dust in her mouth and ears, and the rattle of hoofs behind her maddening Bananas, she nevertheless set herself steadily to overhaul Mme. Rothstein. They approached a narrow gap between the mud walls of two farms, which yesterday had been level going; as they neared it Mme.

de Bulle gave a scream, and Amber saw Ontario rise in a flying jump. Some ingenious Chinese had dug two deep furrows across the gap during the night! Warned in time, Amber gathered Bananas together, and cleared the obstacle, but the unfortunate Dolly Rothstein could not keep her seat, and realised Hawtrey's prophecy by flopping off in a heap. "Are you hurt?" Amber screamed, swinging Bananas round in a short circle. "No—go on!" the other screamed back, and on Amber went. She had lost ground, and gave Bananas his head a bit—phew, Mimi was setting a pace!—Amber hoped she would soon lose her way. But this, like so many human hopes, proved illusory. There now appeared beside Mme. de Bulle another mounted figure. Amber peered through her sweat-dimmed goggles in astonishment; she would have sworn that no one else was ahead of her. But it was not a woman; it was, as she presently saw, Count Herman, galloping easily beside the track and showing his *chère amie* the way.

This roused Amber to something like fury. Setting her teeth, she settled down to ride Bananas as she had never ridden a horse before. Steadily, slowly, she gained on Ontario, using her spurs, but sparingly. There was that rise in the run-in—she would need the last ounce for that. Presently, within three-quarters of a mile of home, Count Herman realised that she was drawing up. "Now use your whip," he called to Mimi de Bulle, before he faded out down a side-track; not even his brass was equal to appearing at the finish as an escort.

But the tip meant for Mimi was used also by Amber. Cautiously she tried her whip. Yes, Bananas responded. She gained. In the gully they were neck and neck. A distant roar greeted them as they swept up the rise. Level, level—would Bananas' nose *never* pass Ontario's? Head down, heels in, her right arm going like a flail,

Amber rode her finish. And her riding won. Mimi could sit on a horse, but she could neither spare it the distressing bumps of her rather loose seat, nor "ride" it. In the last two hundred yards this told, and Amber passed the post nearly a length ahead.

The result of the race created something of a sensation. Though Amber was known and liked, Leicester and Hawtrey had kept her riding rather to themselves; and people who were accustomed to regular wins by either Countess Stefany or Mme. de Bulle were startled by the sensational success of the newcomer. "*Tiens, elle monte à merveille, cette jeune fille,*" observed the French Minister through his cigar—"*Elle a gâché les manœuvres de l'Hongrois!*" Hawtrey's delight knew no bounds. It was genuine and generous, if somewhat proprietary—he had, after all, taken her round the course and helped her to train the pony! "My dear Joe, you make me quite sick," Mrs. Leicester drawled at him, "she *could* ride before she came, you know, and she isn't your daughter." Joe, wounded, blushed the ready blush of the fair-skinned, and turned away without a rejoinder, for once.

"Congratulations, my dear young lady! That was a triumph," said Sir James, thoroughly pleased. He chuckled. "Be careful! Try to limit your successes to horsemanship, or there'll be wigs on the green! Rivals are potential enemies, you know."

"One is born the enemy of some things," said Amber, unexpectedly, startling the Minister by this reply to his airy *sous-entendu*. She stood, hot, dust-stained, her legs still quivering with muscular effort, taking the general congratulations—she did not recoil visibly even under Mimi's effusive kiss and "*Très bien, petite.*" But two she valued more than all the rest put together. One was Henry Leroy's "Jolly good, Miss Harrison—wish your uncle could have seen you." Amber was wishing just the same thing; she would have liked someone of her *own* to be there, someone who really cared; she lifted grateful eyes to Leroy's harsh face. "He's coming next week, you know," she said, happily. At that moment Grant-Howard came up with her coat. "Put this on—you'll be cold in a moment," he said; "and drink this." He handed her a whisky which Rupert carried. "Well done," Nugent said then, as he buttoned her into her coat like a baby, giving her one of his rare illumined smiles, such as he generally reserved for Dickie. It might have been the coat or the whisky, but suddenly Amber felt warmed through and through.

Rupert had held off rather during all this. But later that evening he made his own comments. The whole assembly had been bidden in advance to a "petit cock-tail" at Mme. de Bulle's Peking house. They gathered there about seven o'clock, some still in riding-clothes, some dressed as for a *thé dansant*. Mimi's rooms, though large, were crowded, stifling, and noisy; smoke and the reek of cocktails filled them. The hostess, stout and uncouth, still in her rather dirty riding-dress, made much of Amber with a generosity that did her credit; Amber, incurably humble and bred in a tradition where it was normal for women to ride well, was astonished to find herself treated on all hands with a new deference. Presently Rupert came up and dragged her away. "I've got something to show you," was all he would say; he was arbitrary and mysterious. Rickshas carried them through the windy dusk, starred with lights, to the Southern gateway of the Forbidden City, whose huge bulk stood up, black, solemn, immense, against the last pale light in the Western sky. And now Amber saw what it was that Rupert had brought her out to see. The crows of the City were taking their evening flight, wheeling in vast clouds round and round, to and fro;

K

swinging up in a vertical movement, like flung spray, when they approached the gate-tower, to sink like blown leaves on the night wind. Their numbers, their silence, the strange unanimity of their flight made their motion more like that of some restless element than of living creatures—an element whose restlessness was forever denied by the immobility of the pillared outline of the gate-tower.

In silence they stood and watched. At last, "Well?" Rupert said.

"It's marvellous," the girl breathed; her face in the dusk was pale as a flower—the swift coming and going of her breath told him that she was moved by some considerable feeling. Suddenly he took hold of her arm. "You rode damned well today," he said, "and, damn it, I like you the better for it! But don't you see," he gave her arm a little friendly shake, "that this is worth more than twenty races, even if you *did* ride well?"

Amber did not answer at once. She was conscious of a certain disturbance in herself, partly due, of course, to a young man holding her elbow in the dark; but she was also aware of two distinct elements in Rupert's attitude—his interest in her, and his hostility to one side of her life, horses—which made it hard to answer. And she had a dim instinct that it was rather important to answer rightly. He shook her arm once more. "Well?" he said again.

"Of course," she said. "This is the other thing."

"But Amber, this is the thing that matters," he urged, pressing her arm more firmly.

A confused impulse of resistance stirred in the girl. Her liberty—liberty of thought, liberty of emotion, was somehow being threatened; and she could not go into it blind, she must know where she was first. She must break the spell of the moment, somehow. Crows!

They were only crows! Why were they more important than horses? she thought restlessly, her mind in its simplicity seizing on the concrete to help her in the struggle that she felt rather than understood. But as she looked again at the silent mass of the gateway, impassively resistant to the airy tumult that swept about it, she felt a sudden significance in the sight, and her heart, stirred afresh, cried out within her that somehow these *were* the things that mattered most. Oh, if only she could think of some clever phrase about proportion or something to help her out! Through Rupert's pressure on her arm she could feel his affectionate amusement, his curiosity as to what she would say. He was always so amused and so curious! "Out with it!" he said now, jogging her arm again.

"Everything matters in a way! *I* matter, too," she burst out desperately. "To myself, I mean," she added. Futile remarks! But somehow they seemed to satisfy Rupert.

"Bless my soul, of course you matter—you matter very much," he said. And took her home. But in her subsequent reflections on her day Amber found that their drift had insensibly altered a little. Lying next morning in the large, comfortable and wholly unbeautiful spare-room of the Counsellor's house, looking out through the arches of the loggia at the trees in the garden, just beginning to show a determined tracery of green, sipping the morning tea brought by Chang, the Number Two with the saintly face, she found that it was no longer possible to speculate merely on Benenden the poet, the embittered charming creature, as a person by himself. Curiously, almost against her will, she found that the subject of speculation had become a dual one, Benenden and Amber; Benenden somehow attempting a domination—yes, that was the word—of her ideas, her way of life. This was a new experience; it was stimulating, while it roused the same sense of resistance as before. *Why* did he? Why *should* he? Why not enjoy with her the things they did enjoy together, like the Forbidden City, and leave her in peace about riding? No one else had ever been like that to her—Arthur had never tried to dominate, she thought. But the thought of Arthur plunged her again into a confusion of ideas. To think of him now caused a less sharp, less jagged pain, than it used to. Was she forgetting? Her mind cried No!— but the realisation that she had compared Benenden's attitude with his sent the colour flying into her face. *That* was really absurd! She was interested in the poet as a poet, an exciting person. Anyhow this time, she told herself, she was going to be fearfully careful with all young men—she would make no more idiotic mistakes. She would be very detached. And she wouldn't take things lying down—*she* would be curious and amused, and pry into *his* ideas, and be critical! Yes, she would. And again, suddenly, she wished she knew what Mr. Grant-Howard would say about it all.

Nugent may have had his own ideas about Rupert and Amber, but at this time his thoughts became entirely concentrated on the affairs of the Legation. The day after the Ladies' Hunt the Minister went down with a severe attack of dysentery, throwing a considerable burden suddenly on to his Counsellor's shoulders. At the same moment a burst of political disturbances took place. It was first reported, then known, that Wang, the so-called "Methodist War-Lord," had at last matured his designs on Peking, and was moving troops in the direction of the capital, with a view to ousting Li, the Marshal, who had been in possession for some time. Simultaneously there were sudden outbursts of Communist activity, or activity attributed to Communists; the city police, whose pay was six months in arrears, went on strike; a number of students made a demonstration outside the Prime Minister's house, and before they were dispersed by the troops, leaving the corpses of immature girls and boys lying in the dust of the roadway, the Prime Minister himself had fled to the Legation Quarter. From thence he issued a circular telegram, deploring his own incompetence and lack of skill in the management of public affairs, which had led to these disorders, and announcing his resignation to make way for a more worthy successor. Such an announcement was of course quite in order; according to Chinese ideas it was both dignified and statesmanlike; but owing to the depletion of the public coffers and the uncertainty as to the military situation, the more worthy successor was slow in making his appearance, and in the meantime current negotiations had to be conducted with whoever could be prevailed upon to undertake them. And then one of the Chancery clerks took smallpox.

Nugent was of course one of the very few Europeans in Peking to whom the political disturbances made any difference whatever. But with the illness of Sir James and the archivist it was otherwise. Illness *matters* in China; and smallpox in the compound was no joke. The small society of the Legation, disturbed and alarmed, looked round for a cause for these misfortunes, and found it in the presence of Amber's Bong. A deputation of Legation ladies, headed by Mrs. Hugo, waited on Joanna, and begged for the Bong's removal. Joanna was incredulous, but felt obliged from diplomatic motives to do as they wished, and told Amber that it must go. "But it's absurd," protested Amber; "my poor yellow griffin! He's brought *me* luck anyway; look at the race!" Joanna secretly agreed with her, but insisted, and Amber dutifully undertook to remove the offending image. But

where was it to go? She couldn't bear to lose sight of
such a treasure altogether. She took counsel with
Dickie, who felt he had a vested interest in the "hem,"
and Dickie had an inspiration. If they *must* part with
their precious creature, let it at least do a useful service
in his secret war against the Soviet Embassy! So the
Bong was taken down to the "forpress," a string was tied
round it, Dickie climbed up his favourite tree, straddled
the glassless patch of garden wall, and attached the string
to a branch which overhung it; then with infinite precaution the Bong was lowered into the other garden,
where, as Dickie said triumphantly, it could "harry the
Sovieps."

"Good riddance," said Hawtrey, who had assisted at
this ceremony. "You know, my dear Miss Amber,
people may say what they like, but there *is* something in
these local beliefs. I'm much easier in my mind now
that Mr. Bong's gone to our Bolo friends, ha-ha! I've
known cases in Uganda . . ." He dwelt on them. "I
never care to mix myself up with things we don't understand—don't really understand, you know. You never
know."

"Uncle Joe, do you think he coulb reach us from there?"
said Dickie unexpectedly, capering beside him as they
crossed the lawn.

Joe glanced meaningly at Amber. "No, not from
there, Dickie, old man," he said airily.

"He mipe gep *me*," said Dickie, with half fearful interest, "when I go to my forpress."

Hawtrey swung the child up on to his shoulders. "He
won't 'gep' you," he said. "You're too small beer—
minuscular beer! No one wants minuscular beer!"

How nice he was with the child, Amber thought,
watching Dickie's small dirty hands ruffling his sleek red
head, unrebuked. And she liked him better still when

next moment, with the obvious intention of turning the child's mind off the previous conversation, he began: "Here Dickie, see if you can say this. 'John Nott could not knit, so he invented a knitter which he called the Nott Knitter. But the Nott Knitter could not knit knots, so John Nott had to knot the knots which the Nott Knitter could not knit.'" She and Hawtrey laughed helplessly when Dickie began to recite this epic; the "Mop Mipper" displayed his funny speech to perfection. He wanted to take out his "plape," but Hawtrey wouldn't allow this, and there was scuffling. Yes, fearfully nice—nice with children and horses. How odd that he should be "barely human" as Rupert said, in society. Thinking of Hawtrey and the child, Amber forgot all about the Bong.

Chapter Eleven

THE Temple of Heaven lies on the south side of Peking, within the boundaries of the Chinese City, but outside the Tartar Wall. To reach it one passes through the Chien-mên, the great green-tiled gateway near the railway station, and down the long shabby street known as Chien-mên Wai—"outside the Chien Gate"; as we say "Bishopsgate Street Without" in our own City of London, once, like Peking, a walled town. The straggling one-storey shops of Chien-mên Wai give place gradually to a collection of small mat-sheds and wooden booths, cumbering a great dusty open space, strangely resembling a suburb of broken-down chicken-houses: finally these also cease, and the imperial road crosses a stretch of ground empty of all save the rubbish of a great city, haunted by yellow scavenging dogs. In the middle of this waste, roads branch east and west off the great highway—that on the west leads to the Temple of Agriculture and the place of execution, that on the east to the Temple and Altar of Heaven. Here, near the intersection of the roads, on a fine afternoon, may be seen one of the most enchanting sights in Peking—the exercising of the cage birds. Down the Chien-mên Wai, silent, grave and dignified, in black or grey gowns, passes a steady stream of middle-aged men, each carrying a cage and a little stick like a wand. On reaching the appropriate spot, the cage doors are opened, and each feathered occupant hops daintily out and perches on the wand: with a quick deft movement, the owner tosses the bird into the air, where amid a crowd of others it flies up into the sunlight: fluttering, wheeling, chirruping, the whole sky is full of wings and song and glad freed creatures: below upturned faces watch the pretty sight, pleased and benevolent smiles on the usually impassive countenances. Then, at some signal, the birds drop down out of the airy throng, each to his proper owner, perch again upon the lifted wands, and hop back, docile and content, each into his own cage. It is one of the strangest and loveliest displays of intimacy and sympathy between man and the brute creation: not an isolated instance of power over animals, but a whole city-full of burghers who know their bird companions, and are known of them as friends.

Turning east at this crossways, a road leads across the open space to a gate in a high wall, within which lies the Temple of Heaven. Not immediately within, however. The Chinese have no taste for the crudity which permits access to a private house, let alone to a holy place, directly from the public highway. A sandy road leads from the outer gate through a large park to an inner wall, roofed in sea-green tiles, and behind this inner wall lies the temple itself. Through the park runs the track where Hawtrey had brought Amber to ride, but of what lay beyond the sea-green top of the inner wall she knew nothing.

Rupert's desire to witness the effect on Amber of the first sight of this shrine was natural enough. Among all the buildings of the city perhaps in the whole world the richest architecturally, the Temple of Heaven most stirs the eye and the mind. It contains two things in themselves supremely lovely—the snow-white Altar of Heaven, rising in three circular terraces with carved balustrades to a white platform at the summit, and the Temple of the Felicitous Year, raised also on terraces of white marble, and surmounted by that triple dome of indigo blue tiles which catches and holds the eye in every view southward over Peking, like a dark jewel. And lovely as these things are, they gain enormously from their setting and arrangement. The round altar stands in the centre of a square paved enclosure, whose four low walls are coped, each in a different colour, with tiles which glow like precious stones. The blue-domed Temple is approached by a great causeway, raised many feet above the ground, which stretches the whole distance, nearly half a mile, from the Altar to the shrine. And round both, sheltering lesser buildings and filling most of the inner park, stand groves of huge ancient junipers—so that scarlet walls, coloured tiles and white marble alike have for their background endless masses of that peculiar silvery green, a green so dark that it is almost grey, and the air of the whole place is filled perpetually with their aromatic fragrance. Those incomparable builders, with their passion for space and their deep sense of the value of the things of nature, thought nothing of walling in a park three miles round to hold one temple, used for ceremonial only twice a year, and set about it the trees of the forest to add to the beauty of worship.

But the most striking thing about these buildings is their extreme simplicity, a simplicity reflecting the old uncomplicated monotheistic worship of *Shang Ti*, "The One Above the Earth," which goes back four thousand years. The mind cannot resist a tribute of astonished admiration to the austere and pure conception which gave to Earth's greatest altar no roof but the sky, surrounded it with the three hundred and sixty pillars of the terrestrial degrees, and approached it by the triple gates of the Four Winds of Heaven. No flimsy trappings or ritual furniture disturbed the purity of the marble circle, no priests intervened—bare under the sky, it awaited the feet of the Son of Heaven as, alone, he climbed the steps at dawn to make atonement for the sins of his people. And when, proceeding along the marble causeway, he went to worship and give thanks in the Temple of the Felicitous Year, it was again in a single circular room, under that dome whose intense colour recalls the sky which roofs the Altar.

Now it lies desolate. The great tiled brazier where the bull-calf of pure colour was consumed as a burnt-offering is cold from year's end to year's end: the bronze baskets for burning the rolls of tribute silk—most civilised and innocent of sacrifices—are rusty and empty. Tiles drip off like water, slowly and continually, from the perished cement of walls and roofs; foreigners picnic and boil tea-kettles everywhere: some Americans once gave a dance on the Altar itself—a vulgar outrage which did at last rouse the Chinese to close the Temple for a time. For the most part, however, beyond erecting a booth for the sale of tickets at the entrance-gate, the heirs of so much beauty do little for its preservation. It belongs to the unworthy past, which the new officialdom of the Republic would willingly forget—a benighted past, unlit by electric light: a slow past, unhastened by the telegraph and the internal combustion engine. But Nature, more tender than mankind, has come quietly in to cover the slow ruin of man's handiwork. Big soft primulas, like auriculas, conceal the brilliant fragments of coloured glaze at the foot of the walls, and droop over the half-empty moat which surrounds the Hall of Abstinence, where the Emperor fasted through the night before the sacrifice: anemones, of a more imperial purple than those which the Berkshire villagers believe to spring only from the short turf of their downs where once the blood of Danes was spilt, grow in great tufts among the pale dead grass beyond the causeway; and in spring the groves of junipers are carpeted all through with great drifts of a wild crucifera, a foot or more high, in every tone of mauve and lilac and white, so that the fragrant shade is lightened from below with a glow or pale colour.

Through these groves Rupert and Amber came walking on the day after the ejection of the Bong into Soviet territory. The sky was soft with spring, and the warmth, only gentle as yet, brought out the scent of everything— the dust of the track, the faint sharp smell of dry grass, the incense of the junipers, the scentless freshness of the innumerable flowers. Rupert watched the girl, walking beside him, as he led her carefully by a route where the whiteness of the Altar would burst most suddenly on her vision. She had taken off her hat, and flecks of sunlight now and then caught that hair which was just *not* the perfect Titian red—above the mauve flowers, below the dark branches, her colour had a perfect setting. "The pre-Raphaelites ought to have painted her like that," he thought. But no: except for the marvellous colouring, it was not a pre-Raphaelite face; there was no die-away heavenliness about that firm chin, raised now as with lifted head she frankly snuffed the flying odours of which the air was full; nor about the decided nose with the bump in it, and the rather wide mouth. It was an honest, sensible, sensitive face, Rupert said to himself, reflecting as plainly as a mirror the clear simplicity within; a seeking face, looking for something it had yet to find. For what? Knowledge? Experience? Well, those she lacked, certainly. For love? All women were always looking for that—poor fools! A delicious fruit, love—quickly eaten, and giving you a frightful pain afterwards. But they never understood that; never realised, even, that the better the quality of the fruit, the worse the after-effects. They always imagined that if the fruit were big enough and juicy enough, it would last for ever and leave no pain behind! Ludicrous belief! And the worst of it was, this everlasting hunt of theirs for love made women quite hopeless companions, muddled up such intellect as they had and sent it twisting and doubling in all directions: you couldn't be honest with them, or they with you, so long as love was even a possibility. Not even with women like Lydia, with all her courage and detachment; not even she had *l'esprit libre*. Poor Lydia! he thought, sighing gustily. And women caught and entangled you in this hopeless maze of theirs, snared you with an emotion which they knew all about, damn them!—and then held you with pity and weakness. Oh, never again, except in marriage; marriage was some security, from yourself and from them; marriage was the solution. Find the right person, carefully; and then with cleverness, with patience, it could be made to go. Look at Nugent and Joanna—sound, jolly, stable—as good as it could be. Joanna *was* a bit *terre à terre*, but that was all the better really—you couldn't have *two* Nugents in one ménage. But marriage was so final—that was the devil of it! And meanwhile one was still interested, still curious, still liable to be excited. One wanted to see what was *in* them, each fresh person; to watch them in action, see how they worked. It was *oneself* really, from which one could never get free.

He realised suddenly that they were nearing the edge of the trees. "Shut your eyes," he said to Amber. "Here, give me your hand. You're not to open them till I say." So blinded, he led her out to the space round the Altar; she opened her eyes on gleaming ascending circles of white marble, the sky over them and the trees behind. Carefully, thoroughly, he showed her everything, explained everything, covertly studying her face all the time. He was pleased with her for refusing to set foot on the topmost platform of the altar, though she climbed the steps to look at it. Then he led her along the causeway, towards the blue dome which glowed like a triple sapphire ahead of them all the way; took her across the moat and into the Hall of Abstinence, where lilacs in the courtyards made the air almost intolerably sweet with their piercing fragrance. But then she asked to see the Altar again, and they went out into the open space to the south of it, and sat on the steps of the underground furnace which used to heat the square of soil on which the Emperor's pavilion stood when he robed himself for the ceremony. So far, though eager and appreciative, Amber had said but little; now, as they sat in the sunshine, looking across at the white marble against the grey trees: "I wonder if S. John the Divine could ever have seen it," the girl said.

"Why in the world S. John the Divine?" Rupert asked, surprised.

"It's so like his vision of the Holy City, in some ways," she answered. "Those four walls round it—in the sun, their tiles *are* like jewels—the jewels in the twelve foundations of the wall: do you remember?"

Rupert didn't—his acquaintance with the Apocalypse was of the slightest. "Tell me," he said.

Still gazing in front of her, Amber repeated that string of glorious names. "The first foundation was jasper, the second sapphire, the third a chalcedony, the fourth an emerald, the fifth sardonyx, the sixth sardius, the seventh chrysolite, the eighth beryl, the ninth a topaz, the tenth a chrysophrasus, the eleventh a jacinth, the twelfth an amethyst."

"By jove, they are good words!" Rupert said, when she finished. "Say them again." Amber did so. "But it isn't only the stones," she said at the end. "It's the gates too. Don't you remember them? 'On the east three gates, on the north three gates, on the south three gates, on the west three gates'—and 'Every several gate was of one pearl.' Those Gates of the Winds look just as if they were carved out of huge pearls, from here. It made me wonder if he could ever have seen or heard of this, and that had given him the idea."

"I must read the Apocalypse," said Rupert briskly. "I'd no idea there was anything half so good in it." He lit a cigarette. "No, S. John can't have seen this," he went on, "because this actual building only dates from the fifteenth century. But of course the ritual goes back well into pre-Christian times, and I believe the earlier altars were on the same model; the Chinese don't change much—their ceremonial hardly at all."

"So he might have seen something like it?" Amber pursued.

"There was nothing to stop him, if he chose to come," said Rupert. "The great trade-routes from China to Persia were open then, in fact I believe the journey was easier and safer than now."

Amber was charmed with this information. But Rupert went off on another tack.

"You seem to know the Bible very well," he said. "Are you religious?"

This is always an extremely awkward question, especially to the shy. Amber was nonplussed for a moment, but happily recalled her determination to be curious and ask questions herself.

"Medium," she said. "Are you?" she then asked firmly.

To her secret delight, Rupert also hesitated.

"If you mean, do I believe in the Virgin Birth and the whole bag of tricks, the answer is No," he said at length, with his usual explosiveness. "And I don't go to Church, as you may have noticed. But I *don't* concede that the people who do have a monopoly of religion."

"Of course not—there are Buddhists and all sorts,"

said Amber amiably, her desire to agree with people appearing in spite of her. Then she remembered her resolve again, and said: "You mean you have some sort of religion of your own?"

He glanced at her, a little surprised at this manifestation of enterprise. "Everyone has something they live to, some sort of standard," he said. "Mine wouldn't be accepted by the straight legitimate religious as a religion. But then I don't accept theirs."

This was not taking them very far, Amber thought; she had a feeling that Rupert was evading something. Her courage was limited, and she was wondering if she could screw herself up to another question, when he went on: "The important thing in life seems to me to be willing to accept experience—*all* experience. So many people refuse experience, for one reason or another: either because they're playing for safety, or because of some inhibition. If I have a religion, it is just that—to accept experience." He sighed gustily, thinking of his recent meditations as they walked through the junipers, and said—"But *I* don't always live up to my creed, any more than anyone else."

Amber was thinking about the refusal of experience, and said nothing. Rupert mistook her silence for criticism and said, rather provocatively—"The worst of the pukka religions is that they make a positive virtue of refusing whole categories of experience. They believe in blinkers! Like that appalling saint or pope or whatever he was, who rode along the north shore of the Lake of Geneva with his eyes on his mule's withers, for fear he should be distracted by the view of Mont Blanc and think worldly thoughts. My God! As though the view of Mont Blanc isn't enough to *lift* one to Heaven!"

"But that's very old-fashioned," the girl protested; "no one thinks that nowadays."

"Not about Mont Blanc, but about other things they do," Rupert asseverated. "Church people, I mean."

"Rupert, they don't. It's all rubbish. Why, I heard Dean Inge say in a sermon how people ought really to *use* that Collect about so passing through things temporal that they finally lose not the things eternal. He said they must pass *through* experience, not pass *by* it. And what's more, he mentioned that man on the Lake of Geneva as an instance of how not to do it!" said Amber triumphantly.

"Then he's a very sensible man," said Rupert, smiling at her flushed face: it was delicious the way any excitement brought her colour flooding up. "Is that your religion too? Because if so, we rather agree."

Amber considered. She had seized on that point impulsively as an argument, but on thinking it over she was not perfectly sure that Rupert and Dean Inge were really talking about the same thing. Though she had remembered the sermon, Rupert's words had given a fresh possibility of meaning to it. Up to now she had made, she realised, a rather limited application of the Dean's words about experience. Rupert, she was sure, was thinking of the whole of life, as it came—including what Hawtrey referred to mockingly as "old Rupert's experiences, ha-ha!" Was it possible that they were really the same, that life was all *one?* Because if so . . .

"Well?" said Rupert.

"I haven't finished thinking," the girl said, pushing back her hair off her forehead with an impatient gesture.

"You mean you don't know what your religion *is?*" said Rupert, not unamiably.

"No—I'm thinking what exactly refusing experience is," she answered.

"It's every form of Safety First," said Rupert. "Shy-

L

ing off something because you think it will hurt or is wrong. And in my opinion the trouble with religious people is that they often cover up what is really a form of cowardice by postulating that what they're afraid of is wrong. They're afraid of sex, so they call sex wrong. Actually it's a normal part of life, as well as one of the great purveyors of experience, damn it!" He blew again. "Or one shies off a relationship with a person, for fear of being hurt, or drained dry. Well, that's refusing experience. But if you refuse it," he turned brusquely on her, "at least know *why* you're refusing it, and don't pretend you're doing on moral grounds what you're really doing from cowardice. Isn't that right?" he said, as Amber said nothing. "What are you thinking about?" For the girl was staring at the Altar with a half puzzled, half far-away look on her face.

"I was wondering if it wasn't as bad to refuse religious experience as to refuse sex experience," she said thoughtfully. Rupert laughed—for all her simplicity, she was a shrewd hitter.

"Is that meant for me?" he asked.

"Not specially—though I think you're rather unjust about religion," she said, turning her candid eyes to him. Something in her face disarmed him suddenly.

"Amber dear, I didn't mean to hurt you, and I hope I haven't"—she made a negative movement of her head. "All I meant really is that religious experience is only for some people, whereas what you call sex experience"— the thought of the words on her lips made him smile, involuntarily—"is universal, and can't be denied."

"Oh, but surely, in some form or other, religious experience is universal too," the girl protested. "I don't mean Church services—I don't know quite *what* I mean! Except—the spirit has its adventures. And they can't be denied either. Only I don't quite know where one leaves off and the other begins. Or are they all mixed up? I *can't* express myself!" she broke off, rather embarrassed at having said so much.

"I think you express it very well," the young man said. He was curiously moved by her simplicity and candour; and clearly, in her rather childish way, she thought for herself. He had expected to provoke some completely second-hand cliché, and had got instead a mouthful of genuine, if uncertain, thought. As they walked back through the junipers, where the low light, slanting in under the boughs, caught and lit the tallest flowers like lamps, he thought with approval of the solidity and directness of her mind, untutored though it was. But Amber walked in a strange mental dazzle and confusion, corresponding to the dazing beauty about her, with which she continued to wrestle all the way home. Something in her rose eagerly to hail and greet Rupert's doctrine of the acceptance of all experience. In spite of her perception of the injustice (and even ignorance) of his views on religion, in spite of her much vaguer sense of his evading some issue, she yet felt that *this* in him was vitally right, and that in himself also was something of vital value. She was too young, and as yet too incompetent at the difficult business of knowing people, to be very precise about her reasons for this. But she was aware of a new and growing desire to live up to Rupert's standard, in this particular; to be, in this, the sort of person Rupert would approve. Only—now she went back to the phase of thought where Rupert's impatience had interrupted her—if life was somehow all one: if *all* experience was to be passed through, not by: if it all had value, then what became of her recent decision to watch her step, not to let herself get involved with any more young men—in fact, not to get hurt again as she had been hurt with Arthur?

Oh, it was all so difficult. She must have more time to think. Perhaps it was just as well that she was going to Uncle Bill the day after tomorrow. There she would see it all more from a distance, she thought, her eyes resting on the roof of the Chien-mên, green with the dull dusty green of August elms in the afternoon light, as the two rickshas sped swiftly between the trams. But she would miss all this, she thought, a few moments later, as the coolies swung in at the West Gate of the compound, past the sentry and along the dusty road under the pale fresh pattern of the mimosa boughs. And there would be less chance than ever of getting to know what Mr. Grant-Howard thought about it all.

"Now for some tea—I shall take it off the Erh-ch'in-ch'ai too," said Rupert, as they stepped out of the tilted rickshas and went up the steps between the clumps of irises. Liu opened the door to them, fresh creases of worry marking his yellow face, which wore permanently that look of intelligent concern so often to be seen on the faces of monkeys; he followed them discreetly into the drawing-room, where tea was laid, but untouched: the room was empty.

"T'ai-t'ai not got?" Rupert asked the servant in sur-prise: it was long past tea-time. Liu moved a hand upwards.

"T'ai-t'ai with Small Mastah; she welly sick," he re-plied. "Tai-fu come."

"Oh Lord, what can he have picked up?" said Rupert with a groan; he knew Peking, and had acquired the dis-mal dread of the doctor's sudden presence in a house proper to China. At that moment Nugent came in. He walked heavily, like a man who is dead tired; the expression on his face shocked Amber.

"What's wrong with Dickie?" Rupert asked quickly.

"He's got scarlet fever," said Nugent; he dropped into

a chair like a person hardly conscious of what he was doing. "His temperature's a hundred and four."

"Oh God!" said Rupert. Then he made some cheerful remarks about recent recoveries. "You've got Hertz, I suppose?" Nugent merely nodded, and Rupert expressed his strong faith in Hertz. Amber went to the table, made tea, and gave it to the two men in silence. She was thinking, though she tried not to, about the Bong.

Chapter Twelve

NUGENT GRANT-HOWARD tilted his topi over his eyes as he left the black patch of shadow outside the Chancery porch and started on his short journey back across the compound. Behind him the typewriters clattered, and through the open windows of Hawtrey's room came a buzz of voices and Hawtrey's laugh at its most artificial—Joe was interviewing a correspondent; before him the path shimmered in a haze of dust and heat. He walked slowly along the hot gravel, past the Legation Theatre, past the fives-court and the chapel; the scent of the acacias swept in hot waves across his face, the whole compound was full of them, swam in their honeyed perfume. At the corner of the square, Mrs. Hugo accosted him—"Oh, Mr. Grant-Howard, how is the dear little boy?"

"He was much the same this morning, thank you," said Nugent, in a colourless tone—he listened with an unmoved face to her expressions of sympathy with Joanna. What a cold man! she thought to herself, as he raised his topi and walked on along the square, already a dusty green. At the end of the stable drive, old Wang, the *mafoo*, appeared suddenly from behind a bush; he had a tiny cage in his hand, containing a small greenish bird. With a low bow he tendered it to Nugent. "For small Grandfather. She welly like. Sing!" Nugent, embarrassed, took the bird and thanked Wang. The old man lingered, one slippered foot tapping nervously, his old parchment face wrinkled with uncertainty. "Small Grandfather more better?" he ventured at last.

"A bit better I think, thank you, Wang," said Nugent warmly; but the words knocked at his heart as he spoke them. He would have to get a lot better to get—— Oh God, why could one not stop thinking those things? He walked on, up the curved drive to his house. On the front door was pasted a notice: "*Maladie contagieuse dans la maison—prière d'attendre la réponse au dehors*"; it was repeated in German and in English. Nugent didn't go in that way; he walked round past the irises and peonies, up on to the loggia by the garden steps, and through his study into the hall. The sharp clean smell of carbolic met him there. He turned into the drawing-room to look for Joanna, but she was not there; sighing at even this minute disappointment, he went to wash his hands. In the outer hall lay a little heap of cards—he tossed them over. "To enquire"; "To enquire"—people were very assiduous; "With kind enquiries"—who *could* that be, using the reply for the question? Mrs. Lexham?—one of Joanna's missionaries, no doubt. There were two pots of flowers: a tree of tiny roses—charming—who was that? Anna Stefany—a nice creature! And a great mass of lilies from Lydia Leicester, with a scrawl on the card—"So terribly sorry. *Do* have Hertz."

"Well, we are having Hertz," Nugent muttered to himself. As if in answer, the small greenish bird emitted a little bubble of sound, four notes of astonishing power and sweetness, and then was silent. Nugent started; he had forgotten the bird. He must see to it. He went to ring the bell, but Liu came softly across the hall, unsummoned. "Liu, this must have food and water," Nugent said; "do you know what it eats?"

"All right—can do; I buy food—I fix," said Liu, taking the cage. He smiled suddenly at the bird. "She welly good bird; sing welly loud; Mastah welly like."

"Put it in my study," said Nugent, and went upstairs.

The smell of carbolic was stronger here—the passage leading to Dickie's room was closed with sheets; Chang was spraying them with solution from a bucket. Chang had been chosen to wait on the sick-room; he was gentle, silent, neat-handed and assiduous. He carried the trays to the table in the corridor behind the outer sheets, and Sister Helga, the gaunt tall Pomeranian, with her ugly aristocratic face and clever tender hands, emerged from the inner pair and took the beverages for Dickie, the little special meals for herself. Joanna was allowed into this sort of ante-room in the corridor; there she held endless colloquies with Sister Helga—but Nugent, who had to carry on with his work in the Chancery, was obliged to stay outside. He heard voices within now; Joanna was there. Well, there was nothing he could do, and he had better not interrupt; he sighed again, and went down-stairs. Fearful, this uselessness, this helplessness. His mind tormented him with pictures of Dickie, whom he might not see—in pain, tossing, frightened, fretting for his mother. Though that nurse certainly inspired confidence; she obviously knew her job.

Restless, he went out on to the loggia. Joanna would be down to lunch, anyhow—and probably Hertz would be in again. Mechanically his eyes followed the gardeners, snipping the faded heads off the bright ribbons of pansies that edged the beds. Hertz seemed to know his job too—but how utterly one was in their hands! There was Dickie, his son, his life, his immortality, in pain and in danger; and all his hope, all his slender chance lay with strangers. He, Nugent, who would have worked his hands raw, given his hands, eyes, anything to save him, could do absolutely nothing.

From across the Jade Canal Road came the little vague tune played by the bugles of the Japanese Legation Guard; it filled the sunny air, pervasive, insistent, like a small pointless pattern of spangles—curiously irritating now, though when he was happy he had hardly noticed it. Now four times a day it fretted him; he wondered if Dickie was disturbed by it. His room was on the other side, but that silly little sound, like the smell of the acacias, filled the compound. He saw Amber coming across the garden, from under the trees on the upper lawn. She had not had scarlet fever, and Dr. Hertz would not hear of her going to Uncle Bill, who had returned the previous day, till she was out of quarantine. She came slowly up the loggia steps and sat down.

"Is there any more news?" Nugent said.

"Doctor Hertz has found out how he got it," the girl said. "It *was* his little city."

"Not really?"

"Yes—he enquired in the market; he found out which stall Liu got them at, and there have been six cases of scarlet fever in the man's house—there are two there now. He called a second time to tell us," the girl said.

In the first burst of distress Joanna had been inclined to attribute the disaster to Dickie's visit to the Forbidden City, but Dr. Hertz soon exploded that theory. The maximum period of incubation, he explained, was ten days, and it was more than a fortnight since the demonstration. It was considered important to discover the source of infection, and the servants were questioned and their homes visited. Dickie was always in and out of their quarters, and he had played with Cho Sur, Chang's little fat four-year-old son; but there were no cases of scarlet fever among their families. Hertz had pounced on the toys the previous day, and asked if they had been disinfected—Joanna was incredulous, but Hertz was insistent.

"Yes, so they do, bring toys—and from where do they come, these toys?" he had said, shaking his head.

"What's been done with them?" Nugent asked now, looking at the empty corner.

"I've just been burning them," Amber said. "I must go and wash my hands," and went indoors.

A moment later Joanna came out. "How is he?" Nugent asked at once.

"He's quiet—he feels the heat rather, Sister says."

"What's his temperature?"

"Still a hundred and three, but Hertz says we must expect that," said Joanna. Her voice was very steady and quiet; she sat still in her chair; a sort of controlled strength breathed from her. Nothing could appease Nugent's distress, but somehow her mere presence was comforting to him.

"Did he say anything else?"

"It *was* the toys," said Joanna slowly.

"Yes, Amber told me. It seems most extraordinary that they could carry it."

"Oh no those little straw figures, and people peeling in the house! It's obvious. I suppose I might have thought of it," she said, still in that steady voice. "Or asked someone. I'm sorry, my dear." There was the tiniest quiver in her voice then. But before Nugent could answer: "They must be burnt," she said, in the same level tones as before, looking round.

"Amber's done it," said Nugent.

"Oh—how sensible of her. By the way, Nugent, can you take her for a walk after tea? It would do her good. Hertz says she ought to keep as fit as she can—it all depends on one's power of resistance whether one gets it or not."

"Oh, very well," said Nugent. He didn't want to go for a walk, but if it was useful, it would be as well to do it. And of course they must take proper care of that nice child. It struck Nugent suddenly that since that time on the boat he had made no attempt to find out how she was getting on. The load she carried, whatever it was, she had had to shoulder quite alone all these weeks, among people who were really strangers to her—or at least, he thought rather remorsefully, who had allowed her to remain fundamentally strange to them, for all the apparent intimacy of their common life. He had noticed that both Joe and Rupert were rather taken with her, but young men were more apt as a rule to multiply a young woman's problems than to mitigate them. With perceptions sharpened by unhappiness he remembered her as he had seen her off Sumatra, quivering under some defeat at the hands of life; and this was the person who since had been launched into a new world without any shield of strong affection and certain interest behind which to seek shelter and help in need. His imagination, working with the violent intensity created by emotional stress, saw her suddenly as all youth, involved in its own battle; saw her bright head unhelmeted among the spears like the head of the boy in Paolo Uccello's picture in the National Gallery, gallant and resolved, but peculiarly defenceless. It was one of those curious flashes of vision to which Nugent was given, which do for some people illuminate the theory on which their relations with another are built; and in spite of his own anxiety he had a quick impulse to try to find out how the girl was really faring in that inner life which our theories seek to penetrate.

The summons to lunch broke in upon his thoughts. It was a cheerless meal. Nugent crackled his thin toast and nibbled it perpetually; Joanna spoke once about the flowers; but no one troubled to eat much of the four delicious courses which the servants set before them. While they were having coffee on the loggia, Dr. Hertz was announced. He came out on the heels of the

servant, and after a hasty greeting to Joanna, stood pulling various objects out of the bulging pockets of his grey
alpaca jacket, while he explained his errand. He had
just got at the hospital the pathologist's report on a
rubbing of Dickie's throat. "There is the Klebs-Loeffler
bacillus present, in quantities," he said gravely. None
of his hearers knew what the Klebs-Loeffler bacillus por-
tended, and he was obliged to explain that it was the
germ of diphtheria.

"Do you mean that he may get diphtheria?" Joanna
asked quietly.

"No—he has it now," the Doctor said. "This is
quite usual here," he went on, turning to Nugent, from
whom a sound like the shadow of a groan escaped at
the words. "For this we take the rubbing. I shall
give him now the anti-dipterie injection, and Schwester
Helga shall use these sprays." He put some small
bottles on the table. "We shall go up now, yes?" he
said to Joanna.

"One moment," Nugent said, rising and taking him
by the sleeve. "You say it's quite usual here to have
both things together, scarlet fever and diphtheria?"
He spoke slowly and judicially, as Amber had often
heard him speak when discussing some point of Chinese
politics with Leroy or Benenden—somehow his use of
that manner now turned her sick with pity. Hertz
nodded—his kind heavy face was creased with distress
and concern, tiny beads of perspiration powdered his
large pale cheeks and forehead.

"And such cases are—successful?" Nugent pursued,
still in the same Socratic manner.

Dr. Herz raised his shoulders with a curious distressful
movement of impotence.

"It can be so—yes. Naturally it is more grave. One
can promise nothing yet. There is a chance. I give the

injection now—in twenty minutes I have an operation."
He turned into the house.

"Don't come up," said Joanna, putting her hand on
Nugent's arm, and speaking with a sort of assured finality.
Over his shoulder she threw a glance of entreaty at
Amber. Amber understood. Dickie had had his T.A.B.
inoculations on the boat, and the prick of the needle
always made him scream; he had a nervous terror of it.
Joanna wanted Nugent removed out of earshot somehow,
while that injection was given. Regardless of Amber,
she pressed a kiss on her husband's forehead and followed
the Doctor indoors.

Amber cast desperately round in her mind for some
pretext, and found one. "Mr. Grant-Howard, I'm not
much good at bonfires; could you come up with me and
see if those little toys are burning properly? I'm rather
afraid of the gardeners rescuing some and taking them
off," said Amber, warming to her theme, "unless we do
it thoroughly."

Sighing, Nugent rose without reply and followed her
across the heat of the lawn and into the upper garden,
where behind the septic tank, screened by a hedge of
thujas, was the rubbish-heap, the bonfire and the nursery-
beds. The gardener, his pigtail looped round the crown
of his straw hat, was grafting chrysanthemums on to tall
stout-stalked plants grown for the purpose. Amber's
fire had burned well; with a stick she pushed the few
half-consumed fragments of the pretty toys into the red
ashes, prolonging the operation as much as possible.
Then she suggested a visit to the greenhouse to see
how the geraniums were coming forward. On the
way thither Nugent broke his silence, which she found
so oppressive. "Have you ever had diphtheria?" he
asked.

"No—my sister did," Amber replied.

"Did it hurt?" Nugent next enquired.

"She said it was like a rather bad sore throat," said Amber, as they entered the greenhouse.

"Ah, said Nugent. "Did she have that membrane thing in the throat?" he asked, as they stood between the stagings, which were full of flowers just coming into bloom. Amber thought not. While she forced herself to give a cheerful account of Gemma's illness, she was appalled by Nugent's evident suffering. He walked round the greenhouse, going through all the motions of one who admires the flowers, even touching one now and then; but it was clear to her that he hardly knew where he was, that he simply did not see the blooms before his eyes. There was something frightful about these mechanical actions, performed while he spoke continuously of diphtheria. She got him out of the greenhouse somehow. Oh, it was all very well to talk about the pangs of motherhood, the girl thought, seeing for the first time the terrible thing that fatherhood can be. Far worse to be a father! Joanna was busy, occupied, able to do things all the time that related to Dickie—ordering meals, drinks, medicines; organising the household, in touch with the nurse. It was the father who bore the brunt of the terrible helplessness. And moved by an overpowering impulse of pity, she turned her clear eyes on to Nugent and said, "You know, Mr. Grant-Howard, Dickie has always looked a very strong child to me. I don't mean fat and robust, but strong in himself. And I believe those children get over things much better than the big fat ones."

Nugent turned and stared at her in a sort of surprise. "What do you mean by strong in himself?" he asked.

"It's something about his hands, and the look of his skin and eyes," said Amber earnestly. "He looks—resistant. I do really think he ought to get over it."

"That's very interesting," Nugent said, but his tone was less dead than a few moments before. "It's curious that you should have got that impression of him. Most people think he looks so delicate—and he does seem to get whatever's going."

"Yes, but doesn't he get over whatever's going too?" Amber persisted. "Really, I don't think you should worry too much," she said, looking at him steadily, as if she was trying to *force* hope and comfort into him with her eyes.

"I won't," he said, and for the first time that day he smiled at her. "I'll go across now and do some work," he said, more briskly, "and after tea you're going to take me for a walk."

When he had gone, Amber sat on the loggia and took up some sewing. Well, that was done all right. They hadn't heard a sound. Presently Joanna came out, and said she was going to lie down for an hour or two; "Yes, he was really very good," she said, in reply to a question of Amber's, "but he does hate it so." She half closed her eyes.

"We went and finished burning the toys," said Amber. "Mr. Grant-Howard has gone back to the Chancery now."

"Yes—I want you to take him out after tea, Amber," said Joanna. "Take him a good long walk—to see something, if you can. It will do him good." And away she went, poised and controlled, leaving Amber looking after her with admiration.

Mrs. Grant-Howard had only been gone a few moments when Benenden came round the corner of the house and flopped into a chair on the loggia, where he started to fan himself with his black felt hat. (He refused to accommodate himself to local usage, and spurned a topi.) "Well, how is he?" he said gloomily.

"He's got diphtheria as well as scarlet fever," replied Amber.

"My Christ! Poor little beggar!" Rupert groaned. "I saw Nugent crossing the compound, and hid. I didn't dare to ask for news."

"Ought you to be here?" Amber said. "You know we're in quarantine." She shifted into a chair further away from him.

"Oh, it's all right in the open," said Rupert. "What does Hertz say?"

"He said there was a chance," Amber said.

"Oh Lord!" He put his head into his hands and groaned again. "He'll never recover—people hardly ever do, and he's such a little chip of a thing. It will just about kill Nugent," he said, raising his head and staring at her. "He's perfectly dotty about all his children, but Dickie has always been the pick of the bunch to him." He sighed, lit a cigarette and a moment afterwards threw it away, shifted the cushion in his chair and then flung it away too. "I can't *bear* this to happen to him," he said. "Nugent's not like ordinary people. Half the men here would hardly care after a week; their wretched wives would mind, but they wouldn't suffer really. But Nugent!"

Amber was touched by the depth of his sorrow and affection, but found his company extraordinarily depressing nevertheless; she was really relieved when he took himself off.

The heat was still considerable when Nugent and Amber set out in the car after tea. Nugent had suggested that the Temple of Heaven was as good a place as anywhere, and they walked briskly round the track through the outer park. It was already much hotter than when Amber and Rupert had been there only a few days ago. Peking was stoking up, as Joe called it. The white dust

rose about their feet in the open stretches, and hung in a
shallow silvery cloud where they had passed. At first
they walked in silence. Amber was thinking what a
God-sent opportunity this walk would have been to discuss some of the many things on which she wanted Mr.
Grant-Howard's opinion; but her shyness quite apart,
she felt that she could not trouble him now with her
own concerns. She was therefore both startled and disconcerted when Nugent turned suddenly to her with,
"What do you make of Rupert?"

Amber considered rapidly on which aspects of Rupert
she most wanted illumination. They crowded into her
mind pell-mell, confusing her, and as she was never
much good at expressing herself with any precision—
"He's nicer to places than to people," she brought out
at last.

Nugent laughed, and she was so pleased to hear him
laugh that she forgot to be embarrassed at having
probably said something silly. "What precisely do you
mean by that?" he asked.

"He isn't irritable with places like he is with people,"
she answered. "And he—he accepts them as they are."

"Doesn't he accept people?"

"Oh no—you *know* he doesn't!" the girl said. "People
like you he does, whom he is frightfully fond of, but other
people——" She paused, caught as usual between the
flood of her ideas and the lack of words in which to
clothe them. "He weighs and balances, and suspects—
no, he thinks the worst." And seeing Nugent looking
a little incredulous, she repeated some of Rupert's ad-
monitions to her on the day she had tea with him.
"Even if people *aren't* nice all through, the nice bits of
them may be real," she wound up. "I don't see what
one gains by being so—scrutinising as he is."

Nugent was interested in these criticisms, which he

M

saw were genuine, and not part of the usual defensive apparatus of the sophisticated young woman. Hoping for more, he said non-committally, "I certainly think it's not necessary to *en vouloir* people for qualities they haven't got."

"I think it's even more unnecessary to *en vouloir* them for things they *have* got," returned Amber with unexpected readiness—she was thinking of Rupert's hostility to her interest in horses. Nugent, however, did not know this and said, with an evident placatory intention —"I think perhaps he felt you might need advice, and that's why he lectured you. He does hold forth, rather. Do you dislike him?" he asked her, then.

"Oh *no*," the girl said readily. "I like him very much. I didn't mind his lecturing me. But I'm not sure that I agreed with the lecture. Of course I'm not very experienced," said Amber simply, "but if I were as old as Methuselah I shouldn't want to go about distrusting everybody as he does."

"Why do you listen to him?" Nugent asked, as they passed into a patch of deep shade between two plantations of young conifers. He was interested, and yet half discouraged by her incompetence at expressing herself. The young were very difficult to talk to!

"Because he talks to me! And about interesting things. Most people don't—not to me," said Amber, causing Nugent a prick of remorse. "But I don't know whether to believe him or not," she went on thoughtfully.

"Oh, why? He's more than truthful," said Nugent.

"He quarrels with himself," the girl said. Nugent laughed out. "No, but he does! At least, things in him quarrel with one another," she persisted. Nugent agreed, still laughing. Rupert need not complain so much of her lack of discrimination, he thought; she had got on to the fundamental contradictoriness of *his* character

pretty shrewdly, however oddly she expressed it. He
was surprised at her being able to see so clearly in the
case of a person with Rupert's degree of charm; usually
women were simply bowled over by him.

"Mr. Grant-Howard, may I ask you something?" she
said now, turning to him with a clear seriousness in her
face.

"Yes—go on."

"It's about accepting experience," the girl said. "I
can see it's a good principle to; but a kind of experience
that one has had, and knows it's dreadful—is it very
safety-first to try to avoid that again?"

There spoke the burnt child, Nugent thought—and in
safety-first he recognised one of Rupert's pet clichés.
What *had* he been saying to her?

"I don't think much good comes either of seeking experience or avoiding it," he temporised. Oh, well, let
her have it—she meant her question, and must have a
real answer. "Yes, I think one must accept it. You
go along like this"—he waved his stick ahead of him,
where the track, emerging from the deep shade, stretched
away into the distance, dappled with the light shadow
of young willows, till it curved round out of sight—"and
just meet what comes. And remember, the terrible
things are what *make* people. The unlucky ones who
only meet easy things always remain undisciplined by
life—they've never really grown-up."

Amber made no reply—he saw her staring ahead down
the curving track, as if watching the approach of a whole
procession of invisible crises; he was reminded again
of his thought before lunch, and the pitiful gallantry of
youth. Suddenly he felt that she had the capacity, not
too common, of really being forged by life, of taking a
fine temper; something in the set of her head, the whole
tone of her, gave him this impression with the clearness

of a spoken phrase. It moved him to further utterance. "There's more to it than just accepting," he said. "One has to be willing to embrace experience, to let it do its work in you. Of course that's what the Bible means by dying to live. And even while that's going on, to be what Marcus Aurelius called 'always the same man.'" He stopped suddenly, remembering that in his catalogue of disasters to be so endured, the most human of philosophers put last and worst "and in the death of a child." Oh, could one be the same man in such a case? Was he now to be called upon to practise his own doctrine? His anxiety returning, unconsciously he walked faster, and Amber quickened her pace beside him in silence, thinking. Strange that he should use that expression about dying to live. She had always applied it only to what she thought of as religion—dying to one's sins, and all that. But Mr. Grant-Howard was clearly using it about life in general. Did one, then, only come to full life by death-like pains such as she had suffered over Arthur, such as the silent man beside her was facing even now? She did not phrase it to herself so clearly, but in a dim way she felt these great issues looming about her, saw half-veiled vistas of pain and strength, strangely linked, opening before her. Then about this at least Rupert was right; then experience was one whole; then the adventures of the spirit were received and expressed in quite mortal things like love-affairs and the illnesses of children. Step by step her mind worked at it, as she trod the track beside Grant-Howard, between the young green of the spinneys, with the dry smell of the dust in her nostrils, and the occasional strong resinous fragrance of a single pine-tree. And why Nugent was different to, say, Sir James, was just because of his capacity for embracing experience. And so one must, too—must go forward and meet whatever was coming . . .

Round a curve in the track, with a dull thud of hoofs, a horseman came galloping at tremendous speed. It was Hawtrey. "I'm being bolted with!" he shouted cheerfully as he passed them. Nugent smiled, in spite of his anxiety, at this apparition. Amber smiled too—one always did smile at Joe. But she was aware of a vague sense of anti-climax. Her dim and solemn visions of meeting experience had been suddenly scattered—scattered by the familiar, nice, but slightly ridiculous figure of Hawtrey being run away with, galloping towards them. She walked forward more thoughtful than ever.

Chapter Thirteen

THE next few days passed with the strange and deadly slowness of days of acute anxiety. The diphtheria took Dickie badly. "He's got great lumps, like eggs, on each side of his throat, Miss," Burbidge whispered fearfully to Amber, with the peculiar gloomy satisfaction of a servant with bad news to impart. That nurse, she explained, had let her peep through the sheet and see Master Dickie in his bed. Amber left her, marvelling at this fresh instance of the capacity of maids for knowing everything. Miss Carruthers on the other hand knew nothing—she sat in unwonted and unhappy solitude in the schoolroom, writing interminable letters home. Miss Carruthers did not like Peking. "It's most peculiar, Miss Harrison," she confided to Amber. "The people here seem to have no social sense, if you know what I mean." Amber could not imagine, but she soon learned. "That Mrs. Hugo's maid gives Bridge parties!" Miss Carruthers said, in horrified undertones—everyone spoke in undertones in the Counsellor's house then. "And she actually asked *me*! Of course I refused. The Countess de Gaffi's governess goes, she said. Of course she is only a *nursery* governess, with no qualifications— but still!" Amber, sympathising with her solitude, took Miss Carruthers for walks on the Wall, where they conscientiously gave their acquaintance a wide berth; or played half-hearted tennis with her on the Legation courts. Everything was slowed down and stilled in their lives. The silent servants moved more silently than ever, ceased to display those charming speechless grins with which they were wont to salute the household. Most of all Chang, the Number Two with the saintly expression, seemed to be suffering from some very deep depression. Faithful and assiduous in his duties, his always wistful face now wore a look of settled sadness, and he moved like a man who was deathly tired. He had of course a lot of extra work, and Joanna, noticing his strained appearance, suggested to him in her tentative Chinese that he should take a day off to rest. With a gentle smile he refused, though gratefully. How wonderful their manners were, Joanna thought; just so might a cardinal of ancient lineage express to a benevolent pope his determination to carry on.

Visitors and enquiries were endless. Lydia Leicester and Countess Stefany sent flowers all the time: Mme. de Bulle and Mme. Rothstein called in person more than once. Sir James, now convalescent, came one day, and sat in the garden talking to Amber, the only person who happened to be available. "Most distressing—most distressing," he observed. "This is a most distressing place, Miss Harrison. These Chinese fellohs have no sense, you know. That poor chap Wheeler—the Doctor thinks very badly of him." (Wheeler was the archivist.) "This little chap was such a jolly little felloh. Terrible for Mrs. Nugent."

There you were again, Amber thought — always Joanna! Hardly anyone seemed to realise what Nugent was enduring, except his wife and Rupert. (Amber, characteristically, did not count her own knowledge of Nugent's state of mind.) Henry Leroy came every day; he had had every known illness and scouted the notion of infection. "How is he?" he would ask whoever he could catch: and then sat on in the loggia, saying little, and muffling his booming tones when he did speak. "Sarah had it badly and she got over it," he daily told

Joanna or Nugent; "but it's a beastly thing." Four
times a day the Japanese bugles spangled the hot glittering air with their little foolish pattern of notes; three or
four times a day Hertz came, his face more and more
creased with distress; four times a day the household sat
down to meals in almost complete silence.

Oddly enough, it was Hawtrey who was their main
support, not Rupert. During times of illness the world
becomes sharply divided, for the anxious, into those who
add to their anxiety, and those whose mere presence
mitigates it. Nothing is more curious than to notice who
they are who furnish this rock-like sense of comfort and
assurance. And in this instance Joanna was herself
startled to find how glad she was to see "the tall, rather
unclever one" when he "blew in," as he himself described
it; or even, from her balcony, to hear his high, soft voice
"yarning away" on the loggia downstairs. He and
Rupert were in and out all day long—of the loggia and
garden, not the house: but whereas Rupert sat silent, or
talked in lowered tones, and fretted and fidgeted, Joe
swung in airily, enquired for Dickie with a sort of breezy
confidence, asked for a drink, and chattered away—
retailing scraps of local gossip, telling funny stories, ex-
aggerating, till in spite of themselves they were diverted.
It came to her presently, despite the prejudice that she
entertained about him, that what he was actually doing
was to keep the normal world alive for them in their
isolation; though whether he realised it or not she could
not say. "Oh yes, of course he's doing it on purpose,"
Amber said, when one day Joanna mentioned this doubt
to her. "He goes round collecting stories to tell Mr.
Grant-Howard. 'Must shake old Nugent up, you know;
he mopes, Miss Amber, that's what he does—he mopes!' "
Amber reproduced Mr. Hawtrey's tones with great precision, but with a little uncertain glance at her hostess.

Joanna, however, laughed. "You've got him perfectly, Amber—how do you do it?"

"I—I—I—as a matter of fact, Mrs. Nugent, it's practice—nothing but practice!" Amber answered, still in Hawtrey's manner, and Joanna laughed again. Little monkey! this gift was quite unsuspected. She asked, a little slyly, if Amber could "do" Rupert. With the utmost readiness the girl snatched up a hat and tilted it over her eyes, humped her shoulders, blew, and exclaimed "My good Joanna, if you think poor old James has anything corresponding to what we mean by a *mind*, you're incredibly wide of the mark!" The representation was perfect, and Joanna, weary and overwrought, pealed with weak mirth. Wiping her eyes, "I think you'd better call me 'My good Joanna,' Amber," she murmured, "it does me good." Amber blushed. "Do you mean that? I'd love to." "Yes, yes—and say that to Nugent."

But these interludes of gaiety were short-lived. As the illness progressed, distress gained even on Joanna, for all her stout heart. As for Nugent, nothing seemed to distract him but Wang's little bird. The tiny creature did in fact presently start to sing, in a loud sweet babble of small notes, and Nugent tended it assiduously, taking it out on to the loggia, and feeding and watering it himself. Liu had produced food, as promised—sorghum millet and a green weed: but Nugent was principally diverted by its flesh food. Liu handed him one day, with an air of great self-satisfaction, a small piece of bamboo about four inches long, cut below the knot, and stopped at the other end with a pith cork. "For bird—she welly like—eat meat." He removed the pith cork and shook out into his palm a dozen gentles: "One day two," said Liu. Nugent was charmed to learn that these tubes of bird-food were a regular article of commerce in the Peking market.

He and Amber continued to go for walks, with a good deal of spasmodic conversation. He conducted a sort of inquisition into her life at home, her family and her friends; and Amber, between a sense of flattery at his interest, and the desire to keep his mind occupied, poured out a very full and naïve account of her father and her mother, her horses, Gemma — everything but Arthur. There was soon very little that Nugent did not know about life at Riddingcote: between him and the dark silvery masses of the thujas at the Temple of Heaven were interposed pictures, evoked by her eager and artless words, of the great Cotswold house, the garden and terraces; thronged with clever people, or still, empty and sweet-smelling in the falling rain; most of all, this ardent child, uncertain and unsuccessful, dimmed by the lovely sister, crushed by the overpowering mother—only safe and secure with her horses, her grooms, and the tolerant mischievous old man who must have been, Nugent thought, a very lovable person. He began to have a curiosity to meet Uncle Bill, who so resembled "Daddy"; he felt more urgently than ever a desire to liberate and encourage the spirit of his young companion. She needed a critical freedom from the opinions that had fettered her youth, and with her father gone, there was no one to give it; he tried himself to produce it, with considerable skill. "So your mother goes in for the funnies," he commented, when Amber recited some well-known literary and artistic names as having appeared at a disastrous and thunder-stricken gathering. "Well, the Bloomsburys, then"—as he saw her puzzled eyebrows. Amber listened with a fearful joy; it was at once shocking and delightful to hear these awe-inspiring persons referred to casually as "funnies." "I can't do with them, myself," Nugent observed. "They *will* be clever. Even about life. It's no good being clever about life—one can be sensible about it, or brave, but not clever." Under Nugent's manipulation, through his comments, Amber too saw pictures of Riddingcote form and re-form against the background of junipers, along the dusty shade-spat-tered vistas of the track round the Temple of Heaven, but in a new perspective—the clever people grew smaller, less intimidating, less important, while she herself, Amber, became more solid, less foolish, less negligible. It was marvellous to have her private and hesitant views endorsed by a person like Mr. Grant-Howard — able, brilliant, important, even by her mother's standards. And so nice! In those days of shared distress and en-forced anxiety, the girl's timid, almost latent affection for the older man made a great and sudden growth into con-sciousness and confidence, which increased tenfold the effect of his words and opinions. Affection is almost chemical in its action on the human mind: it acts as a solvent of differing points of view; under its influence the seemingly irreconcilable can mingle and interchange; and like a mordant, too, it *fixes* our acceptance of another's opinion and makes it permanent, dyed in the skein of our thought. Nugent's words, in these long hot afternoons, were bringing Amber out in a place she did not know— where she too had value and merit; where timidity was to be cast aside, and to accept experience and live danger-ously was all-important. But even more than his words, what carried his thought so far and so deeply into her being was the pleasure of his rare smile, and the memory afterwards of his blank fatigued face as they drove back, silent, in the car, his shapely hands absently changing his spectacles—and then changing them back again.

There was a very bad day at the end of that week. For three nights Hertz had slept on a camp bed by his tele-phone, his instruments ready packed, awaiting a sum-mons to come and perform a tracheotomy on Dickie.

Sister Helga did not sleep at all, but lay fully dressed on a couch by the child's bed, a finger on his pulse, watching for the slightest variation in his difficult rattling breath. She had asked for a second standard lamp, beside the one which stood all night on the floor, dimmed with a scarf, to switch on in a sudden emergency. The Counsellor's house was ill provided with these objects; there had been none in Dickie's room, and Miss Carruthers had surrendered hers when he was taken ill. Joanna, unwilling to rob either Nugent or Amber, and not feeling called upon, in her exhaustion and anxiety, to forego the solace of reading in bed, sent a polite note to the local agent of the Ministry of Construction asking for another. This worthy called to enquire into the need for an extra standard lamp, and refused point-blank to send one, observing that they were not officially supplied to children's rooms.

Now Joanna was normally a very equable person, and though not given to *épanchement*, was quite shrewd enough to pave herself a smooth path through life by a cheerful courtesy to subordinate officials, on which she got, as a rule, the usual high yield of interest. And in the ordinary way she was far too sensible to let herself be disturbed by minor affronts. But the grossness of the inhumanity displayed on this occasion, frayed as she was by anxiety, made a most painful impression. She was very angry. She appealed to Sir James.

Sir James was distressed and kind, but explained that he was quite helpless in the matter. He had no control at all over the Ministry of Construction; it was quite independent. Who did control it? Joanna wished to know. Oh, there was a little felloh in Shanghai, a nice little felloh, but he never came to Peking. " But I am paying *rent* for those things—I am paying a hundred and twenty-five pounds for my furniture alone," Joanna at last pro-

tested. "Doesn't that entitle me to one standard lamp
in each room?" "My dear lady, the Ministry of Construction takes the line that no one is entitled to anything, whatever they pay, and that they're exceedingly
lucky to get anything at all. Anyway, you'll get nothing
out of the chap here. The felloh's paid to do this sort of
thing. But Hugo likes him—I can't think why," observed Sir James thoughtfully. "Now look at those curtains of mine"—and he embarked on his own grievances.

Joanna fled from the Ministerial curtains. Anyhow,
Sir James's child wasn't — wasn't perhaps dying, she
thought, forcing herself to finish her mental sentence,
with an angry sob, as she walked back across the square.
On the way she met Rupert. He looked keenly at her.
"What's the matter, Joanna? He's not worse?" "No,
no, I'm only silly——" and she told him the story. "My
God, one of these days I shall forget myself and screw
that chap's neck for him!" Rupert exclaimed at the end.
"Come in here," he went on, leading her into his house,
where he made her have a drink. "Yes—go on; you
need it—I don't care if it *is* before lunch." Joanna mentioned quarantine. "Rubbish—and it's up in a day or
so, isnt' it? You've been shut away from him from the
start."

Her face changed, and he saw that he had said the
wrong thing. "That's just it," she said slowly, fingering
her cocktail glass. "You see, Rupert, if anything—
happens, I shan't have been with him all this time. And
he—asks for me. I hear him. I thought at the beginning that it was right, but now——" She did not finish.

Rupert was firm with her. "My dear Joanna, you've
done absolutely right. It was essential for you to be
with Nugent. Suppose *you'd* got it? Where would he
have been then?"

"I think Amber really does him more good than anyone," said Joanna, rather tonelessly. "Thank goodness she's been here."

Rupert had never seen Joanna in this state of moral semi-collapse—it had somehow never occurred to him that she, judicial and controlled, could know self-doubt or ordinary feminine feelings of any sort. With real insight, however, he met her on the ground she had taken.

"Yes, Amber's a darling," he said warmly, "and she does do him good. Nugent likes studying the young, and she takes his mind off it all. But no amount of young darlings are the same thing as a partnership— you know that! No one else can do what you do for him. By the way," he went on, remembering something suddenly, "a frightful thing has happened. That poor wretched Wheeler is dead."

"Oh *no*."

"Yes—died last night. The funeral's this afternoon. Nugent will have to go."

"Oh, Rupert, must he really? Now?"

"I'm afraid so. Old James isn't fit to hang about in this sun yet. Nugent will have to deputise for him."

"I don't think he ought to have to do that just at this moment," said Joanna, her firmness of mind returning at once to meet this fresh emergency. "Those things affect him very much."

"Yes, he carries a frightfully powerful receiving apparatus. He gets ten times the vibrations that other people do, from everything. In a way it's a disability— but it makes him what he is," said Rupert. He rang the bell, and said something to the servant, who answered it with a promptness which suggested his having been stationed on the mat outside. He went on : "He gets a light—the *real* light—on quite minute things, in a way the rest of us don't. Like this: we were discussing the nature of pathos once, and Nugent said eventually that he didn't know what it consisted in, but how about this for the thing itself?—and he told us how he had seen in the Maryhill Road, Glasgow, a slot machine for packets of chewing gum, and a notice over it: 'Suitable gift—one penny.' Of course he was right; it's the most pathetic thing imaginable: there's the whole of poor humanity in that, striving to express its love through all the limitations that hedge the gift—what it can afford, and what will be suitable. Only who but Nugent would have seen it in a slot-machine in the Maryhill Road?''

The tears stood shining in Joanna's eyes as he finished. The ineffectual love of poor humanity was too much for her just then. At that moment Rupert's boy reappeared, his arms full of electric lamps. Rupert made her choose one, and the boy bore it after them as they walked round to the Counsellor's house. It struck Rupert as he strolled back under the acacias, where the fallen blossoms lay like small curved pebbles of ivory on the path, how great, really, was Joanna's isolation. Possessed of her husband and her children, and possessed by them, she gave nothing to the world in general, and received nothing from it. Nothing to live by, no bread. She was sensible, successful, reliable and kind; but she was strangely alone. One didn't know her—one didn't really want to know her. Bad—bad, thought Rupert, gathering up a handful of the acacia blossoms and studying them as they lay on his hand; it was wrong, it was limiting to live so; all limiting was bad; people should have friends, should let the world in, and go out to greet it. His theory about Joanna developed as he walked—it was the first time he had really applied himself to it. Poor Joanna! He blew, and the acacia blossoms were scattered. He laughed loudly then, and went in to lunch.

Nugent attended the archivist's funeral that afternoon. Seated in a car, he followed the hearse through the teeming streets, resounding with the strong vigorous life and labour and laughter of this alien humanity. He stood beside the grave in the prim little English cemetery near the P'ing-tzu-men, whose unnatural parochial neatness, by contrast with the exuberant disorder outside, created a strangely desolating impression. It seemed lost and unhappy here, under the blazing sun, this small enclosure set apart for the sanctities of his national faith; even the great words of the Burial Service sounded faint in his ears, dulled by the jolly clamour of material existence in all its strength and pervasiveness. As he stood there, hat in hand, correct and formal, with a face as expressionless as brass, he experienced a sort of horror of this land, implacable and indifferent, which menaced not only the life of his son, but somehow by its very indifference sapped the heart of his own beliefs. Here one would have to fight and strive prodigiously to preserve the salt and strength of one's integrity, one's grip on real values. In a flash, in the little forlorn cemetery, with the line of the city wall cutting the sky behind him, so much more imposing and permanent than this plot of ground, he saw the inner reason for many of the features of white life in China which he had already noticed with dismay—the casual inconsequent drifting through a round of pointless pleasures; the moral slackness, the unprecedented reliance on stimulants as a source of vitality. Yes, one would have to struggle, to gird up one's loins, to face the influences which were stronger than isolation. But not here, not now; now he must just stand with his face still, and throw earth on the coffin, and not think, *not* think, NOT THINK of Dickie.

Before dinner that same evening, Amber took a little red enamelled can from the corner of the loggia, and went up to water Dickie's garden. Under the wall of the Soviet Embassy, agriculture and war went hand in hand; beside the fortress two or three asymmetrical plots were laid out in the dusty unpromising soil, in which some flowers and lettuces languished as only plants grown by children do. Since his illness she had watered them every day. She went round by the shadoof to fill the can, and passed on to the upper garden behind the grey thuja hedges; emerging from them, she stood still. There, beside the incompetent little childish garden, the futile fortifications, Nugent Grant-Howard stood, gazing at them. His face was shadowy in the dusk under the trees, but there was that about it which filled the girl with a sort of awe. He was embracing experience. Without a sound she slipped back between the thujas and stole away.

Chapter Fourteen

UNCLE BILL'S house was in a Hu-t'ung off Morrison Street, that curiously hybrid thorough-fare which begins so European, at the end near the Ta Ch'ang an Chieh, with its pavements, its block of flats where the dentist lives, its plate-glass windows in the two shops which purport to sell French dresses; and ends so completely Chinese. Some little distance down it the pavements gradually cease to be paved, and then to be defined at all, and become merely a sort of dusty adjunct to the street, a no-man's-land between the shops —which here degenerate into ramshackle one-storey affairs with scaffold poles leaning against them, and swinging vertical signs—and the roadway itself—a space devoted to the practice of all sorts of minor trades, from the sale of sweets and persimmons to chiropody and knife-grinding. The street carries a heavy volume of miscellaneous traffic. Strings of laden donkeys patter along the gutters, neat-footed and unconcerned; teams of mules, ponies or coolies, or of all three, strain at long low-wheeled carts laden with sacks of flour or baulks of timber, which creak in a hideous treble as they pass over the uneven surface; the skimming rickshas dart up and down, thick as may-flies on a stream; great bundles sway from the shoulder-yokes of carriers as they move with their peculiar unsteady heel-and-toe run. And all this mass of traffic shouts as it goes; men and merchandise are moved to the accompaniment of an uproar like that of a political meeting in Dublin, and the dull rumble of wheels and hoofs becomes a mere ground-bass to a terrific orchestration of yelling in many keys.

But in Uncle Bill's Hu-t'ung it is very quiet. Leaving Morrison Street on the west side, you turn right, and then left, and then right again, along narrow lanes between high grey walls with trees showing above them, where only a casual ricksha passes, and dogs and beggars snooze in sunny corners, till knocking at a scarlet door set with rows of golden knobs in fives, you are admitted to Uncle Bill's dwelling.

It was a regular Chinese house, consisting of nine or ten paved courtyards scattered without apparent plan over a large space of ground, each with three or four one-storey pavilions round it. Those nearest the gate comprised the servants' quarters—it was only after a longish walk through several strangely shaped doors, across a court or two, and along raised verandahs under the eaves of the pavilions that one at last reached the house proper. A court with a trellis of wistaria along one end and a *p'eng*, or straw roof, shading the other, housed the drawing-room and Aunt Bessie's sitting-room; a passage and a verandah led to the dining-room in the next court, on which also opened the apartment which Uncle Bill called his "room," but which Aunt Bessie persistently referred to as his "den." From this a heart-shaped door led, across a small court with a goldfish pool in it, to that which contained Uncle Bill's and Aunt Bessie's bedrooms—beyond this again, or alternately by another route through a miniature landscape and a long passage, one reached a court with guest-rooms, where Amber slept and enjoyed the use of a small sitting-room.

The house had been Europeanised to the extent of putting in electric light and anthracite stoves for heating, but most of the rooms still had their curious pretty wooden lattices in the windows, with soft paper panes, and the baths were the old Soochow tubs of glazed earthenware, three feet high and as much across, sea-green inside and looking like bronze without, with their raised patterns under the dark glaze. Aunt Bessie, whose taste was so catholic as hardly to merit the name at all, combined, in the great L-shaped drawing-room and through the house generally, bright flowered cretonnes and glossy cushions from Harvey Nichols with black-wood furniture, scroll-paintings and bronze pictures—producing a quite bewildering effect of uncertainty and unrest; but the rooms themselves, with their high walls and timbered ceilings, and the stretches of cool rush matting on the floor, remained strangely Chinese, calmly indifferent to the bright unsuitable objects which jostled one another within them.

To this household Amber came a couple of days after the archivist's funeral, when the period of quarantine was well over, and Dickie's recovery a matter of certainty. For Dickie "squeaked through" as Hawtrey said, thanks to Sister Helga. Hawtrey made a Club tale of the Sister's action on that occasion, and indeed it was sufficiently remarkable for its courage and promptitude to be worth the telling. "She was lying by him on her camp-bed, touching his hand, you know, and foxing—she got no real sleep for a fortnight—when she felt him move, and heard him giving a sort of choke. So she switched on the light, and by Jove, if the whole great swelling on his neck wasn't gone! It had burst inside, and he was swallowing away at all that frightful pus and stuff, poor little brute. So she ups with a medicine glass of that black disinfectant that looks like Guinness, Collargol or whatever it is, and pours it right down him, and then a glass of castor-oil on the top of that; and away the whole show goes, Collargol chasing the poison, and castor-oil chasing the Collargol, a regular paper-hunt! And in the morning he was as right as rain."

This, if a picturesque, was on the whole a veracious account. But what Hawtrey did not relate at the Club, because he had not seen it, was what Amber saw and would never forget—Nugent's daybreak face at breakfast, after hearing the news, and Joanna's look, all that day, of utter weariness and deep content. "It's like coming out of a tunnel," the girl said to Rupert later in the day, turning back to look at the house, as they strolled together in the garden. Rupert stood still and stared at her for a moment. "You're a good friend," he said at length, before he went away.

So Amber settled down in the Hei Lung Hu-t'ung, and proceeded to adapt herself to the way of life prevailing there. Aunt Bessie was a kind, cheerful and exceedingly guileless person, who since her marriage had entirely ceased to exercise any capacity for independent thought and judgement that she might ever have possessed. "Bill says," "Your Uncle says," represented her final arbitrament on human affairs, great or small. Her warm and childless heart delighted in young people, and in seeing young people enjoy themselves—but she rated her own powers as an entertainer of youth very low, and with some reason. Her own life was governed by her two absorptions, Bill and Bridge. For Bill she entertained, at a particularly luxurious table, the Peking t'ai-p'ans (business men) and their wives, and his racing friends—the Rothsteins, the Leicesters, the Stefanys. For her own amusement she played Bridge daily. Either in her drawing-room, or in some other woman's, she sat down immediately after lunch at a small green table, where she remained till it was time to rise and dress for dinner, comfortably absorbed in cards and post-mortems of hands. Her mornings were spent in the usual Peking pre-lunch

industry of writing chits, and in attending to her household. This she did exceptionally well; all the hetero-
geneous furnishings of her many courtyards according
to their nature shone, or glittered, or were clean and fresh,
or stood in their proper places. She loved flowers, and
was clever at them; the courts in the Hei Lung Hu-t'ung
were full of great tree-paeonies in tubs; oleanders and
myrtles bloomed at the entrance to each pavilion; dwarf
rose-trees made a pattern of pinks and reds against the
blue curtain of the wistaria.

Aunt Bessie was delighted to have Amber, and extremely anxious that she should enjoy herself. Secretly
the good lady rather disliked Lady Julia, while at the
same time she thought her wonderful and important, and
courted her good opinion—a state of mind which in spite
of its inconsistency is very common. She had seen very
little of Amber, and had been mildly dreading to find
something of her sister-in-law's chilling superiority in her
niece. But Amber's simplicity and good temper soon
dispelled this dread, and the pair got on very happily together. Amber for her part was charmed with the house.
She loved the privacy of a whole courtyard to herself,
loved the running through two or three others to meals,
or to fetch a pocket-handkerchief; loved the courtyards
themselves, with their unexpected profusion of flowers in
a setting of architectural formality; she even enjoyed the
quaintness of her lofty china bath, and of a bathroom with
a paper door. One night the electric light fused, and they
had to fall back on candles; she had the ill-luck to set
her bathroom door alight as she passed, and in two minutes the frail thing had burnt to the ground. Amber was
much distressed—but by eleven o'clock next morning a
new door of bamboo and paper was erected in its place!
There was a spaciousness, a leisureliness about life in the
Hei Lung Hu-t'ung which reminded her of her feeling on

that day when she first drove through the by-ways of the
Tartar City, going to lunch with the Leicesters. There
was a special pleasure about breakfasting under the *p'eng*
in the cool mornings, and later sitting down to sew under
an oleander, and laying her scissors on shallow marble
steps; it seemed easier to learn Chinese when each time
she raised her eyes from her book she looked across a goldfish pond, which reflected the stiff artificial shapes of the
paeonies, to a green-tiled roof with Bongs on its corners
and painted eaves below.

Besides all this, on coming to the Hei Lung Hu-t'ung
she immediately plunged with Uncle Bill into the world
of horses. The Spring Race Meeting was imminent, and
the hopes of Uncle Bill's stable were set high on two ponies
in particular—on Northcliffe for the Mandarin Stakes,
the biggest race of the year, and on a black griffin, called
Berry, for the Maidens Plate. Griffins, it should perhaps
be explained, are ponies newly come down from Mongolia, which have never raced; to show their status their
manes and tails are often left long, the latter looped up
with bright braid, though their small bodies are clipped
and groomed to a high gloss. Berry had come down in
the autumn draft, and in his early training had shown
an unusual turn of speed, but Old Bill's illness had seriously interfered with his progress. And there were rivals.
Mme. de Bulle's Huron had carried off the Mandarin
Stakes the previous year, when M. Rothstein's Cointreau
was third. Cointreau was running again, and Rothstein
was also alleged to have a marvellous griffin called Crème
de Cacao—all his stable were called after drinks—whose
form was being kept very secret. Henry Leroy, whose
stable rejoiced in diplomatic names, had entered a horse
called Ambassador for the Mandarin Stakes, and was
training a couple of griffins for the Maidens, Envoy and
Extraordinary, but no one yet knew which he would run.

Mme. de Bulle's jockey, Tom Shaw, was already up from Shanghai, and installed in her villa among the willows at P'ao-ma-Ch'ang; Dickie Roberts was as usual riding for the Rothsteins. Leroy always rode his ponies himself, and such had hitherto been Old Bill's habit; but this year it was deemed imprudent that he should, and to a long lean boy called Mulholland, from the Central Asiatic Bank, the Press stable fortunes were entrusted. Mulholland had a little racing experience, but not much, and had to be trained as well as the horses.

Old Bill's equine activities were all carried on from his temple at P'ao-ma-Ch'ang. Here he and Aunt Bessie spent their week-ends, and in such times of emergency as the present, several nights in the week as well. It was a real temple, dedicated to some obscure divinity with a long and unpronounceable Chinese name, whose image, lofty and gilded, half filled one large pavilion in the main court. On certain days in the year the monks from whom Uncle Bill rented the place came to this pavilion and performed rites with incense, the big drum and the round bronze gong on its silken pedestal; otherwise it was used as a dining-room. The pavilion opposite contained a large living-room and a couple of bedrooms; in a smaller court behind were the bathrooms and a guest-room or two. Both courts were paved with flagstones, which Aunt Bessie had removed in places to make room for flower-beds; out to the north her single form of genius had created quite an English-looking garden, with walls, borders and flowering trees. Here Aunt Bessie was generally to be found, in leather gloves and a shady hat, labouring herself, and directing the operations of a very old man whom Hawtrey called the King of Spain, because of his spindly moustache, which hung down in two threadlike strands of black hair far below his chin, like a thin double beard, and looked rusty at the ends, as if it had been singed. "Listen to Auntie B. singeing the King of Spain's beard!" Hawtrey would call, when sounds of objurgation in Aunt Bessie's rather shrill Chinese floated over the garden wall—and Amber, in spite of his folly, laughed at him.

Uncle Bill, however, was seldom seen in the garden. From a *chaise longue* on the narrow verandah in front of the sitting-room he would occasionally point the butt end of his cheroot in the direction of a bed of wallflowers or stocks in the courtyard and observe, "Bessie! those flowers are a most appalling colour." But such destructive criticism was his only contribution to horticulture. His domain was the stables, a range of mud-built loose-boxes in a large walled yard, shaded by willow trees. There he might always be seen on a Sunday morning, in very shabby breeches, an aged Terai on the back of his head, a cheroot in his mouth, examining the various ponies which stood tied to rings in the yellow-washed walls, with Kuo, his head *mafoo*. Kuo had a deep brown and inconceivably wrinkled face, made further remarkable by one of those beaky noses which are occasionally, and surprisingly, to be seen in North China. He was a rather unusually good *mafoo*, a fair horseman and an artist in feeding. His *mao-ping*, or defect, was opium—as a head groom, with seven or eight men under him and considerable opportunities for squeeze, he was rich enough to indulge in a bout every five or six weeks. On such occasions he vanished entirely for a couple of days, to reappear in a dazed condition, with a complexion almost literally pea-green; till the effect wore off he was quite useless. But his master weighed his devotion and the aforementioned good qualities in the balance, and found it on the whole worth his while to keep Kuo. When the groom recovered from an opium bout, Bill rated him vigorously and at length; Kuo was abject to the point of

tears, and promised never to fall again; both men knew
perfectly well that the promise was worthless, but both
it and the previous scolding were essential to the preservation of mutual self-respect. Uncle Bill had lived for
twenty years in China, and not in vain. Indeed he definitely preferred the Chinese way of life in many respects
to the European. It was because of this preference that
he retained so many purely Chinese features in his house
in the Hei Lung Hu-t'ung, such as the Soochow bath-
tubs, which up-to-date Chinese themselves would spurn
today. At the temple at P'ao-ma-Ch'ang Chinese food
was often served at the evening meal; Uncle Bill was as
deft with his chop-sticks as any coolie, holding his bowl
of broth-flavoured rice well up under his chin, and shovel-
ling the contents into his mouth in a steady stream which
reminded Amber of the jet of earth which pours out behind a terrier at a rabbit-hole.

The temple stood on a small eminence near the road;
behind it the ground dropped away in a long gentle slope
towards the racecourse road and the big swampy pond,
so good for snipe in early autumn, which lay close to the
racecourse itself. There, outside the stable wall, were
several jumps, mud walls and *kaoliang* fences, over which
he trained his paper-hunters. The *mafoos*, exercising in
a circle, as their custom is, had worn in the loose dusty
soil a hard-beaten track in an irregular ellipse round the
jumps.

On this manège, one morning about ten days before
the race-meeting, a string of ponies, muffled in blankets
against the early chill, was moving slowly round with a
mafoo at the head of each animal, awaiting Kuo. Presently he appeared, coughing and trembling, and the
procession moved off down the slope towards the racecourse. Kuo had only just emerged from one of his
bouts, and had had a worse dressing-down than usual,

since the moment for such indulgence was peculiarly ill-chosen; he looked weak and ill.   But he had strength and spirit enough to yell directions to his underlings with his wonted ferocity.   A moment later the notes of a hunting-horn, rather hoarse and flat, resounded through the temple.   They woke Amber, and she groped sleepily for her watch.   Needlessly—for the next moment Haw-trey's voice was uplifted outside her door.   "Amber! Half-past six!   Don't be late!" and then she heard him in the next court, "Auntie!   Six-thirty!   Jump to it!"

Amber rose and hurried into some clothes.   Hawtrey and Mulholland had come out to the temple the night before, and they were going down to the course to watch the trial gallops of Northcliffe and Berry.   Bill himself was riding, and Kuo, as well as Mulholland; Hawtrey was to function with the stop-watch.   For some weeks before the meeting the racecourse, in the morning, is always the scene of great activity, the various stables training and trying out their own horses, and trying to get slants on the form of the horses of others.   Most people are satisfied to begin about eight; but Uncle Bill, largely in order to avoid undesirable publicity, began much earlier than anyone else—it was currently re-ported in Peking that during the last fortnight he gal-loped his ponies in the dark.

It was not dark, however, when the temple party crammed themselves into the open tourer and drove off. The clear light poured over the fields, where the tender green of springing crops showed delicately against the brown newly raked earth, the still tenderer silver of budding willows against the pale early sky.   The lake was steaming gently among its reed-beds as they passed it; a couple of duck flew up off the water, with a scatter of bright drops.   Hawtrey was apparently inspired by the brilliance and freshness of the early hour; he talked

incessantly, relating the latest information as to Mimi de
Bulle's griffin, St. Lawrence. "I don't think much of
him—I wish you could tell me what Crème de Cacao's
time for his last quarter is," Old Bill grunted. Then he
gave his chuckling laugh, which reminded Amber so
much of her father. "It always seems so absurd that
Mimi's horses should be called after lakes and rivers—
water, in fact; while Rothstein, who is an unusually ab-
stemious man, calls his after drinks."

"I expect Rothstein does it out of compliment to his
wife, ha-ha-ha," was Hawtrey's comment.

"Good! We've got the place to ourselves," Bill observed as they arrived. The horses were waiting under
a group of willows down by the paddock. While Bill
and Mulholland went over to them, Hawtrey escorted
Aunt Bessie and Amber to a favourable station by the
rails, close to the grand-stand, which stood up, white,
clean and empty in its new paint in the morning light.
Coolies with paint pots were at work on the *pari-mutuel*
buildings behind them, and were erecting mat-sheds for
luncheons under the willows beyond the stand. Hawtrey
adjusted his field-glasses, got out the stop-watch, and
explained the proceedings to Amber. "Each of those
white posts over there is a furlong post. Bill may want
their speed over the whole mile or whatever he's taking,
or just for the finish, say for the last quarter. So you
set this needle here" . . . he went off into technicalities.
Presently Bill rode up.

"Now Joe," he said, in his loud emphatic tones, "we're
giving Northcliffe his full mile and a half. I shall take
him round for the mile and Kuo will bring Walters in
at the three-quarters post and give him a finish. I want
the last two quarters. Doesn't matter if you take the
first mile too—but Mulholland won't press him then.
But it's the finish we want. See?"

Joe saw, and Old Bill rode off. He was so broadly built, though spare, that walking he struck the beholder as a short and even rather an awkward man; but on a horse he gave at once that definite impression of being one with his mount which in itself amounts to grace, or at least gives the eye a pleasure of the same quality. Craning over the rails, watch in hand, Hawtrey waited for the start, and accurately clicked off the watch as the two ponies got away. Round the double circle of white rails they sped, flicking past the furlong posts one after another, down past the watchers by the grand-stand, out towards the willows in the distance, and back round the curve again towards the winning-post. As they passed Amber watched Mulholland appraisingly; he rode well, a nice easy seat; he wasn't fussing the horse, but he was in command. Presently Kuo, on Walters, joined them from his allotted position, and Old Bill pulled out. Joe started another watch going, to time the last half mile. But it was soon evident that something was going wrong, even at that distance. "What on earth is Kuo doing?" Amber exclaimed, as the *mafoo* shot two lengths ahead. "Sshh!" said Aunt Bessie. Joe clicked his stop-watch; and then said "Hell!" very loudly. "Sshh, Joe!" said Aunt Bessie again. No one heeded her. For the groom, having succeeded in checking his horse, instead of keeping abreast of Northcliffe and giving him a race, pulled up, and in a moment or two dismounted. Mulholland rode on alone. "Thirty-three— take it down, Auntie," Joe called, "thirty-two—got that? —thirty." He clicked the watch as Mulholland passed the stand. "Well, that's a washout," he said handing it to Aunt Bessie. "What that hoodoo Kuo is thinking of!" He strode off up the course towards the groom, who was leaning over the rails at the further end of the straight, apparently being sick. Old Bill galloped past in the same direction, with a face as black as thunder. Other grooms ran up, pattering over the grass in the black sateen slippers which look so odd under jódhpores. The women waited, while comminatory sounds floated down to them on the clear morning air. "Your Uncle will be so disappointed," said Aunt Bessie distressfully. Amber thought that disappointed was rather a mild word for Uncle Bill's state of mind, judging by the tones of his voice that reached them. Then Hawtrey came back, giggling.

"What's wrong with Kuo, Joe?" Aunt Bessie asked.

"The lunatic! He's as sick as a cat. He wanted to get over this last bout quickly, so he says he went to a magician, who gave him a potion made of lion's bones or something, to set him up. 'Tajen, he has mixed a sick man's bones with the bones of the lion'—that's what he keeps saying. He swears it's entirely the magician's fault."

Amber laughed. However, from the training point of view the morning was disastrous. And the second gallop was no better than the first. The griffin Berry was to have two companions for a one-mile scurry, and Kuo being out of action, Hawtrey was called in to ride. He gave Amber and Aunt Bessie the most minute instructions in the use of the stop-watch before he went off to the paddock. But Amber's rather considerable experience of horses had not hitherto extended to timing; and though she and Aunt Bessie clicked, and stared across the white circuit of the course at the furlong posts, and jotted down seconds on a pad with the utmost fervour, their results were greeted by Hawtrey with yells of derisive laughter, and by Old Bill with the gloomy statement that they were impossible. Berry galloped beautifully—but as no one knew precisely *how* beautifully, it was felt that the morning was wasted. As they got into the car to drive back to the temple the Rothstein ponies were arriving at the course, and the party all stared eagerly at Crême de Cacao, a blue roan of a peculiar mauve tinge. Hawtrey suggested remaining to take his times secretly. "No use," growled Old Bill. "Ee-tzŭ knows you by sight" (Ee-tzŭ was Rothstein's head *mafoo*) "and he'd see you got nothing to do you any good. Tsou, Chang!" The chauffeur drove off.

Three mornings later, in Peking, Old Bill's stop-watch was missing. When Wang, his Number One, was summoned to explain the loss and institute a search, it transspired that Wang was missing too; breakfast was served by the Number Two. "Have go out" was all that could be got from the servants, and Bill went off to his office mystified. When he returned at lunch-time the watch was back in its place in the drawer in his "den," and on his table lay a slip of paper with several sets of figures on it, neatly dotted down. "Lai!" roared Old Bill, and Wang appeared, immaculate and complacent. *Nakö piao*, he explained, indicating the paper, showed the very great swiftness of time in which Lo Lao-yeh's peach-flower pony had passed the second, third, fourth, fifth, sixth, seventh and eighth white sticks that morning. (Lo was the Chinese version of Rothstein's name.) Hearing from Chang, he proceeded, looking more complacent than ever, that the Grandfather desired to know this, he had taken the dial and a ricksha, driven out to P'ao-ma-Ch'ang, and with the dial made this computation. "Hao!" (It is well) said Old Bill shortly, and Wang withdrew. When he had gone Old Bill studied the figures again. H'm! It was pretty much what he expected— but fast! "Wang's probably got it right," he said to Hawtrey and Mulholland later at the Club, when he had shown them the paper. "There's very little the Chinese don't know about horse-racing—they're all as mad on it as Yorkshiremen." And then he gave his chuckle. "We'd have done better to take him the other day, instead of Bessie and Amber."

"Can Berry better it?" Hawtrey asked.

Uncle Bill sipped his drink. "No wise man ever prophesies in China," he said with his usual loud emphasis. "Time will show."

Chapter Fifteen

ON the last Sunday before the Spring Meeting in Peking, the morning gallops at the racecourse lose their professional status and are elevated into the dignity of a social function, which is attended with enthusiasm by many who never otherwise leave their beds before 10 A.M. and have neither stake nor serious interest in the subject at issue—the horses. This gathering was spurned by such serious spirits as Henry Leroy and Old Bill, but the Leicesters had invited Amber to go under their escort, and she accordingly found herself, at about 9.30 on this particular May morning, seated at a small white table in front of the grand-stand, eating grilled kidneys in company with a largish party which included the Rothsteins, Hawtrey, and Dickie Roberts, and at intervals watching the rather lackadaisical gallopings of various ponies through the screen of pink geraniums which fringed the white rails. On this occasion the gallops are rather a farce—there is too much publicity for serious business; but when Crème de Cacao idled past, she rose, like his owner, to admire his peculiar beauty of shape and movement; then she settled down again, a contented spectator of the scene about her.

It was undoubtedly a pretty one. The graceful little grand-stand with its attendant buildings, the rails of the course, the paddock, stood up, gay and snowy in their fresh paint from turf which had been brought by diligent watering to some semblance of greenness, against a fragile background of tall willows, the undersides of their leaves showing white too as the morning breeze stirred them. Oleanders and pink geraniums bloomed everywhere. The masses of flowers on the scheme of green and white, the groups of people at little tables, eating such an unwonted meal as breakfast in the open air, above all the extraordinarily brilliant light, gave to the whole picture a certain theatrical quality, a novel and rather moving, though artificial, gaiety. Without nervousness, now, Amber observed all this, while she ate, and chatted with M. Rothstein; she knew these people, she had no need any more to look round for someone to make her a personal safety. Since leaving the Legation and coming to Uncle Bill's she had been living mainly in the safe world of horses and those who deal with horses—but, oddly enough, during these weeks, she had felt increasingly that this world was less safe, and the other less dangerous, than she used to think. She had become aware of a certain sense of division in her life, particularly when she met or visited the Grant-Howards—on the one side they and Rupert, and all that they, somehow, were and meant; on the other her uncle and aunt and the Leicesters, the de Bulles, the Rothsteins and the rest. What exactly she meant by this division she could not frame to herself with any definiteness, but that she went from one sort of world to another was certain, even if she made the transit by the mere crossing of a room. Hawtrey alone seemed to bridge the gulf between the two, and yet—oh, so oddly!—without knowing there was a gulf to bridge. Affectionate, amiable, extravagant and witty, he moved from one to the other, unaware of the difference. Yes, unaware—that was what he was; he was being gallant now to Dolly Rothstein with precisely the same lively folly that he would show to Joanna at dinner, or to Aunt Bessie at lunch, or to her, Amber, in a few minutes. Well, no—not to her; he was a little different to her, and at the thought the honest colour stirred in her face, even while she smiled at the memory of his absurdities. And yet he was shrewd — painfully shrewd; the sweeping veracity of his comments on the *t'aipans*, and the racing set, had startled her more than once.

When they rose from the table, the Hamburger took her off to the paddock. Amber had become rather a favourite of his, and as they looked at the ponies, and Amber praised their points with some discernment—"Do you want to make money?" he asked her confidentially. "Oh yes," the girl answered gaily. "No, but if you do, seriously, I tell you something. You keep it to yourself, of course." He leant to her ear. "Back my griffin on Friday. You can make enough to buy yourself a good horse. The odds will be long. No one knows his form but Roberts and I."

As Amber thanked him, Mimi de Bulle came up with Tom Shaw. "Sec*rets*, Monsieur Rothstein?"

"I give Mademoiselle a tip," said Rothstein, raising his Homburg. "To back St. Lawrence!"

"Ah! You hear?" she said to the jockey, triumphantly.

"Morning, Mr. Rothstein. You got some nice little horses here," observed Shaw, paying no attention whatever to Mimi. Her enthusiasms bored him, and his chilly ignoring of them in public was, as Hawtrey often said, almost conjugal. He and Rothstein studied Cointreau now, raising his cloths. "H'm—funny; he reminds me a bit of Bengal," Shaw said at length. Bengal was the name of the best race-pony then in China—probably the best that Mongolia has ever produced. "Know what district he came from?"

Rothstein didn't. The peculiarity of racing in China is that it is impossible to tell the pedigree of any given pony. Stallions are not at stud; they run with the mares on the Mongolian uplands in flocks, like sheep, and the geldings alone are sold to the European dealers who go up to Hailar and Kalgan in the early autumn. Thence they come down in great droves, and are parcelled out between Peking and the Treaty Ports; but for the individual buyer in those places each purchase is a lottery; the pony, selected on his appearance, may prove a second Bengal or a complete dud. The dealer himself may know that a given pony came from the flock of a khan in a particular district, and ponies from certain districts have fairly defined characteristics, like the height and carriage of the head, suggesting a touch of Arab blood, of the Hailar ponies; but more than this can never be known, and even so much only by personal acquaintance with, and veracity on the part of, the dealer himself.

Mimi, soon bored by any other ponies than her own, dragged Amber off to look at Huron. Presently they were joined by Shaw, and Mimi introduced Amber to him as "Beel's niece." "Seen much of your uncle's stable this spring, Miss Harrison?" the jockey asked as they strolled back towards the enclosure. "I hear he has a good griffin for the Maidens."

Amber was not to be drawn. "No, very little," she said civilly. Shaw glanced at her pretty blank face with a sort of respectful amusement. He knew quite well that she had spent most mornings on the racecourse for the last month. His wide close-fitted mouth shaped the syllables "Good girl," silently; he had formed the habit of thus communing with himself with his lips, and it afforded him much relief. On reaching the Enclosure, Amber looked about for the Leicesters—it was nearly eleven and she judged they would soon be leaving; but loud screams from Mimi announced the arrival of François de Bulle with some commodity which was anxiously enquired after. "No—you don't go, Miss 'Arrison—you come and drink good luck to Huron.

'Arry! 'Arry! Come too!" she screamed to Leicester, who was idling, cigar in mouth, among the pink geraniums by the rails, with a curious air of solitude. Laughing and screaming, Mimi collected a considerable multitude round several little white tables. They had assembled, Amber presently found out, for the purpose of drinking champagne, and for the next half-hour they drank the healths of Mimi, her horses and her jockey, and of one another, with a good deal of banter, much of it aimed, rather openly, at Mrs. Leicester, who had gone off to the paddock with Bruno. Watching Harry's face, Amber was first embarrassed, then discomfited. For some weeks now M. Bruno's magnificent presence had caused her a definite discomfort—but whether more on Harry's account or Mrs. Leicester's, she could not have said. The world of horses and those who dealt with horses was not, it seemed, such a safe place after all—not here in Peking; nor wholly a happy one. Looking at the scene about her, the pretty flowered enclosure, the smooth curve of the course with the graceful groups of willows drooping above the white rails, she felt a swift distaste for it all; it was too glaring, theatrical, too highly coloured for real life; and this party, drinking champagne in the open air in the freshness of the morning, was like the company in some vulgar farce. Hawtrey, watching the shifting colour and the movements of lip and eyebrow in her face, realised that something was upsetting her, and made a well-intentioned effort to distract her mind. "This is quite an experience for you, my dear Amber, isn't it, ha-ha?"

"Oh, do shut up!" the girl answered explosively, irritated beyond endurance for the moment by his clumsiness. Hawtrey shut up, with a certain complacency. In his experience, when they started being cross to you it was rather a good sign.

Chapter Sixteen

THE private preoccupations of those who set out in a stream of cars for P'ao-ma-Ch'ang on the Friday after Amber had had the valuable experience of drinking champagne out-of-doors at 11 a.m. were quite as various as might be expected. Mr. George Hawtrey's principal concern was somehow to see enough of Amber to push forward what he regarded as his recent advantage. Aunt Bessie was thinking about her lunch-party at the temple, and whether the King of Spain would have tied up those stocks in the garden before they returned to it. François de Bulle's meditations revolved round the question of whether he had really provided sufficient champagne for lunch, and the effect of a possible failure of some horse on Mimi's temper. Sir James Boggit, smoothing his white top-hat in his saloon car, alternated between deciding that he really must have a new one for next year and hoping fervently that this manifestation of *le sport* would produce no "incidents." Rothstein, cigar in mouth, was thinking—quite legitimately—about his ponies, registering a resolve not to let Dickie Roberts out of his sight for a moment, and to keep him away from the women and the wine; Shaw, on the other hand, was concerting schemes to keep Mimi away from the horses. Nugent Grant-Howard was fidgeting as to whether Dickie (who, white but effervescent, was to be allowed to come for the morning and to lunch at the Harrisons' temple) would get too hot, too cold, or too tired: Joanna was wishing Nugent wouldn't fuss—it was so bad for the child—and expecting to be pretty thoroughly bored, an expectation in which Rupert seconded her. Miss Carruthers was thinking bitterly that Mr. Grant-Howard placed very little reliance in one, and arranging in her mind the sentences in which she would later point this out to his wife; at intervals the consciousness that she had forgotten her face-powder surged up, drowning all other feelings in the certainty that her nose would shine. For the rest, broadly speaking, the men were thinking about their bets and the women about their clothes.

"What are you going to wear, my dear?" Aunt Bessie asked Amber with maternal solicitude. "Nothing too *old*, I hope." Aunt Bessie liked girls to look fresh and girlish; she was inclined to think Amber's rather sophisticated clothes too mature. She was, however, quite satisfied when her niece finally appeared, ready to start, in a soft lacy affair the colour of pale parchment, with a green hat, green shoes and green parasol. "Hum! You've properly let yourself go, haven't you?" Uncle Bill remarked, looking her up and down. There was indeed a general air of delicate expansion about the flowing softness of the frock, the graceful wide hat, which enhanced the girl's very considerable prettiness enormously —she looked really lovely. "Jemima! Our Amber will make hay today among the lads of the village!" Harry Leicester muttered to his wife, as they passed through the small willow-shaded Members' Entrance after greeting the Harrisons' party outside. "The pretty thing—yes," Mrs. Leicester answered with the warmth that was so engaging in her voice.

Almost the first people Amber ran into among the throng inside were the Grant-Howards. Dickie hugged her rapturously. Nugent looked her up and down, as Uncle Bill had done, and said "I like the frock, Amber." In that curious place, a girl's mind, the conviction of looking really well has an odd quality—it produces a sort of glow, without as well as within. Nugent's words, with the ensuing pretty compliments from the foreign community, touched up the girl's face like some magic cosmetic, and gave her in addition a little dash of assurance, a pleasing uppishness that her manner usually lacked. This was well in evidence by the time she met Rupert.

"Hullo, Amber," he said, stopping in front of her. His light eyes looked her up and down too, but he made no remark. Count Stefany, who was with him, produced some gallant exclamation, which Amber countered with admirable coolness by an enquiry for his wife. *Dame!* she was getting an air, the young man thought as he looked at her, and abruptly—"Come and bet," he said. "I want you to make some money for me."

They strolled towards the *pari-mutuel* windows, which extended in a long row between the paddock and the grand-stand, greeted at every yard by acquaintances, catching scraps of talk about horses and riders. Amber consulted her race-card, while Rupert took her parasol. He unfurled it and opened it. "What a pretty brolly!" "Brolly indeed!" said she, with fine scorn. "Well, it's *d'une élégance folle*, anyhow, like its owner," he said, shutting it again. Amber paid no visible attention. "Here you are for the Urga Plate—we're too late for this race," she said.

"What?" he peered over her shoulder.

The girl made a mark with a silver pencil under a horse's name. "That."

Rupert read: "'First Secretary—H. Leroy.' Oh, come off it!" he said, grinning at her.

"Don't be so silly! You *can't* go past a thing like that. And don't shout out names," she reproved him.

They each put five dollars on Rupert's namesake, and then Amber did some considering. The third race was the Maiden Plate.   In loyalty she ought to back Berry, Uncle Bill's griffin: but she believed Rothstein meant business when he gave her the tip about Crème de Cacao, and she wanted to make some money, for a vague reason which was beginning to take shape in her mind.   She finally decided to back Rothstein's griffin to win, and have something each way on Berry.

They watched the Urga Plate from the rails.   Henry Leroy's scarlet-and-white colours hung half-way round the course in a bunch of ponies—then he left the bunch behind, came level with the leader, a grey pony of Mimi's, and won easily by two lengths.   Rupert was charmed— and he was more charmed still when the chalked board was run up and announced that First Secretary was paying $6.25.   He pocketed his winnings with great satisfaction.   "Now what?" he said.   "You evidently know your job."

"Well, you really *must* keep this dark," the girl said. "Just do what I do."

"All right—go ahead."

At a *guichet* marked "Crème de Cacao" Amber put down five ten-dollar notes.   Rupert gaped.   "I say, aren't you going rather a burst?"   "Put your winnings on," was all she said.   He did so, obediently.   She moved to another window and put ten dollars each way on Berry.   He was amused at the way she took command— he liked her certainty: he always did like certainty.   And he was enjoying strolling about with her in this crowd: heads turned after her, he caught muttered remarks: she was enchanting today.

The *pari-mutuel* windows were now crowded, and people were flocking into the stand: with "the Maidens" imminent there was a slight tension about the crowd that had been lacking before.

"Let's go up for this—I must see," the girl said.   They

climbed the stairs to the stand and found places with some difficulty.

From the top of the stand the whole course was spread out below them like a painted diagram. A roar of voices floated up from the enclosure below, where the bright dresses among the flowers made a changing pattern of colour, deepened here and there by the light shadow of the willows—the pattern spread up past the luncheon *p'engs*, an oblong of pale gold straw, and at both ends faded out into a solid line of blue, where the Chinese, yelling and chattering, hung on the rails. The sharp green and white oval of the course stretched out from beneath their feet into the landscape, and returned to them again; between the groups of willows which fringed it, out in the fields, the figures of peasants were quietly at work. Overhead innumerable kestrels, hovering and planing, cried their brief complaint in the blue.

Most strange it is how the same place, seen by the same person, but in two different moods, can wear so different an aspect. This scene, from which Amber had turned in revulsion on Sunday as vulgarly theatrical, was charming today. But now Rupert was beside her, muttering his little short revealing phrases, isolating the two of them in an increasingly intimate companionship. When Hawtrey had tried to annex Miss Harrison for a visit to the paddock, Benenden turned him off with an abrupt— "No, Joe—we're a combine today, Amber and I: we're making money. Don't disturb us." "It requires concentration," he said to the girl, "doesn't it?" Amber only laughed: in her little mood of successful haughtiness she would not be at the pains of framing a reply. But the whole thing was delightful. It would be too much to say that she had missed Rupert, these last weeks: rather he had been squeezed out, to a great extent, by absence and by other interests. Now he was squeezing his way in again, and she was only to realise later that he came to a place prepared for him. For the moment she merely enjoyed the unmistakeable flattery of his fun and amiability.

A stir, as of a breeze, passed over the stand: the crowd thinned in the enclosure, thickened at the rails—the field was passing up to the starting-point. The streaming manes and brightly braided tails of the griffins gave them a wild look, in odd contrast to the conventional dress of the jockeys, as they cantered past, a gay file of colours—Shaw on St. Lawrence, in maroon and gold; Dickie Roberts in pale blue on Crème de Cacao; Mulholland, looking nervous, on Berry. (The Press stable colours were, very appropriately, black and white.) Leroy had scratched Extraordinary and was riding Envoy, a white pony. After a false start or two, the withered Mr. Heseltine got them away. There was some jostling among the bunch of ponies, Amber could not see clearly what, in the scramble for the rails, but as they swept round the curve beyond the paddock they gradually spaced out—Berry and St. Lawrence neck and neck in the lead, with Berry on the rails: then Envoy and Crème de Cacao, and several more lying all together. In this order they ran till the fifth furlong. Now Berry bit by bit cleared St. Lawrence, and came on leading. Roars rose from the stand—"Bill has it! Berry has it!"—yells from the blue line at the rails about "*nakö hei ma*" (the black pony). But what was this, shooting out from the group, passing Leroy's red and white, overhauling St. Lawrence? Benenden put up his glasses. "Gosh! It's our friend," he said, as he saw the pale blue of the rider. It was, indeed — at amazing speed Crème de Cacao passed his rivals: now he was only a length behind Berry, now level; then, still apparently without effort, galloping easily, he drew ahead and won by three lengths.

Standing in the crowd, which screamed congratulations in four tongues, Amber and Rupert watched Dolly Rothstein lead the pony in. She didn't do it very well, Amber thought—flamboyant, excited, she laughed, waved, patted the pony, patted the jockey, gave little cries of triumph. But the girl's heart went out warmly to old Rothstein as he stood rather impassive, cigar in mouth, with a quiet satisfaction on his pale heavy face. "Good, Roberts," she heard him say, "very judicious." But the effect of the whole episode was to give shape and precision to the vague idea which had been forming in her mind earlier. This was no less than the ambition to buy a griffin of her own, train it, and run it in the Maidens next year. Waiting in front of the *pari-mutuel* board, to see what Crème de Cacao would pay, she thought it all out. The stable was the difficulty—the branch of an oleander tickled her cheek, and she moved impatiently to one side. She would have to take someone into her confidence about that, either Uncle Bill, or someone like the Leicesters. And a jockey. Perhaps . . .

The chalked boards ran up. "Swelp me!" said Rupert. Crème de Cacao was paying $11.25. Amber had cleared over 500 dollars, Rupert 250. He took her elbow. "Good girl! You and I are some combine, aren't we?" The words set a little pulse flickering in her throat, but—"*I'm* the managing director," was all she said. They went and leaned on the rails again, among the geraniums and the oleanders, till the crowd round the tote should have thinned; the smell of crushed turf, the faint smell of the flowers, rose in their nostrils. "Well, no firm could wish for a better," Rupert said, after a pause. But he wasn't exactly laughing as he said it. The girl looked out over the course at the kestrels still wheeling in the blue overhead, at the light striking like great chords through the distant willows. Lovely it was, moving—she could almost hear the chords of light vibrate from sky to earth, as she heard the high notes of the kestrels. It was beginning again; the world was stirring into music again. But how *did* one know if it was real? Or rather, if it was based on anything? And what did one do till one knew? Confused, dizzying, thoughts that were half emotions and emotions that were sketches of thoughts wheeled in her like those brown birds—there, that one—now a spray of oleander hid him behind pink blossoms, as thought faded with a touch of Rupert's hand again on her arm. "What thinking?" he asked her.

The intimacy of the babyish phrase sent fresh little waves of warmth stealing through her. Startled, with her usual lack of presence of mind, she blurted out the truth—"I was thinking how little I know."

"H'm," said Rupert. "Except about horses, yes." He studied her as she leant against the rails, delightfully dressed, her lovely skin and hair most wonderfully shadowed under the green hat, her eyes still on the wheeling birds. "I'm not sure it isn't time I started to teach you," he said abruptly. And again he wasn't exactly laughing.

They all lunched with the Harrisons—the Grant-Howards, Rupert, Hawtrey, Mulholland and the two Stefanys. Most people in Peking always invited Herman and Mimi de Bulle together, and if they couldn't ask Mimi—as on this occasion it was obviously useless to do, since she had her own *p'eng* and party—they did not invite Count Stefany either. But such nuances either escaped Aunt Bessie or she sublimely ignored them: she liked Anna, and invited her and her husband together. And, Aunt Bessie being Aunt Bessie, together they came.

It was already too hot for lunch in the courtyard—they sat in the pavilion, and the gilded image presided solemnly over the meal. But only the image was solemn

—and Mr. Hawtrey. Joe was feeling distinctly miffed.
There was Amber, looking charming, really charming,
prettier than he had ever seen her, even when he had
visualised himself, on the drive out, escorting her, his eye-
glass in his eye, through the paddock and the enclosure;
and that infernal Rupert had mopped her up completely
for the whole morning. He couldn't get a seat by her
at lunch, even; she was sitting between Stefany and Mulholland, and talking to Herman about the exact proced-
ure for buying griffins. But his jealous and experienced
eye noted with concern her dreamy expression in pauses
of the conversation, and how when Rupert spoke she
listened, whoever he was talking to. Damn and blast!
Something must be done about it. Rupert would charm
the eyes out of anyone's head if he gave his mind to it.
Look at Mme. de Clarens—look, indeed, at poor Lydia,
till Bruno came along and went one better! Though
what they saw in Rupert, apart from his brains, really
beat Joe. Relatively, he was a small man! It was very
odd.

He fared no better in the afternoon, however. Rupert
continued to monopolise Amber; together they wandered
about, betted, stood with heads together over the race-
card; together engaged in conversation with other people,
only to move off again side by side. By the end of the
day it was a source of comment—nothing escapes notice
in Peking. "*Enfin, elle s'affiche trop avec ce jeune homme,*"
Mimi observed virtuously to Count Herman. "*Qu'avez-
vous donc, Shaw?*" for the jockey burst into a guffaw.
"*Ah, ça—mais pour les jeunes filles c'est autre chose,*" she said,
drinking some more champagne, which in the de Bulle
p'eng took the place of tea. Champagne no doubt accounted for this frankness. And François' fears were fulfilled—the defeat of St. Lawrence had upset her; she
vowed that Roberts had fouled the pony at the start.

There were, in fine, the makings of an incident, and rumours of it reached Sir James, spoiling his tea.

But nothing of this touched Amber. A return to her former uppishness had seemed the best treatment of the situation, on the whole. "You are in your element in all this, aren't you?" said Rupert to her, with a lazy mixture of mockery and approbation, when she had successfully squeezed a tip out of Dickie Roberts in the paddock—"I believe a racing-stable is your spiritual home." And some movement of contrariety checked her first impulse to tell him how much less at home she had felt lately in the world of those who dealt with horses. She agreed. "You don't look the part, you know," he said. "What part do I look?" she wanted to know. Rupert hesitated for once. "No part—yet," he finally brought out. "You look very pretty indeed," he said then, with firmness. "Are you vain?" he asked. Her answer—"I should like to be," set him chuckling with its candid unexpectedness. "Well, do be—you've every reason to."

Joe's turn only came that night. He craftily arranged with Aunt Bessie to call for Amber—Joe had a car of his own—take her to the Rothsteins' party at the Peking Hotel, and bring her back. Aunt Bessie accepted this escort gratefully. It was nice to have someone steady, like Joe, to look after the dear child. The Rothsteins' parties were sometimes rather rackety, she believed.

The struggle of the human heart to make its own meaning clear to itself is not, as a rule, the simple matter that in fiction it is represented to be. It is generally a slow and tortuous business, confused by irrelevancies like pride or caution, held up by the competition of other interests, worried by the intervention of the questioning brain; pushed forward, on the other hand, by all sorts of accidents. Actually it was Mr. Hawtrey's own endeavours to improve his position which in this case opened Amber's eyes as to where she stood. Seated at a table for forty, in the vast, skilfully illuminated dining-room at the Hôtel de Pékin, behind the screen of conversation, the pretty finished façade of her appearance and her smile, she was working away at her theory of Benenden, fitting into it the events of the day. He had said this, and that—"You look very pretty indeed," " I think it's about time I started to teach you." She did, as it were, sums with them, carrying forward the debit or credit balance of previous conversations, previous reckonings. Teach her what? The mere thought of one possible answer to that question set up a curious stifling pulsation within her. But she still conceived it to be in her power to go forward or back, or remain placed; still imagined that her heart would answer to the helm. Now and then—for the talk was mostly of horses —she drifted off into a contented recollection of those five hundred dollars, and the griffins she could buy; then she came back to Rupert again. And then the music began.

M. Rothstein had done himself rather well on this occasion. The immense table not only carried vases of roses — the whole surface was strewn, thickly as they would lie, with lilies of the valley. Men filled up the champagne-glasses almost between every mouthful; the chef had been subsidised, so had the band. Half-way through the meal the White Russian *chef d'orchestre* stepped out with his violin, came and stood by the table and began to play the "Chant hindou." The melody, heavily sweet as the overpowering perfume of the lilies, stole round the table, with the ring of well-fed and satisfied faces, the shirt fronts, the shoulders and the jewels—carrying a hint of unseen beauty, like the night wind off some tropic shore. It filled Amber with a strange languor; leaning back in her chair, holding a

spray of lilies, she surrendered herself to the exotic sweetness.   This sort of music was new to her—at home, apart
from jazz, it was the clear cool purities of Mozart or Bach
or Corelli with which she was familiar.   This saccharine
sensuous stuff took her by surprise, had her at its mercy.
This then was the land into which one might be led, this
place of dim enchantments.   Rupert's face swam before
her, his light eyes, his smile; his voice, caressing and
mocking, was in her ears, his hand on her arm.   As air
led on to air she found it harder and harder to reply to
remarks addressed to her, to hear what was said, so
caught was she in her dream.   When, with the advent
of coffee, the *chef d'orchestre* returned to his place and
couples began to move out into the room she hardly
noticed it—she started when Joe touched her shoulder
and said "Come and dance."

Mr. Hawtrey did not dance unusually well.   He was
in time, steady and safe, but there was a military firmness about his tread, and a tendency to emphasise the
less subtle rhythms with a vertical movement of his
partner's hand which made his performance not quite
the poetry of motion.   Nevertheless Amber went off
with him very contentedly—she loved dancing, she was
very fond of Joe, and she had a slight sense of having
neglected him rather severely during the day.   Rupert
was not here, so by all means dance with nice old Joe.

But she became aware, bit by bit, that there was something odd tonight about nice old Joe.   Wrapped again
in her dream, in the lulling movement, she only noticed
vaguely, at first, that he was being nicer than ever; retailing flattering remarks that this one and that had
made about her during the day.   Well, there was
nothing in that; so did her other partners; her host
actually insisted on taking a turn with her, and quite
touched the girl by his pleasure on hearing that she

P

had taken his tip to the tune of fifty dollars. But when after an interval she danced with Joe again, absent and dreamy as she was, the meaning of his little enquiries, his little half-tender jokes slowly dawned on her—Joe was making love to her. Startled, she realised that this was quite unambiguous; there was no need for theorising here. But while she listened with a gentle smiling indifference which Joe interpreted as encouragement, secretly she was suddenly busy on a new occupation, trying to guess what it would have been like if this had been Rupert; what words the poet would have used instead of poor old Joe's circumlocutions and conventional phrases. Ah, now her heart within her uttered at last—when Joe said, "You are quite lovely—and people love what's lovely, you know," it left her unmoved; but when Rupert said "What thinking?" her very blood had altered its beat. Now she knew—and with the knowledge came a sudden startled shyness. She had a secret to defend—and with an innocent craft that would have drawn tears from stones, she was a little more actively nice to Joe.

These tactics, however, had their disadvantage. Joe had a great belief in striking while the iron is hot, you know! On this occasion, unluckily for him, the iron was much cooler than he thought. Going home in the car, without warning, he expertly gathered Amber to him and kissed her. Surprised and disconcerted—"What *are* you doing?" she said rather indignantly, freeing herself. Joe, seeing that he had bogged it, was a little indignant too. "Well, you needn't be so high hat about it, Amber darling." Amber was instantly penitent at his hurt voice. "I'm sorry, Joe, but—don't."

"Why not?" Argument, Joe knew, was sometimes fruitful. But it wasn't in this case. Amber wouldn't argue. How indeed explain how trivial—and therefore how unendurable—were anyone's kisses, compared to one of Rupert's little shakes of the elbow? "Just don't," she said simply, "please, Joe." And Joe, who was also learning something that night, said "Very well, Amber."

What he was learning was not her secret. Not given to self-analysis, or analysis of any sort, he was quite unable to diagnose his own state, far less hers. He must, he innocently supposed, give her more time. But he *was* surprised at one thing—simply that he found he wanted her to have what she wanted, even if it was not to be kissed, more than he wanted to kiss her. This was novel and puzzling to Mr. Hawtrey. He thought about it all the way back from the Hei Lung Hu-t'ung to the Legation compound; he thought about it as he walked up to his bungalow door and fitted his latch-key into the lock. Then he forgot it, because some fool had bolted the door. Swearing, he rattled the handle, and eventually pulled it out by the roots; furious, he stormed round to the servants' quarters, still waving the handle, and knocked up the frightened boys, who flew in a body to open the door. The lock being broken by Joe's strength, they had to let him in by the French windows on the verandah. Next morning Mr. Hawtrey held a Court of Enquiry, which revealed that his Number Two was the culprit. So he administered justice, with his usual mixture of shrewdness and jocularity. He had lost "face" by being shut out—Number Two must lose face too. Amid the grins of the assembled staff he dressed the boy in his own sheepskin coat, stood him face to the compound wall, and taking his Chinese crossbow, he fired off two or three of the large clay balls which are the ammunition of this weapon in his direction, from a distance of fifty paces. At that range the balls could not hurt. The other servants looked on, giggling discreetly—the fantasy and ingenuity of the punishment devised by the Number Four Envoy tickled their curious but lively sense of humour, and enchanted them. Then Mr. Hawtrey, much pleased with himself, went in to breakfast, and began again to think of what Miss Harrison wanted.

Chapter Seventeen

FROM the middle of May onwards the temperature in Peking mounts sharply, first to the lesser heat of June, then to the *Ta Shu*, or Great Heat, of July, when the rain begins, ushered in by the spasmodic thunderstorms of the previous month. In June, looking out over the plain from some high point in the Western Hills, from above Pa-Ta-Ch'u or from the Emperor's Hunting Park at Hsiang-shan, the watcher sees no city, but a great wreathing of smoky white, as of a vast bonfire —the sunlit dust lifted from the unpaved streets and open spaces of the town by the hot noonday wind. At sundown, when the wind has dropped, those who walk on the city wall to catch what movement of air there may be, what hint of coolness, find the sun-baked flagstones still warm beneath their feet; while to their nostrils mounts, more potent even than in the streets below, that peculiar stew of smells—of cess of men and animals, of charcoal fumes, of cooking with strange fats and strange condiments, of remembered dust, which is the summer atmosphere of Peking. This penetrating compound of odours, sweetish, sourish, indescribable and unforgettable, reaches even to the roof-garden of the Peking Hotel on those hot nights when the European population assembles there, to dance listlessly on the polished concrete, or to sit languid round tables set against the garish trellis of artificial roses, drinking something; while the band brays and the lights glare, till they are lowered for a waltz and he who cares may see the stars, brilliant above the few lights of the city. And going home to bed, even with doors and windows set wide and the irritant whirring of an electric fan matching the ceaseless rattle of the crickets outside, the reveller's bedroom thermometer will still show him, at one in the morning, an implacable ninety-five degrees. Each open piece of ground is a furnace; wonks and coolies lie panting in every patch of shaded dust; sweat streams from hairless bodies burned copper-colour with the sun, the thick coats of donkeys are dark and smooth with sweat.

As if in some secret rhythm with the earth's relation to the sun, with the rising temperature, Amber's need of Rupert mounted then like a slow tide. With its emergence into consciousness at the Rothstein's party, this emotion had become as it were vocal; she could no longer ignore it for any length of time. On the hotel roof, at night, she watched his white coat among the dancers; Rupert refused the indignity of a monkey-jacket, and wore what Hawtrey derisively described as a "dentist's coat." When he was in another party she watched with soft torment—she could not help herself—his smiles, his queer humorous grimaces to his partners, wondering what he was saying, why laughing; when he was in her own, the waiting for him to ask her to dance brought always a slow agitation, an almost physical pressure over the heart. When they did dance, it *was* the poetry of motion; Rupert, on any showing, danced divinely, with an almost inspired subtlety of step and rhythm—the contrast of his jerky acid comments with this smooth movement had something drily stimulating about it, like old brandy. (Only Amber knew nothing about old brandy.) To meet him unexpectedly made her almost dizzy. Now, too, she welcomed any reason that took her to the British Legation—sought, indeed, occasions for going. Poor human heart! The portals of Paradise had now become that squat, grey gateway, guarded by the *k'ai-mên-ti* in his long gown, the sentry in his summer drill.   She never entered that gate now without a glance across the square, green at last, towards Benenden's house, remembering, with the heart's passionate sense of treasure spilt, of pearls flung down unregarded, the day she took tea with him there, when he scolded her for her amiability and said he should call her Amber.

A bazaar at which Amber was to sell and Mrs. Grant-Howard to preside furnished the occasion for several visits to the Counsellor's House.   One morning at the beginning of July Amber went by appointment to discuss some business in connection with it.   Liu, with his monkey-fied smirk of welcome, said "T'ai-t'ai lai" and left her in the drawing-room.   It was too hot to sit outside now after 10 A.M., and the windows were closed for the day's heat, the *lienzas* of the loggia lowered against the glare. While she waited for Joanna, Amber wandered round the familiar room in the gloom, noting its contents.   Hullo, there was a new book!   Two!   Amber had been long enough in China to pounce on a new book with avidity— she pounced on these.   A novel—and a small thin book in a buff cover: "*China Hand.   Rupert Benenden.*"

The girl sank down on a chair where she was, opened the book and began to read.   Actually she had never seen any of Rupert's poems before; she had been too shy to ask Rupert himself, and his works were apparently not among those indispensable treasures from which Nugent could not be separated, which she had once carted into the study next door.   Like most people, she turned at once to the title poem, which was not the first, and read:

> In your pale room
> Are books, flowers, pictures, firelight on the wall,
> Perfection—when you are there.
> But half the time you are not there at all,

Although you lie extended in your chair
Blowing out smoke.   Where?
Where has your mind gone grumbling off alone?
Now last night it was here
Speaking to mine in every change of tone,
In every silence; and the words you said
So carefully in general, were my own.

Well, I shall leave too!
Low in my chair, blowing out smoke, *I'll* go!
Slip through your white wall—
Perfection even can pall
And books, flowers, pictures, firelight—
The uncertainty of passion most of all.
I'll go across the world, to real things.

I know a bench below a green-tiled wall.
Beyond the cobbled path the tall maize swings
Shivering, rustling, drooping under the stars.
Out from a doorway shoot two yellow bars
Of dusty lamplight.   To and fro
Threading the dark I see the fireflies go,
Living sparks, reddish.
Up the street
There is a shuffling sound of slippered feet
And voices keening—"Ai-yah!   Ai-yah!   Ai!"
They say that selfsame cry
Has mourned the dead here for four thousand years.
I only know it fills
The valley trough between the stony hills
And hits the sky
And falls again like rain.
It brings no sense of tears
But ageless human pain
And man's submission.
A man was tortured to death this afternoon.

Quite close by
I hear large bodies bumping, a camel's snarl,
The hot dark night is full of acrid smells,

Dust, wood-smoke, donkey-dung, the camels themselves.
Bong! go the temple bells.
I must turn in soon.
We did a solid thirty miles today;
I shall sleep log-like in my folding bed,
My book will go unread.
Look, there's the moon!
Rum now, and one more gasper, and to bed.

But in the morning I shall go
Down to the river and throw
My clothes off on the stones, and soap, and scrub
Under the sun—no polished taps or tub!
The hurrying cold blue of the stream
Will rinse and lave me, silvered with the gleam
Of the fresh morning of a long hot day—
We'll sleep another thirty miles away.

What did you say?
Oh, I was thinking.   Not of anyone.
No, things, real things.   Not pictures, books or flowers!
Of long hot hours
And the hot China sun
And camels, and tall maize and *kaoliang*—
What is it?   Oh, a thing you wouldn't know,
A real thing; what they use to make a *p'eng*—
And of the smells of dust and donkey-dung.

Good night!   I must go.
No, not tomorrow.   Tuesday?   I don't know.
I might.
Wednesday?
All right.

To read the verse of a person you know is like seeing
them in a new and revealing dress, like bathing-things or
riding-clothes—it gives a new picture.   There is something about the actual form of poetry which makes for
revelation, some strange compulsion in that way of
using words which, almost without our volition, forces
out the half-recognised realities of the deeper ranges of

thought and feeling and leaves them bare for all to see. But poetry does more than this mere laying bare—it crystallises the revealed emotion into a thing with shape and form of its own, a new entity, which is everyone's possession; poetry makes public characters of the heart's secrets. That bad poetry does this less than good is obvious; but that all poetry, whether good or bad, does it to some extent is one of the mysteries of the poetic form. And when we say that a prose writer writes like a poet, or that his writing has a poetic quality, we mean just this—that he, somehow, also presents us with these new entities of expressed emotion, instead of merely picturing for us emotions and actions. Those who wish to keep their secrets should not write poetry.

So when Amber, sitting where she was in the dim room, read this poem of Rupert's through, she did so with a thirsty expectancy of learning more about him. Actually her first impression was that the poetry itself was rather bad; it was not in the least like Tennyson's, which Amber secretly adored; it reminded her faintly, on the contrary, of the productions of her old enemies, the clever young men at Riddingcote. She read it through again—and this time, in spite of its roughness and jerkiness, she realised that it did at least say something with quite peculiar clearness—etched for her a little picture of a hot night in a Chinese village that she could *see*. And dimmer, but more potent, was the suggestion of the troubled relationship with some woman, who drew him and yet irritated him; from whom he turned to real things. "The uncertainty of passion most of all"—what lay behind that? Here, large as life, was the Rupert she knew, irritability and all; but here was also a life of his that she didn't know, from which she was excluded. With a long sigh she turned the page to the next. It was called "In Self-defence." She read it.

Keep out!   Keep out!
Do not come in!
Keep out, I say!
I will not have you in my mind—
Leave the door—go away.
While you are just outside,
Just there—close, near—
I cannot see the words upon the page,
I cannot hear
The ringing pauses of the sentences,
There is no meaning in the sounds I hear.

I will *not* have you in my mind.

There!   You are gone.   Now all is clear.
Now meaning flows and words ring.
Now I can hear a bird sing.
Now I am free, and now I can be kind.

What, again?   Go, go, go, go!
Why do you haunt me so?
You turn my world to slag when you come in—
Filling my mind
Till I am smitten blind
Seeing only you—and not as I would see,
But bitterly—a burning pain.
O, go away again!
Keep out, keep out!   I will not have you in.
I want my world of simple things—
Food, friends, books, thought—
In which a bird sings.
Why should you make it ashes, grey?
Leave me my world.   Go—go away.

In her mood of expectancy, unusually receptive, these
lines hit Amber with extraordinary violence—in the
darkened quiet room they reached her mind almost with
the painful force of a scream.   Bad they might be—that
they were authentic, expressing some tormenting reality,

she could not doubt. Because she knew it so well herself! Oh, she knew so terribly well that struggle to defend the mind from the invasion of another; knew how words do lose their meaning, how the printed page swims and fades under an intruding picture. Sitting there, she realised with a startled pang of fright that it was really against *this* domination that she had struggled when she argued with Rupert that night, watching the crows at the gate of the Forbidden City—not merely against his point of view. And as the mind in panic flies from fear to fear, from dread to past experience, so now her old misery about Arthur stood up before her afresh, as it were visible—outside her now, rather than part of her, but still a shape of anguish.

As usual, she struggled with herself—no heroine of Jane Austen's had a greater passion for "subduing her agitation" than poor Amber. She looked about her, as if to draw support from the homely details of the familiar, rather ugly room; gazed at the dark velvet curtains that framed the windows, at the narrow stripes of light traversing the lowered *lienzas*. Absurd—to be flung into such a fuss over a poem! She read it again, determinedly. But for once her small experience matched Rupert's too closely for her to be able to minimise it as she would have wished; she sighed again, thinking with naïve surprise—How odd that men should feel this too! She tried to combat that curious sense of panic which the thought of Arthur had intensified—the sense of a threat to her happiness. Why, because it had gone wrong once, it should always go wrong! Absurd again! But she had a sense of groping in the dark. She needed so to *know* Rupert, know him all through—and she didn't. Think as she would, weigh and examine as she might, he always baffled her. Now he was one thing, now another. These poems threw light—but only on his power to suffer, and his intolerance of suffering. What sort of woman had done this to him? And—with a shoot of pain—who?

She started violently as the door opened. Joanna came in, summery, neat and cool, but looking very disturbed; she apologised for being late—"I was with poor Chang."

"What's wrong with Chang?" Amber asked—the Number Two with the face of a saint was a great favourite of hers.

"Oh, it's so awful," Joanna said. "His little Ch'o Sur is dead."

"Oh *no*—when?" Amber was deeply distressed. Little fat Ch'o Sur was Chang's only son; she knew him well; he had often played with Dickie, with curious dignity and solemnity, in the compound and the upper garden.

"It was while Dickie was ill—that's what makes it so frightful," said Joanna. "But no one told me—how could I know? I thought Chang looked very tired and miserable, and I begged him to take a day off, but he wouldn't—and the child died"—her voice shook a little —"when he wasn't there."

"What was it?" Amber asked.

"I can't make sure—I wish I was better at Chinese! From where he put his hand I think it may have been appendicitis. I only found out just now, when I was sorting Dickie's things. His dressing-gown had shrunk when it was disinfected, and I thought it would do for Ch'o Sur, so I sent for Chang and told him. His poor face all crumpled up, and he said '*Ssǔ-loh!*' " (He's dead.)

"But why didn't he tell you?" Amber asked.

"I know—that's what I said to him," said Joanna, unaffectedly dabbing at her eyes. "And do you know what he said? The T'ai-t'ai was such a kind T'ai-t'ai and she was *hen chao-chi* (very worried) about Young Master and he knew she would be very sorry if she knew, so he wouldn't say anything to me, for fear of causing me any more distress. He went and let his child die without seeing him again, rather than trouble us!"

"Good Heavens!" said Amber. "Oh, *poor* Chang. He simply worshipped that child."

"If he'd been with us years and years, like the Hugos' boys, or the Leroys', I could understand it better," said Joanna, "but we've only been here a few months—we'd no sort of claim on him. It's incredible."

"He really *is* a saint, like his face——" Amber was beginning, when the *lienzas* were pushed aside and Dickie dashed across the loggia and hammered on the French windows to be let in, shouting something indistinguishable.

"Go round! Go round!" Joanna called through the glass, waving towards the front door. Dickie continued to hammer and shout; but as his mother continued to wave, he eventually gave in and went. "I can't have him in and out here all day—it makes the room so hot," Joanna said. "He oughtn't to be out now, either—I wonder where Miss Carruthers is?"

At that moment Dickie burst in, this time by the door from the hall. His face was scarlet—he was gibbering with excitement. "The soldiers are in my forpress!" he at last brought out.

"*What* soldiers?" Joanna asked tranquilly.

"Ours! The Guarb!"

"Oh nonsense, Dickie—what *do* you mean? Stand still, Mr. Fidgets," she adjured the child, who was tugging at her hand and bouncing up and down.

"Come and see! Come and see! They've gop guns! They're fighting the Sovieps!" Dickie squeaked.

Miss Carruthers appeared at the door. "Break is over, Dickie—come back," she said repressively.

"What is all this about soldiers, Miss Carruthers?" Joanna asked.

"Oh, *I*'ve no idea, Mrs. Grant-Howard. I saw some men up there, so I came away."

"*Do* let's go and see!" said Amber. "May we, Dickie and I? Just for a minute?"

"You're as bad as Dickie, Amber," said Joanna, smiling tolerantly. "All right. They won't be five minutes, Miss Carruthers," she said easily. Joanna had learned out of long experience never to seek to placate governesses—"Their maw is so ravening for that," she said frequently to Nugent, "if once you begin."

Amber and Dickie ran out by the front door and round the corner of the house towards the garden. The drive, passing the portico, swept on behind a group of trees to a private gate into the Jade Canal Road, only used for the exit of cars at garden parties and receptions. The first thing Amber saw was a group of soldiers and a couple of machine-guns by this gate, of which the little panel which Dickie called "the person-gape" stood ajar. But Dickie tugged her on towards the upper garden. What thrilled him was the noble use to which his "forpress" was being put at last; it was this which he desired Amber to see. As they crossed the lawn Amber caught a glimpse of the servants standing in a chattering group at the corner of the house next to the kitchen compound, from which a small door led through into the garden. Clearly, she thought, as she hurried along with Dickie, something was up. They passed through the bushes and trees which masked the grey ugliness of the Soviet garden wall, and emerged into Dickie's private territory. Soldiers in khaki, sure enough, with fixed bayonets, were lined up at intervals along the wall, while a sergeant and Jimmy

Briggs, the most junior lieutenant of the Legation Guard, stood a little back, their solid boots heedlessly planted in Dickie's flower-beds, gazing over the bristling glass into the tree-tops of the Soviet garden. A Lewis-gun was ensconced in the dug-out.

"What *is* happening?" Amber asked of Briggs, without the ceremony of a salutation. He swung round to her.

"Good morning, Miss Harrison," he said, with a certain dignity.

"What are you doing?" she asked again.

"There's something going on in there"—he nodded at the Soviet wall—"that's all we know. So we're just standing-to to see that no trouble comes our way." He spoke paternally; then moved a step aside and lowered his voice. "We haven't heard what they're up to, but you never know with these chaps. We had it reported to us some time ago that the glass had been removed from the wall in one or two places to facilitate a crossing— there's one here." He nodded again towards the wall. Amber's laugh pealed out. "But Dickie did that!" she said.

Briggs looked disconcerted. "Removed that glass? Are you certain, Miss Harrison?"

"I mocked ip off with a brick——" Dickie was beginning importantly, when a soldier came up and saluted. "If you please, sir, there's something afire inside there— you can see if you come a bit further up."

Briggs, followed by Amber and Dickie, set off in the wake of the soldier, scrambling along the dusty and neglected hinterland which lay under the wall, past the kitchen garden and the septic tank, through a thuja hedge, and into the Leroys' garden, where there was a similar waste behind the shrubbery. From here, through a gap in the trees, they could see smoke pouring out of a low chimney, from some building that was hidden from view;

here too they found Burbidge and Mrs. Hugo's maid, in giggling conclave with another sergeant. While the sergeant saluted and Briggs put up his field-glasses to stare at the smoke, Amber turned to Burbidge. "Do *you* know what it's all about, Burbidge?"

"Not much, Miss. That sergeant he's a proper clam!" said Burbidge, in a hissing whisper. (Amber thought the sergeant was traduced by this statement, judging from the glimpse she had caught as they came up.) "But the boys say, some of them, that the Chinks are in there chasing these Communists."

One of Amber's impulses overtook her. This was *fun*; and it was a pity not to get one's money's worth out of fun. Glancing round to see that Dickie was out of earshot, she turned again to Burbidge. "I'm going round to the front of the Embassy to see," she said. "Would you care to come, Burbidge?"

"Yes, Miss," said Burbidge, with alacrity. With a comprehensive and discreet "So long!" to the military, she faded out through the bushes. Amber dragged the protesting Dickie back to the house, telling him that five minutes were "well up"—then she collected a hat and parasol and slipped out. She had forgotten entirely about Joanna, about Chang and the bazaar, about Rupert's poems. Burbidge was waiting for her in the drive. At the gate they took a couple of rickshas. "Mei-kuo-Fu," Amber directed—the American Legation was almost opposite the Soviet Embassy.

Chinese ricksha-coolies are well accustomed to hastening to the scene of any disturbance. In a country where all war is waged by mercenaries, who are liable to be purchased by their opponents at a moment's notice, and where battles are often brought to a halt by a downpour of rain, the steady conviction which makes fighting a serious, and therefore a dangerous, matter is almost wholly lacking; in its place there is a volatile curiosity, a trivial desire to "look-see" when anything unusual is toward. The sound of firing anywhere at once sets a tide of rickshas flowing in that direction, some full of sightseers, others empty, but hopeful of picking up a fare, if only a frightened policeman or a corpse. So Amber's and Burbidge's coolies merely grinned and jabbered very contentedly to one another as they pattered up the Jade Canal Road and turned into the western end of Legation Street.

Some little distance along it a cordon of Chinese troops barred the roadway. "Mei-kuo-Fu," cried the coolies to the soldiers. "Mei-kuo-Fu" said Amber, getting out and tendering a card—on which, after a little hesitation, they were allowed to pass through on foot. Within the cordon the crowd was considerable; they pushed forward, but could see nothing. "Let's try to get up there, Miss," said Burbidge, indicating the steps of the Asiatic Bank. They were pressing towards them, when Amber caught sight of Mulholland at a window. She waved to him, and a moment later the Bank door opened and the young man emerged, came down the steps, and drew them up and into the Bank, where he took them to a window which commanded a view of the entire proceedings.

"What is it all about?" Amber asked—for the fourth time that morning—as they stood with Mulholland, staring out over the crowd in the street. More Chinese soldiers were grouped in force both at the main entrance to the Soviet Embassy and at a smaller gate which pierced its wall some distance further along. Hampers stood in piles outside the smaller gate; some stuffed with papers, from others the soldiers were pulling small red flags and waving them with contemptuous amusement.

"They're howking out the Communists, I'm told," said Mulholland.

"But the Chinese troops aren't allowed in the Quarter!" said Amber, in surprise.

"Well, there they are!" said the young man cheerfully. "And that's not the Embassy; all that further gate is the Chinese Eastern Railway buildings; there's a drive and a wall between it and the Embassy proper. It used to be the barracks, you know, when they had a guard; then they leased it to the Railway people. They say," he went on in a lower tone, "that all these Communist doings lately have originated in there, and the Chinese are fed-up. Don't blame them."

Amber, as she listened, began to remember things. At the time of the Minister's illness, before anxiety about Dickie swallowed up everything else, there had been—yes!—quite a lot of talk about Communist activity in connection with the Soviet Embassy. Those dead students! She was about to ask Mulholland some further question, when a fresh disturbance became evident in the crowd outside—cries of "*Hai-yo ikö!*" and "Here come some more!" arose, the latter in richly American accents. The gate was opened, and out through it came a file of soldiers dragging three prisoners, two men and a woman, all Chinese. Their clothes were torn and dishevelled, the woman's hair hung loose; but most horrible of all to Amber were their faces. They were contorted and green with terror; the woman and one of the men were giving low appealing screams; their captors were laughing. While they were being handcuffed, Amber suddenly noticed a new sound, which she was conscious of having heard for some moments without giving it her attention; she craned her head out, and spying about, identified it with the ticking of a cinematograph camera, worked by a man in horn-rimmed spectacles perched upon a wall to her right. The idea of perpetuating those agonised faces appalled her. "Who in the world is doing that cinema-thing?" she asked Mulholland.

"Oh, that's the movie-man from the *Dollar Princess*, the American cruising-ship," he replied. "Most of this crowd down there belong to her too. They're up here for three days—changed their date so as not to miss the executions of those bandits tomorrow; they ought to have gone to Shanghai first. They're getting double value! They sent in here and telephoned round to the Wagons-Lits for him as soon as this show started."

Amber felt suddenly sickened. It had seemed exciting enough at a distance, but the "fun" was not so funny when there were living prisoners screaming with terror within a few yards of her, and other people photograph-ing them. "I should like to go away now," she said to Mulholland, even while she could not help watching the three prisoners being thrust into a car and driven off.

"I say, I'm not sure that you'd better," said the young man. "There's the deuce of a crowd down there. Wait just a bit. They've got twenty-five out now—there can't be many more to come. It'll be clearer presently."

Even as he spoke, a fresh sound of screaming, appal-lingly clear, rose above the wall across the street; next moment the gate opened again and four more prisoners were brought out. The crowd shouted; the cinema clicked; Amber turned away her eyes. She *must* go! She remembered now that Joanna was waiting for her, remembered Chang and his sorrow and silence, remem-bered that she had read Rupert's poems and something had frightened her—she couldn't for the moment recall what. "I'm going," she said briefly. "Mrs. Grant-Howard is waiting for me. Thank you so much for bringing us in. Come on, Burbidge."

"Yes, Miss," said Burbidge.

They pushed their way out, down the steps and through the crowd, on whose fringe they found abundant rickshas. "What a morning, Miss!" said Burbidge cheerfully, as they bowled again down the Jade Canal Road; "those poor creatures, they did look green!" Amber shivered and made some brief sound of assent. She was trying to remember what it was that had flung her into such a panic when she read Rupert's poems—the heat, the sun, the excitement, the varied emotions of the last two hours had given her a violent headache, thrown her mind into an extreme confusion. *Before* Chang, *before* Dickie and the soldiers, *before* those terrible green faces, *before* those Americans and their cinema—why couldn't she keep her head clear? A fright—and it had been silly. What had she been afraid of? Oh, she remembered—she had been somehow afraid of Rupert. But the potency of the fear was gone—these other things, that living panic, had obscured it. What a morning, indeed!

Chapter Eighteen

THE raid on the Communist Headquarters was a perfect god-send to the dinner-tables of Peking. Though in public Ministers might think well to assume *visages de circonstance* when speaking of it, in private they found it an endless source of good stories. Every day fresh titbits emerged. There was the matter of the fire in the Military Attaché's office. The Chinese raiding party had kept rigidly to the premises of the Chinese Eastern Railway, which were, strictly speaking, no longer diplomatic territory, till the officer in charge saw, as Briggs and Amber had seen, smoke pouring out of some building in the Embassy proper. He saw it with dismay; for he was afraid that some zealots among his troops had exceeded their instructions, trespassed, and committed arson. Fearing complications, he sent a water-party across the road and over the Embassy wall to quench it. The officer in charge of the water-party found, to his extreme surprise, the Russian Military Attaché in his shirt-sleeves, armed with a petrol-can and a pitch-fork, burning papers in his office as hard as he could go. The water-party quenched the flames and carried off the papers to the Yamen, where their subsequent examination produced some interesting results which immediately became common property. It was alleged, for instance, that most of the T'ing-ch'ais (messengers attached to the various Chanceries, whose duties include the distribution of the mail and of visiting cards) had made a practice of selling the contents of the waste-paper baskets of their respective employers to the Bolsheviks.

This caused a great sensation among the uninitiated at the Club.

Then there were some accounts of expenditure, which revealed that the unfortunate students who were shot down during the demonstration outside the Prime Minister's house had been paid fifty cents (some said as much as seventy-five cents) apiece to walk in the procession which ended so fatally for many of them. "Yes, but what you don't realise," Uncle Bill said in loud judge-matic tones to Amber, when she expressed her astonishment at anyone's being willing to run the risk of being shot for about 1s. 5½d., "is that *money here is the basis of life.*" (Uncle Bill had a way of making many of his remarks sound like the text of a sermon.) "Money here is the basis of life," he repeated. "Everything in China has a money value, even a display of patriotism—if you can call it patriotism," he added gloomily. "I don't suppose half of them knew what they were demonstrating about." Quite a flutter was produced, too, by the wide-spread rumour that among the Military Attaché's extraordinarily miscellaneous collection of documents were plans of the dinner-tables at most of the larger diplomatic parties in Peking, showing who had sat next to whom, with notes of the conversation! Nothing had given Mr. George Hawtrey so much pleasure for a long time as to be taxed, as he now was, with being among the notables whose hospitality was of so much account. He ragged Mimi de Bulle, who was considerably piqued that her table apparently went unmapped. "*Les Bolcheviks ne s'intéressent pas aux chevaux, ma chère!*" "*Évidemment, mon cher Joe, chez toi on ne fait que la politique!*" replied Mimi scornfully. "*A moins qu'on ne fait un peu l'amour!*" retorted Joe, undaunted, whereupon she screamed at him de-lightedly.

Sir James, however, was, as usual, worried by all this.

He had conscientious scruples (not shared by all his colleagues) about sending off hasty telegrams on partial or inaccurate information, which might call for a subsequent contradiction. You couldn't send rumours to the Foreign Office, and at first there was very little else to send. "Poor old James," said Rupert to Joanna, over a cocktail, two or three days after the raid, "he got a nasty jar today. They sent him a stinker of a telegram" —("they" is the official description of Downing Street abroad)—"this morning, asking him why the devil he'd allowed forty-eight hours to elapse without forwarding full information."

"Poor Sir James! How ridiculous!" said Joanna compassionately. It is a curious and interesting psychological phenomenon that the most loyal and dyed-in-the-wool Foreign Office officials, on being sent abroad, rapidly develop a certain tone of superiority, even of slight acidity, towards "they" (or them), which infects even the womenkind in a Legation. "What did he say?" she asked, stitching away at her embroidery.

"Oh, he showed it to Nugent, of course, and old Nugent said 'I should reply: "Cannot send full and accurate information till the torturing of the prisoners is completed. This will probably take about ten more days." ' Nugent thought that would give them something to think about —and actually it's strictly true. But of course James wouldn't—he's too *protocolaire*."

The final sensation was the ejection of the Bolshevik Mission and the closing down of the Embassy. And oddly enough it was only then that anyone remembered the Bong. Hawtrey and Amber were both lunching with the Grant-Howards the day that the news came out, and the talk of it was general. Dickie sat quietly eating his dinner—he and Miss Carruthers had dining-room lunch when there was only a small party—but presently he looked up from his plate and said loudly "Babby!"

"Yes, Dickie?"

"Have the Sovieps gone?"

"Yes, old boy; gone bag and baggage."

"Then *we* semp them!" said Dickie triumphantly to Amber. "With the hem!"

"By jove! So you did!" said Hawtrey. "I say, Nugent, that's really very remarkable, you know—most remarkable. ' *C'est un coïncident!*' as François would say."

The placing of the Bong in the Soviet Embassy garden was news to Nugent. It certainly was a rather impressive coincidence. He used it in one of his frequent endeavours to amuse his chief. "You don't want me to tell the Foreign Office *that*, my dear fellow, I hope?" said Sir James, rather caustically, when he had heard the tale.

"It would be quite as rational as most of the reasons we give for anything that happens here," observed Leroy, who was present, "and make a damned good story."

As a damned good story, though excluded from official despatches, it went the rounds of Peking; to such an extent that Amber began to fear that some inquisitive person would steal her precious image, which she still privately called her "griffin." "Let's get it back," she said at last to Dickie. Dickie agreed with enthusiasm. Again the problem arose of where to bestow it for safe-keeping. They dared not have it in the house. Eventually Amber hauled it up—she wouldn't allow Dickie to touch it—and perched it among the creepers on the flat roof of the septic tank. "There! Now it can cast spells on the sewage!" she said triumphantly, surveying the small ginger-coloured object. And there, unknown to anyone but the two conspirators, the Bong remained.

Though these stirring events offered a surface distraction, which perhaps she unconsciously welcomed,

Amber remained much preoccupied with Rupert. Her sense of her need to *know* more, to have more fuel for the ceaseless consuming activity of her mind about him, increased steadily, and the chance and scrappy meetings in company, though delicious, were from this point of view merely tantalising. This feeling was now intensified by the prospect of being separated from him altogether for some time. The annual exodus of women and children from Peking to the sea, to Wei-hai-wei or Pei-t'ai-ho, was imminent, and the Grant-Howards had invited Amber to join them at the latter place. Aunt Bessie had accepted for her with relief; Uncle Bill, having been away for more than three months in the spring, did not care to leave his business again so soon, and nothing would have induced Aunt Bessie to leave him. A temperature of 105 in the shade meant nothing to her, dauntless woman; but for Amber it was different —she thought the dear child looked a little pale; it was a delightful plan. Amber thought it a delightful plan too, at first; but the delight was somewhat dimmed when she learned that Rupert was not going to Pei-t'ai-ho at all. He was staying in Peking to help Nugent, who would be in charge while the Minister took his holiday. Oh, if she could somehow see something of him before they went! If only Rupert rode more! She was always being asked to ride by Joe, by Mulholland, by M. Leopardi; with one or other of these she went for innumerable hot dusty *tête-à-tête* canters, out to the Princess's Tomb or the Wang Hai Lou, in the late afternoon, when the westering sun turned the dust to a golden fog, against which the little everyday groups of peasants—women washing by a canal, children chattering round a sweetmeat-seller, a dung-carrier pitching his evil-smelling basket on a bank to gossip to a water-carrier—detached themselves with the sudden blurred significance of the ink-blue figures on a Japanese colour print. And always, seeing them, her instant wish was that Rupert could see them too. But Rupert's riding was restricted almost entirely to what Hawtrey contemptuously called "healthful hacking" on the glacis.

It appeared, however, that Benenden himself felt that he ought to see a little more of Miss Harrison before her departure, for one day at the Legation when the Coal Hill was mentioned, he turned to her with his usual abruptness and said, "That's a thing you've never seen, Amber. You ought to see it. Let's go. Tomorrow?"

"Tomorrow's the bazaar, Rupert," Joanna reminded him.

"Well, how long does the bazaar go on? Not after six, surely?"

Quite till six-thirty, Joanna thought. "Well, we'll go then—it'll be all the cooler," said Rupert easily. Amber murmured something about being late for dinner. "No, that's simple—I'll give you a bite at my place when we come back," he said. "I'll call at the Wagons-Lits for you at a quarter to seven. That'll be all right, won't it, Joanna?"

"Yes, perfectly," murmured Joanna abstractedly—she was counting napkin-rings on the loggia. Amber was a little startled at the suggestion of dining alone with Rupert at his house, but she chose, rather wilfully, to regard Joanna's vague rejoinder as a sanction for the whole plan. More wilfully still, she merely told Aunt Bessie, on her return to the Hei-Lung Hu-t'ung, that she should be out to dinner next day. If Aunt Bessie had asked any questions she would have answered them truthfully, but Aunt Bessie didn't—it was natural enough that Amber should dine with the Grant-Howards if she was late at the bazaar, as she comfortably assumed was to be the case, and she left it at that. And with her

heart singing Tomorrow, Tomorrow, Tomorrow, in a
silly little soundless tune, Amber, behind her mosquito
curtains, fell asleep.

The Mei Shan, or Coal Hill, is a part of that astonishing group of pleasaunces—there is really no other word
to use for them—which stretches all down the eastern
side of the Imperial City. The Chinese system of building towns one within another, like a nest of boxes, is exemplified in the royal habitations. The vast enclosure
of the Imperial City holds within its crimson walls, set
like a jewel in a bed of greenery, the immense oblong of
the Forbidden City itself, roofed with gold, girdled with
its moat and isolated by that forbidding rampart of grey
stone from which look down, at the four corners, the
golden pleasure-domes; but it holds also temples, theatres,
gardens, groves, libraries, with acres of latticed apart-
ments for soldiers, for eunuchs, for concubines; and for
the recreation of the Imperial inmates, pleasure-grounds
of unbelievable extent, containing above all those two
indispensable elements in the Chinese conception of
terrestrial beauty, hills and water. (The very word for
landscape in Chinese is *Shan-shui*—hill, water.) Three
large lakes stretch down in a linked chain of shining surfaces from the Pei Hai, or Northern Sea, to the Nan Hai,
or Southern Sea; their shores and islands bright with the
tiles and marble of pavilions, and gentle with willows,
their stillness reflecting the remoter images of the Coal
Hill and that other eminence which is crowned with the
immense whiteness of the Dagoba.

These lakes and hills are all made by man. It was the
rulers of the Chin dynasty, in the twelfth century, who
first conceived the idea of bringing the waters of the Jade
Fountain from the foot of the Western Hills, miles away,
to ornament their capital, heaping up the soil thus dug
out into artificial mounds from which to behold their

new creations. Later monarchs extended the work; Kublai Khan laid out his gardens round the Pei Hai, sending back to the uplands of Mongolia, legend says, for the roots of a particular blue flower to adorn them, so that his children might grow up familiar with one beauty of the steppes which he, as a child, had loved.   There is a certain pathos about this home-sickness of conquerors, which recurs again and again in Chinese history—the *lou*, or two-storey pavilion which Ch'ien Lung built among the Sea Palaces in order that his Stranger Concubine, the Zungarian Princess, might gaze upon the western horizon, reflects the same feeling; the Chinese still call it "The Home-looking Building."   Ch'ien Lung, whose very name has become the hall-mark of some of the loveliest things in Chinese art, was a Manchu: it was his predecessors, that dynasty of incomparable builders, the Mings, who for the most part gave to the Forbidden City its present form, and enlarged the small ponds and mounds of the Chins to their present proportions, including the Coal Hill. And there it now stands, with its five little summer-houses adorning its five little summits; not much visited by foreigners, since one can do so only if armed with a special permit obtained through the Legations; entirely solitary, save for the knot of soldiers who guard it, spitting and gambling in the gate-house porch, and for the innumerable crows which roost in the great trees behind it, standing lonely in the tangled and deserted park.

Punctually at 6.45, Rupert called for Amber at the Wagons-Lits Hotel. He found her among a crowd of women who, the poorer greedily and the richer resentfully, were buying blotters, paper-knives, ash-trays, fancy pencils and cretonne knitting-bags for the benefit of some missionary effort in Szechwan. She looked flushed and fagged, and doubted whether she could leave her stall.

Rupert, however, was firm and Joanna complaisant, and she was packed into a ricksha and carried off. The rickshas sped through the haze of suspended dust, golden where the low sunlight caught it—down the Jade Canal Road, across the Ta Ch'ang an Chieh, down the Nan Ch'ih Tzu, till a leftward swing brought them out beside the moat of the Forbidden City, now a forest of pink lotuses, standing two or three feet clear of the water, like delicate carved and tinted candelabra above their crowding leaves. Amber caught her breath and gazed; till this moment she had not seen the holy flower, whose represented shape is omnipresent in China, growing, green and free, in masses wide as the reedbeds round an English mere. The rickshas stopped, and they stepped out, Rupert dragging after him a lively cocker spaniel.

'Why, that's Touchy's dog! What did you bring him for?" Amber asked, stooping to pat the pretty creature.

"Because I couldn't get a *piao* in the time," said Rupert. "You have to have one here. But this chap may do the trick for us. Come on, o' man!" So saying, without giving Amber time to ask how a spaniel could replace an official permit, he led the dog over to the gateway and banged on the wooden door.

A soldier in the usual dirty grey cotton uniform opened it. Rupert asked with assurance for the Number One man, and stepped inside, dog and all; Amber followed. Instantly two or three more soldiers sprang up and came forward, demanding the *piao* and protesting violently that the place was closed. "*Teng-i-teng*" (Wait, wait), said Rupert easily, and explained that he must speak with the Number One. Meanwhile, the soldiers looking on suspiciously, he made the cocker sit up; took off his hat, and set it on the dog's head. Bimbo sat like a rock; the soldiers began to grin; Rupert picked up a fan which lay on the ground, furled it, and set it across the cocker's shoulder like a gun—the soldiers chuckled. *"Shih kö ping"* (He's a soldier), he said, and the group, including the Number One, now arrived, laughed with childish delight. While Rupert made Bimbo balance a lump of sugar on his nose a violent discussion broke out as to what this strange animal was. *"Shih kö kou!"* (Is dog); *"Pu shih kou!"* (Not is dog); *"Shih kö yang hsiung!"* This latter view, that the long-coated spaniel was really a "foreign bear," finally gained acceptance. But by this time the official guardians of the Coal Hill were so entranced by the performance provided, that when Rupert showed the Number One his card with his rank in Chinese on the back, and expressed a wish to stroll up and look-see, his request was granted with '*Haos*' and bows, and he and Amber, followed by Bimbo, passed out of the court and began the steep ascent.

At first, as usual, Rupert was conscientiously the showman. Even as they climbed single file up the little pathway, trodden in the rank wiry grass of the hillside, he began to tell of the flight and suicide of the Emperor Ch'ung Cheng, the last of the Mings, when the Manchu conquerors were at the gate, to this, one of his favourite haunts, where he hanged himself from a tree. "Sit down a moment," he said, pulling her down beside him on the steps of the pavilion, as they reached the first little summit. "You're puffed. Now look."

Amber did not need the injunction. She was seeing Peking as she had never seen it. Their seat on the shallow marble steps of the pavilion commanded a view of the whole great oblong of the Forbidden City, spread out below them like a child's city of bricks on the floor, but curiously foreshortened; the yellow roofs at the further end were piled upon one another in a rich golden confusion, which made it hard to identify them. There were the pleasure-domes at the corners, and that splash of dark green was the thujas of Xanadu; there was half the great tent-topped gateway, with just a hint of the two others behind, through which Amber had come that first day; right out beyond, a dim smear of green marked the gate-tower of the Chien-Mên, another stage on the Imperial road southwards towards the Temple of Heaven, whose blue dome was faintly visible, like a dark sapphire, in the haze of the southern horizon. To the west of the Forbidden City itself lay the lakes and the Sea Palaces, gleaming through a sort of haze of willows— myriads of willows, drooping to water golden with sunset, overhanging walls of marble and crimson, brushing against strangely shaped tiled roofs of amber, of seagreen, of plum-colour. Their summer foliage, a peculiar dusty shade between fawn and silver, their extraordinarily elusive delicacy of form and outline, made them a perfect setting for the architecture, at once definite and fantastic, which they companioned with their grace. Is it because they grow so freely in North China, or because their budding wands are the symbol of rebirth in spring, and so of immortality, or for this more subtle reason, that the Chinese have showered willows all over their landscape?

But it was not only the willows that fascinated Amber. Beyond the golden central block of the Forbidden City, beyond the outer oblong of the Imperial City, whose outline was traceable at intervals, lay Peking itself, to east, to west—the whole southern half of the capital. But it didn't look like a city at all. Seen from this height, it appeared more as a vast wooded plain—like the vale of Moreton from Stow, or the Thames valley from Long Crendon; so great is the cumulative effect of the trees which stand, scarce noticed from below, in every courtyard of house or temple. What a city, the girl thought, gazing out at it in the late light that deepened

and enriched every colour with thick gold, touched
every shape into solidity with dense blue shadow. She
gazed and gazed, thinking—how incredibly perfect to be
seeing it now, in this miraculous light, and with him!
And with the thought she turned to Rupert, hoping to be
able to get a look at his face, to set it for ever in relation
to this vision of the wooded city, the golden palace, the
dream-like lakes among the silvery willows.

But Rupert was watching her, and when she turned
she met his challenging eyes, his amused affectionate
smile. "How you do love it; don't you?" he said. "It
was worth bringing you here."

"Why don't you write a poem about all this?" the girl
asked, looking away again—Rupert's eyes were a little
too challenging, too keen.

"I have—one or two. What do you know about my
poems?" he asked.

"I read some the other day at Joanna's."

"Which did you read? Did you like them?"

"I like the one about the village frightfully," said
Amber cautiously.

"About a *village*? What *do* you mean? None of them
are about villages," said Rupert vigorously.

"Yes—one called 'China Hand' was," asserted Amber.

Rupert laughed. "Oh, that. But that wasn't about
the village, it was about a woman."

"It was more about you than about the woman," said
Amber, with a sense of hardihood. He laughed again.
"Love-poems are apt to be more about oneself than about
the woman," he said with his curious harsh abruptness,
"because when one's in love one's so cursedly obsessed
with one's own sensations."

"But you don't call that a love-poem, do you?" asked
Amber in genuine astonishment.

"Of course. What else? What would *you* call it?"

R

"Not that; it was so—discontented; angry, nearly."

"My dear girl, love makes people discontented and angry," he said, turning round to stare at her, half mockingly. "You'll make plenty of people discontented and angry before you've done," he said, smiling into her eyes.

"But why need one be *angry*? That's what I don't see. I don't call that loving," protested Amber, disregarding the last part of his words.

"It may not be loving, but it's love all right," the young man asserted. "I was angry with that woman, although I loved her like mad, because she was a shifting tease." He frowned, pushed back his hair, as though to brush away some disturbing recollection; then he sprang up. "Come round to the back—you haven't seen that side yet," he said, and reaching down he took her hand and pulled her to her feet. Still holding her hand, whether forgetfully or on purpose Amber didn't know, he led her along the little crest of the hill, past the pavilions, and a few feet down the further slope to where a piece of marble, half-bedded in the soil, offered a low seat. Amber sat down, and he threw himself on the ground at her side.

The outlook on this side was rather more restricted. It was a strange place to find in the heart of a city. The trees and the thick thorny underbrush that grew between them entirely hid whatever wall there might be on two sides of the enclosure, for aught that one could see the park might stretch for miles in that direction. Crows were flying in in thousands from the north and west, and settling in the tree-tops with an immense clamour; on the dry turf at the edge of the wood two or three rabbits, with a single long black stripe down their backs, were hopping about. Bimbo set off in pursuit, and was recalled with difficulty. Amber, lovely as she thought the place, rather regretted the interruption of the move; she had been learning some rather important things about Rupert, she felt; she would sooner have stayed where she was. But when Bimbo had been brought back and made to "sit" beside them—"Did you read any others?" Rupert asked, pulling the dog's ears.

"Yes—one called 'In Self-Defence.' "

"Well, what did you make of that?"

"I thought it very good," the girl said slowly. Somehow, sitting here *with* Rupert, with his face quite near to look at, she felt a great security, from which she looked back with surprise at her fright over that poem when she first read it. It was an additional safety, in some odd way, to talk of it to him. "Very good," she repeated.

"Why? What do you know about it?" he asked, as if surprised at her commendation. She did not answer immediately, and in a moment he went on, as if he didn't want an answer—"That's an angry one, if you like. I'm surprised at your liking it."

"Oh, but it's true. And it isn't angry—it's only what you call it—self-defence. People can't help struggling for existence," said Amber, without choosing her words.

"By George, you *do* know something about it!" said the young man, staring at her in astonishment. He continued to look at her in silence for a moment; when he spoke again, she had a feeling that he was saying something different from what he had meant to say.

"So you think it's allowable to resist love, but not to hit back if you're hurt—is that it?" he asked. Amber nodded. A certain breathlessness made it difficult to speak. Rupert was talking now with a seriousness that was new to her, and he was talking of love. As if fascinated, she watched his hand on the dog's neck, moving among the silky curls in such skilled caresses. It was as though that hand had something of its own to say to her—some message different to his actual speech. But now he was speaking again. "I daresay you might manage to love and be hurt without hitting back," he said. "You're very generous—I can see that. You'd probably be rather a safe person to love." He paused— and Amber sat listening to the noise her heart made, in the enormous silence that his words left behind them. Suddenly he shifted his position, leaving Bimbo; propped on an elbow, he looked up into her face. "But you'd get possessive in the end," he said. "Even *you* would—you all do."

"Do we?" Amber said.

"On the whole, yes," said Rupert with finality. "I suppose love is the devil, for you as well as for us, and you can't help it. But I think women have a sort of dishonesty in love that men don't. *I* don't know!" He got up, as if to close the argument. "Come on— let's go and have a bite of supper, Amber; you must be starving."

The "bite" consisted of hot soup, a variety of cold deliciousnesses, an iced *soufflé* and a bottle of Lieb- fraumilch in a bucket of ice. Everyone lives well in Peking, but Rupert's food was in a class by itself; the perfection of all the accessories to the meal was some- thing to which Amber was quite unused, even at Lega- tion tables. She sat in a curious state of consciousness, like that we experience in some kinds of dream—at once intense and remote; everything Rupert said seemed to come from a long way off, and yet to be charged with significance; she heard her own replies, saw her own and his gestures, as through a sort of haze. But the haze was partly one of enchantment; there was something sweet and frightening about the intimacy of the whole

Chapter Nineteen

DURING the next two months Amber gave way, in an unprecedented manner, to the evil habit of day-dreaming. At Pei-t'ai-ho, by the sea, she rode, walked, played tennis, swam four times a day; was taught to dive without her hands by Sir James Boggit, and to open her eyes under water and catch falling coins and cups by George Hawtrey; ate enormous meals, relished the rain when it rained, revelled in the sun when it came out again. She learned the correct seat on a donkey, well over the tail, and so mounted hooshed along the narrow field paths between the tall maize and *kaoliang*, or down the sandy donkey-track that runs throughout its length beside the one long road which links together the three miles of villas of the pleasant straggling wooded resort. She also learned never to put on anything but a bathing-suit or a wrapper till 5 P.M. and became quite accustomed, on that same road, to ride about in a ricksha with a bathing dress and a painted paper parasol as her only costume on her way to bathing-parties at other people's *p'engs*. Like everyone else, she consumed quantities of ginger biscuits and cherry brandy on the beach at these parties, before riding back, damp but warm, the way she had come. Her creamy skin turned a deeper cream, her bronze-red hair grew bleached on top; freckles assembled not only on the bump on her nose, but all down her arms and even, as Hawtrey pointed out, on her insteps and shins; colour came back into her cheeks. She was strong and fresh and amused and occupied. But she was not fully satisfied or con-

tent; a hidden hunger gnawed her; and for false contentment and illusory satisfaction she turned to dreams of
Rupert. Drowsing on her hot bed during the siesta in
the darkened room, sitting out in a *chaise-longue* on the
terrace after supper, by sunset and moonrise, while
Hawtrey dabbed the ankles of the ladies with Muscatol
against the mosquitoes, lying on the short turf above the
rocks at Lighthouse Point, she deliberately surrendered
herself to dreaming of Rupert.

Day-dreams are peculiar things. Essentially of course
they are merely an expression of one's hidden wishes; but
that curious engine, the human mind, imposes on them
certain limitations. To satisfy it, even in their own in-
substantial fashion, they must be in character, wearing
the aspect of known reality; in their fragile and unreal
sort, true. The mind, then, seizes on the known reality
as the raw material of the fabric which the heart has
bidden it to rear; broods on it, works on it, speculates
on it; living as it were in closest contact with the object
of its desire, it makes the utmost use of every fragment
of knowledge, every word, look, tone, change of expression or shade of temper. Out of these the dreamer
creates his beloved illusion, remoulding nearer to the
heart's desire his actual experience. But he may never
falsify this experience, or the dream withers; he can only
amplify it, project the known further, so to speak, along
the lines of possibility into the wished-for unknown. And
this imperative need to keep the dream as real as possible,
this patient and concentrated brooding on the secret
possibilities of known aspects, does often bring about in
the dreamer a quickness of perception, an interior knowledge, which may stand him in good stead in actual con-
tacts. But the dangers outweigh the advantages—too
often the reality, less pliable, cannot be moulded to
the dream; and he falls back from it disheartened, in

exhaustion, nervous and mental, into lassitude and listlessness.

Amber passed her late summer, then, in day-dreams. And the wish round whose fulfilment they hovered was that Rupert should be fond of her as she was of him. But she was under the compulsion already pointed out to keep the dream true, to continue the phantasy along the lines of the reality with which she was familiar. For two months she stood staring, as it were, at the Rupert she knew, seeking to see if this thing was in him; listening in her mind to forms of words in which such an admission could come living from his mouth, examining and discarding sequences of events which might bring it to pass. Love has no more pathetic manifestation than this fantastic imagining—its only sterile activity. And by the end of the summer Amber had practically decided that that could be; that what he said and did and was, showed it to be within the limits of possibility, at least.

Both Joanna and Hawtrey, watching the girl's occasionally absorbed and withdrawn face, wondered what it was that held her thoughts in such a spell. Joanna briskly assumed that it was "one of those two"—those two being of course Rupert and Hawtrey; and for all his cleverness and his devotion to Nugent, she hoped it wasn't Rupert. There was something difficult and hard about him, she considered; he might be unreliable. (Joanna had by this time naturally heard of his past affair with Mrs. Leicester, which did not incline her very particularly in his favour.) Whereas Joe, in spite of his rather naïve airs of a *galantuomo*, *was* reliable, she thought; he was just the sort of man, once married, to spend the rest of his life carrying his wife's gloves and fussing over her health and complexion; besides—her mind just brushed this in her rapid review—he was a Duke's cousin and very rich. And cleverness and insight weren't everything in marriage—in fact, quite definitely, you *could* have too much of them, as of all other good things.

Mr. Hawtrey, for his part, though inclined to fear the worst, thanked Heaven for these good weeks without his rival, and made the most of his opportunity. But only within the limits which Amber had imposed; it was strange to himself, this new harness which bridled him— the wish to let someone else have their way. And how odd her way was! Strolling along the paths of the Legation Compound, or sitting on the little plank seats above the sea, they wasted long precious hours of fragrant dusk or divine moonlight (which had been far better spent in kisses, his arm round her delicious slimness) discussing horses! Mr. Hawtrey really deserved (and certainly gave himself) a good deal of credit for his self-restraint on these occasions.

It would, however, have been a great mistake to imagine that these dreams and yearnings made Amber actively unhappy, or that she pined. On the contrary there were moments, especially on wet and rough days, swimming out alone into the sea, surmounting near dark and foaming horizons, when she experienced a strange sense of triumph and conquest, an almost spiritual exaltation; when she told herself that *nothing* mattered, while there was sky and sea and strong conscious motion; that she could face not getting Rupert, even, if these things endured. She remembered then Nugent's words about embracing experience, and made them part of her contest with blown spray and towering crests; returning to breakfast with a conquering air that startled Joanna, and set Hawtrey's heart hammering. Hawtrey too was, in a way, a source of pleasure to the girl; there was something both comforting and supporting about his unfailing good-temper, his real kindness, his constant readiness to further any and all of her plans; while his

physical splendour, as he dived, swam, or stretched upon
the shore, was a thing to make the beholder feel that
Nature was somehow richer than one had supposed.
She confided to him her scheme for getting a griffin, and
Joe, while inclined to feel that racing was a man's job,
and better let alone by the women and children, nevertheless offered all sorts of assistance. He would see about
griffins in Tientsin when the draft came down—he was
sure he could arrange a stable; he would help with
training.

The one thing Joe would *not* do—there are limits to all
devotion—was to accompany Amber on her longer
walks. Quite a short residence in North China has the
effect of depriving Europeans of the use of their legs, and
everything but the mildest of strolls is looked at askance.
Amber had not yet reached this stage, and her passion
for long walks was regarded as a form of mania, and not
so harmless at that.

She had set her heart on walking along the eleven
miles of shore to Ch'ing-wang-tao—not because she
wanted to see it, but because it is most desirable to walk
to a *place*, in China, in order to get a roof over your head
for the three hours in the middle of the day when ex-
posure to the sun, even in a topi, is dangerous; and because there were lovely sand-dunes on the way; she had
seen them over and over again from Lighthouse Point.
This project encountered almost universal opposition.
Sir James thought it *outré*, and spoke vaguely of possible
bandits—"and you'll ruin your pretty complexion, my
dear child. Take me a good ride instead." Joe refused
point-blank to go: he also worried over Amber's complexion, and premised quicksands along the shore.
Amber found her only ally, most unexpectedly, in Burbidge. Burbidge would love to go; she liked a good long
walk; it would make a change. This reinforcement

enabled Amber to get her way with Joanna; a donkey and donkey-boy were engaged to show the way and carry the lunch, and at six o'clock one morning they set out.

The eastern sun was level in their eyes as they crossed the neck of land which joins Lighthouse Point to the coast, and skirted round the seaward end of the ridge behind the village. Beyond this point all was new and unexplored, and with considerable exhilaration the pair trudged along the faintly defined track across the saltings, sand-flats and water-meadows which formed a sort of neutral territory between the sea and the land. On the right lay the blue and sun-warmed waters of the Gulf of Pechili, lapping idly against a long curve of dazzling white sand which faded away, in the distance, into a faintly pencilled dark bluff with tall wireless masts rising from it—their destination; on their left stretched a low line of dull green, the edge of the endless marshy plain which here separates the mountains from the coast —a line made soft and undecided by innumerable knots and tufts of small silvery willows, their rounded tops as light and shapeless as lumps of green cottonwool. Now and then they came to a wide stretch of water, where one of the coastal rivers ran out; these looked formidable, but, perched in turns on the donkey, Amber and Bur-bidge, the latter with shrill peals of amusement, forded them dry-shod, while the donkey-boy splashed alongside. Amber was very happy. The place had a curious simple loveliness, a landscape reduced to its barest essentials; the low flat planes of white and blue and dim green were restfully satisfying to the eyes, the solitude and silence, in which the light clop of the donkey's feet on damp ground matched the gentle hesitant plash and rustle of the break-ing and retreating water, most soothing to the spirit, after the rather concentrated companionship of the Legation bungalows. Burbidge was an ideal companion;

she seldom spoke unless first addressed; if she did volunteer a remark, it was of a shrewd obviousness which was as soothing as silence, and funny as well.

After some miles of going they reached the sand-dunes, and Amber insisted on turning aside to explore them, indicating to the donkey-boy that he should wait on the shore. The dunes ran up, in curiously steep and mountainous shapes, to a height of over a hundred feet in places, but the wonderful thing about them was their colour. They were not yellow or fawn at all, but a sort of peach-pink, fading to purest white; all through them grew great tufts of stiff prickly grass of a bright silverblue, like sea-holly; here and there in the hollows, most surprisingly, were little pools of water, overhung by those same silvery willows which grew in the marsh. A pink landscape with sky-filled pools, bordered with blue grass and set with silver willows is really something to exclaim about, and Amber exclaimed. "Yes, Miss," said Burbidge temperately, when called upon to share her enthusiasm. "It does get into your shoes, though, doesn't it, Miss?" Amber laughed, and struggled up the tallest crest in sight. From its summit she looked out over the whole expanse of the coastal plain, from north to south, as far as the eye could reach, of that cool green; behind it rose the mountains, fantastically steep, of an improbable blackish blue. But now her eye was caught by a nearer sight—the donkey and the donkey-boy, trekking placidly inland through the dunes. She yelled to them, waved and pointed towards the shore; but though the boy turned and looked at her, he continued quietly on his way. There was nothing for it but to follow, and shouting down to Burbidge directions as to the easiest way to take, Amber set off in pursuit. When she reached the tracks she sat and waited for Burbidge, then they went on together. Now a near-by rattle broke out, as of rifle-fire.

"I hope we aren't coming to a battle, Miss," said Burbidge. Surprised and uneasy, they walked forward, till rounding a shoulder at the end of the sandhills, the reason for the boy's manœuvre became plain to them. In a clearing among the reeds and bushes, numerous American soldiers were carrying out musketry practice with both rifles and Lewis-guns, firing seawards; to continue along the shore would have been to cross their line of fire. Following the donkey, Amber and Burbidge skirted round the rear of these military exercises, and presently reached a green embankment stretching right and left across the plain; climbing it, they found themselves on the metalled track of a railway.

It was now nearly nine o'clock, and getting hot; they were hungry, and decided to breakfast. The donkey-boy produced the food, and squatted down at a little distance with his own "chow"; seated peaceably on two sleepers, Amber and Burbidge ate tomatoes, buttered biscuits and hard-boiled eggs. While they were thus employed a man on a bay pony came cantering along below the embankment and hailed them. "Say, you seen a grey pony loose anywheres?"

"No," Amber called back.

The man rode up below them and halted. "Well, I guess he ain't gone far. You taking a walk?"

"Yes—we're going to Ch'ing-wang-tao," Amber replied.

"You come all the way from there this morning?" the man asked in surprise.

"No—from Pei-t'ai-ho."

The man whistled. "Gee! You girls are some walkers, ain't you? How do you figure to get back from Ch'ing-wang-tao? Train?"

"No, we shall walk back," said Amber, amused.

The man gaped at her. He was a tall, fair fellow,

good-looking; his flat-brimmed pointed hat revealed him for an American soldier, but the rest of his dress was of an almost cinema picturesqueness, consisting of a khaki jumper much patched in odd colours, opening down the chest on a singlet, and a pair of loose blue twill trousers.

"Well, you must be pretty smart walkers," he was beginning, when Amber interrupted him.   "Look, there's a grey pony, over by the trees!"   She pointed.

"That's the cuss!" said the man, and wheeling his horse round he went off in pursuit, disappearing among the scrub.   Amber and Burbidge continued their breakfast —they had reached the coffee stage when their new acquaintance appeared again, a couple of hundred yards further up the line, leading the grey pony; he dragged it up on to the embankment, handed it over to a Chinese, and then rode slowly back towards them.   On reaching them he dismounted, put his horse's reins over his boot, and sitting down on the edge of the embankment pulled out a packet of Lucky Strike cigarettes, lit one, and proceeded with the conversation where he had left it off. His curiosity was insatiable, though quite inoffensive; to meet two women breakfasting on the permanent way of the Peking-Mukden Railway was apparently something of an event in his life, and he was determined to make the most of it.   Time seemed no object to him; when Amber offered him a cup of coffee he drank it gratefully, and when the little caravan set off again on its way to Ch'ing-wang-tao he declared his intention of "coming a piece" with them.

After following the embankment for half a mile they turned down off it and took a track through the green scrub of the plain.   Presently they reached a little river, and when Amber prepared to mount the donkey to ford it, at the donkey-boy's request, the American observed, "If you kin ride, you'd better get on my hoss and cross both at once." Nothing loth, Amber mounted and splashed through the ford, while Burbidge followed on the ass. The American waded. They were still close to the railway, and at this moment a goods train came rattling over the bridge above them; the "hoss," startled, plunged wildly forward; Amber let him out along the track, steadied him, and wheeling in an open space, brought him to his master again. The Yankee grinned approvingly at her. "You surely can ride! I thought I'd lost two hosses this morning, when I saw him quit off." He made Amber remain in the saddle, while Burbidge rode the donkey; strolling beside the pony, he discussed "hosses" with this startling young person who set out to walk twenty miles for pleasure, and rode a strange pony with perfect assurance in a summer frock and tennis shoes. And from this chance encounter something rather important emerged for Amber. Her new acquaintance proved to be a horse-master and vet, attached in those capacities to the American troops in China; every autumn he went up to Jensi, far beyond Kalgan, to buy ponies for the army. When, seizing this heaven-sent opportunity, she confided to him her secret ambition to buy and race a couple of griffins, he entered into the scheme with enthusiasm; promised to choose her out two of the likeliest he could find and bring them down for her to Peking. They might cost her, he said, as much as a hundred and sixty dollars apiece; Jensi was a long way off, but the ponies there were big, and the little ones "'re no use to our boys." He and Amber exchanged addresses, scribbled on bits of sandwich-paper; his name was Johansen, she found, a Swedish-American, which accounted for his fairness and height. He was as charmed with Amber as she was with the prospect of getting two choice griffins chosen by an expert; when they came to the wide river outside Ch'ing-wang-tao he insisted on taking her camera and walking across the viaduct on the sleepers, in order to get a photograph of her riding through the water below. Beyond this river they took to the shore again, and Amber amused herself by jumping the pony over the small streams which cut the sand into shallow steep-sided channels, smacking him on the quarters with her soft felt hat to make him move; Johansen watched her, smiling, and observed, somewhat to Burbidge's horror, that she was "a great kid."

They parted by the Japanese wireless station on the outskirts of the town. The day was clouding over, and soon a drizzling rain began to fall. Amber and Burbidge conscientiously examined the coal-stained harbour, the pier and the railway sidings, which were as dull and ugly as those of any other small seaport; then they took a couple of rickshas and drove round the rest of the place. It failed to please. The villas of the Kailan Mining Administration employees stood, commodious, neat and dull, along straight sandy roads among groves of acacias.

"It puts me in mind of Woking, Miss," said Burbidge; and indeed, except for the prevailing tree being the acacia and not the Scots pine, the residential quarter of Ch'ing-wang-tao is exactly like the suburbs of Woking. They lunched in the only hotel they could find, a very "family" affair with a strong resemblance to a boarding-house at Margate; lay down for a couple of hours on two *chaises-longues* in the verandah, and then set out to find the donkey-boy and return home. The donkey and his attendant were to have met them by the pier at three o'clock, but there was no sign of them there. They waited for a quarter of an hour. "Well, we can't hunt for him all over Ch'ing-wang-tao," said Amber finally. "We'll leave him to find his own way back." They started homewards, but as they approached the wireless

S

station they saw, lounging on the sand under the barbed-wire fence, first their new American friend, and then the donkey-boy and his charge. Whether the donkey-boy liked Johansen's company, or whether he had decided that the American and his own patrons were now one unit, it was impossible to discover—anyhow there he was, and for the first four miles of the homeward road Amber, as before, rode the bay pony, and Burbidge the ass. At the sand-dunes they parted from the American for the second time. "Well, you'll get me two really top-hole griffins, won't you, Mr. Johansen?" said Amber, smiling up at him.

"Sure thing! I'll get the hosses to match the girl!" said the American, wringing her by the hand. "S'long, Miss Harrison! S'long, Miss Burbidge!" He swung himself over the bay pony and disappeared in the direction of the camp.

"What sort of a man should you suppose he is, Miss?" Burbidge asked, as they plodded, a little stiffly, along the shore track. It was clearing from the west, and the sky in front of them was a flare of gold under the departing clouds, throwing a lurid metallic lustre on the green of the willows, and making the brackish pools dazzling.

"Well—apart from being very nice—he might be almost anything, Burbidge. I believe the Marines come from a very good class; schoolmasters and all sorts of people volunteer to come out here, just for the fun of it."

"He was very free-like in his speech to you, Miss," said Burbidge, a little dubiously.

"Americans are very democratic, you know, Burbidge," said Amber sententiously; "I'm afraid you're not."

"Well, no, Miss. But then you see I've always been in very good service," said Burbidge complacently. And Amber thought, for the twentieth time that day, that

Burbidge was really better company than almost anyone
at Pei-t'ai-ho. She was what Anna would call "zo
genre." Then her thoughts drifted off to company *not*
at Pei-t'ai-ho—to Rupert, away in Peking. But that
afternoon her thoughts were peaceful ones. Mile after
mile, along the shore, while the glory in the pools grew
stronger and the green line of marsh vegetation turned
to translucent enamel, she walked in a sort of dazed contentment, bred of nearly twelve hours of hard exercise
in the open air, of lovely new sights, of one ambition
realised, of another brought a step nearer. It was
enough, during that long trudge home, to know that
Rupert was alive in the same world—this world which
held so much of serene beauty: the golden stretches of
water, the black cattle grazing on the amber grass of the
salt-meadows. She loved, and she could wait; for the
moment this was enough; the heart sang a still song,
clear and gentle as the flooding light on sea and land.
And delicious when she got in was the cocktail on the
verandah, solicitously administered by Joe; the hot tub
in the sparrow-splash in the little tiled *cabinet de toilette*
attached to her room; the coming out, lazy, cool, and
ravenous, to dinner on the terrace, to be plied with
food, with wine, and with questions. The story of
Johansen went down well; when the Minister strolled up
after dinner to enquire and to collect a fourth for bridge,
he was greeted with a variety of accounts: "They got
mixed up with the American Army, Sir."—"My dear
Sir James, she got off with a vet.!"—"We swopped
addresses, Sir James!" But when Sir James, having
made a suitable diplomatic joke about this new Anglo-
American *rapprochement*, carried Mrs. Grant-Howard off
to the ministerial bungalow for bridge, Amber told Joe
about the griffins, which she had suppressed at dinner.
"I *wish* I knew where to keep them," she ended up. "If

I have them at the Temple, they won't be like my own horses."

Then Mr. Hawtrey had an inspiration. "Why shouldn't we run a joint stable, together?" he said. "I could definitely lease half his stabling from Harry, and we could keep two or three *mafoos* out at the Insects, to run the race-ponies; quite separate from my string at the Legation." He expounded the scheme in detail, thinking it out as he went along, and Amber, tired as she was, caught his enthusiasm. "But what shall we call it?" she asked. "We'll give it some fancy name, like The Press," said Joe. "I've got it!" he exclaimed a moment later.

"What?" Amber asked.

"The Portfolio Stable!" said Joe triumphantly. "And all the ponies Ministers! Minister for War, Minister of Marine, Minister without Portfolio! Ha-ha-ha!" Laughing, Amber agreed. She could think of no better plan, and there were lots of things she would find it hard to manage alone; Joe would be a great help. "Do you think we could keep it a secret?—for a bit, anyhow?" she asked rather wistfully. "It would be so much more fun."

"We damn well will, if you want to," said Joe.

Chapter Twenty

"HULLO, Amber, my dear! Marvellous to have you back! Let's look at you! You haven't half browned your funny phiz!"

This greeting of Rupert's, in the full publicity of the station platform at Peking, caused Joanna to turn her head towards the pair with a slight question-mark about her eyebrows. But Amber was too happy to notice anything. Actually she turned a little pale under her tan when she first saw Rupert—after weeks of dreaming, the solidity of his actual presence was literally a shock. But how much more satisfying than any dream! As they walked along the cinder-path under the City Wall towards the Watergate, exchanging news, comparing notes, with all the zest of two people whose life holds much in common, Amber remembered how she had first walked there beside Rupert, shy and silent, last February, when he asked her if she had feelings about the Flag, and she wondered if he was the poet or not. For a moment she saw him again as she had seen him then, untidy (his coat collar was half turned-up again today!), with his queer mouth and light-brown hair and light eyes—a rather odd, strange man; and—so timid and perverse is the human heart—she had an instant's regret for that day, when he *was* only a stranger, whom she could meet on equal terms, free and independent, and not the person who had put her peace of mind in his pocket. But it was only for an instant; the next minute, with a happy laugh, she put up her hand and turned down his collar—"You *are* untidy, Rupert!" And when

he replied, "Well, damn it, we can't all dress like Joe!"
she laughed again with full content.

There is no better test of how well we like a new place
of abode than to return to it after an absence. And
judged by this test, the Grant-Howards found Peking
to come out very well when they returned there in the
middle of September. Nugent had gone down to Pei-
t'ai-ho for the last three weeks, when the Minister and
Hawtrey returned, and came back with the others. And
when, approaching the east wall of the city, he caught
a glimpse from the train of the Temple of Heaven, a
solitary jewel on the skyline, he felt—rather to his surprise—that little stir of warmth which a man feels when
he nears his home. He, too, remembered his first arrival,
as he sat later that evening in his study, going through
the telegrams—remembered his thoughts and doubts in
this very room—and contrasted with his frame of mind
then this jolly familiarity, this sense of belonging to the
place and in a way owning it; of knowing your way round,
of being established and secure. He had been up to the
stables to see the ponies, who whickered at him from their
dark stalls with delighted recognition—what a noisy
fellow Buick always was!—while Wang and Shang kow-
towed and grinned with an unmistakeable pleasure; he
had gone on to see the Minister, who greeted him with
unusual effusion as "My dear felloh"—an effusion which
lost none of its value in Nugent's eyes when he found that
it arose mainly from the fact that His Excellency was
extremely bothered about "this felloh Li's goings-on
about the Customs." Here was a job of work, a problem
to consider; he had gone over to have a drink with Leroy
and discuss with him whether the Marshal's tendency to
raid funds to which he was not entitled could best be
restrained by a show of firmness or by giving him more
"face." "He's still harping on those aeroplanes, that's

really the trouble," Leroy said. "Nothing will persuade him that we aren't, *sub rosa*, backing Wang." "I thought that was all settled ages ago," said Nugent. "We told him we couldn't do it."

"My dear G.-H., nothing is *ever* settled in this country," Leroy boomed at him. "The great mistake Europeans make in China is to suppose that you *can* get a solution of any question, or that anyone wants it! There's nothing the Chinese like better than a good unsettled dispute, hanging on for years—unless it's a good grievance! It's the breath of life to them—like sermons to a Scotsman, or making money to a Yankee. Talking of Yankees, did you hear what old Schuyler said to the Minister?" He told a funny story, and Nugent presently went home, chuckling to think how like itself Peking still was.

Joanna, after her own fashion and in her own sphere, experienced the same sense of familiarity and assurance. She had learned by now that devotion such as Chang's, on the servants' part, was by no means incompatible with the utmost pertinacity and ingenuity in the matter of squeezing her. No doubt to make up for the lean weeks, almost devoid of entertaining, at Pei-t'ai-ho, on her return to Peking she found the *ch'u-tzu's* weekly totals suddenly mounting sky-high. But now Joanna knew how to deal with him. To complain, to scold, was worse than useless; "face" was the one adequate weapon with which to quell him, and she used it. She invited a small company of intimates—Rupert, Joe, Amber, Mulholland —to lunch. When the second course arrived, she tasted it, put down her fork, and, exclaiming "But this is horrible!" called to the servants to remove it instantly. "Tell cook to make an omelette instead—at once." She apologised to her startled guests—"I *am* so sorry." The *ch'u-tzu*, who according to his custom was peeping through the crack of the hatch to see how the meats of his

preparing were received, departed, chittering with distress, to make an omelette, which shortly afterwards
appeared. Next morning, on her progress through the
back regions, Joanna in due course reached the kitchen,
and received with chilly *hauteur* the kow-tows of the cook,
Leeti-Cook and the three kitchen-boys. She examined
the cook's account, neatly written out in English of a sort
by Liu; then, turning to her Number One, she said in
Chinese—"Considering how the *ch'u-tzu* squeezes me,
I think he might at least not send in not-good food when
I receive guests. Yesterday I must send rice from the
table—I have no face left."

The cook, clasping his hands, pressed forward, wailing
out—"T'ai-t'ai, the food in what fashion not good?"
Coldly Joanna turned to him. "I with *this* man speak"
—she indicated the Number One. "Are you here to
speak or to listen? In my opinion, I am here to speak,
and you to listen." Having thus crushed the cook, who
stood back abashed, she continued, in cold impersonal
tones, her complaint to the Number One. The food was
bad; she said so; had it been good, she would not have
sent it away and thus lost face before guests. She tapped
the account-book; give sight here—how immense was
the squeeze! Great squeeze and exceedingly not-good
food, and face lost, was an exceedingly not-good plan.
Liu was too intimidated to make his customary defence
of the cook, and after scanning the menu for the day,
crossing out an item here and inserting a different salad
there, Joanna left the kitchen. She knew, the cook
knew, and the Number One knew that the dish in question had been, as always, perfect; all three knew that the
others knew it too; but the T'ai-t'ai had inflicted a great
loss of face on the cook. In fact, it was recognised that
she meant business. That week the cook's accounts
dropped like a stone, by over fifty per cent; in a month

or so, Joanna knew, they would begin to creep up again —then she would repeat the farce. Writing up her own accounts, later, from Liu's book, she laughed to herself. What fun it was! She glanced out through the open window—all along the edge of the loggia, and up both sides of the steps from the garden, stood pots of chrysanthemums in full bloom. But not chrysanthemums as we understand them—Chinese ingenuity could never be content to leave a flower with the decorative possibilities of the chrysanthemum to bloom as it chooses. Each pot held a stout upright stalk, like a standard rose-tree, at the top of which bloomed a round bush of flowers. Not all of one sort—grafted on to the branches of the parent plant, a strong-growing artemisia, were bronze, crimson, white, yellow and pink blossoms, in every sort of combination of colour—sometimes two shades, sometimes three or five. Like immense nosegays they trimmed the loggia, with taller ones, three feet high, standing on the steps and in the middle of each archway. The house was full of them too, only for indoors the colours were not mixed—great drifts of white or mauve or orange filled the corners of every room, stood sentinel by the doors, washed round the foot of the staircase. She could smell them as she sat. Heavenly to have these millionaire-like masses of flowers everywhere, Joanna thought, without even having to order them; to enjoy this incomparable service, this perfect food, a whole string of jolly ponies. Peking was really rather good value.

Autumn in Peking is perhaps the loveliest of all the seasons. After the great heat of summer there is something divine about those brisk October mornings, crystalcool, with a tang in the air; the days of brilliant sunshine, hot but not oppressive. The courts of houses and temples are brilliant with chrysanthemums; out in the country the willows spin fine-leaved golden patterns against the sky, shed them, still delicate in decay, upon the quiet waters of canals, upon the earth, returning now again to its beautiful uniform brown. The fields are full of stooping blue figures, lifting the harvest of pea-nuts and sweet potatoes, and later digging out the roots and stumps of maize and *kaoliang* — they bind them in bundles to burn them. Though the crops are not all up yet, the area of rides spreads every day; the leaves of the ginkgos are as primrose-yellow as their tiny golden apples which fell a month before; sometimes there is mist before sunrise. The last of the convoys of solid-wheeled, blue-hooded carts come creaking into Peking along the narrow sandy tracks from the north and west, before the Gobi Road closes for the winter. And upon all these scenes and activities the sun, glorious and splendid, shines all day long, pouring out over the beautiful and busy earth a flood of light of a quality and brilliance beyond European imagining. The great continent of Asia, the greatest land-mass in the world, is cooling down after the terrific heating of the summer—but how slowly and temperately, with what a matchless serenity of atmosphere and light and colour. Here, undisturbed by the turbulence of cyclonic currents, by the intrusion of oceanic winds or moisture, the seasons pass in majesty, still, glorious and slow, with the large royalty of movement of a planet in stellar space.

Mortals use such a combination of cosmic forces for their own minute purposes. The Chinese peasant gathers his harvest — the European employs the perfect weather for expeditions. Early in October a rather miscellaneous party set out from Peking with mixed objectives. Nugent Grant-Howard, Benenden, Henry Leroy and Harry Leicester were going for a few days' wild-goat-shooting to the Kou Wai Miao, a temple in the mountains not far from the foot of the Nan k'ou Pass;

Joanna, Mrs. Leicester and Amber desired to see the Ming Tombs, which lie in the same direction; for the general convenience, and because Leroy wanted to bathe a rheumatic instep, the whole party decided to sleep at the sulphur springs of T'ang-Shan, where there is something in the nature of an hotel. A donkey-train with the men's equipment preceded them, and on Saturday afternoon the party drove off in two cars, Leroy's indefatigable old Dodge, a war-veteran of various Gobi Expeditions, and a hotel hireling.

The road to T'ang-Shan runs north-east from Peking, and swings round a spur of the Western Hills into the great semicircular bay of plain which lies at the foot of the Nan k'ou Pass; T'ang-Shan lies at the eastern tip of this bay, the Ming Tombs within it. Since the Nan k'ou road is one of the great gateways into the Peking plain, the plain below it is frequently the scene of battles for the control of the pass; and owing to fairly recent fighting, the travellers found the road in a very peculiar condition. For miles trenches and small earthworks, flung up just beyond the willows which shade it, bordered it on the northern side; this was merely interesting. What was of more immediate concern was that all the stone bridges had been blown up, and then hastily and incompetently patched with rough wooden structures, which were now in process of falling to bits, so that chasms four and five feet wide gaped in the planking. This necessitated a particular technique for crossing. On reaching a bridge the occupants of the car leapt out, ran cautiously on to the bridge and surveyed it; decided rapidly which was the soundest side, and proceeded to tear up planks from the less good one with which to stop the largest gaps in the other. The chauffeur was then instructed to "stand on the gas" for all he was worth, and the empty car shot at headlong speed across the crazy erection. Sometimes, however, the bridge was definitely non-carrossable, and there was nothing for it but to send the cars smoking and splashing through the fords.

The hotel at T'ang-Shan was a pleasant little place, rather reminding the party of Italy, with its low white-washed buildings round an open courtyard, its arcaded loggias for meals, its oleanders. In the court itself two vast marble basins, at least thirty feet long, steamed under the sky as the glass-green waters of the two springs bubbled up in them; here also were smaller tanks, a couple of feet square, like manholes, for individual dippings; the moment he arrived, Henry Leroy rolled up the leg of one trouser, plunged his foot into one of these, and sat there on its marble rim, smoking a cigar and reading a newly arrived copy of *The Times* with great contentment. Joanna produced her embroidery; Lydia merely lay back in a chair and smoked—there was a curious still look of languor about her, as of a piece of mechanism whose mainspring is missing. Amber, whose heart was teaching her so much, guessed the reason; she felt that she knew just where the almost physical sense of weight and emptiness lay—and forgetting that it was all very wrong, she was simply sorry for Mrs. Leicester. Possibly she would not have been so observant or so sympathetic if Rupert had been talking to her, but he wasn't; seated at a table with bottles of beer, he was en-gaged in one of his prodigious literary discussions with Harry Leicester. "My good Harry, there is *only one* pre-scription for style," she heard him say. "Well, let's have it, Keyserling," said Harry reasonably. Not having read *The Travel-Diary of a Philosopher*, Amber didn't know why Rupert should laugh so much, and even Leroy lower his *Times* to say "Haw! Haw! Haw!" "You've simply got to hold the nose of your mind to the grindstone of an idea, and go *on* holding it," Rupert pronounced.

"Nothing but that will produce a style worth having."
All this seemed to Amber incredibly dull; she was rather
at a loose end, and was wondering how she should fill in
the time till dinner, when Nugent strolled into the courtyard, came up to her and said, "Come and look at the
gardens here, Amber." Delighted, she went off with him.

The gardens of T'ang-Shan have a good deal of *Shan-
shui*, as is only proper. Paths wander among little
groves, round tiny mounds crowned with small fanci-
ful buildings, and past miniature lakes. There are no
flowers. Such gardens suffer less from the onset of
autumn than ours, but there was nevertheless an indefinable melancholy about the place as Amber and
Nugent strolled through it. Dead leaves floated on the
surface of the pools, and lay scattered through the empty
pavilions; the low light threw long shadows behind the
trees; on the evening air hung an autumnal smell of
decay.

"It smells almost like England," Amber said, as they
strolled along the sedgy border of one of the pools.

"Yes, it does. Do you think a lot about England out
here?" Nugent asked.

"Not so much as I did at first," Amber replied.

"Which did you think most about, the place or the
people?" Nugent wanted to know. He paused to light
a pipe, and the leisurely action produced a comfortable
confidential atmosphere which Amber liked; she always
felt tremendously at home now with Mr. Grant-Howard.
She considered her answer, leisurely too. "The people,"
she then pronounced.

"Several people, or one person, really?" Nugent next
enquired. Coming just then to a seat—"Let's sit," he
said. The casual way in which he asked his questions
and then said something else, leaving them in the air,
was very reassuring.

"Why do you ask that?" Amber said—but not, as he realised, in the least defensively.

"Because one so often does think mainly of one person," he answered. "And ever since I first saw you, I got the impression that you were doing it."

"Oh! Why?"

Nugent put another match to his pipe. "Do you remember nearly missing the boat at Southampton?" She nodded. "You said you wanted to buy a book, but when you came on board you hadn't got a book. So I assumed you'd either been seeing him or telephoning to him."

Though she was startled into a blush, Amber laughed. "I'd been trying to telephone to him, but he wasn't in," she said. It was strange to look back now on that misery, strange, too, how comfortable it was to be speaking of it to Mr. Grant-Howard.

"What happened to him?" Nugent asked.

"It was all over—dead—even then," she said. "I was a maniac to try to telephone to him, only at the time I felt I had to." This time Nugent nodded. "One does," he said. "But why was it dead? Or would you rather not tell me?"

Amber did not answer at once. She sat looking in front of her—at the leaves on the pool, at one or two which came floating down, gentle and silent, from the willows which overhung the bench on which they sat. Did she want to tell Mr. Grant-Howard about Arthur? In one way she would rather have talked to him about Rupert and her present problem, but in another way that was impossible. And then, what had happened with Arthur was rather like—no, that wasn't it; the thing was that *she* was the same; she hadn't known about Arthur, and so she had made a mistake; she didn't know with Rupert, and so she was afraid—though less so just lately —of making a mistake with him. If she told Mr. Grant-

Howard about Arthur, he would say things that might help her with Rupert. Yes, and there was more to it than that; she had never really told anyone about it, and somehow she would be glad to—and who was there in the world that she would rather tell than Mr. Grant-Howard? Another leaf came floating down and settled on her dress. She picked it up, and folding it round her finger she said, "No, I think I will tell you."

The story when it came was very much what Nugent had expected, only with a sharper, more tragic twist. He did not remember—men don't remember these things—that when her name was first mentioned between them his wife had surmised that Amber might be running away from a young man, and that he had suggested that she was even more probably running away from herself. But he learned now the truth of both these crude statements, and he saw too, as he had long guessed, that of the two the second represented the more permanent and essential condition. With a courage and a clear-headedness which he could not respect too warmly, the girl made absolutely clear where the cause of her disaster lay—she had made a mistake, and leaned on it, built too high on too frail a foundation; her misery and humiliation had sprung from a situation of her own creating; it was no one's fault but hers. And Nugent guessed, too, that far as she had run from herself, her problem remained the same; he, like Joanna, had watched her with the two young men—he more than suspected that she was in love with Rupert, and well as he knew Rupert, he had not been able to decide how much he cared for Amber. That there was no understanding yet between them he was certain. So when, at the end, she said—"You see, I was such a complete *fool*," he realised how much at the mercy of her own folly, as she chose to call it, she probably still felt herself; throughout, her emphasis had lain,

rather strangely, on her incompetence rather than on
her unhappiness, great as he saw this to have been.

"No, you weren't a fool," he said. "You made a mistake which it's very easy for anyone to make. For some
mysterious reason, it's a form of mistake which is considered to be highly respectable in young men, and rather
disreputable in young women." The judge-like way in
which he made this pronouncement made Amber laugh.
"None of that is the point," he went on. "You say you
didn't *know* him enough. I doubt that. You didn't
know all the facts about him; he was carefully concealing
them, so you couldn't. But don't you think you probably got to know him, as a person, much better than you
would have done if you hadn't fallen in love with him—
more in love with him, perhaps, than he was with you?"

Amber considered this—largely, it must be said, in the
light of her more recent attempts to know Rupert. "Yes,
I expect I did," she said eventually.

"Then I don't see why you call it a wash-out," said
Nugent. "If you believe, as I and most sensible people
do, that knowing people and loving them are two of the
most important forms of human knowledge and human
activity, I don't see what you've got to worry about."
He wanted, quite passionately, to wipe out her sense of
humiliation, of waste; it was the one thing which he felt,
with an urgency that surprised him, that he couldn't bear
her to endure. As she said nothing, only continued to
twist the yellow and silver willow leaf, he went on—
"What makes knowing people so expensive is that to do
any good with it you've got to love them, to some extent.
Oh yes, I know all that in the books about love being
blind—but the fact remains that nothing but love, affection, in some shape or form, gives real interior knowledge.
That's simply a natural law, though the only person
who's really given it much publicity since St. Paul is

Pirandello, and he only by implication.   But Pirandello's implications fairly bite you."

"I've only seen Henry the Fourth," said Amber.

"Well, it sticks out of that a yard," said Nugent. "Don't you remember when they take the psychologist to see how the madman is getting on, and there is he, and the other Doctor, and the Countess's lover and all the rest, fussing about, being clever—but the one person who guesses that Henry has really been sane for years, and is only shamming, is the Countess. She's quite a stupid woman, but she had loved Henry once, and even the poor ghost of that old tenderness gives her vision where the rest are blind."

"Yes," said Amber after a moment's consideration. "I see that now you say it, though I hadn't thought of it before."

"It comes in nearly all the plays in some shape or other," said Nugent. "Pirandello is obsessed by the problem of reality, and especially of how different reality is for each person; but all through his work, if there ever *is* a solvent of differing realities, a fusion of outlook, it's affection that brings it."   He attended to his pipe again. "That's why I can't think it so deplorable when I hear that someone has 'loved in vain,' as it's called," he went on.   "How can you love in vain, if the activity of loving is one of the highest there is?   Loving is an end in itself —why should it lead to anything?   We always think it's wasted unless it leads to marriage.   Well, marriage is all right; it can be a great work of art, it's indispensable to human life at its best, but you can't go harnessing a spiritual activity like love to it alone.   There are all sorts of love that can never be crowned with temporal rewards and successes."

He stopped abruptly, and Amber felt that he had almost forgotten about Arthur and herself.   She dragged

T

him back to her problem. "One *feels* wasted, oneself, all the same, when you love a person and they don't want it."

"Good Heavens, yes! You feel it, of course. It deals a frightful blow to one's whole personality when that happens," he said. "But though you can't be expected to see it at the time, most people are better value for having loved, whatever came of it."

Amber compared this swiftly in her mind with some of Rupert's statements on the same subject. "Even if love makes them discontented or angry?"

Startled, Nugent swung round to look at her. Sitting there, quietly concentrated, with her pretty honest face and clear eyes, her generous mouth, those words struck a note completely alien to her whole being—he could not have been more surprised if a mouse had run from her lips. Staring at her, as she sat absorbed, suddenly he saw that this was Rupert in her; she was giving utterance to his thought, using his words. Oh, poor child! This went deep indeed. Nugent knew that stage of the actual invasion of the personality by another, when the very mind is dyed with that other's attitude and conceptions. So it was as bad as that!

"I don't think loving ever makes a person angry," he said. "That poor word is so misused. Surely only 'Love,' in the Continental sense, does that."

Struck by this, forgetting that she might give her secret away, "That's just what Rupert said!" the girl exclaimed. "How funny!"

"*How* funny!" echoed Nugent, a little grimly.

Chapter Twenty-one

THE expedition to the Ming Tombs ended in the muddle and confusion which so often attend European enterprise in China. The plan was admirable. The donkey-train and the men were to start early on foot, accompanied by Amber, who could not forego the chance of a walk; Mrs. Grant-Howard and Mrs. Leicester were to go later by car with Leroy, who wished to spare his instep—they were all to meet for lunch "at the Tombs." But alas for imprecision! The Tombs surround a large valley; it is three miles at least from the entrance P'ai-lou to the Yung-lou, the largest tomb; and neither Leicester, nor Nugent, nor Rupert, nor Amber realised this fact. It was only when they had walked for some eight miles, and entered, under the walls of a ruined fort, a flat valley studded in the most Claude-like manner with groups of trees, that they grasped the problem, on the donkey-boys enquiring, at a fork of the path, whether lunch was to be at the P'ai-lou or the Yung-lou? They had no idea. In the end Nugent decided to go with the donkey-train to the Yung-lou, which, it was established, was on the way to the Kou Wai Miao; while Amber and Rupert were to be led by Leicester, who thought he could find his way, to the P'ai-lou, there to intercept the car.

Whether Harry really could have found the way soon became a matter of academic interest to Rupert and Amber, since he walked so fast that they lost him in the first mile. After interminable wanderings through the valley, which seemed, and is, a vast place, during which they both got more and more worried and cross, they found themselves, at two o'clock, hungry, thirsty and exhausted, at the P'ai-lou; where, however, there was no car, no friends and no lunch. A peasant, who was quietly rolling the newly ploughed earth round the very foot of the marble pediment of that marvellous five-arched structure, with a stone roller hitched behind a donkey, was persuaded to unharness his ass and trot off on it to the Yung-lou, bearing a note for Leroy scrawled on the back of an envelope, after he had testified to seeing foreign devils in a gas-cart pass that way. And at three-thirty gas-cart and T'ai-t'ais reappeared. They had gone straight to the Yung-lou; one always did, Leroy said so; Rupert and Amber were their poor dears, but they were clearly made to feel that they were also very foolish ones; Harry had not turned up at all, and was so excessively foolish as not even to be a poor dear—he was merely tiresome. Rupert was to hurry up and go on to join the others—he could not miss the way, there was an avenue of marble animals. And after hastily devouring some lunch he did so, with a cheerfulness which in the circumstances Amber felt to be quite heavenly minded. She found it hard to emulate this serenity, or Mrs. Leicester's extreme calm over the temporary loss of her husband; she had looked forward for weeks to seeing the Tombs, and was bitterly disappointed.

On their return to Peking, however, all disappointment was swallowed up in a fresh excitement. Joe came round to the Hei Lung Hu-t'ung after dinner, still in riding clothes and looking darkly mysterious, and demanded to see Amber alone. Her two griffins had arrived, and he had just returned from settling them in at P'ao-ma-ch'ang. There was also a letter, rather grubby from travelling in the underclothing of a *mafoo*, from

Johansen to Amber. The American regretted that he could not leave Tientsin at the moment to bring them himself, but he hoped she would find them "O.K." "I think they are a good pair. I told you I should send a horse to match the girl, and I think he is the best." Joe began to laugh when Amber read this out. "What is it?" the girl asked. But Joe would not tell her—he would only giggle and say that she would see tomorrow, and that her Yankee friend was quite a wit.

Amber did see next day, when Joe drove her out to P'ao-ma-ch'ang, where he had taken a stable, not from Harry Leicester, but from a business man called Miles who was going home for a year. Joe's head *mafoo* was already installed there with his griffins, which had arrived some weeks previously, a dark bay and a white—pending better names Joe called them Port and Folio respectively, but the *mafoos* called them simply the *hung ma* and the *pai ma* (the red pony and the white pony). With thirsty curiosity Amber gazed at her new possessions, as Li paraded them in the stable-yard before her. One was a pale smoky grey, what the Chinese always call a *ch'ing*, or bright pony; the other, as Hawtrey delightedly pointed out, was "the horse to match the girl"—a red chestnut, whose thick furry coat was "just the colour of your nice thatch, Amber." They were both big, for China ponies, thirteen hands three, the maximum allowed by the Peking Club rules. Little else could be seen of them, clad as they were in their bear-like over-coats of long soft hair, but both had good heads. The grey showed temper—he lashed out wildly; "*Yu chin,*" said Li, grinning. *Chin* (pronounced *jin*) is an almost untranslateable Chinese word, meaning both strength and violence—a powerful man or a vicious pony are alike said to "have *chin.*"

And "*chin*" the grey pony continued to show. Clipped

and groomed, he proved a shapely creature; so did the chestnut.   But whereas after a certain amount of training the latter could easily be handled and ridden, the grey pony remained very intractable; his head had to be put in a sack before any European could hope to mount him. Mr. Hawtrey's turn of mind being what it was, it was not surprising that he soon christened Amber's two griffins Gin and Ginger.   Their official names were to be Minister of Finance and Minister of Marine, because one was copper-colour and the other a battleship grey—but Joe and Amber and Mulholland (who had been retained as jockey and was privy to the whole scheme) always called them Gin and Ginger and nothing else.

These two animals now absorbed a vast amount of Amber's time and thoughts.   Griffins arrive rather low, after the long trek down from Mongolia, but gradually they were got into condition.   There was no violent hurry, since Joe had decided that the Portfolio stable should not make a start at the autumn race-meeting, for which Johansen's griffins were in any case too late, and serious training would not start till the spring.   But both he and Amber, to say nothing of Li and Mulholland, had the utmost curiosity to see what the four new acquisitions were "good for," and for this purpose they were steadily trained up to ordinary paper hunt standard.   It very soon appeared that Johansen had done Amber pretty well.   Both Gin and Ginger were fast, much faster than Joe's new pair; and the more speed they showed, the more secretive and cunning Mr. Hawtrey became about them.   Joe had a child's love of secrecy for its own sake, and here there was a real interest involved.   He would not allow Amber to ride either of them in the drag-hunts, and for training gallops he chose the most unfrequented spots he could find—out beyond the Eunuch's Temple, perched on a crag above its persimmon orchards, or away to the north of Maude's bridge. It became increasingly evident that nothing in Joe's stable, Pertinax or any other, could touch the Ginger Griffin for speed; nor could Bananas or Curaçao, a pretty pony which M. Rothstein had presented to Amber. But none of these were real race-ponies, and the great desire of the owners of the Portfolio stable now was to try out Ginger against a pony whose speed was known.

Here Amber came in. Besides training her own ponies, she was doing a lot of riding with and for Uncle Bill, who was preparing for the paper-hunting season. Her light weight, good hands and hunting experience made her a useful, even an ideal person to put up on ponies who were being taught to jump, and she spent hours on the field behind Uncle Bill's temple, controlling the wild and stag-like leapings of some ponies, and discouraging in others, less mercurial, a tendency to butt the jumps down with their chests. In her privileged position, it was easy for her to borrow a pony, even a race-pony, from Uncle Bill, and she borrowed Berry, who had just won two races in the autumn meeting and was still fairly hot. They took him out to a flat sandy stretch of country beyond Maude's bridge, where reasonably smooth going could be obtained for nearly a mile; and there, Mulholland riding Berry and Amber the Ginger Griffin, they tried them out. The result was astonishing. Ginger was not trained to a flying start, and Berry left him at first; but presently the griffin came up, and ride Berry as he would, Mulholland only won by a neck. The Portfolio owners were enchanted. It was clear that in the Ginger Griffin they had a pony with an amazing turn of speed. "If he'll do that when he's not even half trained, what will he do when he is?" said Joe triumphantly.

So far they had kept their stable a secret from everyone

but Mulholland. But certain difficulties beset the path
of pretty young women when they embark on a partnership, even of the most businesslike character, with handsome young men. And these difficulties were not long
in forcing themselves on Amber's notice. That connected with the attitude of other people arose first. Aunt
Bessie, absent-minded and absorbed in her bridge, was
slow to notice anything, but Uncle Bill had sharper eyes.
He observed that Amber, instead of riding impartially, as
before, with Hawtrey, La Touche, Leopardi, Mulholland
and the Leicesters, now rode perpetually with Joe. He
mentioned it to Bessie. "The child is sensible enough,
but people will talk. You'd better keep an eye on her."
Aunt Bessie, thus admonished by the infallible Bill, kept
an eye; she saw, and then she spoke. "My dear child, I
think—you are very young, you know; don't think I think
any harm, but young people—your Uncle thought——"
It emerged gradually from such utterances as these
that what Aunt Bessie and Uncle Bill thought was
that Amber rode rather too much with Mr. George
Hawtrey. Blushing, a little distressed, Amber greatly
relieved her Aunt by bursting out laughing. "Oh Aunt
Bessie dear, it isn't that; there isn't anything in that.
Don't worry." But she had to explain—swearing Aunt
Bessie to secrecy, she did so: "Joe and I have got a stable.
I've bought two griffins and he's bought two. And of
course we've got to ride them, you see. That's all it is."
To make matters more secure (for Amber knew quite
well where the directing mind lay in the Hei Lung
Hu-t'ung), she tackled Uncle Bill as he sat in his
"den." "Uncle Bill, will you keep a secret? I know
you can."

"Oh, I can? Thank you, Amber. Well, I might, if
it's a good one," said Uncle Bill, swinging round from
his roll-top desk. Actually he imagined for a moment

that he was to hear of an engagement that he would have welcomed; he had a great respect and liking for Joe. "All right—carry on," he said.

"Joe and I," began Amber—and Uncle Bill smiled expectantly—"have got a stable," she said, and Uncle Bill frowned.

"A stable! What the devil do you want with a stable? Can't you get riding enough at the Temple?"

"Oh yes, yes, masses, Uncle Bill darling! Don't be hateful! But I wanted to race ponies of my own. That's quite different, don't you see? So I've got some, and so has Joe. We're partners," said Amber eagerly. "We meant to keep it quite a secret, till the spring—but Aunt Bessie is worrying because I'm with Joe so much, so I thought I must tell you both *why* I am."

"H'm," said Bill, and nothing else. After a moment, "Where did you get your griffins?" he asked; there being no satisfactory engagement, his mind turned naturally to the practical and ever-absorbing subject of the horses themselves.

"Joe's came from someone in Tientsin, but an American called Johansen brought me down mine, specially," said Amber.

"Johansen? How in the world did you get Johansen to bring you down ponies? He's as sticky as Hell about selling to anyone but his Yankees," said Bill in great astonishment.

Amber explained. She made Old Bill laugh with the story, and then laid an embargo on him. He was not to *see* her griffins, or ask about them, or anything—"else it will just be *you* training them. Everyone knows you can train, but I do so want to have a try, by myself."

"But I thought Joe was helping you?" said Uncle Bill.

"Oh, Joe!" said Amber.

As she was leaving the room, Uncle Bill called her back.

"I say, Amber—was that what you wanted Berry for, to try out your new Bengals?"

"Yes—and you're not even to *won*der how they stood up to him!" the girl said, coming back and standing beside him. "Promise!" she said, and stooped and gave him an unwonted kiss on his bald patch. Uncle Bill carefully and insultingly wiped his head with a bandana. "You're asking the impossible," he boomed after her, as she ran out.

The other type of difficulty is a more personal one. Amber's reassuring statement to Aunt Bessie was rapidly falsified. A few days later she and Joe took a long ride out beyond the Eunuch's Temple, into the rough stony uncultivated country where the sparse pale bents of wild grass make a sort of veil over the thankless yellow soil, and where sometimes you may see a bustard run, swift as a dog though ungainly as a turkey. Amber was riding Gin; she was anxious to handle him into a more reasonable shape, for he was fast enough to be worth training, though not the equal of Ginger. They were galloping along a track where the ground on both sides was pock-marked with deep pits and hollows, when a crow arose suddenly from a heap of carrion, almost from under their horses' feet. With a loud "Cark!" it spread its black wings like sails, and flapped off. The grey pony took fright—shied wildly, and bolted sideways; the next moment, to Joe's horror, horse and rider plunged together into one of the deep stony pits.

For a wonder, when they were pulled out neither was seriously hurt. The pony had a tear down his shoulder, unsightly but not deep, from a sharp stone, but he was not lame; Amber was limping from what she imagined was a kick on her knee, and had a nasty broken bruise near her right temple—but, though sore and shaken, she declared herself quite able to ride home. Joe really fared the worst—even when the extent of the damage had been fully examined and proved to be slight, he was curiously white, his voice high and unsteady. Nothing would induce him to allow Amber to ride the *Ch'ing Ma* back to P'ao-ma-ch'ang, though the shock and fright had reduced the pony's *chin* considerably—he was temporarily quite docile; she was made to ride Folio, and the little party trotted home very soberly, the *mafoos* in the rear, Joe asking the girl every other minute if she was *sure* she felt all right? He was experiencing for the first time in his life that desperate and agonising concern with the welfare of another human being which love first reveals to most people, and to some first reveals love. He could not forget the horror of the moment when he saw the pony falling sideways into the pit, and Amber along with him—in that instant, in a flash of knowledge, he realised how completely all happiness, for him, was bound up with that bright head which went down among the stones. And in the car, driving home slowly (as he had bidden the chauffeur to do), he told Amber so. He didn't do it very well—Joe's glib phrases deserted him in moments of crisis. "Amber darling, you know you were angry when I kissed you, but this isn't kissing. I—I—I wish you would marry me—I do love you so. Won't you? I'm sure I could make you happy—I would take care of you for ever."

Poor human love, so eager and so self-convinced!— poor words with which we dim its glow! Pathetic belief in our own competence at the great task of loving! Mr. Hawtrey, like the rest of us, exemplified all these things when his turn came. But his sincerity was for once evident, and the refusal which Amber had to give caused her some genuine distress. "Oh no, dear Joe, I couldn't, possibly. No, don't—I *know* I couldn't." And when Joe pressed her, still, even in this moment of clearsightedness, slightly under the influence of his theories about how to deal with women, she turned him off with the practical. "Do let it alone, *please*, or I shall have to chuck the stable. I told Aunt Bessie there was nothing in us, when she fussed." Joe had to laugh. "But there *is* something in us, Amber, *mein liebstes Herz*."

"Not unless you make it! No really, Joe. Promise to let it all alone till after the races, anyhow. Do please."

And Mr. Hawtrey, thinking that this sounded rather like hope, but still more under the influence of his strong desire to let his dearest heart have what she wished, promised.

Amber was a good deal disconcerted by this episode for several reasons. It disturbed her theory of Joe as a person who, though kind, though devoted to her, and of whom she was very fond, was in some way emotionally negligible. His white face, his uncertain voice, the un-mistakeable accent of deep feeling when he proposed to her, all went to disprove this idea. And that fact made it both unfair and unsafe to use her friendship with him as a sort of smoke-screen for her love for Rupert, as she had tended to do. But on the other hand she *couldn't* give up the stable. It was all very difficult. For her own part she cared hardly at all for public comment on herself and Joe, while she shivered under the very thought of it in connection with Rupert; but she was honest and generous enough to credit Mr. Hawtrey with feelings as sensitive as her own (in which she was to some extent mistaken) and felt that she must protect *his* secret too. She must no longer say airily, on a day when she had had a stroll with Benenden and a ride with Hawtrey, that she and Joe had had "*such* a ride to So-and-so"—she must mention both, or neither.

And it was just at the moment of its removal that she was forced to realise how much she needed a smoke-screen to hide herself and Rupert from the hard amused curiosity about any form of love-affair which is the breath of life to the bulk of Peking society. A few days after her tumble she was bidden to a party at M. Bruno's. It was a "cocktail and *zakouska* party," with two forms of invitation card; which began as an ordinary At Home at six, but continued, for those who received invitations to that effect, as an evening entertainment nourished by a cold-supper bar. Amber and Rupert were among the privileged few who received such an invitation. The Bessarabian had a house in the East City, small, but decorated and furnished with real virtuosity; his walls of golden silk, his ivories, his jade and bronzes were famous even among Chinese collectors, whose icily artificial politeness about the artistic acquisitions of foreigners is normally the most crushing of social experiences. His food and drink matched his dwelling—people usually found it convenient to accept M. Bruno's invitations.

But the evening brought Amber a double shock. When the earlier guests had filtered away, Joe and the Grant-Howards along with them, the remainder assembled round the *zakouska* tables, with a pleasant and rather conspiratorial sense of selectness, to eat caviare just come in by the Trans-Siberian railway, *vol-au-vent* of quail and white truffles, great helpings of Strasbourg *pâté*, and Bosnian figs in ginger syrup—and to drink vodka, champagne and Russian brandy from the Imperial vineyards at Erzerum. Afterwards they drank coffee in a room furnished with low opium-tables and piles of cushions on the floor. The company consisted mainly of what even Amber's inexperience recognised as the less *rangé* elements of Peking society, and in a mood of peculiar recklessness at that—the scraps of conversation which she caught from time to time were in a vein not usually to be heard at Legation entertainments.

She was slightly discomfited at finding herself in such a gathering with no support but Rupert's. And it was then that she got her shock. She was sitting with Rupert when Mme. de Bulle came by. The lady greeted them with her usual crude archness—"*Vous voilà très bien installés, tous les deux!*" Then, with a glance of evident intention—"*Plus ça change, plus c'est la même chose, hein?*" she said to Rupert. Amber followed the direction of her glance and saw Mrs. Leicester standing a few paces away. And in a flash the meaning of Mimi's gibe broke on her. Perhaps in England she might not have taken the point, but in this gathering she could not miss it. Of course!—and while Rupert, admirably collected, drawled out some casual reply, the girl's mind went flying back over the past, finding incident after incident which bore out this new discovery. Mrs. Leicester's strange remarks to her at that first luncheon with Hawtrey, and her advice to stick to people like Joe; the way Rupert sighed and said "Poor Lydia!" the day she quoted her to him, at tea in his room—and other small things, looks and words and avoidances, unnoticed at the time, but which now took on a fresh significance. She was thankful when Rupert soon afterwards took her home. Bowling through the cold starlit lanes and *hu-t'ungs*, past draughty open spaces where the marble of temple gateways glimmered faintly across the grey ground, Benenden was silent—no cheerful words, called forward and back, broke the steady patter of the coolies' feet. Even when he dropped her before the red door in the Hei Lung Hu-t'ung Rupert did not speak; but she heard him shout a final "God Bless!" as the red doors slammed.

Chapter Twenty-two

I T was some time before Amber could get over M. Bruno's party. The certainty which had come to her there, that Rupert had once been in love with Mrs. Leicester, was alone enough to keep it in the foreground of her thoughts. In theory of course she had always recognised that Rupert must have loved other people, but to be brought face to face with the fact, and the actual object of his late affection, caused her a distress which surprised her. She watched Lydia now when they met with a painful intensity, as if there must still be about her some visible trace of Rupert's love. She read the poems again, looking for her there; ashamed of so pitiful a curiosity, she could not refrain from dwelling on Mrs. Leicester in conversation, and piecing the results together. Rupert had known her in London, before he went to China—the "pale room" might be hers; her lapses into vagueness fully justified "but half the time you are not there at all." Though then he didn't know about Chinese villages, reflected Amber, innocently unaware that dates mean little to poets; and that woman he had called a shifting tease—surely this was not the Mrs. Leicester she knew? But she *had* shifted; she had changed to loving Bruno, incredible as this seemed to the girl. And had Rupert suffered then as she suffered over Arthur? And was he, too, feeling "safety first" about anyone else? Was that why he was so changeable, said so many things which *might* mean all she hoped and might, again, mean nothing but general amiability? Ignorant and innocent as she was, the theory, sharpened by this new distress, took on an edge which cut pretty near the truth.

Besides this, she was profoundly disconcerted to find that she and Rupert should have attracted attention. Waking early, she would lie staring into the glacial darkness of her bedroom—Uncle Bill, like the Chinese, did not believe in overheated houses in winter—tormented by those flashes of preternaturally clear and remorseless vision which assail the undefended mind at 5 A.M.—thinking, that to be *affiché* with her like that might well frighten and irritate Rupert, and drive him away. She found it hard to reply with easy unconcern when the ladies of Peking said to her—"You see a good deal of Mr. Benenden, don't you?" Often they said she saw a good deal of Mr. Hawtrey, it was true; but though she minded that less, she disliked it, as she disliked all the misplaced archness of the T'ai-t'ais. No one in Gloucestershire had ever commented on her and Arthur to her face like that.

She was really rather glad when chance gave her an occasion to speak of it all to Joanna. She had been lunching with the Grant-Howards; Mrs. Schroff made some joke to her about Hawtrey in Joanna's hearing, and even her dear Touchy, when she asked some small favour of him just as he was leaving, said—"Why not ask Joe? Isn't he your devoted slave? I'm sure he can't refuse you anything."

"Damn the man!" exclaimed Amber when the door shut behind him, and she was left alone with her hostess. "Joanna! You heard Touchy, and you heard that inane Mrs. Schroff. People talk like that all the time here—they *never* did at home! Does it matter? Is it my fault, or are they being silly fools?"

"The standard of gossip is higher in Peking, and the standard of"—she nearly said "decency," but changed it to "manners"—"lower, than in any other place on earth, I should say," replied Joanna, with unwonted energy. She realised a number of things that Amber had not said—how much the girl wanted a lead, how very little use Aunt Bessie would be in such matters. And her resentment about Peking manners was quite unfeigned. She had been there long enough to understand the causes of that curious intellectual and social disintegration which affects so many white women in China. With servants so abundant and so excellent, even on the narrowest income, as to make housekeeping a pleasurable trifle, with no duties to the poor or to dependants, with few books, and in many cases with no children to occupy them, they are left with vast tracts of leisure, which they fill with bridge, flirtations and rather malicious gossip.

"You can write off four-fifths of what they say," she said. "But actually, though it's natural that you are thrown together a good deal with those two, I have thought lately that you were seeing rather a lot of George Hawtrey, myself."

Once again the secret had to be sacrificed. "Well, you see, Joe and I have got a joint stable," Amber said. "That's why."

Joanna's eyebrows said "The devil you have!" but her mouth merely observed "Oh, have you? What fun!"—which made it all the more startling when the next moment she asked, "Do they propose to you much?"

The colour flew into Amber's face, even while she could not restrain a laugh. "Well — yes and no," she said, rather hesitatingly; "not *much*," she ended, more firmly.

"Well—" Joanna reviewed the girl's colour, her laughter and her hesitation, and decided that it was the wrong one, from Amber's point of view, who had proposed; whichever that might be! "Yes, I think you'll have to publish your stable," she said with decision. "It

U

won't stop these women talking—nothing will do that, but it will give you a good answer about Joe. Do the Harrisons know?"

"Oh yes—I had to tell them, because Auntie B. fussed," said Amber.

"One mark to Auntie B.!" said Joanna amiably. "I shouldn't worry about it if I were you," she pronounced finally. "Young men have no reputations, and there's no question of your being silly enough to risk yours. Riding is intensely respectable, thank goodness! But come to me if there's ever anything you want to ask, won't you? Now I *must* go and ride."

Amber left the Legation a good deal comforted, and set off in her ricksha for an afternoon's Christmas shopping. She was having some crystal trees made for the Grant-Howards, at Tai's in Morrison Street, and the alabaster pots for them had to be chosen. This done, she went on to the bookshop, housed among the coiffeurs' establishments on the ground floor of the Peking Hotel, to choose a novel for Uncle Bill. Which led to another knotty problem. What about Joe and Rupert? It would be awful, if they were to give her presents, to have none for them; on the other hand it would be even more awful to butt in with presents to them if they had not thought of giving her any. Poor Amber—these Victorian scruples complicated life for her greatly. In the end she bought *Toi et Moi*, which she wanted badly for herself, to give to Rupert at a pinch, and a new horsey book on the Forward Seat, to which the same applied, as an emergency gift for Joe. Dickie was having a party on Christmas afternoon, and if her presents were needed, she could take them then, she reflected, as she sat huddled in a ricksha, driving up the Hata-mên to the French *Confiserie* to get Dickie's chocolates, and some red caviare for Aunt Bessie's dinner that night. The *Confiserie* was crowded—there was paper holly on the counter, and a general Christmassy feeling about the place; Amber felt a little thrill, half home-sickness, half pure happy excitement, as she stood waiting to be served. One has to be much more than twenty-two to lose that peculiar thrill of expectation, the wonder as to just how affection will manifest itself tangibly in gifts. Surely *he* would give her one? And Joe, too?

Amber need not have worried—they did. Her place at the breakfast-table on Christmas morning was piled with packages and flowers. Peking society goes rather a burst over Christmas; pot-plants and chocolates are cheap and non-committal, and Amber was much more popular than she knew. "But how extra*ord*inary!" she kept on saying, as she turned up the cards of her various acquaintances, like Major La Touche, Mulholland, Mimi de Bulle, M. Leopardi, the Rothsteins and Countess Anna, on rose-trees in pots, on baskets of *glacé* fruit, on bottles of French perfume. But when she had carried her presents off to her sitting-room, flitting to and fro, singing, through the bright cold courtyards, it was over three in particular that she at last sat smiling by the stove. A T'ang horse from Joe, which Uncle Bill said was a real beauty, a collector's piece; Pirandello's plays in translation, from Nugent Grant-Howard; and Rupert's present, a bird in black crystal on a little carved wooden stand—a lovely piece of craftsmanship, with that indefinable amused sophistication about it which is so intensely Chinese. She studied the card which came with it, reading it over and over again—"To wish you all the luck in the world, in real things. From R. B. B." Of course, the bird was a crow—he was reminding her of that evening at the gate of the Forbidden City after she had won the Ladies' Hunt, and their argument there; he was having a dig at her love of horses. How like him! But was that really all? "All the luck in the world"—it was a warm, a comprehensive wish, she thought, reading it once more—seeking, the gift received, to draw the richest possible treasure of assurance from the manner of its sending, as older people have been known to do.

She took her two books off to Dickie's party that afternoon. Dickie had insisted on a battle as his celebration of the season of peace and good-will, and the entire personnel of the Legation, male and female, marshalled themselves in two armies, whose objectives were to defend a hundred green flags in the "forpress," and to capture a hundred red flags from the Chancery Porch, the G.H.Q. of the opposing force, nearly a quarter of a mile away— and vice versa. For over an hour the grown-ups reverted to childhood; the compound rang with shouts and cries, and with startling reports from a huge supply of Chinese crackers, imported by La Touche, and let off by privates at intervals; prodigies of valour and cunning were performed by everyone. The Bishop, hotly pursued by the Military Attaché, eluded him by leaping into a car on the Square and out again by the other door; Sir James executed a brilliant coup by driving up to the Chancery porch in his own car, snaffling a dozen flags, and driving off with them to the Leroys', whence, concealed in an umbrella, he took them by way of the shrubbery and the septic tank to Dickie's stronghold. Drawn by the noise, a crowd of curious Chinese gathered in the Jade Canal Road, in the hope that another raid like that on the Soviet Embassy might be taking place in the Ying-kuo-Fu—they melted away, regretfully, when the k'ai-mên-ti informed them that the foreign devils were merely having a difference-not-big strike-shoot (the Chinese version of a sham fight). Amber's military exploits were negligible —she was generally, Joanna noticed, being chased by either Joe or Rupert, or both, so hotly as to make her a useless combatant. But she enjoyed herself prodigiously. Rupert was in a heavenly temper, and when she was periodically captured, and marched off to imprisonment at the Chancery headquarters, there were intervals of conversation in which to tell him how much she liked his crystal bird and—rather ostentatiously—to praise Joe's T'ang horse.

That night there was a small dance at the Legation, after Sir James's dinner to his staff. "Who in the world put you on to Geraldy?" Rupert asked Amber, when he had thanked her for his present.

"Oh, you *hadn't* got it already?"

"No no—but I'd seen it. It's damned good—I'm frightfully pleased to have it. But how did *you* know of it?"

"Why shouldn't I know of it?"

"Because it's not exactly a *livre de chevet* for *jeunes filles*," said Rupert.

"Nugent lent it me. I think you're being rather Victorian," said Amber, a little affronted.

"Come on and dance and don't be silly!" said Rupert, putting his arm round her as the music started again. "You know perfectly well that if there *is* an unshorn Victorian lamb in Peking it's you, you blessed child."

This, as a matter of fact, was perfectly true—and truer then than it had been six weeks before. The shock of the Bruno episode had driven the girl back on to the old conventional preoccupations from which contact with Rupert had begun to free her, and had roused into activity a latent reaction against the moral carelessness about her. These influences, too, blew like an east wind on the confidence which Nugent had tried to create, and revived her natural uncertainty. But that night, dancing and arguing with Rupert, she could even forget

Lydia Leicester, and she finally went to bed in that very rare state of human blessedness, of thinking that it was hardly possible to be happier than she had been all day.

In that she was wrong. There was a night, a few weeks later, when she lay down in such a blinding extremity of rapture that for hours she could not sleep. At the Great Cold, that year, snow fell in unusual abundance. It fell on a Friday, and riding was impossible over the week-end; on the Saturday morning Rupert sent a chit round to the Hei Lung Hu-t'ung to ask Amber if she would care to go for a walk on the Wall that afternoon, to see the city under snow. Without waiting to write a note, she scrawled a rapid "Yes, rather—2 o'clock," against her name in his well-known green chit-book.

The unfamiliar white streets, stained brown with traffic in the centre, the delicious unwonted dampness in the air, filled her with physical pleasure as she rode in a ricksha to the Legation, where she found Rupert waiting at the entrance. They drove on to the Watergate, and struggled up the ramp on to the Wall. Tracks were visible—someone had been there before them, and as they walked along the huge flagged top, broad enough for two lorries to drive abreast, they presently came on Dickie and Burbidge, engaged in a smart snow-balling encounter with the two or three Marines who guard the American wireless station and the barbed-wire barrier which closes the European section of the Wall at the end nearest the Ch'ien-mên. In theory Europeans are not supposed to pass this barrier; in practice the more enterprising do—Rupert and Amber had already taken several strolls beyond it, along the little paths, used by goats and goat-herds, which wind between the growth of thorny vegetation that has sprung up between the flagstones, turning the neglected summit of the great rampart into a wild pasturage, where hoopoes flit in spring, and where in autumn a crop of "Peking dates," the stony fruit of a wild thornbush, is gathered, to be crystallised by the sweetmeat-sellers, stuck on wands, and sold to the urchins of the city. After a brisk exchange of snowballs with Dickie, Rupert, to Amber's great relief, withstood the child's entreaties to be taken with them, and they squeezed through the barrier and set off by themselves. They passed round under the great crimson pillars of the gate-tower of the Ch'ien-mên and ploughed along the narrow path—the stems of the bushes stood up, brown and bare, above the dazzling surface, with here and there a withered fruit clinging to them, or a frayed brown leaf whipping in the wind; the crenellated parapet, roofed with snow, cut a white mediaeval pattern against the blue of the sky. Amber wanted perpetually to stop and look through the embrasures at the city below, where the roofs, emphasised by their white surfaces and the shadows under their deep eaves, took on a new importance of shape, their strange curves standing out sharply among the faint pencillings of the bare trees.

"They look like masses of sabots!" she said on one of these occasions, gazing down at them.

"What extraordinary things you think of!" Rupert said.

"Well, but don't they?" she persisted, turning her face, vivid with cold and exercise, back to him.

"Of course they do—only no one but you would have thought of it," he answered, with one of his sudden brilliant smiles. "Come on, *piccolina*—I want to get to the corner, and we've none too much daylight in hand."

Happy, stirred by his smile, his use of the pet name, enjoying this common enterprise, Amber pushed on behind him. Out beyond the Shun-chih-mên it was all new to her. They were approaching the south-west corner of the Wall; in the great angle below it, the city thins out vaguely into scattered houses and temples among open stretches of ground, with ponds and thickets —a strange sight within the walls of a town. Amber would have liked to linger and look, but Rupert was talking, and she would not have interrupted him for anything. They had got on to poetry again, by way of a discussion on the peculiar excitement caused by the sight of snow, and Rupert was maintaining that excitement was essential to poetry. "It just depends on whether you are capable of being *really* moved and excited by the visible world, whether you can write nature-poetry or not. Most people can't—places only move them in connection with some other emotion; whereas anyone can get excited about a person," he said, talking with the peculiar brusque roughness which Amber had come to connect with his feelings being roused for any reason. "That's why good nature-poetry is so rare."

"But *you* get excited about places," Amber said.

"Yes I do; but I get a damned sight more churned up about people—unluckily!" Rupert answered, as if moved by some recollection. "I wish I knew *why* one does. My God, what an amount of blood and sweat one puts into it! For months on end you can't digest what you eat, you can't do your work properly, you can't read a book—you're only really alive for the hour or two in the week when you see her, the rest of the time you're suspended in a sort of blind craving, like a desert thirst. And you turn your life upside-down, chuck up all sorts of good things, simply to be near her—and then find that it's all a plant, or that she's changed her mind and wants someone else!" He took off his hat and rumpled his hair; he spoke with extraordinary bitterness. "And when you've died a thousand deaths from misery, and are sane again, you look back and see that you acted like a complete maniac, literally like a case of insanity. God, what a waste of energy it all is!"

Amber listened to this outburst with the sharpest sensations of pity and pain. She felt certain that he was telling her about Mrs. Leicester, in all but name—to be near her he had got himself transferred to China, only to find that she preferred Bruno. *She* had deprived him of rest and food, filled his mind, upset his work—how incredibly he must have loved her! The pain was almost stifling as she thought: he can never love anyone else like that! But pain was conquered almost at once by an overpowering pity. She wanted quite terribly to comfort him, to make him see, as Nugent at T'ang-shan had made her see, the other side of what looked like waste and defeat; and under this impulse, in her simplicity, it never occurred to her to hesitate to speak on behalf of love to a person as shrewd as Rupert, with whom she was in love herself.

"I don't believe it *is* waste," she said.

Rupert stopped to turn and look at her. "You don't? Didn't you think it waste when your love-affair went wrong?—whatever did go wrong with it—you only said it was over."

"Yes, I did at the time, but now I see that it wasn't," said Amber.

"Why wasn't it?" said Rupert, with curt incredulity, walking on again—they were practically at the corner of the Wall now; immediately in front of them rose a small wooden hut, and piled about it great heaps of square-hewn timbers. As they approached, the door of the hut opened, and an ancient Chinese emerged, muffled in leggings and a sheepskin coat; he bowed and grinned at them, amiably.

"Because——" Amber was beginning, intent on her theme, when Rupert interrupted her.

"Half a moment—we must have a word with the old boy. This is where the corner-tower was, you know— he lives up here to guard the old timbers."

Amber didn't know. She had, however, suffered before under Rupert's habit of breaking off the most absorbing conversations in order to show her something, and submitted with admirable patience to being introduced to the old man—who, leaning against a notice which forbade smoking, in Chinese and three European languages, accepted a cigarette himself, and looked mildly on while Rupert lit one—and to being told the story of the demolition of the tower. There were till recently towers at each of the four corners of the city walls, and nine gates in the sides; but when it was proposed to make a fourth gate in the south wall, to relieve the congestion of traffic, it became necessary, it appeared, to pull down one of the towers, since thirteen was the correct and fortunate number of towers and gates, and to add another would have brought ill-luck.

"That's *feng-shui*—geomancy, you know," said Rupert airily, in conclusion. "You must consult the *feng-shui* experts before you start on any building. The last Finance Minister but three told me solemnly that China would never be solvent again till they moved the new Ministry of Finance, because the *feng-shui* is all wrong— it stands near a cross-roads, and the money has four streets to roll away by!"

Amber laughed. "Better put it down a blind alley next time," she said, moving over to one of the piles of timber near the parapet. Mounting the timber and looking over, she cried out in a different voice, "Oh, Rupert, *look*!"

He came and stood beside her. Beneath their feet the much lower wall of the Chinese city abutted against the one on which they stood, and ran out into the fields before turning south, with a little erection near the angle, the gate-tower of the Hsi-pien-mên; up to the north the grey line of the Tartar Wall stretched away, austere and dark above the white fields. There was something beautiful and sustaining about that huge line of masonry, imposed with such majestic decision on the snowy land-scape. And round the white plain, in a great arc, stood the Western Hills, magnified by the snow into such an unexpected height and splendour as to lift the spirit suddenly. As they stood looking at it all, in silence—"Now tell me why you say your affair that went wrong wasn't a waste," Rupert said, brushing the snow off the parapet so that they could lean their elbows on the wall.

"Because—Nugent said it to me, and I'm sure he's right," the girl said, a little hurriedly. "Love isn't wasted just because it doesn't lead to marriage or any-thing. It's worth while for itself. And besides, you can never really know people without loving them in some way, and knowing people *is* worth while, even if it's very—very expensive." She paused; her impulse had lost its momentum during the check and the discussion of *feng-shui*, and she felt that her hasty *réchauffé* of Nugent's views was not very telling; she glanced nervously at Rupert. But he was listening quietly and seriously; there was no sign of the inquisitive amusement she dreaded. "Go on," he said.

"That's most of it—I can't put it like he did. But I'm sure it's true. So you see, Rupert dear, even if she did turn you down, and you were so miserable, it was all right; you *knew* her more—it *wasn't* a waste," she said, turning to him now and speaking with the utmost con-viction the lesson she had learnt.

"Amber dear, it's a fearful thing to know some people too well," he said slowly. "Nugent is probably right about love and knowing coming to the same thing—but what if love only shows you abysses?"

His words, his tone, silenced the girl. She had been reading Nugent's Pirandello to some purpose, and understood in that moment that this was a case where two realities, hers and Rupert's, differed so widely that her words could not help him. Daunted by a sense of defeat, unexpectedly the tears stood in her eyes; she turned away her head and looked up the line of wall dominating the cold white fields. "I'm sorry," she said simply, when she had steadied her voice.

Perhaps she had not steadied it as well as she thought. "Amber!" said Rupert suddenly, in a tone she didn't know. "Amber, look at me!" And when she did not at once do so, his arm came round her and turned her forcibly towards him. Holding her, he studied her undefended face. "I thought so," he said at length. "Amber, my dear, do you know that you are a *complete* angel and darling?" He continued to hold her and look at her; then, deliberately, he kissed her cold bright face. "You know I *do* know you—rather well," he said. Shifting his arm from her shoulders to her waist, he turned her round to face the mountains, their snowy summits shining in the level rays of the low sun. "Look at that!" he said, and kissed her again. "And we both love the same things really, don't we?"

She had no words to answer with. The world had turned to music—the snowy city, held by the strength of the impassive wall, the mountains of an incredible pearl-colour, shining across the blue-white of the darkening plain, all these flooded into her consciousness, to ring there in an incommunicable harmony of bliss. It was so, then; Heaven had opened; here was certainty, rapture and peace. No words and no need of words—only silence, in which that sense of music was spreading like a

flood.   Driving home in two private rickshas which they
found waiting outside an opium-house, she was glad to
be alone to listen.   Oddly enough, the thought of Pei-
t'ai-ho, and all her doubts and questionings there, returned to her vividly on the ride—but she felt an almost
patronising pity for those poor old days.   Now she *knew*.
Lying awake, that night, too overwrought with happiness for sleep, she went over in her mind, again and again,
those moments on the Wall—Rupert's arm round her, his
kiss, his words, his strange new voice as he said "Amber."
The more she thought of them, the more utterly satisfying they seemed.   It was true he had not mentioned
marriage; but what of that?   That wasn't the main
thing.   He loved her, and she loved him.   They loved
the same things, too.   Towards morning she sank into
an unconsciousness that was hardly sleep, so vivid still
in it was the sense of a pure space walled in with hills of
pearl, ringing with music, in which a face leaned above
her and a new voice spoke the ultimate secrets of love.

Chapter Twenty-three

WHILE a theory is in the making, the maker lives, if it is an important one, in a state of tension and uncertainty, balancing probabilities and weighing hypotheses; but once it is completed it ceases to be an intellectual exercise and becomes part of the solid foundation on which we build up the rest of life.

So Amber now stood four-square on a new happy certainty which released fresh energy for everything else. The training of the griffins went steadily forward. She was much at the temple, eating Chinese chow and sitting round the blazing fire at night, while Aunt Bessie played patience, Joe talked, and Uncle Bill, with great concentration, worked through piles of papers; and waking in the morning in a room so cold that she had to hide her nose in the bedclothes to thaw the tip till the boys came in at 6 A.M. to light the coke fire. Their batterings and bangings in the grate she heard with warm, sleepy pleasure; they roused her to another spell of delightful activity—not, as so often in middle-age, to a weary bracing of oneself to shoulder the drab burden of another day.

She saw, if anything, a little less of Rupert than before —she was so busy with the horses, as the cold un-spring-like March of Peking came on. Rupert knew about the stable, which had become an open secret, and actually showed a rather detached interest in it, spiced as usual with a certain animus. "Coming to skate at the Pei-Hai tomorrow, you?" he would ask at the close of some evening gathering, as he helped her into her cloak or saw her to the car—"or have you got to jockey?" "Oh, Rupert, tomorrow I *must* ride—it's Gin's day for his long gallop. Can't we go Thursday? They'll only be exercising with the *mafoos* then."

"No, Thursday I'm playing badminton—never mind," Rupert would say, a little sourly.

"Rupert dear, you know I'd love to—but I must ride Gin myself, now Mulholland's laid up." (Mulholland had influenza that spring.) "Joe's too heavy."

"Yes, yes—okay by me," Rupert would answer. And Amber would drive off, still in reasonable contentment. It was frightful to miss a walk with Rupert, or to *contrarier* him in any way, but it didn't matter. They were *safe*; nothing really mattered any more. She had become as blandly unquestioning now about Rupert's state of mind as she had formerly been scrupulous, scrutinising and doubtful—nothing shook her serene, unreasoning security.

Nugent, watching her, did not share this security. He saw that something fresh had happened, something to give her that still look of supported happiness. But he looked in vain for signs of its equivalent in Rupert—in Joe he never even sought for them—and speculated, a little gloomily, as to what was going on. Then the Marshal's renewed activities in connection with the customs revenue took him away to Shanghai, and for three weeks he was too busy to think much of anything else.

He returned on a Saturday, and on Sunday he and Joanna drove out to one of M. Rothstein's paper-hunt lunches. "The niece has arrived," Joanna said to him on the way.

"What niece?"

"The Minister's niece."

"Didn't know he had a niece," said Nugent, looking vacant.

"Nugent, you are vague!   He's been talking about her all the winter."

"Not to me," said Nugent.   "What's she like?"

"I haven't seen her yet, but Rupert says she's rather nice; he knew her in Washington."

"Why Washington?" Nugent wanted to know.

"The mother's an American—she married James's brother. He's dead—George Boggit, you know. She's madly rich, I believe," said Joanna, producing these rather disjointed items of information like one who consults a card-index. "Anyhow, she'll be there today."

"Then we can give her the once-over," said Nugent. "Is the mother here too?"

"Oh, rather—a portentous woman; I called on Thursday, but the girl was out," said Joanna, thus completing her *compte-rendu* of the female Boggits.

In the crowded rooms at the Rothsteins' villa Nugent had an opportunity to study these new additions to Peking society.   He soon saw why Joanna had described Mrs. Boggit as portentous.   She was a big, tall woman with an imperial profile under iron-grey hair, superbly dressed, holding her massive figure magnificently; not palpably American in appearance, except for the excellence of her clothes and carriage, not noticeably so in her speech, save for its torrential and overpowering abundance.   She talked in long sentences, like an orator at a public funeral, a thing English people never do; even to hear it makes them wriggle internally, and Nugent, sitting next to the lady at lunch, wriggled and even writhed before the meal was out.

Miss Daphne Boggit was quite different.   She was small and pale and perfectly European in every way. Her light hair was smeared round her head as close and shining as treacle; her scarlet lips and nails, her clothes, her smile, her gestures, all had the hard smooth finish of a piece of highly polished cornelian. This was her first introduction to Peking in bulk, as it had been Amber's last year, but unlike Amber, she was wholly at her ease, accepting introductions with cool poise, making little remarks, and talking to Rupert, Nugent noticed, as an old friend. He had some speech of her himself, and listened with rather sour amusement when she made to him three or four brief pronouncements on Chinese character and politics. A regular pseudo-highbrow, he said to himself, listening to statements whose origin he recognised, with all her gambits taped out. "You read ——, I see," he said rather unamiably, naming a well-known writer on China. She was unabashed. "Yes—but he's the goods, isn't he?"

"If you like publicists' opinions, yes."

She was quick, he granted, in her attempt to recover lost ground. "What do *you* recommend, instead?"

"Personally I prefer the views of novelists, if you must take things at second-hand."

"Ah—because Art is more disinterested?"

God, what a girl! It *was* rather near to what he meant, which added to Nugent's distaste.

"No—because their eyesight is better—and often their prose," he said, escaping.

Waiting for the start below the Ta To-tzu, in the sand and the bitter wind, Nugent observed that Benenden was again with Miss Boggit, explaining the proceedings and showing her round. Suddenly he remembered their first paper-hunt last year, and how Rupert had then squired Amber; and a little chill of apprehension ran through him as he heard the newcomer repeatedly drawling out "But Rupert——" with that rather adenoidal inflexion, placed at the back of the nose, which so many young women seem to regard as a social asset. Amber was with Joe, who was going to ride Port in a paper-hunt for the first time; presently they came up together, Joe in his old orange waistcoat, and Nugent noticed with fresh distaste how the newcomer ran her eye over Mr. Hawtrey's splendid presence with cool practised appraisal. Joe apparently noticed it too—during the little spate of talk following the introductions he bent to Nugent's ear, muttering, with a nod in Miss Boggit's direction— "Straight from Tsavo! Pure-bred man-eater." Nugent chuckled—this vein of rather vulgar shrewdness was, to him, one of Joe's most endearing traits. When Joe went off to mount, Amber, who was also in riding-dress, took off her fur coat and handed it to Rupert—"Hang on to that, Rupert, will you? I'm just going to have a last look at Port." There was a confiding simplicity about the action, small as it was, which revived Nugent's sense of apprehension—as Amber and Joe walked off together he heard Miss Boggit say to Rupert, "Is she one of his sweetie-pets?"

"No—they're running a stable together; she's a marvellous horsewoman," Rupert replied, in a rather cold voice, which Nugent heard with relief.

"Oh, is she? She's *quite* terribly pretty," observed Miss Boggit. "That baby manner suits her too—rather clever."

Rupert made no reply; the riders were beginning to line up, and he pointed out the various notable figures to his companion. Amber presently came back for her coat, and stood with them as they watched the start. Port took the first jump beautifully, and she turned to Rupert with some enthusiastic comment.

"Yes—marvellous," Miss Boggit said. "Rupert darling, how much longer must we go on lousing around in this appalling wind and this *das*tardly sand? Can't we go and sit in a car till they come back?"

"No, you must see the finish," said Rupert firmly.

"It's quite against the rules to sit in cars. You can walk about." And walk about they all did, till the race finished. Joe was fourth, but was "on the card" and seemed very well satisfied.

As the Grant-Howards drove home: "Well, what do you think of them?" Joanna asked her husband.

"She's got thick ankles," said Nugent non-committally. Joanna, as they lurched over the well-known bumps in the dusty road beside the canal, stared out at the now familiar spectacle of the ice-cutters hewing at the harvest of putrid ice, which looked deceptively blue and clean, and the women at the water-holes hauling up dripping wicker buckets, which left a trail of dark round spots in the deep dust as they were borne up the bank. Presently she spoke again. "I shall dislike it very much if that little *arriviste* does Amber down," she said.

Nugent was startled. Joanna had never spoken so definitely about Amber and Rupert before, and some curious half-shy delicacy about the girl's concerns, since he had received her confidence at T'ang-shan, had prevented him from opening the subject.

"Oh, you noticed them too?" he said, really rather relieved to get Joanna's opinion.

"*Not*iced them!   It was like Writing on the Wall," said Joanna. "I wish it was Joe," she added in a moment, "he's as stupid as an owl, but still——"

Nugent found this inconsecutive utterance perfectly clear. Remembering Joe's remark about Miss Boggit, he repeated it to his wife, and they laughed together. "Yes, Joe's got that kind of sense," Joanna said. "Rupert hasn't. He's morally *very* stupid, you know, Nugent. He's not independent—and then he's so cross!"

Nugent, for once, did not defend Rupert from this general indictment, and they drove home in rather gloomy silence.

During the next few weeks nothing occurred either to relieve or to intensify Nugent's sense of a menace to Amber's happiness. The thing remained, apparently, where it was. Mrs. and Miss Boggit of course completely permeated Peking, as Joanna said—staying with the British Minister, they had to be asked to everything, and were to be met everywhere. Rupert, like everyone else, both met them and entertained them; but not more than Joe, who did his bit in keeping up the Legation traditions of hospitality by giving magnificent lunches and dinners for his Chief's guests. (This did not prevent him from referring to the girl as "Yellow Chartreuse," "Gold Flake," and similar uncomplimentary titles.) So far as Nugent could judge—and he made a point of seeing a good deal of her—Amber noticed nothing; her serene contentment and unconcern suffered no perceptible change; her talk was all of her ponies and their progress. And then something happened which she *did* notice.

Acting on Leroy's suggestion that it "might be as well to see what a bit of 'face' would do" in the way of making the Marshal more amenable to advice, Sir James gave a party at the Legation for Li. It took the form of a dance, with supper and a band, brass and champagne being known to be two of the European inventions which appeal most to the Chinese. Now there are certain difficulties attendant on entertaining high official personages in China. To show them due courtesy, you must meet them at the outer gate, and escort them personally through your household courts. This would be easier to arrange if you could know to within an hour, say, when they are likely to arrive. But you cannot. Invited to dinner at 8.30, a Chinese may easily seek to give himself face by arriving, bland and gracious, at 9.20; or, to show his friendly eagerness for your society, he may equally well turn up half an hour or more too early. On this occasion the reception was due to begin at 10 P.M., but just before half-past nine, while the ladies were still drinking coffee in the drawing-room, the spies posted by the Military Attaché for the purpose came hastening with the information that the Marshal was even then entering the compound. There was a general *sauve-qui-peut;* the ladies, carrying their cups and dropping their spoons, fled into an ante-room, to leave the great salon vacant for the formal reception; the Minister nipped briskly down the steps and across under the lighted *t'ing-erhs* to the outermost one, there to greet his guest; servants in red and blue silk robes lined up in the great halls, or collected the coffee-spoons; Leroy, the Military Attaché, Mr. Hugo and the vice-consul all attended on Sir James, to act as interpreters and to do the requisite "getting-together" with the Marshal's staff in Chinese. Slowly, solemnly, with bowings over clasped hands, with salutes, with the light shuffle of slippers and the firm tread of uniform boots, with rustlings of brocade robes, the procession passed through the red-columned *t'ing-erhs,* up the steps, and into the Great Envoy's residence.

The Grant-Howards, coming across from the Counsellor's House at a quarter to ten, according to plan, were greeted by a spectacle which did not wholly accord with the European idea of a friendly diplomatic reception. All round the Minister's house, and stretching away up the dimly lit road beyond the Chapel, was a fleet of motor-cycle combinations, with a machine-gun mounted on the side-car of each, manned by soldiers in uniform. "Gosh —he's rolled up already," said Joe, who was with Nugent and Joanna. "Look, there's his car; come and see it." He proceeded, coolly, to point out to them the more peculiar features of the vast bullet-proof saloon: the quick-firer on the windscreen, where happier people carry a spotlight, the quick-release bullet-proof shutters worked by a handle in the roof, the silver spittoon set in the floor. Two or three revolvers lay among the priceless sable rugs on the seat. "In his home town the old boy never leaves his *yamen* without four of these—all the shutters are up, and no one knows which he's in," Joe informed them. The outer hall of the Legation was thronged with soldiers, armed with rifles and revolvers; smoking, spitting, they filled the air with a reek of garlic and cheap American tobacco. It was like passing through a barrack-room to a ball. Joanna sniffed, daintily. "They're very amusing people," she said resignedly.

Inside, in the great drawing-room, they made their bows to the Marshal. This renowned war-lord, who had fought his way up from banditry in a small way to the position, practically, of an independent monarch, this fierce soldier, ferocious slaughterer of his rivals, startled Joanna even more than his idea of a suitable escort to an evening party. She saw a little old gentleman in a robe of gentian-blue brocade, with a mild face, like that of a benevolent Oxford don, small beautiful hands, and a very quiet gentle smile. He was talking, rather haltingly, to Sir James, Leroy interpreting, or turning to chatter fluently with the Military Attaché, for whom he had a great liking, no doubt because of the latter's delightfully intimate connection with those modern weapons of precision which have such an attraction for war-lords.

Sir James stepped forward to greet them. "Now do your stuff, Mrs. Nugent," he said urgently to Joanna, "he likes talking to *t'ai-t'ais*." Thus adjured, Joanna made her first essay in *k'o-ch'i-hwa* (politeness-talk). This consists in *dénigrer*-ing yourself and your possessions, and lauding to the skies those of the person you address, and is an indispensable preliminary to conversation in polite society in China. (If you wish to speak seriously about anything, after some minutes of flowery compliments you

say "*Pu k'o-ch'i!*" (not politeness) and then get down to
it.) So Joanna, who had carefully mugged up the requisite phrases, when the Marshal complimented her on
her extremely rudimentary Chinese retorted that it was
more fitted for the ears of *mafoos* (grooms) than of a
T'a shuai (commander-in-chief). The Marshal, purring
visibly, enquired after her virtuous and high-born children; Joanna thanked him for his gracious condescension
towards the abject offspring of an unworthy mother,
who were, beyond their deserts, in health. After some
minutes of this, while the Military Attaché and Leroy
stood by, grinning at her struggles, and the Minister,
relieved from the labours of an interpreted conversation,
talked to his other guests, the Marshal, to Joanna's great
embarrassment, expressed a wish to drink her health.
Whereupon they moved off in solemn procession, accompanied by a large group of staff, both English and Chinese,
to the buffet, where they drank champagne, touching
glasses with many bows. The Marshal then embarked
on a long story, which soon became too complicated for
Joanna's small vocabulary—on their return to the drawing-room, she asked Leroy what it had all been about?

Leroy gave his cavernous chuckle, and muffled his
boom to what he regarded as an undertone. "It was
about his health," he said. "He was telling you that
for years he was too ill to drink champagne; but then he
consulted a magician, who gave him a broth of stags'
bones—and after that he got quite well, and had six
children!"

By this time the general company had assembled, and
dancing had begun. The Marshal, surrounded by his
suite, watched it from a sofa with absorbed attention.
Joanna, who was not an ardent dancer, presently found
herself sitting by Lydia Leicester. Her attitude towards
Lydia was a fairly even mixture of liking, pity and

disapproval. While she could not condone the behaviour which rumour freely attributed to Mrs. Leicester, she could not help pitying the suffering and humiliation which she divined behind that gracious and beautiful exterior. When she was actually in Lydia's company, pity and liking were generally uppermost—she was so intelligent, had such a well-bred simplicity of speech and manner, and was, occasionally, so witty. As they sat together now, Mrs. Leicester amused her companion by her penetrating but not unamiable comments on the dancers as they passed. Presently Amber came by with Mr. Hawtrey.

"That pretty child!" said Mrs. Leicester. "I should be much happier if she would marry Joe and have done with it."

"Why?" Joanna asked, interested in spite of herself in Mrs. Leicester's views of Amber.

"Because I think she needs safety. She's one of the ones who are simply *made* for pain about people, till she gets some solid anchorage." She turned her immense clear eyes on to her companion. "You know," she said, with that sincere simplicity which Joanna could not help finding so attractive, "I'm sometimes afraid of her falling in love with your husband. She thinks there's no one like him. Of course the idea never enters her head, and that protects her—but if it ever did, I believe she would find she cares for him more than she knows."

Joanna heard these sentences with most unusual sensations of discomfort. She respected Mrs. Leicester's intelligence too much to write off the idea as folly, and her good-breeding enough to realise that if she wished to convey a warning about Nugent's own feelings, this would be the way she would choose. Done as it was, there was no loophole left for a rebuff, even had she felt any inclination to administer one.

"I think the protection probably *is* enough," she said, careful to speak slowly and thoughtfully, as if she were considering someone else's concerns. "The force of an accepted convention is a very powerful defence." She paused, as if thinking again. "Do you really feel, though, that George Hawtrey is the right person for her?" she asked, turning the conversation in a channel easier for herself.

"I'm afraid *Rupert* won't marry her, though he's a fool not to take the chance, in my opinion," said Mrs. Leicester. "Look at that! That's the third time running." They both looked at Benenden and his partner as they passed. Miss Boggit danced with her face pressed into Rupert's shirt-front—occasionally she tilted it up at a provocative angle to gaze at him, then she turned it down again. There was something about the whole aspect of the pair which made Joanna wholly sympathise when Mrs. Leicester said—"The little bandit!"

Joanna and Mrs. Leicester were not the only people to notice Rupert's dancing with Miss Boggit. Amber had gone to the Legation ball with the keenest expectations of pleasure. She remembered the dance on Christmas night, and had promised herself a repetition of that happiness, only more so. But after one dance with her, Rupert made none of the usual assignations for the next but two, and so on; he said, rather vaguely, that he must do a bit of duty now. And when she saw him steering the wife of the Iberian Minister about like a ship, she felt no surprise. But then she saw him dancing with Daphne Boggit; and again, and then again—and still when he passed her in the doorway or in the corridors where one sat out, he did not come and ask her for another dance. Amber could not understand it. Was he just being extra discreet? Using Miss Boggit as a smoke-screen, as she had used Joe? But need they be *so* discreet? To leave

room for the dances she was counting on, she had been
rather vague with some of her earlier partners about what
Touchy called "second editions," and half-way through
the evening there came a moment when she realised, in a
panic, that Rupert really wasn't going to dance with her
again; and that, failed by him, she might have to endure
the humiliation of being seen to be without partners.
People were drifting off to the buffet and the bridge-
tables—Aunt Bessie had settled down to play long ago;
in the great white-and-gold room the crowd of couples
was much thinner.

All this was not lost on Nugent. He had watched
Amber's eyes following Rupert, as he passed her without
a word; and he saw, in that panic-stricken minute, the
fear begin to dawn in her puzzled face. And suddenly he
felt that he could not bear it. Looking ahead, he put all
possible future pain for her into that moment. She must
not be allowed to see it, to realise it; not all at once; not
then. He went up to her and asked her for a dance.
And for the rest of the evening, whenever she was free,
he danced with her. He talked, involving her in long
arguments about books, giving her amusing criticisms on
people—anything to keep her mind occupied. He succeeded—it was hardly possible not to be interested by
Nugent, if he gave his mind to it; and the flattery of this
unwonted attention, and the interest of his conversation,
really did for the time prevent the girl from watching or
thinking about Rupert, as Nugent saw with great relief.

But his rescuing enterprise had one repercussion which
he could not have foreseen. Joanna, with Mrs.
Leicester's uncomfortable remarks still fresh in her ears,
saw first with surprise, and then with an odd little prick
of concern, her husband dancing repeatedly with Amber.
But for that conversation with Lydia, she would have
thought nothing of it—as it was, not all her affectionate

common sense about Nugent, the ripened fruit of years of sympathy, loyalty and good-tempered comprehension, could quite exorcise that prick. Such moments do come to the most sensible, the most secure, the least exigent of wives—and they have to occur a good many times before they can be taken quite as lightly as they deserve. Two of the Minister's guests at least took away a source of thoroughly uncomfortable meditation that night.

For in spite of Nugent's efforts, Amber finally went home a good deal distressed. Quite at the close of the evening she had one more dance with Rupert, which, though good in its way, mainly prompted comparisons with the many more he had had with Miss Boggit. He was lively and amusing, too, but she missed a particular tone to which she had become accustomed. As they were moving back to the ball-room Count Herman intercepted them, and speaking to Rupert, briefly confirmed some previous assignation. "I have arranged it for next Thursday—you are free then? Good. You will find it surpassingly interesting—it is a unique experience." He bowed and passed on. Most innocently, most naturally, Amber asked Rupert what this unique experience might be—it had been quite openly spoken of, and she never dreamed that her question could be unwelcome. To her immense surprise he turned to her and said, with a rather patronising smile, "My dear Amber, little pitchers shouldn't have such long ears!"

Blushing with mortification, she stared at him, speechless for a moment. Then—"I'm sorry," she said, angrily. "You choose such odd places to discuss your secrets," and walked away, her lips quivering with vexation. Prickly though he often was, Rupert had never done this to her before. It was a deliberate snub. And she had done *nothing* to deserve it! How could she guess it was a secret? She went home miserable.

Chapter Twenty-four

RUPERT'S snub to Amber had been prompted mainly by a momentary embarrassment. He had not felt equal, on the instant, to explaining to the girl that he was going under Herman's escort to visit the Sing-Song houses of the Chinese City—those curious places of entertainment which are so often referred to by Europeans, but into which so few of them ever in fact penetrate. The plan had long been arranged, but somehow or other the episode of Amber's question had taken a good deal of the edge off his enthusiasm for the expedition. He realised at once that he had behaved badly, and would readily have tried to put things right, given the chance—but he did not meet Amber during the next few days, as he expected, and when he finally both wrote and telephoned to the Hei Lung Hu-t'ung, he learned that she had gone out to the Temple for a week. A letter of explanation would be making too much of the whole thing, and there was nothing for it but to blame Amber for her sensitiveness, Herman for his tactlessness, and to feel thoroughly disgruntled with himself for something which he did not specify very precisely.

He set off, accordingly, in a rather bad frame of mind, but hoping vaguely to be distracted from his mental discomfort. As the two rickshas passed down the broad street outside the Chien-mên, he noticed how much denser and livelier the crowd was by night than by day, and a faint infection of interest took him. They turned into Lantern Street, where each shop displays an array of lanterns and lamp-shades of every shape and colour;

overhead the fluttering banners proclaiming the names of the proprietors almost touched, making the narrow street look like an arcade. The crowd was denser than ever here, and the rickshas had to pass in single file, with loud cries of "lend your light!"—once Rupert lost sight of Herman altogether. But after a few moments they turned to the left into an almost deserted lane, lighted only by an occasional lamp hanging from a dilapidated pole, where they moved more swiftly and again close together.

"*Na-i-kö hu-t'ung?*" (Which street?) panted Herman's coolie, pausing. Like all his kind, he knew the habits of his master to perfection, but there were four or five streets in the neighbourhood, any one of which might have been selected for the honour of a visit. On being told "to the Han Chia T'an" he trotted forward a little till Count Herman bade him stop. "We'll walk," he said.

Getting out, they turned down a narrow alley, followed by the rickshas. On either side were open doorways illuminated from above by clusters of round lamps of frosted white glass. The few Chinese they met gaped with curiosity—a verminous beggar pestered them for alms. Humming and tapping his teeth, a trick of his when undecided, Stefany murmured the names of the houses as they passed—"The Pa Fung Yuan—no, not there; the Yin Ts'ai Ke; these are all famous, you know, some of the most popular in Peking. No—we will go to the Lotus Spring."

At the entrance to the Lotus Spring Rupert observed several small brass plates, each engraved with two or three Chinese characters, hanging above the door. "Those are the names of the girls who live there," Herman explained. "Come on in."

Passing through a narrow passage and round two

corners, they found themselves in a small and rather dirty paved court, half open to the sky. Round the sides ran a dark green wooden verandah, on to which opened the windows of the ground-floor rooms; a rickety staircase led up to a second floor, and in one corner was a large dust-bin and a pile of coal briquettes. In a sort of combined office and kitchen at the entrance to the court a number of servants were gathered, smoking and drinking tea; one of these, clearly the head janitor, recognised Count Stefany and emerged in haste, bowing and rubbing his hands. "Ah, Mr. Ssŭ!" he said.

"Mr. Ssŭ has come!" shouted the others, grinning.

"Guests!" shouted the janitor in loud tones; immediately a tall man in a grey gown strode into the courtyard. "Guests!" he too shouted in a long-drawn wail—"Gue-e-e-ests!"

"Coming at once," piped a chorus of shrill voices from all sides of the court. Rupert's interest was fully aroused now—this was definitely amusing and Hassan-like.

"Which room, Wang?" asked Count Herman of the attendant. "Here," said the man, ushering them through an open doorway across which hung a white sheet; he stood at the door and held the sheet aside. By this time a queue of girls had formed up in the courtyard. Rupert saw at a glance that they were all young and attractive, and dressed in the unvarying style adopted by well-to-do Chinese women in the evening—a straight close-fitting dress of brocade reaching nearly to the ankles, buttoned on the left side, and shaped high at the neck into a stiff two-inch collar. To his surprise, he experienced a curious feeling of embarrassment—but whether it was the numbers of the girls, their difference of race, or their perfectly dignified appearance which caused this unexpected sensation, he could not have said.

Wang called the girls up one at a time, by name, and

each in turn paused at the door for a few seconds of scrutiny by the guests, standing in attitudes of flower-like grace, with an exquisite nonchalance which was yet strangely courteous. The fifth in the queue walked straight into the room and sat down without a word.

"This is Yin T'ai," said Count Herman, as the other girls continued to halt and pass on. "She is an old friend of mine; it is not possible for me to call anyone else here. But which do you like? You must call one of them."

"Oh, the one in black," said Rupert rather desperately. The last girl had by now vanished.

"There were two in black," Wang said gravely, "which one do you wish, Li Tzu or Hsiao Feng?" Both were recalled, after much shouting, and Rupert, again embarrassed, indicated Li Tzu without really looking at her. She also entered then, and sat down as Yin T'ai had done.

The room in which they sat, though clean, was rather like a bed-sitting-room in a third-class Continental hotel. A brass bedstead, a wardrobe, a dressing-table and a side-board constituted its main and most garish features; in the middle stood a table covered in oil-cloth, and four wooden chairs. A Chinese note was struck, however, by the presence of two large brass spittoons, and by the absence of any shade over the powerful electric bulbs which glared above the table as though in readiness for a major surgical operation. As they sat down to this table an old *amah* in black trousers and a short black coat shuffled in with four cups of tea, which she placed before them: to these she added a saucer of sun-flower seeds, a tray of caramels, and a tin of Three Castles Magnum cigarettes. "It is a long time since you have been here, Mr. Ssǔ," she said; "Yin T'ai has waited every day for you." She screwed up her eyes and beamed expectantly. The girls giggled.

"I was here a fortnight ago," said Count Herman, replying in Chinese to her banter. "I am sure Yin T'ai has so many sweethearts that she has almost forgotten me." The girls giggled again.

A second *amah* now appeared, accompanied by a small girl of about ten, who, it transpired, was Yin T'ai's younger sister. They both sat down on the bed, which jingled disconcertingly, and stared with unblinking intentness at the two visitors.

"Do we have an audience all the time?" Rupert asked, glancing at the newcomers.

"Oh yes, rather—they come and go as they like," replied Herman; "there is no such thing as privacy in Chinese life. Besides, this is the first time you have been here, and you are a foreigner, so everyone in the house will want to come and look at you, and then discuss your visit for days." His rather malicious smile appeared. "If you commit some *gaffe*, or make an amusing mistake in your Chinese, they will enjoy it for weeks."

Rupert's slight sense of embarrassment was not much relieved by this helpful information. He turned to Li Tzu. By any standards she was an undoubted beauty. Her shiny black hair was bobbed and drawn back behind her ears in carefully tended waves; her nose was straight and chiselled, and dimples showed in her cheeks at every smile. But it was the eyes and mouth that were her most arresting features. Her eyes were large, but half-veiled, as though to keep some secret to herself—a strange contrast to the flaunting scarlet of her lips, which curved in a broad line, half-disdainful, half-inviting, but always restrained and self-assured. For the rest, she had that curious poise and grace which is the heritage of all Chinese women.

"How old are you?" Rupert asked her—it was the first thing that came into his head, but it happens to be one of the most correct opening gambits for a Chinese conversation.

"Eighteen."

"And where do you come from?"

"Soochow."

"Nonsense," interposed Herman. "They all say that. Soochow is where all Chinese beauties are supposed to come from. Her parents are probably shopkeepers in Shanghai."

"And how old are you?" Yin T'ai asked now of Rupert.

"How old do you think?"

"Forty-nine."

"Forty-seven," Li Tzu put in.

Rupert had little personal vanity, but this unflattering consensus of opinion was rather a shock. Herman laughed at the sight of his face.

"It's your hair," he said. "By their standards it's fair, which is the same thing as white hair to them, and can only mean age. You ought to feel complimented that they didn't say sixty."

"I am thirty-two," said Rupert firmly, to the two girls.

"And what do you do?"

Rupert was unprepared for this. "I am a merchant," he said, on the spur of the moment.

"No use saying that," said Herman in English, again with his malicious smile. "They will know exactly who you are within twenty-four hours."

"Well, you explain to them, then, that I do so much commercial work at the Legation that it comes to the same thing."

"Right. To be an official will give you immense face."

The girls accepted Mr. Ssu's explanation without comment. It took them ten minutes, however, to be convinced that Rupert had no wife and family. "To be a bachelor at thirty-two is incredible here," said Herman.

Y

From the courtyard came the sound of voices and laughter, evidently of new arrivals, for "Guests" wailed Wang's voice again. "Back in a moment," said Yin T'ai and Li Tzu, dropping their cigarettes and hastily examining their make-up in the mirror on the dressing-table. As they ran out of the room another girl, in a plain cotton dress, with a pale featureless face came in, and calmly began to select an armful of clothing from the wardrobe. The two *amahs* appeared to object to this, and for some minutes a heated argument took place, which Rupert, fortunately for him, could not understand, though he caught the words "dog" and "grandmother." When she departed, triumphant, and they were left alone with the two old *amahs*, Herman turned with his smile to Rupert. "*Eh bien, mon cher*, what do you make of it all?"

"It's most interesting—and even odder than I expected," said Rupert. "The girls are lovely, of course. But what does it all amount to? *Are* they prostitutes? One imagines so."

Herman blew out a cloud of smoke. "In the West," he began sententiously, "chastity is enjoined by religion, but here it only depends on social convenience. Many of these girls have young lovers—'little white faces,' they are called—whom they often support out of their earnings, and many of them have a 'patron' among their clientele. But they are not here for that purpose at all. These places are not *maisons tolérées*. These girls are simply professional entertainers, and they work every night from about seven to one."

"Most extraordinary," said Rupert.

"Not really," said Herman. "As you know, the Chinese have nothing which corresponds to our club life. Instead, a few friends go out together to one of these sing-song places to chat, and to play mah-jongg or poker. Some prefer to hire a room in a restaurant and call the girls out to join them for an hour or two.   Nearly all the important political and military leaders amuse themselves in this way, and discuss their affairs at the same time.   In fact they often transact their most important business on these occasions.   Anyone who takes the trouble to make a tour of this district now and then, and to become friendly with some of the girls, can often pick up a lot of useful information."

"H'm," said Rupert.   He thought he began to see why many of the diplomats in Peking saw so much of Count Herman.   But he was really more interested for the moment in the sing-song industry itself.   "And how do the 'patrons' get hold of the girls?" he asked.   "How does one become a regular patron?"

"It's a tremendous business, that," said Herman. "Up till quite recently the set series of formalities to be gone through before you could make a sing-song girl your mistress was almost as elaborate as marrying a wife.   It is all designed to give the girl face, of course.   First the *amahs* have to be taken into your confidence—and bribed. Then you must give a series of banquets to the house she lives in—the expenditure on each of these must not be below a certain prescribed minimum—and several mah-jongg parties on the same scale.   There is an appropriate and prescribed period of waiting, too, and finally the auspicious day must be chosen."   He smiled again. "Very unlike Europe, isn't it?   No hurry, no furtiveness. The wooing of a courtesan in China is much more decorous than many marriages in America or England."

"Quite right, too," said Rupert.   "It's partly the hurry and furtiveness that make prostitution in Europe so disgusting.   But why do you say up till quite recently?"

"Ah, because now, since the hard times began, the formalities are being relaxed a little.   For a Chinese-speaking foreigner who is thoroughly conversant with *li*

—you know what *li* is—the rules of courteous usage—
things are getting a good deal easier."

By this time the recently arrived party had settled down
in an adjoining room and were making a deafening noise
playing a game rather like "Up Jenkins." Two players
each raise a clenched fist, and straightening as many
fingers as they choose, simultaneously guess at the combined total thus exposed. "Two, seven, three, three, nine."
Through the wall it sounded like an auction. Then the
thin piercing screech of a Chinese violin was added to the
hubbub, the bow scraping across the strings like a car-
penter's saw, with no tune perceptible by a European.
The shrill voice of a girl joined in, equally tuneless though
less harsh.

"For Heaven's sake don't let them do that in here!"
said Rupert, putting his hands to his ears. "Hullo—
here's another! To what do we owe this pleasure, do
you suppose?" he asked, as a rather impish-looking girl
came in, sat down at the table with a familiar smile, and
began carelessly to crack sunflower seeds.

"That is the one who was quarrelling with the *amahs*
just now," said Herman.

"*This* one? Nonsense, Herman. Look at her face!"

"She has just, so to speak, constructed it," said Count
Herman. "You must remember that China knew more
about the art of cosmetics two thousand years ago than
Paris knows today."

"It's incredible," said Rupert, still gazing at the girl.
"What about our two—are they as plain as she was without make-up?"

"No—Li Tzu and Yin T'ai only need quite a little
powder and lip-stick—nature has treated them well,"
observed Herman.

"By the way, were those huge jade bracelets Li Tzu
was wearing real?" Rupert asked.

"I understand that she has no 'patron,' therefore the bracelets were certainly imitation," said Count Herman. "But that reminds me of a rather characteristic story. There used to be a girl in the next house to this, called Mei Yu, who had a pair of jade garters worth at least twenty thousand dollars. They were a present from her 'patron,' a general from Hupei. He could afford expensive presents because he had made enough out of the opium revenue in his province to build a whole house of jade, if he wished. Naturally the garters made the girl famous and popular; any party which she condescended to attend even for ten minutes was a success. In the same house was another girl called Hua Ying, in whom a young foreigner became rather interested. Presently this youth had to go away to Honan on business; he was bored there, and one day he sat down and just *pour se désennuyer*, wrote Hua Ying a long and ardent love-letter in quite good Chinese. When the letter arrived here it created a sensation; naturally she showed it to the whole street. No sing-song girl had ever received such a letter from anyone, least of all from a foreign devil. Soon the sing-song houses in Shanghai and even in Canton were discussing the story, and suddenly it became evident that Hua Ying's name was made. Everyone sought her favour, and presently she accepted the attentions of a certain political agent of the Hupei clique in Peking, and therefore of the same party as Mei Yu's patron."

"Well, and then what?" asked Rupert, as Herman paused to light a cigarette. He thought the story rather dull, like the evening itself; a sing-song house was about as exciting as a Mothers' Meeting.

"Ah, now we come to it," said Herman. "It is this which is so characteristic. Mei Yu felt that Hua Ying's success was making her lose face; her garters were supplanted in the public estimation by Hua Ying's love-letter.   So she tried to arrange an intrigue for her rival's downfall.   Unfortunately the plot was too complicated, like all Chinese plots; Hua Ying became suspicious, and one evening there was an open quarrel and the two girls scratched each other's faces terribly before they were separated.   Soon all the sing-song houses were divided into two camps.   As you know, mediation is at once a fine art and a staple industry here; naturally all the various interests involved employed the most renowned professional peace-makers, but without success.   And then, of course, the 'face' of the two Hupei patrons, the general and the official, became involved."

"Oh come—not over a sing-song girls' quarrel?" said Rupert incredulously.

"But most certainly!   Here things are like that.   In the end Mei Yu somehow succeeded in discrediting Hua Ying, and that was the end of the comedy in the sing-song houses.   But not in Hupei!   Hua Ying's defeat involved the public prestige of her patron, the Hupei official, for the whole town knew the story.   He lost so much face that he had to leave Peking.   He went back to Hankow, officially for a short holiday; but as soon as he got home he revenged himself on the general by getting him dismissed on a charge of treason to the Hupei government.   It's a fact," said Count Herman, smiling at Rupert's astounded stare.

"Well then, the general, of course, had no option but to change sides, and offer his services and his fifty thousand useless troops to some other provincial clique.   All that was some time ago.   But the general will attack Hupei as soon as the summer civil-war season opens; he badly needs to recover his opium revenue, but what he wants even more is to be able to execute the political agent. So there will be one more war in China because of a foreigner's idle love-letter to a sing-song girl."

"My God! And these people belong to the League of Nations!" was Rupert's only comment.

Count Herman became sententious again. "My dear friend, that is just what makes world politics so interesting at the moment. The West is now enslaved by its own American-born idealism; the East goes quietly on its millenial realism. But the East is quite astute enough—in China, anyhow—to exploit this situation by doing noisy lip-service to Western ideals, for which in reality it does not care two hoots, and so adding to the difficulties of those Western nations whose hands are tied in the East by a set of new conceptions which are barely valid yet even in Europe, and here are simply an absurdity." He smiled finely. "And the cream of the joke is that America, who started the whole game, has drawn her skirts aside, refuses to touch the League with a barge oar, and has her Nicaraguan expedition as and when it suits her. But *still* she is the rallying-point for this lip-service in the Far East, and comes out with some highly sanctimonious pronouncement whenever any member of the League she will not join attempts to act in accordance with facts as they are and not with a sentimental idealism. For us outsiders, this is very funny. Your statesmen do not appear to notice all this," he concluded.

"Our poor wretched statesmen——" Rupert was beginning, when Yin T'ai and Li Tzu returned. They complained of the rowdiness of the other party and Li Tzu suggested that they should all adjourn to her room for another cup of tea. Just as they were about to go the face of a young Chinese, adorned with horn-rimmed spectacles, was poked round the door.

"Hullo, Charlie!" said Count Herman. "Come in."

"Hullo, Mr. Stefany," replied the newcomer. "I heard there were foreigners here and I thought maybe it was you. Got up from Tientsin this evening, and just came out here to see the girls. Gee, I'm glad to see you again." Herman introduced Rupert. "Glad to know you, Mr. Benenden. Say, how d'you like China? Find it pretty slow here, I guess, in some ways, don't you? I've been eight years in the States—went through College there. Here's my card."

He handed Rupert a large piece of pasteboard on which was printed:

> Charles (Ch'a-Li) Wang,
> B.A. Memphis College, U.S.A.
> The Oriental Emporium, Tientsin.

"Speak Chinese?" Mr. Wang went on. "Bit, eh? Mr. Stefany's is wonderful. What d'you think of the Chinese girls? Pretty cute, some of them, hey? But you gotta know how to handle them; no rough stuff like in the States. Guess I know how all right. You sweet on this girl?" He indicated Li Tzu. "You leave it to me —I'll fix you up."

Rupert declined the offer. Mr. Wang pinched Li Tzu's cheek; the girl shrank back with a pout of annoyance. "Well, I'll bet she's pretty inexperienced any way," continued Mr. Wang, ignoring her. "You come down to Tientsin and I'll show you some fine girls." He glanced at a square gold wrist-watch. "Gee—nine-forty-five. Guess I must rush; got a date along the street. So long, Mr. Stefany—Goodbye, Mr. Benenden." He was gone.

"There's the new China," said Count Herman. "Most of them are like that—amusing perhaps, but quite unreliable; they think only of pleasure. The American-educated ones are the worst—they have none of the charm and dignity of the old-style Chinese left."

"God, no," said Rupert. "If America were as near China as Russia is, the whole place would turn into one

vast Y.M.C.A. in no time. Praise Heaven for the
Pacific, for China's sake."

Voices and steps announced the arrival of more guests
in the courtyard. "We may as well go," said Count
Herman, "we've been here over an hour. They will be
delighted to see you if you come again, but for Heaven's
sake don't try to come alone, or you may commit some
gaffe that it will take me a month to put straight."

The two girls accompanied them to the outer door and
waved after them as they rode off, with repeated cries of
"Come tomorrow," the stock phrase of the sing-song
houses for "*au revoir*."

"Well, what did you think of it?" Count Herman asked
as they drove down the ill-lit lane towards Lantern
Street. Rupert considered. For him the most striking
feature of the whole evening had been its colossal dullness.

"I am very glad indeed to have seen it," he said. "I
don't think I should ever care to become an *habitué*,
though I imagine that one misses most of the point unless one is really fluent in Chinese. They wouldn't talk
such bromides all the time with you, would they?"

"No, not quite," said Herman. Rupert could hear
that he was smiling again. As they turned into the
glare and the curious harsh noise of voices in Chien-mên
Wai, he reflected that the very dullness of the whole thing
had been interesting in itself. But the thought just
flicked him, as he stepped into his house, that it was perhaps hardly worth having hurt Amber for.

Chapter Twenty-five

THE Minister's party for the Marshal took place in the middle of April. The races were, as usual, early in May, and during the intervening three weeks Amber actually never saw Rupert alone at all. It is not easy to see anyone alone in a place where (*a*) you cannot dine at a small restaurant, because there are no restaurants; (*b*) you cannot go to a theatre, because there are no theatres; (*c*) you cannot go to a concert, because there are no concerts; (*d*) it is no good going to the cinema because there is only one, and everyone else will be there too. All the usual resources of the engaged or the would-be engaged being thus denied one, there remains only to walk or to ride. To arrange a walk, where no one does walk, is to make a rather definite *démarche*, lacking the helpful element of an excuse; while to conduct an emotional crisis when riding a China pony is an experiment which few will attempt twice.

Quite apart from these difficulties, Amber was more occupied than ever then with her griffins. These last weeks were the most crucial ones of the whole training period; and, as luck would have it, Joe could hardly help at all. There was a "hoosh" on in the Legation. The Minister's party for the Marshal had failed of its object, or rather had succeeded only too well; encouraged by the face there gained, Li had suddenly become more than usually truculent about the revenue; he had sent a defiant message to Wang, his rival, and the city was full of rumours of another attack by this worthy. Everyone in the Legation was working from 9.30 in the morning

330

till 11 at night, and Amber and Mulholland had to manage as best they could. Mulholland, occupied by day in the Bank, could only get out for the early gallops; the general supervision of the feeding and exercising, in fact the whole management of the Portfolio stable devolved on Amber.

It was, then, in no fit of pique that she had gone off to the Temple, but merely in order to be on the scene of her labours. Uncle Bill was there, occupied in the same way —Mulholland slept in the country when he could, more often dashed out in Joe's car, galloped, and dashed back again. Gin and Ginger were both entered for the Maidens, appearing formally in the lists as Minister of Marine and Minister of Finance respectively. Gin was a form of insurance, a second string; he had come on well in the last few weeks and ran very level. He could not touch Ginger at his best, but the chestnut had developed a temperament, and there were days when Mulholland could get nothing out of him.

One morning a few days before the races Amber walked out into the stable-yard at 6 o'clock, munching a piece of chocolate, swung herself into the saddle, and cantered off down the track towards the racecourse. The Portfolio ponies were there when she arrived, but not Mulholland. Giving Bananas to a *mafoo*, she strolled about, waiting for him. As last year, the stand and buildings were newly painted, white and fresh; coolies were planting pink geraniums all round the enclosure, and setting tubs of oleanders in position. Leaning on the rails, her thoughts ran first on the ponies, waiting down by the paddock. *Her* ponies, *her* grooms, *her* jockey! It was the most heavenly fun to be running a racing-stable of one's own! She wondered, for the thousandth time, whether the Ginger Griffin could possibly win. That new white of Mimi's, St. Jean, had done some terribly good last quarters lately, Joe said. And Fine Champagne, Rothstein's entry, who was coloured like Bananas, looked very fast. Ee-tzŭ was a wonder at training—she wished they had a *mafoo* as good. Oh well, no good worrying—she was certain not to win it, with all these experts to compete with. "Make up your mind to it," she muttered to herself.

She looked at her watch—6.25—Billy was late. Others, Leicester for one, would be coming presently, and she wanted to be finished first. Thinking of Harry reminded her of Lydia, and the thought of Lydia led on to Rupert. It was horrid, not seeing him all this time, with that quarrel unsettled between them. She had been furiously angry with him at first—how dared he speak like that to her—how could he? But in time her anger had cooled; she was prepared to believe that she had perhaps been tactless, or that something was worrying him that night. As soon as all this was over, she would see him and put everything to rights, she told herself; it was such a small thing, it couldn't really disturb their happiness for long. "A safe person to love"—he had said once that she would be that. And so she would be—she would make a safety for him, a refuge from his own bitterness, and let his love of "simple things" and of lovely places expand and grow in peace. *She* would never be a shifting tease. As for his dancing so much that night with Daphne Boggit— she drove the pricking, uncomfortable little thought resolutely away. Surely she could stand up to a little thing like that; she must be prepared for such episodes, lots of them—Rupert being Rupert—if she was to build a haven for his spirit.

She was so lost in her thoughts that she never heard Mulholland approaching. The young man, coming up to the figure by the rails, in the old breeches and pull-over, actually hesitated a moment before he spoke to her, so held was he by the lovely expression on her face. When at length he said "Morning, Amber," she turned at once, smiling; but the strangely beautiful look of vision and purpose vanished.

"You're late," she said.

"Yes, that idiotic chauffeur of Joe's has ditched the car again—I had to walk from the corner."

"Oh, poor you! Well, come on; let's begin."

Stop-watch in hand, Amber stood at the rails. She knew all about timing now; concentrated, businesslike, she watched every detail of the start, saw just how neatly Mulholland got Ginger away. Billy *had* come on as a rider since last year. Round the course they went, and Amber took the times. After they passed the post she made some notes on a pad, then walked down to meet Mulholland.

"Well?" he asked.

"Two-twenty. He'll have to do better than that to win."

Mulholland grunted. "He wasn't keen," he said. "I can't think what's wrong. He did better than that three weeks ago."

"Let's look at him," said Amber. Together they studied the pony—he turned his head and talked to them in low confiding little whickers.

"Chatty chap, isn't he?" said Mulholland, patting the pony's neck. But Amber continued to look at Ginger with a little puzzled frown.

"I wonder if we've trained him a bit too fine," she said at length. "I've known that happen at home. Li!" she called. The head *mafoo* came up, and waited expectantly. How *did* one say "trained too fine" in Chinese? She found a round-about formula, and put the point to Li. Rather to her surprise, he pounced on it. *Nakö huang ma* (the yellow pony) too much gallop, he opined;

gallop more less, gallop more better. And eventually it was decided to leave Ginger completely quiet for the few days that remained before the race.

As they left the course they met Harry Leicester's ponies coming down. They stopped and talked with him for a moment. He expressed the view that Low, Uncle Bill's griffin, was going to "scoop the Maidens." He asked after Gin and Ginger. "We're rather blighted," Amber said truthfully, "we think Ginger's stale."

"Overdone it a bit?" said Harry. "H'm—pity. Amateurs often do. What does Li say?"

"Li agrees."

"Well, they don't know much," said Harry consolingly. "Good luck!" He raised his hat and went on. A moment later he called after them—"I say!"

Amber turned Bananas round and went back. "What is it?"

"Listen!" said Harry, cocking his head like a clever dog.

Standing on the road in the sunshine, they listened. The air was full of small sounds—a blue magpie was clattering in the willows, making a noise like a bird-scarer's rattle; kestrels cried overhead, a coolie was hammering at a *p'eng* behind the palings; down in the paddock a pony whinnied, and a *mafoo* spoke to it. There was nothing unusual about any of these; they were the common cheerful accompaniment of a morning in the country. Amber stood puzzled, when—"There!" said Leicester, holding up his hand.

A very low faint bumping sound made the air tremble for a few seconds—it seemed to reach them as much through their bodies as through their ears, coming from nowhere in particular.

"Hear it?" said Harry.

Mulholland nodded. "What can it be?" Amber asked.

"It's guns," said Harry. "I heard last night that Wang was going to get a move on. Seems to be true."

"Where is he?" Mulholland asked.

"Somewhere down the Hankow line. He's got three or four heavy howitzers on trucks. I suppose he's having a stab at Li's positions down there—I heard he was going to."

"Who from?" Mulholland asked.

"As a matter of fact it was Stefany," said Harry. "He's generally pretty well informed, too, though I never ask where he gets his stuff. Well, I must get on." He rejoined his ponies.

Amber and Mulholland went on their way; they were both stirred by the indefinable excitement which any sight or sound of war arouses. "Will it upset the races?" Amber asked, a little anxiously.

"The *races*? Good Lord no!" said Mulholland, so emphatically that Amber felt slightly foolish. She had not been long enough in China to realise how incredibly trivial war is out there, to Europeans at any rate. At the corner they found Joe's car, which had been released from the ditch with the aid of several farm teams and a number of coolies with spades. Mulholland drove off, but Amber, finding herself near the Portfolio stable, decided to go on there and have a last word with Li about Ginger before returning to breakfast. The stables lay just behind the vacant villa, which usually stood, blank and shuttered, a weather-stained Union Jack drooping from its gable. Today, however, she noticed with surprise that the back door was open, and a ricksha standing in the yard; as she rode up two Chinese popped out, and seeing her, popped in again. Wondering what was going on, she called for a *mafoo*, and dismounting, walked into the house.

A most peculiar scene met her eyes. The villa had been left partly furnished, curtains and carpets rolled up and piled on the scanty furniture. But these remnants of European occupation were now almost hidden under a mass of strange objects, most of them manifestly Chinese —lacquer chests for clothes, cloth bundles which she guessed to contain ivories or porcelain, clothes themselves, lamps and bath-tubs, the long wooden cases of scroll-pictures, all heaped up in indescribable confusion. In every room it was the same. She ran the two Chinese to earth in the bathroom, which was stuffed almost to the ceiling with baskets of pea-nuts and sweet potatoes, and asked them what they were doing. They grinned sheepishly, muttered something about *"Ping"* and escaped. Puzzled by this extraordinary phenomenon, Amber went across to the stable and questioned Li. Li put on an expression of studied vacancy. He knew nothing at all; he knew not what men come; he knew not what plan. More puzzled than ever, Amber gave her final directions, and returned to the Temple, where over breakfast she recounted these events to Uncle Bill.

To Uncle Bill the connection between the sound of guns and the accumulation of Chinese possessions in the villa was as clear as daylight. "Oh Lord yes, they're putting their stuff there for safety," he said—"they always do that if they can when there are troops about."

"But the house is empty—it isn't a bit safe," Amber objected.

"Oh yes it is—far safer than their houses," boomed Uncle Bill. "It's got a foreign flag over it—it won't be touched. Leave 'em alone—they'll do no harm. When the fuss is over they'll cart it all away again, and leave everything tidy." After breakfast he went out with

Amber on to the manége and stood listening. Yes—
remote and faint, hitting their senses all over like light
muffled blows, came that distant reverberation.

"H'm," said Uncle Bill. He appeared to consider.
"You say Leicester got this from Stefany? Then it's
pretty sure to be right—if he *can*, Wang'll come on up.
He's wanted to for months, and he got those extra Hupei
troops a time back. Now look here—there are several
things to be done. It's always well to be prepared."

"Yes?" said Amber. She expected to be bundled off
into the city, where Aunt Bessie had remained the previous night for bridge, and waited in docile dismay.

"Have you got all the frocks and things you'll want for
the races out here?" Uncle Bill asked.

"No," said Amber, astonished.

"Well, you'd better take the car and go in and get
them," said Bill. "If the gates are shut later we may
have a job to get in and out. And tell Bessie to get her
things too, and to come out after lunch. I shall want—"
he recited a list of his requirements. As, a little later,
Amber drove off—"Remember to tell Bessie we're nearly
out of gin," he shouted after her. In the car Amber
giggled to herself. Blessed Uncle Bill! Enchanting
China! Where else in the world, with a possible siege
impending, would one carefully arrange to assemble oneself and one's drinks *outside* the city, so as not to miss a
race-meeting? It occurred to her that she ought to tell
Joe, and when she got to the Hei Lung Hu-t'ung she
rang up the Chancery. Rupert answered the telephone.
"Yes? Oh, it's you. How are you? All right?" He
sounded hurried and *affairé*.

"Yes, rather. Could I speak to Joe?" said Amber,
anxious to make it clear that it was not Rupert she
wanted.

"He's with the Minister, I'm afraid. Any message?"

"Yes. Tell him——" She paused to arrange her message.

"Well?" said Rupert, rather impatiently.

"We think Wang's probably coming up."

"My dear child, we've had nothing but rumours about Wang all this week," Rupert interrupted. "That's nothing new."

"Oh, all right!   Only you can hear the guns, out there. Tell Joe to ring me up—I won't keep you!" said Amber.

"What's that?" Rupert began, but Amber rang off. Tiresome, irritable creature he was!   Five minutes later Joe rang up.

"I say, what's all this you've been telling Rupert about guns?"

"Oh, nothing—only Harry says he heard from Count Stefany that Wang is really on the move, and you can hear the guns clearly out at P.M.C.   Look here, Joe——" She told him their plans.   "Can we take anything out for you?"

Joe was rather upset.   "I say, do you think that's really wise?   I mean, if anything's going on, I should have thought you'd have done better to be in the city, you and Auntie, anyhow."

"Mind the women and children!" Amber mocked. "Don't fuss, Joe!"

"I'd come out myself, only we're so damned busy," grumbled Joe.   "Rupert and I were working till midnight last night.   And if this old Methodist brute really comes up, there'll be more telegrams than ever.   How loud were the guns?"

"Not loud—sort of hitting you," Amber replied. "And the Chinese are cramming Miles's villa full of stuff —I saw them."

"Hern Jé!   That looks like business," said Joe, and went off to spread the news in the Chancery, while Amber

and Aunt Bessie packed their race frocks, collected plenty
of gin, and drove out to the temple.

For the next four or five days gossip in the Club was
fairly evenly divided between the prospects of a siege
and the prospects of the various ponies for the Maidens,
including Ginger. There had been a good deal of speculation among the regular race-owners in Peking about
Miss Harrison's griffins, after it became known that she
was starting a stable; the fact that she had got them
through Johansen leaked out, and Mr. Hawtrey's secrecy
fanned curiosity. Rumours had gone round that the
chestnut really was something out of the way. During
the next day or so, however, it became widely known
that the Portfolio pony was overtrained and stale, and
might be discounted. Gossip to this effect depressed
Mulholland rather, but Joe took it very cheerfully.
"Nonsense, my dear chap. Club chat won't affect the
pony's form, and we shall all get a longer price. Excellent thing."

Out in the country, that mutter of guns to the South
continued, always getting a little louder and clearer;
small parties of soldiers, wearing the Marshal's pink arm-
lets, appeared in the villages, and presently wandered on
again, weary and inconsequent. In the City it was re-
ported officially that Li was maintaining his positions
by the railway and had repulsed Wang, but old hands
like Uncle Bill, seeing these parties, drew their own con-
clusions. Without doubt a retreat was in progress.
For one panicky day the city gates were shut, but on
Wednesday, two days before the races, they were opened
again. Bill went in to Peking to glance at his neglected
office, and Amber begged a lift too—she wanted to cash
a cheque, for betting purposes.

Amber's financial arrangements were a little on her
mind. The stable had worked out rather more expens-

ive than she had anticipated. The two griffins, at $160 each, had mopped up over three hundred of her five hundred dollars; her share of running costs for the six months had been another three hundred—she was now down on the thing. For the moment she was all right, and if Ginger *had* won, as she had half hoped he might, she would have recouped herself. As it was, he probably wouldn't. She sat in her ricksha in frowning calculation as she drove to Legation Street. Should she put her shirt on Ginger, or not? She couldn't afford to lose a lot more; but unless she put on a good lump, she wouldn't cover her losses if he *did*, improbably, win. Entering the bank, something caught her eye which for the moment drove her problem out of her head. It was a printed notice, standing at intervals along the counter, and ornamenting the walls:

"Friday and Saturday, the 7th and 8th of May, being the occasion of the Spring Meeting of the Peking Race Club, the bank will be closed on those days."

As she stood at the counter to cash her cheque, still staring, enthralled, at this remarkable pronouncement, Mulholland came over to her. "Hullo! how is he?" he asked.

"He" could only mean one creature.

"He looked very spry and jolly this morning," the girl answered. "Li is rather braced about him. I say, Billy, what *is* this?" She indicated the nearest notice.

"That? What about it?" said Mulholland, surprised.

"You don't mean to say the whole Bank shuts for a day and a half, just for a race-meeting?"

"Of course—always. Obviously! I'm riding, and so are Reggie and Nobby, and the T'ai-pans always go out. And no one would come here anyhow. How much, Madam?" said Billy gaily.

"I suppose I'd better have three hundred," said Amber rather gloomily—and took her money and went.

In Peking, where up-to-date clothes are unobtainable, the best-dressed women are always the newest arrivals. This time, therefore, Amber was perforce denied that small extra reassurance which she had derived at last year's races from being ideally dressed. She had had the parchment frock tinted a pale green, and it looked very nice—but she experienced a faint dissatisfaction with it when in the enclosure she encountered Daphne Boggit, her yellow fairness emphasised by a white tailor-made, manifestly Paris, and *du dernier bateau*. She had too many other preoccupations to think long about it—it just took that final edge off her general sense of satisfaction about the day before her: of really having a pony running in the Maidens, and of being about to see quite a lot of Rupert, and get everything happy again. Rupert had been booked for luncheon in the Ministerial *p'eng*, but lunch was no good for talking anyhow; there would be heaps of opportunities beside that. He would want—even Rupert, today, *must* want to come to the paddock, and see Ginger, who was after all to run in the big race. ("Gin *can't* win, and Ginger *might*, if he's in form—so we lose nothing by letting him try," Joe had said.) And this year, more than ever, Rupert would be watching the race with her, she thought, as she stood soon after her arrival by the rails, looking out over the course. As last year, kestrels cried overhead, and shafts of light made blue dusty caves in the silvery green of the willows—how well she remembered standing there with Rupert then; and her sense of security returning with the memory of what lay between, she thought—Today will be lovelier still!

Joe joined her as she stood, her eyes ranging over the enclosure, seeking Rupert. Siege or no siege, the Lega-

tions seemed to have closed down almost as completely
as the banks. Sir James was there, splendid in a new
white top-hat; the German Minister was getting a tip
from Rothstein, the French and Italian Big Envoys had
their heads together over a race-card, though, as Joe
observed, they were more probably discussing the prestige
of *la race latine* than bets. At intervals the noise of guns
bumped across the conversation—no longer a faint vibra-
tion, but a heavy definite booming. But no one appeared to pay the least attention to them. People came
up and greeted her, with enquiries about her pony.
"Going to beat your Uncle, Miss Harrison?" Shaw
enquired, with a knowing look. Amber hoped so.
"Well, Mademoiselle, are we to bet on your Finance
Minister? He has a rich sound," Sir James enquired.
"Yes, *do*, Sir James, and bring me luck." But still there
was no sign of Rupert.

Ah, there he was, coming in now. "I must put something on for the Urga Plate," she said, to excuse her
movement, and walked across towards the *pari-mutuel*
to intercept Rupert. She was herself, however, intercepted by Mrs. Boggit, within a yard of where Daphne
stood, and so witnessed their meeting. "Hullo, Daphne!
You look rather marvellous in white." He said "Hullo"
to Amber too, when he noticed her, but said nothing
about her dress, and went on talking to Daphne. Amber
went and put ten dollars on a pony of Rothstein's, still
accompanied by Mrs. Boggit; she remembered how last
year she and Rupert had made every bet together, and
a little chill of disappointment crept over her.

Joe now summoned her to come to the paddock. Mrs.
Boggit expressed a great desire to come too, and they
moved off together. As they passed Rupert and Daphne
—"Daphne, Miss Harrison is very kindly taking me to
see her griffins," the lady said. "I hear they are mar-

vellous. I think a beautiful horse—Good morning, Mr.
Benenden!—is one of the most moving things in creation,
Miss Harrison; I have always been a passionate lover of
horses."

"Are you coming, Rupert?" Amber said—the question
was almost forced out of her by the chill at her heart, born
of something in Rupert's look and tone—a look almost
of obedience—as he spoke to his companion.

"Yes, rather—in a moment—don't wait for me," he
said. "Do you care to come and look at them, Daph?"
he asked, as Amber moved away. The girl heard her
distinct—"Not in the least—horses bore me to tears," as
she followed Joe and Mrs. Boggit through the crowd.

Down under the willows in the paddock the ponies
for the Maiden Plate were being led round in a ring,
Ginger among them. Amber watched them with a
mixture of emotions. Her natural pride and excitement
and pleasure at the sight of her own pony, at the favourable comments which he aroused, were all mixed in with
an impatient distressful wonder about Rupert. Surely
he wouldn't not come and look at her pony with her, just
because that girl didn't want to? But if he didn't come
soon he would be too late, she said to herself, glancing
at her watch. Oh, today was not going at all as she had
expected!—and something burned and thickened in her
throat as she remembered her happy hopes. Passionately the surface of her mind argued that it was nothing,
his lingering with Daphne, the way he spoke to her,
looked at her—but deep within her a voice that would
not be silenced cried that all was somehow lost, and
disaster upon her.

"Well, now for it!" said a voice beside her. It was
Mulholland, a little pale, taut and nervous, come back
from weighing-in, and prepared to mount. Instantly
Amber forgot her own troubles. "Billy, don't worry!"

she said warmly. She gave him her hand. "The best of luck."

"You know I'll do it if I can," said Mulholland, eyeing her ardently.

She watched the race from the lower part of the stand —but with Joe, not Rupert. In a burst of desperate recklessness she had put two hundred dollars on her own horse—let it be all or nothing! Rupert had not come down to the paddock—she could see his head now, a few seats away, turned constantly towards a white figure beside him. But she had no eyes for anything else when she saw the Ginger Griffin pass up to the starting-point, her own orange racing-colours matching his flaming coat. He was cantering quietly, apparently in a good mood— when they took up their positions she saw that Mulholland had drawn a fair place, third from the rails. Now they were off; clear, thank goodness! Down past the stand in a racing thunder of hoofs they came; Mulholland was giving the horse his head, but whether to get the rails or in order not to upset him she could not tell; actually Ginger was leading by half a length from St. Jean, who lay next. Now, as they swept round the curve by the paddock, Mulholland got the rails fairly, and St. Jean dropped back a length. If Ginger *could* stay the pace——! Her race-glasses to her eyes, she looked apprehensively in the following bunch of ponies for Roth-stein's pale blue—yes, there was Roberts, nursing Fine Champagne, no doubt, for a spurt like that which brought Crème de Cacao in first last year. Oh, Billy was mad to have started so fast, she thought, as they streamed up the opposite side of the course, the chestnut still in front. There, she knew it! Breathless, she saw the pale blue stealing up the string of flying colours— now Roberts drew level with St. Jean, now he had passed him, and was closing up on Ginger. She lowered her glasses and shut her eyes—she could not bear to see it happen! The rising roar of voices about her was like the sea in her ears, meaningless—no, what was that behind her? "The chestnut has it!" "The chestnut wins!" "*C'est Ministre qui gagne!*" She opened her eyes to see her pony pass the post three clear lengths ahead of Fine Champagne.

Chapter Twenty-six

"BY God, we've scooped it!" Joe gave her a staggering thump on the back. "We've done it, Amber!" Dizzy, incredulous, she smiled vaguely at him. "Come on," he said, in his excitement actually putting an arm round her to draw her from her place.

"Come on where?" she asked.

"Darling, you've got to lead him in!" said Joe. "You're all addled! Jump to it!"

Passing out on to the course by the gate under the Stewards' box, congratulations shouted at her on all sides, again her unhappiness was driven underground by the excitement of the moment. Rather soberly, she led the pony in; but when a tumult of acclamation broke out as they passed through the crowd, she could not restrain a rather startled smile. Amber never was any good at assessing her own position—she realised nothing of her popularity; now, receiving what was really an ovation, she was as surprised as she had been over her Christmas presents. The win was wholly unexpected, but it was a popular one; her prettiness, her youth and enterprise made her success delightful to people who would have been left cold by another win of one of the old guard. A little tingling glow came over her again, as, during the unsaddling, people thronged round to congratulate her—the Leicesters, the Stefanys, Bruno, even Mimi. *"Ce poney est merveilleux, Mademoiselle—mes félicitations!"* said François, with a rather timid glance at his wife. "Well, Miss Harrison, I thought your jockey was

346

crazy for the first half mile—but, by George, he knew what he'd got under him!" said Shaw. "That's a damn good pony." As soon as she could, she went off to pat and thank Ginger, who stood, dripping and quivering, in his box. "You lamb!" she said, stroking his neck, darkened now with sweat. Ginger made a low cheerful reply through his nose. Here she was found by the other riders. "Well, I think you deserved that, Amber," said Uncle Bill, "and he's a corker, your Minister."

"Mulholland was a bit rash, Miss Harrison, in my opinion—but it came off all right. I'm as pleased as if I'd won it myself," said Leroy. This was an unusually long speech for Henry, and Amber was pleased. When she got Mulholland to herself she thanked him. "But you frightened me out of my wits at first, Billy."

"Well you see, I knew at once that he *was* keen," said Mulholland, "and I was afraid of upsetting him if I started monkeying about with him, so I thought I'd better let him out and chance his keeping his lead. It wasn't conventional riding, I admit."

La Touche, who was one of the Stewards, came up at this point. "I thought you'd like to know his time, Amber."

"Oh *yes;* what was it, Touchy?"

"Simply marvellous — two-seven. It's within two seconds of the record!"

"I say, we must go up and see what he pays, Amber," said Joe. The Portfolio stable went back *en masse* to the space in front of the *pari-mutuel*, and waited in some suspense among the crowd. When the board was run up it was evident that the rumour of the pony's staleness, disseminated by Leicester, had produced precisely the effect which Mr. Hawtrey had anticipated. Minister of Marine was paying $15.25. Amber's reckless bet had brought her in something over $3000, more than three hundred pounds. Nugent came over to them. "Amber, my dear, I am most frightfully glad—and glad I followed my sentiments and not the experts, and backed your horse!" Sir James came up, his hands full of notes —"Well, I obeyed you, Mademoiselle, and I am grateful for the tip." As she and Joe left the *guichet*, Joe stuffing wads of her notes into his breast pocket—"I shall look like a pouter pigeon for the rest of the day, Sir," he said to Sir James—they encountered Rupert, still with Miss Boggit in tow. "Well, Rupert, did you back my pony?" Amber asked, gaily.

"No—you never gave us the tip," said Rupert. Amber's gaiety froze a little at the "us." (Who had said, last year, "We're a combine, Amber and I"?)

"Rupert is a most miserable guide to the turf," drawled Miss Boggit. "We've lost on every race so far."

"Well, Amber, I congratulate you," Rupert said warmly. "I am most frightfully glad. Now you've got your heart's desire, haven't you?"

For a moment she simply stared at him, unable to speak. Was this stupidity or cruelty? "She's got three thousand dollars and the best griffin in Peking, anyhow," said Joe heartily. And whether this was accident or cleverness Amber didn't know, but she had never felt more grateful in her life to anyone than she did then to Joe.

She made some excuse to turn away with him, but as she walked she could hardly see for the tears which burned behind her eyes. Her heart's desire! When all was lost, irretrievably, unmistakeably now. He hadn't come to the paddock, he hadn't cared to be with her to see the race, his very congratulations mocked her. Not even the surface of her mind could contend any longer against the evidence of her senses. How, why, when this change had come over him she could not guess; and though for

weeks to come her heart would not cease to ask those
questions, and find no answer, for the moment she could
only concentrate on getting through the rest of the day
without showing her desolation—the day that should
have been one of the happiest in her life. The bitterness
of that thought she dared not look at. But where could
she look without meeting some reminder of her lost joy?
She was at the mercy of her surroundings—the smell of
crushed turf, a spray of oleander against the sky, the
high notes of the kestrels, the willows beyond the course,
all rang with a faint echo of the music they had first begun
to make for her there, last year.

It was lucky for Amber, really, that the day should
have ended on a note of unwonted excitement. At lunch
at the temple there was an empty place. "Who's missing?" Amber asked Joe. "I can't remember."

"The M.A.," said Joe gaily. "He's gone off to the
War!" Amber paid no attention to this—she knew
vaguely that to go in Pullman cars to look at battle-fields
was part of the duties of a Military Attaché, and assumed
readily that to go and listen to artillery might also be his
job. On their return to the course the guns were silent
for the time being. After a couple more races Rothstein
took her aside, rather mysteriously.

"Miss Harrison, that is a beautiful pony of yours. Do
you want to sell him?"

"I've never thought about it," said Amber, surprised.

"Well, if you do want to, I will give you a cheque for
fifteen hundred dollars now."

"Fifteen hundred? But that's fantastic!" said Amber.

"Perhaps so—perhaps not. From one race one cannot
be sure. If he is what I think, it is not so fantastic.
But you will have many offers for him; and probably
they will not be so good as this."

"May I think it over and let you know?" Amber said.

"If we do sell him I should like you to have him, because I feel I owe him to you."

"How so?"

"You gave me that tip last year, and I got him with the money I made on Crème de Cacao."

"Oh! That was nothing. Well, think it over—but at any time, I would like the first refusal of him."

As he spoke a loud booming shook the air; it was renewed again, and yet again, and then shivered away into silence.

"That was much nearer," said Rothstein tranquilly, as people in England speak of a thunderstorm. "They are moving up, apparently."

To Amber there was something fantastic about the rest of the day. The later races were run on ground shaking with the roar of artillery, and Gin, her grey griffin, won the Stewards' Cup soon after they began to hear the machine-guns. She was the owner of two winners, she had made—with the prizes—over £350, and had the chance of selling her pony for another £150. And she was as miserable as she had ever been in her life. Just before the last race, when the rattle of machine-guns had become like a ceaseless rhythmic crackling of fire-wood, Uncle Bill left a conclave with the Minister, Joe and Mr. Hugo, and came up to her.

"We're going back to Hei Lung Hu-t'ung tonight, Amber. The Minister prefers it, as they seem pretty close. But I expect you'd like to stay for the last race, wouldn't you?"

"I don't really mind. I think I'd better go and pack," said Amber.

"That's all done," said Bill. "Bessie has gone on with the car to take the things, and Joe says he'll take you."

"Oh, all right," said Amber indifferently. She really only wanted to get away quietly by herself, to stop having to talk and smile, and to be able to look her position in the face, to ask herself those questions which here she dared not even think of. But it might be conspicuous to go away now—and it was only a little longer. So she stayed, in the gradually thinning crowd, and watched the last race, feeling the muscles round her mouth stiff with smiles that had to be made with conscious effort. When she and Joe got into the car she sank back in her corner and closed her eyes. Heavens, how her head ached! Well, it was over now—now she could rest; Joe wouldn't mind.

"Tired?" Joe asked.

"No—yes; headache. It's the guns, I think."

"I expect you *are* tired—you've been pretty hard at it these last weeks. But it was worth it, wasn't it, darling? Two winners! Marvellous."

"Yes, rather—it's been wonderful," said Amber, trying to put enough enthusiasm into her voice not to damp Joe's satisfaction. Dear Joe—it wasn't his fault that this day of days had been so wretched.

"Darling," Joe began again presently, a little hesitatingly, as they swayed along the sandy road between the fields and the rows of willows, "darling, last autumn I asked you something, and you said 'Leave it till after the races.' Well, we've won the Maidens now, and——"

"Oh Joe, not now! Please not now," the girl almost moaned, putting up a protesting hand.

Mr. Hawtrey captured the hand. "Yes, now, sweetheart," he said, gently but determinedly. "I love you, and I want to marry you. I won't hurry you, but I've waited six months and not said a word, and now I'm asking you again. I know I'm not a brain, and all that," said Joe simply, "but I'm sure I could make you happy, and I can never be happy myself unless I do! After all, we like the same things, don't we?"

At that, to his great astonishment, the girl burst into tears. "Oh no, no!" she sobbed. "Oh no! Not that! No, no, no!" She seemed quite beside herself—her sobs were almost uncontrollable; her words made no sense at all. She's utterly overdone, he thought—the heat and the excitement, and those beastly guns! Very gently, with a skill born of experience, Mr. Hawtrey contrived to slide an arm round Miss Harrison's waist in such a way that, though they were in a stream of cars, it would not be unduly evident to outsiders. "There, now, sweet love—there," he soothed her.

"No!" she cried, almost with violence and sitting bolt upright. "No, Joe, I tell you! I can't marry you—and you're not to say that! Do you understand?" She was quite hysterical. "You're not to—I can't—I can't *bear* it!" she sobbed, sinking back again in a sort of collapse.

Joe was both hurt and distressed by this. But his concern for Amber outweighed all other feelings. "All right, dearest—I won't, I promise. Just sit quiet and don't talk—there's a darling." Still sobbing, she lay with closed eyes, while with his free hand he stroked hers, gently, as it lay in her lap. Poor darling, poor love, he thought, watching her white face, as her sobs came more slowly—all his personal hurt and disappointment melted away, but a new pain forced its way into his mind. This was love! She wanted someone she couldn't get. Was it Rupert, with that new girl of his, damn him? They had seemed very thick, he and Amber, about Christmas time, but lately it seemed to have worn off a bit. Or was it someone else? Looking round among her friends, only one other person presented himself as in the least probable—Nugent! Oh, perhaps! Girls did do that— fell for married men. And Nugent was much more attractive than he probably realised, with his curt masterful speech, his intelligence, and the way he under-

stood people. And she was always there. Perhaps it
was Nugent. Anyhow, he thought bitterly, it wasn't
him, Joe! That was all sure, and he had best make up
his mind to it. No good going on trying while she was
as much in love as this. Stubbornly he took his pill,
sitting there in the car, his eye-glass stuck firmly in his
eye, his white top-hat set at a jaunty angle, his arm
round the person he loved, who loved somebody else.

2 A

Chapter Twenty-seven

MR. RUPERT BENENDEN'S engagement to Miss Daphne Boggit was announced a week after the races. The intervening days saw a new war-lord established in Peking. It seemed to happen very simply, really. The guns boomed away outside the city for a couple of days, some of Wang's commercial aeroplanes flew over the town and dropped a bomb or two, the city gates were shut. Then, one evening, as Nugent and Joanna drove out to dine in the Tartar City they found Morrison Street full of groups of soldiers, each group, as a rule, running behind a donkey hung round like a Christmas tree with rifles, clothes, tin basins and bags of meal, which dropped off it at intervals —the Marshal's troops, it proved, retiring. And next day, going out to ride at the Temple of Heaven, they met, overshadowed biblically by a high-hanging cloud of dust, Wang's troops marching in, singing Moody and Sankey hymns as they went. And that was all. There was no proper siege, no actual bombardment, and nothing much in the way of a battle; there seemed no particular military reason why Li should have gone out, or Wang come in. Nugent, remembering Count Herman's story, which Rupert had passed on to him, supposed that it had all been arranged in some sing-song house. Anyhow it made no difference, so far as he could see, to anybody but the shopkeepers, who found themselves obliged to accept a different paper currency from the newcomers, and landed with large stocks of the old one, which for the time being they could not easily dispose of.

But even that would soon be adjusted by some indescribable Chinese method. One could not blame the European community, he thought, for being—as they were—far more interested in the engagement, and in the other important piece of diplomatic news, that Mr. George Hawtrey was to be transferred to Madrid, since to the inhabitants themselves the change-over was of so little moment.

Nugent's first reaction to Rupert's engagement was one of sheer dismay. The little he had seen of the girl he disliked; she was not in the least good enough; she would stifle the difficult best in Rupert, and bring out all his facile worst. It was a bad show. But his more immediate concern was Amber. She must hear the news in the easiest way for her. Rupert had come in person to tell him, and the moment he left the room, Nugent, changing his spectacles, rang up the Hei Lung Hut'ung. "Morning, Amber. What are you doing to-day?"

"Well, nothing, actually, till this afternoon—I said I'd go to Anna's cocktail party then."

"Would you like to cut that and come for a ride with me? I've found a place I want to show you."

"Yes, I'd love to—but I've no ponies here, and we can't get out, can we?"

"We don't have to go 'out,' and you can ride the Mishu pony. Meet me outside the Hata-mên at five, will you?" And when she agreed—"Right. Well, I must work now," he said. "By the way, there's a piece of what *I* think bad news. Rupert is engaged to that girl—he's just told me so. I don't much like it" — and rang off.

That was all he could do. Ensure that she took the knock alone, not in a crowd, with a few quiet hours ahead of her; not to get over the worst of it—that, he knew, would be in the long weeks to come—but to recover from the actual shock, and to get her poor little face well set to meet the world. Nugent had never forgotten her dive into the carriage at Fenchurch Street, within a few minutes of his first setting eyes on her, of which he had divined the purpose. Poor little wretch! What a thing to meet twice over. Well, he would probably hear all about it this afternoon—indeed, he would see to it that he did; she couldn't go bottling it all up. Sighing, in the dim light behind the *lienzas* in his green-washed room in the Chancery, Nugent changed his spectacles again and went back to his work.

When Nugent rang off, Amber hung up the receiver and went to her own courtyard, where she sat down on a step in the shadow of the loggia. In the patch of sunshine in the centre of the court two or three small blue dragon-flies, brilliant as jewels, poised and darted above the warm brown depths of the goldfish pool, or made flashing excursions towards the delicate carved stiffness of the two tree-paeonies by the doorway, whose great scentless flowers were each as perfect and solid as if made of ivory. There is all the difference in the world between listening to your heart within you crying that all is lost, and hearing the fact baldly stated in a reliable voice down the telephone. This was really the end; now there was no longer any room for secret unbidden gleams of hope. Without knowing that she watched them, her eyes followed the dragon-flies, rested on the flowers, during the hot hours of that morning—it was only years afterwards that she realised why she disliked the sight of blue dragon-flies, or why even a picture of tree-paeonies filled her with a vague discomfort. In those hours, she asked herself again and again those questions which at the races she had not dared to face. Why had he changed? Was it her fault this time too? Where had she gone wrong?

She remembered with something like agony those occasions when she had gone to train her ponies instead of walking or skating with Rupert. At the time it had seemed right and even inevitable to do that—had it really been a grave mistake? But if he loved her he must have understood why she did it—and she had been so certain that he loved her. Had she been wrong ever to be certain? Oh, but that she could not do!—when she tried to examine the grounds for her certainty, to recall those moments on the Wall, such an extremity of misery overcame her that the sensation was almost one of physical torment. She couldn't, she wouldn't remember that— not now—that must remain inviolable, untouched! She moved, in her pain—got up, went into her room, drank water. It was no better in there; she felt cold; she went out again with a hat, and sat in the sun. It occurred to her, in the shock of this second defeat, that perhaps she was really the sort of person whom nobody could go on loving—no real person, like Rupert or Arthur; only very, very simple people like Joe. Then why had he taken so much interest in her at first, been so persistent about seeing her? She thought of their walk at the Temple of Heaven last year, and suddenly she remembered the resolution she had begun to break that day, to watch her step, to keep clear of young men. She had been right, right, right! She would have avoided this misery if she had stuck to that. But then she remembered, too, that she had really definitely decided to break it because of what Nugent said. Nugent must be right—he was always right; *he* could be trusted utterly. Thinking of Nugent, for the first time she wept, her head sunk on her knees as she sat beside the goldfish pool. In all her misery and mortification, she clung desperately to the thought of Nugent; and how he had said that this was the right way to live.

The south-eastern quarter of the Chinese city in Peking is a place little visited by Europeans. There is nothing particular to take them there, and the dust of the rutted road which leads out to the inconspicuous gateway of the Chiang-Ts'o-mên is seldom stirred by the wheels of foreign cars or the feet of foreigners' horses. To the Chiang-Ts'o-mên, however, Nugent took Amber that afternoon, riding across the open fields and through the woods of small trees, where the few houses are clustered together like country villages and the city is completely lost sight of, till with a shock one comes on the Wall again, reflected in the reed-fringed waters of the swampy mere that lies near the gate. They turned there, and rode back by another route which brought them to the foot of a small pagoda, standing isolated among the fields. It was very ruinous. Its little stone frills were crumbling and broken—weeds had taken root in the neglected stone-work and hung wreathing down in places over the creamy walls, adding to its derelict look. But it had nevertheless a curious desolate grace. They dismounted, and gave their horses to a couple of peasants who had left the hoeing of their crops, as usual, to come and feast their eyes on *wai-kuo-jen*. Nugent led her over to a bit of broken stonework, the footing of some ruined wall, and they sat down on it. In front of them lay a little group of graves, the rough earthen mounds still decorated with willow-wands and sticks frilled with paper, stuck in the top; about and between them, more peasants were hoeing the rows of winter wheat.

"How much more *gemütlich* that is than our way, isn't it?" said Nugent. "Instead of the dead all huddled together in a damp solitary churchyard, where people only go once a week, if that, to lie out in the sunshine in their own fields, with their families working round them, day in and day out."

"Yes, much," said Amber. Then, feeling her answer rather inadequate: "What are the willow-wands for?" she roused herself to ask.

"They put them there at Ch'ing Ming," said Nugent. "Stefany was telling me about it. Ch'ing Ming is the Spring Festival; a sort of Easter, May Day and Arbour Day combined, when they go out to visit the dead, and give them food and money and so on for the next year in the other life. The willow is the symbol of immortality, because it is the first living thing to bud afresh in spring."

Amber said nothing. You couldn't say "How interesting!" to Nugent, and her mind felt quite empty, squeezed dry by the pressure of one continuous train of thought.

"Amber, how much has this about Rupert hit you?" Nugent asked her then.

She turned away her head—he saw her hands moving in her lap. "It's rather—beaten me up," she said, in a stifled voice. "Why? Could you *see*?" she said, in tones cold with desperation, after a moment.

"I shouldn't have, but for what you told me at T'ang-shan, and for knowing Rupert so well."

"Oh, does he go in for this sort of thing?" she asked, with icy bitterness.

Nugent put his hand on her arm. "Amber, my very dear child, not that way," he said. He had never, he realised, heard her say a bitter thing before, and it moved him more than anything else could have done. "Won't you tell me about it, quite quietly? It's him I'm sorry for, and so must you be."

"I *can't* understand it," the girl burst out. "If I could understand it I shouldn't mind so much. You see, I thought it was all right—I felt so safe. I didn't worry when I couldn't see him and go for the walks he wanted.

I *had* to train the ponies; but when people love one another they understand about things like that."

"What made you think he loved you?" Nugent asked.

"I suppose it was my mistake," said Amber, wretchedly.

"Well, tell me." Gradually he drew it out of her—the story of Lydia, the talk on the Wall, and how the world had turned then to music; her engrossment in the ponies afterwards, the breeze over her question about Count Herman. As she spoke her manner became quieter—once she cried a little; it was clear that to get it all out afforded her some relief. Presently she said a thing which struck him. "I believe I shouldn't have made whatever mistake I did make if I could have *known* him better—but he's afraid of being known." He realised at once that this was true; it was one key to Rupert's character. But to the question which he knew was tormenting her, what her mistake was, he could give no answer.

"You may find that out sometime," he said, "but it's not really important, because it may not have been anything in you at all, but something in Rupert. And you may have been perfectly right in believing that he did love you. One can't always know these things. What *is* important is that you shouldn't be either embittered or intimidated by all this. Do you remember something of Rupert's that I quoted to you on the boat?"

"The traveller?"

"Yes. There are bags of gold to bear home even from these sort of journeys."

She stared at it. Were there really? even from these deserts of pain?

"There are," he said, answering her unspoken question. "So don't regret, and don't forget. By the way, when were you thinking of going home? Would it be a good plan, do you think?"

Amber had thought of it. Her year was more than

up, and now that Joe was going back, there was not much
point in keeping on the stable, she said. Nugent pointed
out that Mrs. Hugo was going home in just under a
month, so that she could count on an escort. They
agreed that it would be as well to take this chance.
There was a pause, and then Amber said, quietly and
thoughtfully—

"I came out here to get away from Arthur, and now
I'm going home to get away from Rupert; but how am I
to get away from the thing in me which makes these mistakes? How am I ever to know if it's real or not, when
everything turns luminous and sings?"

"That's in you—so it's always real, to that extent," he
told her. "But it isn't the important thing. It doesn't
matter."

"Doesn't *matter*?" She stared at him.

"No—it's heavenly, but it's quite irrelevant to loving
anyone, really and truly. It isn't the thing that lasts.
It may be the prelude to what lasts, but it's quite independent of it." He pointed to the blue figures of the
peasants among the graves in front of them. "There are
four hundred millions of those people, and they have the
most perfect family life in the world. But it isn't based on
music—nearly always their marriages are arranged for
them. It's based solidly on loyal love and affection
growing up through the years, as all good marriages
must be, ultimately, however they begin." He paused.
"I often think," he went on, "that we sacrifice a lot of
time and a lot of happiness in Europe to the theory of
romantic love."

Amber sat looking in front of her.

"And yet you told me to accept experience," she said
at length.

"Yes, certainly—since that is how we all live. You
can't, being a twentieth-century Englishwoman, get

your mother to arrange a marriage for you with a suitable man you've never seen—and you couldn't settle down in it if you did. But you will be twice the wife to somebody because of Arthur and Rupert."

"Why?"

"Because you'll be twice the person. At present, like everyone else, you *want* the world to be made luminous and sing—in fact, you want it more than most of us. And I can tell you that it's not important, till my tongue falls out, but you won't believe me. The only way to learn that particular truth is by having that experience and losing it—as you have been doing. That in the end will give you freedom."

"Freedom from what?" she asked.

"Yourself—and our Western tyranny of romantic love. Incidentally you learn a lot about loving each time, too; but the main thing——" he paused, looking ahead of him.

"What is the main thing?" she asked, as he did not go on. In spite of his brusque words his face had a curious visionary look, very unlike a Counsellor's, as he stared at the sunlit Chinese graves.

"Look at those willow-wands," he said. "How like the Chinese and their sweet, unfathomable good sense! The commonest of all the trees, the simplest of all natural facts—it buds the first in spring! That is their symbol of immortality." He took off his hat, and sighed—the hair above his ears was greyer than fifteen months ago, when she saw the lilac-blossom stuck in it, the day after they reached Peking. "One can die, and yet be immortal, here and now," he said. "That is the main thing, Amber."

She did not know why the tears stood in her eyes then. Something about him moved her extraordinarily; she was reminded somehow of that evening when she saw him standing by Dickie's garden, during the child's illness. The unconscious undertone of resistance to what he had been saying gave way—something melted, broke, flowed in her; her resentment, her despair, her mortification yielded to some gentler, truer impulse.

"Mr. Grant-Howard, I will try!" she said impulsively. "You have been so good to me."

"Give me a kiss," he said gently, and kissed her. "You're a brave child," he said. "Be stout-hearted."

Chapter Twenty-eight

THE train shrieked, puffed and lumbered its way out of the Ch'ien-mên station, with Mrs. Hugo's, Miss Harrison's and Mr. George Hawtrey's heads projecting out of three windows, one behind the other. Nugent and Joanna stood on the platform, waving, with half Peking waving round them. Peking runs rather to farewells—there was a carriageful of bouquets for Amber and Mrs. Hugo, books and endless back-slappings for Joe. As the train disappeared a loud sobbing lamentation burst out—it was Mimi de Bulle, suddenly overcome by the loss of *"Ce cher Joe!"* *"Il était tellement sympathique!"* she wailed. Mrs. Leicester glanced round at her with a faint shrug of distaste—then continued to gaze after the train. Her lovely still face gave no clue to her thoughts—perhaps she was thinking of her words to Amber over a year ago, and wondering, since she left Peking engaged to no one, if she was leaving it with a broken heart. Or perhaps she knew. M. Rothstein turned away, cigar in mouth, genuine regret on his face —he liked that nice little girl. But he had got both her griffins, and one of them was going to be another Bengal. Uncle Bill and Aunt Bessie moved off together. "We shall miss her, Bill, shan't we?" said Aunt Bessie.

"I wish she'd marry Joe!" said Uncle Bill.

Joanna and Nugent, walking behind them along the cinder-path with Sir James, overheard, and smiled the same smile at Old Bill.

"If she marries Hawtrey he'll be an extremely lucky felloh," the Minister observed in an undertone to Joanna.

"She's a delightful girl: healthy interests, you know—those ponies, and learning Chinese—and pretty manners. I like a girl like that." Joanna had a moment's wonder as to whether he liked his own niece so well. She soon learned. "I wish Daphne was more like her," Sir James proceeded regretfully. "It's all dancing, and those very odd modern books, with her — really deplorable, the books are, Mrs. Nugent."

Joanna could well believe it. They parted from Sir James at the Water-gate, refusing a lift, and walked in the blazing sun down the Jade Canal Road and in at the "person-gape." On the way—"I shouldn't wonder if Joe does get her to marry him in the end," Joanna said.

This utterance was rather unexpected to Nugent. Since that day when they discussed Miss Boggit on the way home from the paper-hunt Joanna had said very little about Amber—indeed she had almost seemed to sheer off the subject. And, with all Joe's good qualities, he still didn't *quite* see Amber marrying him—though anyone might do far worse. It would be much better, anyhow, than Rupert marrying Miss Boggit; that was simply a catastrophe. Already the mere fact of Rupert being engaged to someone he so much disapproved of had cut Nugent off from the old freedom and fearlessness of intercourse with him; they could not speak freely on the subject which was presumably nearest Rupert's heart at the moment—at least he, Nugent, couldn't. He felt himself a little chilly and bereft: Joe, comic and reliable, gone; Amber gone, with her confiding eagerness and the warmth of her affection; and left with him in this alien world, of all these friends, only Rupert, whom he had loved so well and so long, in whose companionship he took such delight, but now self-bound to a person who could only mar his best qualities and separate him from his more valuable friends. (Nugent naturally placed himself in this category.) Thinking all this, he said nothing; Joanna, however, proceeded with her train of thought undisturbed: "I'm sure he'd do her better than that idiotic Rupert, though she was so frightfully in love with him."

"Why do you think that went wrong, really?" Nugent asked as they mounted the steps of the loggia—it was perfumed by the pots of stocks standing along its outer edge, and he sniffed the scent gratefully.

Joanna sat down in a long chair and took off her hat.

"One of the things that irritated him was that she would *express* things, I'm sure," she said.

Nugent stared at her. "Why shouldn't she express things?"

"She didn't do it very well," said Joanna—"a cleverer person would have kept her unfinished ideas to herself, at least with Rupert."

"But he was tremendously interested in a lot of her ideas," objected Nugent.

"I said her *unfinished* ones," said Joanna evenly. "Rupert loves definiteness." "Then of course he was maddened by all the business about horses," she went on.

But a new idea had struck Nugent, and he let the horses slide. "Did that irritate *you*?" he asked suddenly.

"No," said Joanna sincerely. "I liked her enormously, and her least baked ideas were worth much more than the slick little second-hand gobbets that that wretched Daphne hands out, as if they were so profound! But it was bad technique to unload them on to Rupert. Daphne has caught him by her absolute certainty about every-thing, I'm sure. Amber was always so uncertain. So long as anyone is certain, even about nothings, even if they're wrong, it will do for him!" She spoke with a sort of exasperated contempt.

Nugent considered this. There was, as usual, a good

deal in what she said. "You sound as though you really disliked Rupert," he said at length.

"No," said Joanna, "I don't dislike him. His mind is perfectly charming—it's like an incredibly ingenious machine for turning out amusing ideas. But I disapprove of him completely."

"Why?"

"I hate his cold curiosity. He can't let people alone—he's as inquisitive as a Chinese, always poking and investigating and trying to make them function, to see how they work! And doing it without real affection. You never saw that, because you're as blind as an owl about people you're fond of, and besides, he doesn't do it with you—he's a little afraid of you. But that's what he was doing to Amber—at first, anyhow."

"Oh come, he wouldn't do that — *really*, Joanna!" Nugent expostulated.

"Well, he mightn't be absolutely deliberate about it, because he's so careful not to know himself too well," Joanna conceded. "But he does do it, and he did do it to her."

But Nugent was reminded of Amber's remark about Rupert—"he's afraid of being known." He repeated it now to his wife.

"Of course!—and the greatest protection against being known is to refuse to know yourself," said Joanna. "That was very sharp of her. She was curiously intelligent sometimes. When did she tell you that—lately?"

"Yes—just after the engagement was announced. I took her a ride on purpose to give her a chance to talk about it if she wanted to—and she did."

Joanna smiled. "What are you laughing at?" Nugent asked.

"I was only imagining you cross-examining her,

because you thought she ought to talk about it," said Joanna, looking very much amused. When Nugent changed his spectacles and looked Socratic, she knew that, as Joe would have said, she had got it in one. He did so now.

"I think it did her good to get it out," he said very judgematically.

"Dearest, I'm sure it did—poor little mite!"

"You see, she had told me about her other young man in England, before," said Nugent. "I didn't tell you about that, because it was her poor wretched little secret; and I didn't tell you about Rupert this time, because while she was still here, the fewer people who knew more than they could see, the better for her. Now it doesn't matter. But her real trouble is that she feels she's been a flop, twice—and that's rather hard to get over."

"Yes," said Joanna thoughtfully. "She depends far too much on what other people think of her—she doesn't go ahead on her own enough. And she's madly generous-minded. That's where she has it over all the Ruperts in the world! Lydia Leicester was perfectly right about her being *made* for pain with people, till she gets some security. That's why I think Joe would make her such a good husband."

"When did Lydia say that?"

"Oh, at Sir James's party for Li." Something in the course of this conversation with her husband had drawn the small sting out of Mrs. Leicester's other observations on the subject of Amber — Joanna could contemplate them serenely now. She smiled again, a very little, thinking that in her place Amber would certainly have poured out the whole story. Well, that might be generous, but it would be bad technique—some day, if she ever married, she would have to learn about the many silences which love and loyalty impose. Meanwhile, in this restored ease, Mrs. Grant-Howard turned back to the subject of Benenden. "Nugent," she said, "you asked me what *I* thought about Rupert and Amber, but what do you think yourself?"

"About why it went wrong?"

"Yes, partly."

"I simply don't know. I think a lot of what you say about Rupert is probably true. But I don't know how much he was ever in love with her. If I even knew that, I could have answered one of her worst questions."

Joanna guessed what that question was. But she did not seek to verify her guess—Nugent ought to be allowed to respect the child's confidences.

"Do you think I'm too hard on him?" she asked—"or do you agree that he's too experimental?"

"I agree——" Nugent stopped, took off his spectacles and rubbed his eyes, a frequent gesture of his when his ideas were refractory. "I agree with you about his not being willing to know himself—what I'm less sure about is the reason. But I think I do know it, more or less."

"Well?"

"Rupert's a very *conscious* person, and he's afraid of letting himself be much interested in moral questions— well, in the things of the spirit, if you like—for fear of where they might land him. But unconsciously, like everyone else, he *is* interested in them, so that in itself ties him up in a good many knots. And I believe he only lets his interest in those things express itself where other people are concerned—he puts *them* under a microscope to study spiritual values. That's what makes him what you call so poking and inquisitive."

"Um," said Joanna. She balanced a comment, and then decided, in the interests of married life, which to her were paramount, that it would be better to bring it

2 B

out. "That's a little hard on the person who's put under the microscope, isn't it?"

"Yes, it may be," said Nugent.

"Well, he won't find exactly a plethora of the spiritual graces to study in Daphne B.!" said Joanna.

Nugent grinned—he enjoyed it when Joanna was spiteful. "No, he won't," he said. Then he sighed— "Poor old Rupert."

Dickie came tearing down from the upper garden, his jaw working with some piece of news. "Amber's left her hem behind!" he shouted, as soon as he got within earshot.

"What do you mean?" his mother asked, as he came up.

"Come and see! Come on, Babby!" Nugent rose and went with his son, in response to urgent tugs. Dickie led him to the septic tank, against which stood a wooden box. "Ip's there still—she's forgop ip," he said, pointing to the roof. Mounting on the box, Nugent saw that the Bong indeed sat there, a malevolent ginger-coloured object among the green creepers. He had forgotten all about it. Now he eyed it thoughtfully, while Dickie told him the story of its return. Curious, the number of unpleasant things that *had* happened since Amber brought it out from the Temple of the Ancestors. It had done down the Soviets, it had pretty well done down Dickie— and since she brought it back again, Amber's own happiness had been crashed.

"I think the Soviets can have it back, Dickie," he said —"no, I'm sure Amber didn't want it." He picked up the thing gingerly, carried it along the path, and pitched it over the wall into the deserted garden of the Soviet Embassy. A tinkling crash announced its final demise. "Poor Amber!" Dickie muttered, still unconvinced. He could not imagine why his father rejoined "Poor Rupert!"

Chapter Twenty-nine

VERY occasionally there comes towards the end
of January, even in London, one of those fine
mild days, soft with an almost tremulous softness,
when the air speaks of spring. Amber's wedding-day
was one of them. She sat, that morning, at the window
of her room in Grosvenor House, looking out over the
Park, where the mist seemed to hold the faint sunshine
steady among the bare boughs of the plane-trees, and the
delicate light made London's buildings beautiful and
dignified as those in one of Canaletto's pictures. She
was wishing that it wasn't a London wedding; she would
rather have been married at Riddingcote. But it had
had to be hurried on when Joe's appointment was suddenly
changed from Madrid to Adis Ababa, because they must
be married before he went; and what with the difficulty of getting a trousseau in a hurry from down in
Gloucestershire, and the inconveniences of a winter
wedding in the country, Lady Julia had decided firmly on
London, taken a flat, and dragged Amber up to live, the
girl felt, with dressmakers, for the next few weeks.

Sitting in the enforced idleness which custom decrees
for brides on their wedding morning, Amber was also
wishing that she had heard from Nugent. She had written
to him as soon as she was engaged, two months ago, via
Siberia, and if there had been no hold-ups, and he had
replied by the same route she might have expected an
answer by now. She wondered if her letter had made
him understand why she was so sure it was all right, her
marrying Joe. She was still sure—but somehow it was

hard to be married without his approval; she had lived so much by Nugent and his precepts, all these last months. Well, never mind, she thought—she knew it was all right. Her mouth set in a firmer line than it had ever shown in Peking, as she sat there in the window.

It was all right for Joe too, really, she believed. She had told him the limitations he might expect of her love —"I'm not *in* love with you, Joe—do you understand?" She thought he did—Joe had been learning a lot of things even before they got engaged, as well as since. He had learned, for instance, that it cut no ice at all when he told her that he had no eyes for anyone else—she knew that only too well. God, he must have known some awful duds of women! It was some time before he could be persuaded that she really was not jealous of other women, or even of his Club! But since they were engaged she had found out that there were some things that Joe knew by himself. When, moved by conscientiousness, she enquired if he were sure he was really happy and satisfied, his answer was always the same. "Darling, I never think about those things. When I can look at you, I'm happy. And if I can do anything to amuse you and make *you* happy, of course I'm content. I love you. But I think you do too much, you know. Can't you cut out——?" etc., etc. There was something extraordinarily lovable and restful about this simplicity—thinking of him now, she smiled. She would be very safe with Joe, and very happy. And even she, with all her lack of subtlety, could surely make Joe happy if, as she was doing and would do, she gave her whole mind to it. She thought of what Nugent had said about Chinese family life, and her mouth set again in lines at once firm and content. Nugent had been right—that terrible laying the world aside, the world made light and music, had given her a sort of freedom that she had never known before. This she was too wise to try to explain to Joe, but this too, like the Athenians, he ignorantly worshipped, saying—"I can't describe it, but there's a sort of other-worldly look about you now, that you hadn't before." She reminded him, she learned, of Watts' Sir Galahad in Eton Chapel, which had caught his early aspirations and fixed them. Amber felt that Nugent would say that it was probably better to have seen these things in terms of Watts than not to have seen them at all. And then she would laugh, and thereafter scourge herself for an intellectual snob, setting up to be so much better than Joe, with all his loyal unselfish patience.

The opening door made her turn her head. Joe stood there. "Darling, what *do* you want?"

"To see *you*!" he said, shutting it cautiously and tip-toeing across the room. "Where's Mamma?" he asked, kissing her.

"Somewhere about—she won't approve of you coming here this morning."

"I know—I put on sneakers on purpose." He displayed a pair of crêpe-soled shoes complacently. "Leave her to me," he said. Amber laughed—Joe handled Lady Julia as she had never dreamed that mortal could. "But look, sweetheart, I've got a good excuse. I just went round to the F.O. for my letters, and here's one for you from jolly old Nugent, enclosed in one to me. So I brought it along. I thought you'd want it to be married on!"

"Angel!" said Amber, stretching out her hand for it.

"Ah! But what do I get for it?" said Joe, holding it out of her reach.

"Name your price!" said Amber. "The firm's rich!"

He gave it into her hand, putting his other arm round her. "Lovely one! If you only knew *how* rich the firm is!" he whispered.

The door opened again, and there stood Lady Julia; her eyebrows would have quelled a whole brigade. "Morning, Mamma!" said Joe, springing up and giving her a hearty kiss. "I'm acting postman! No complaints, I hope? I found a letter for her at the Office, so I brought it round at once."

"Oh, thank you, George. But she ought really to be left now," said Lady Julia, "the dress-maker will be here very soon with her frock."

"Right.—I'll be off. Make her maid rouge her up a little, Mamma—she looks pale. *Auf Wiedersehen, mein liebstes Herz.*" He was off, Lady Julia following him out—"See him safely off the premises!" Amber grinned to herself. Then she turned to her letter.

It was a long one. From the first line Amber was re-assured—Nugent understood. He was very glad indeed —"As for your Uncle Bill, you would have been touched at his pleasure; I met him the day they got your letter, and he made me drink a champagne cocktail on it!" Then, after good wishes, Nugent turned to another matter. "I think it may do you good to know the answers to two of the questions that worried you so much last spring. Rupert went and had dysentery the other day, rather badly—we shoved him into the German Hospital, and Hertz pulled him through, but we were all a good deal worried about him. Emetine and a diet of *hsiao mi* brought him low, and anyhow dysentery is a disease of the will, as I found out last summer—all inhibitions leave you for the time being—so one day he was moved to tell me the whole story from his point of view. I may tell you at once that you were not mistaken that time—he was in love with you; I think perhaps more than he himself realised then. But you know Rupert— do you remember how you told me once that he quarrelled with himself? And that he picked and chose and thought the worst of people? He wants everything at once, and everyone to be all of a piece—absurdly, at his age. And though he respected your mind and loved your generosity—he mentioned that—your inexperience fretted him. And there were the horses. He has always had a regular phobia of sporting people—did you know that his Father was an M.F.H.?—and he ran away with the idea that if a person cared about horses at all, they could care for nothing but horses. Of course you were very absorbed in your stable then—and that girl came along, and briganded him. (He didn't tell me that, of course, but *cela se voyait*.) So that was that."

Amber put the letter down and looked out over the Park again. Yes, that was that! But Nugent was right—it did do her good to know that she hadn't been mistaken, that there had been a foundation for that unbelievable bliss. It was irrelevant now, of course—and yet perhaps nothing in one's life was really quite irrelevant. Poor Rupert! Oh, poor Rupert! A scatter of bright drops fell on the window-seat. She took up the letter again.

"I think I must tell you that that is off, thank Goodness. I didn't much like that young woman. I think it was her controlled certainty about everything that caught him; it went one better than his own dogmatism. I'm glad it's over—I don't believe he loved her much. But I expect the experience has been good for him—he will look deeper next time. I think loving you did him more good—and will go on doing so."

She turned a page, but did not at once read further. So he wasn't engaged to that girl any more. If she had known that two months ago, would it have made any difference? Answer! Answer! said her heart. But Amber didn't answer just then—she went on with the next sheet of Nugent's letter.

"I expect you will always love Rupert a good deal—
and I daresay he will you, more than he thinks. But
you will do better with Joe. You've taught him some
of the things he most wanted to learn, which no one
had taught him before. Lots of women would simply
have plundered him, and mocked him while they did it
—he's that sort; but with you he will be safe. He is
more defenceless than Rupert. But don't be afraid or
ashamed of loving Rupert still—in fact it's usually a
great mistake to be afraid or ashamed of loving anyone."

There it was, her answer. Probably she always would
love Rupert a good deal, but she loved Joe very much,
and she would do better with Joe. Besides Joe did need
her more. Nugent was right, as always.

Lady Julia bustled in, sumptuous in a wedding-gar-
ment. "My dear child, they are here with your dress!
Haven't you changed your underclothes yet?"

She was engulfed in clothes; the room billowed with
tissue-paper; her own maid and Lady Julia's ran to and
fro; the dressmaker put on her wedding-dress, Gemma
pinned on her own diamond brooch for her "something
borrowed." Then the hairdresser tackled her coppery
mop, putting a pink printed cloak over her shoulders to
protect her dress. Amber laughed into the glass—the
pink made her *too* hideous, with her hair! She shut her
eyes to avoid the screaming clash of colour.

Curiously, when she did that, she saw two places, perfectly clear, in her mind—a pool on a road with stars
shining up from dark water, and a young moon between
the thin branches of alders—and a little hut standing in
an empty space on a great fortification, which looked
out over a snowy plain to mountains shining like the
battlements of Heaven. And clear and far, but not
faint, the echo of the music with which those two places

rang was in her ears, unearthly lovely, unutterably sweet.
Yes, there was that! Such music draws tears to the eyes
just because of its sheer loveliness—it isn't that one needs
it! Amber gave her head a little shake. "*One* moment,
Mademoiselle!" the coiffeur implored—"just to adjust
the veil." No, she didn't need it—it was a thing by itself,
and she had had it, anyhow. All was well. She had got
that freedom—the freedom that Nugent, staring at some
grave-mounds stuck with willow-wands, away in Peking,
at the other side of the world, had said was the main
thing. And suddenly she saw him again, sitting there,
with his tired face and his greying hair and his shapely
hands, and realised, with a little stab of comprehension,
something she had never understood before—how easily
Nugent could have made the world sing for her! She
opened her eyes to stare at this idea; from the mirror her
face stared back at her, veiled now, crowned with green
and white flowers. Oh yes—the wonder really was how
he had managed not to! She took up his letter and
began to read it again. Absorbed, she never noticed the
coiffeur give his handiwork a final pat; bow, scrape and
withdraw. Oh wise, dear Nugent! Grateful as she was
to him for so much, she was now most grateful of all for
this. "In fact," she read again, "it's usually a great
mistake ever to be afraid or ashamed of loving anyone."
In this too, all was well; he had himself given her this en-
franchisement. Darling Nugent!

Suddenly she remembered something. Joe wanted
her to have rouge on, and they'd forgotten it. She threw
back her veil and hunted in the drawer—where was the
blessed stuff? She practically never used it. Ah, there
it was. Darling Joe—he should have a blushing bride if
he wanted one! She dabbed and rubbed and powdered
—yes, that would do. She went back to her letter.

"Now, dear child, we ought to start," said Lady Julia,

coming in. "Good heavens! What has happened to your veil? Agnes, here, quickly!"

"It's all right—I've only been putting some rouge on," said Amber. While her mother fussed, and the maids tweaked the veil, she slipped Nugent's letter into the front of her dress. Then, smiling, she went off to marry Mr. George Hawtrey.